Deadly
Excitements

Deadly Excitements
Shadows and Phantoms

Robert D. Sampson

Bowling Green State University Popular Press
Bowling Green, Ohio 43403

To Frank Hamilton, artist extraordinary,

whose magic dots delight the heart.

Acknowledgements

Magazines and covers were copyrighted, as cited, by:

Blazing Publications, Inc., proprietor and conservator of the representative copyrights and successor-in-interest to Popular Publications, Inc., for *The Spider* © 1938, renewed 1966.

Better Publications, Inc., for *The Ghost Super-Detective* © 1939; and *Captain Future* © 1943.

Conde Nast Publications, Inc. for *Doc Savage* © 1933, by Street & Smith Corporation, renewed 1961 by Conde Nast; *The Shadow Magazine* © 1938 by Street & Smith Corporation, renewed 1966 by Conde Nast; and *The Whisperer* © 1940 by Street & Smith Corporation, renewed 1968.

Fiction House, Inc. for *Action Stories* © 1943

Phantom Detective, Inc. for *The Phantom Detective* © 1934

Standard Magazines, Inc. for *Five Detective Novels* © 1951

Ziff-Davis Publishing Co. for *Fantastic Adventures* © 1958

* * * * *

My thanks to all those who opened the pages of their publications to these essays, and who have spent so much of their time and treasure enthusing over yesterday's glories. They have given much more than you can realize and it is with gratitude that I thank:

John Gunnison, *The Pulp Collector*

Tony Hardin, *Xenophile*

Tom and Ginger Johnson, *Echoes*

Howard Hopkins and Chuck Juzek, *Golden Perils*

Edward T. LeBlanc, *The Dime Novel Round-Up*

Frank Lewandowski, *Nemesis*

J. Grant Thiessen, *The Science Fiction Collector*

Guy Townsend, *The Mystery Fancier*

Robert Weinberg, *Pulp*

And, particularly, Lianne Carlin, who started me off by accepting a piece on The Phantom Detective for *The Mystery Readers' Newsletter*.

The following articles were first published in the places shown and occasionally read as they do now:

"Face Changer," *Golden Perils* Vol. 3, #13 (Spring 1989)

"Jesse James' Ferocious Exploits," the *Dime Novel Round-Up* #568 (August 1984)

"A Bow to the Wizard," *Skyrack* (March 1972)

"Ghost Story," *Pulp*, Vol. 1, No. 5 (Winter 1973)

"Sex and the Spider," *Echoes* #2 (September-October 1982)

"Yes, I Know Exactly What it Is," *Echoes* #24 (April 1986)

"Fourteen Issues," *Xenophile* #22 (March-April 1976)

"Pretend Not to See Her, She's A Scarlet Adventuress," *Nemesis Inc.* #13 (Fall 1982)

"The Second Time Around," *The Pulp Collector*, Vol. 1, No. 1 (Spring 1985)

"Sea Stories," *Xenophile* #33 (July 1977)

"Crime Busters," *Xenophile* #38 (March-April 1978)

"Guy's Ghost," *Echoes* #22 (December 1985)

"The Murder Cases of Pinklin West," *The Mystery Fancier*, Vol. 8, No. 1, (January-February 1984)

"Rings of Death," *The Mystery Fancier*, Vol. 10, #1 (April 1988)

"Grace Note," *Xenophile* #17, (September 1975)

"The Tall Man," *The Man Behind Doc Savage*, Chicago: Pulp Press (1974)

"About Senorita Scorpion," *Echoes* #20 (August 1985)

"You Red-Headed Girl of My Dreams," *The Pulp Collector*, Vol. 1, No. 2 (Fall 1985)

"You Mean You Found That Jewel At A Flea Market?" *Echoes* (June 1982)

"How To Deal with Dud Issues," *Echoes* #8 (August 1983)

"The Real Reason Argosy is Better Than Fantastic Adventures," *Echoes* #18 (April 1985)

"Disguise Is Pretty Impractical," *Echoes* #15 (October 1984)

"Why All Those Magazine Covers of Girls in Space Are Dead Wrong," *Echoes* #25 (June 1986)

"Memoirs of a Doc Savage Reader," *The Science-Fiction Collector* #14 (May 30, 1981)

Contents

Contents

In Appreciation Of 10-Cent Pleasures

The pieces that grace these pages are about that elder art form, the pulp magazine. For that reason, a few words of introduction are in order, since "art form" and "pulp magazine" are rarely linked in the same sentence—or the same thought.

The pulps were inexpensive magazines printed on coarse paper and flaunting brightly illustrated covers. Almost entirely devoted to popular action fiction, they appeared in the pale dawn of the Twentieth Century and vanished some sixty years later, as silently as they came. To this day, we have no exact account of the titles issued. A thousand? Fifteen hundred? Twice that number? And where have they all gone, those millions of copies, hurled out by the presses and distributed world-wide, as prevalent as oxygen. They have gone, at any rate. Gone permanently.

The pulps expressed no rare aesthetic aspirations. Quite simply, they were commercial productions, published to make money by selling fiction to a public that still read. Reading is now an obsolete skill, superseded by pictures on a screen. At one time, however, people read by choice—for amusement. How alien that seems to our enlightened present.

The magazines they read contained light popular fiction. It was entertaining, not particularly complex, and inexpensive. Priced for casual purchase, casual reading, and equally casual discard, the magazines were as impermanent as teen-age slang.

Impermanence is the curse of magazine fiction. Whether printed on slick paper or pulp paper, fiction gleams a moment and is gone. Like the dime novels, the story papers, the yellowbacks of yesterday. Skilled professionals produced the magazines; artists and writers of ability contributed to them. But the end product was written on air.

So the pulps have vanished. Once a world-wide phenomena, common as the contemporary paperback, the pulp magazine has become nearly invisible. And that is a distinct loss. For the magazines glowed with their own peculiar atmosphere. Like a carnival, they promised much. And if that promise was forever larger than life, as promises tend to be, still the heart remembers the pulps with affection.

Perhaps that is a consequence of reading great numbers of them when young. The fiction you first discover for yourself somehow blends into your bones. Granted that fiction, in some form, seems a necessity to growth, like sunshine and pizza. That is fiction in the widest sense, for fiction comes packaged in many different forms, various as colors in the sky. Each generation favors one form over all the rest, and smiles, with quiet superiority, at the enthusiasms of the past. In this age of paperbacks and television screens glowing with dreams, such fictional forms as the chanted epic and the half-hour radio drama are obsolete. As is the all-fiction magazine printed on pulp paper.

That's only to be expected. The medium changes; only fiction endures.

The pulp magazines, then, were vehicles for selling fiction to the public. Like plastic toys and varieties of cup cakes, the magazines were product. That they were also an art form was beside the point. Perhaps the subject might be debated late at night, when the boys gathered in the back room around a pitcher of iced tea. But few seriously accepted the idea.

By nature, the pulps were informal publications, effervescent and raucous, lacking social prestige. They were fiction in old jeans and tee shirt. The covers were garish, the story titles often sensational. Through them pulsed action, conflict, melodramatic violence, an incessant thunder of deadly excitements. It was obvious, urgent, and often improbable, but it was also story-telling at a high level, with narrative complexity, freshness, and unexpected intensity.

That otherwise substantial people, fifty years later, would collect these magazines, and reread them, and gloat over their covers—that never occurred to those producing them. That well-meaning drudges might examine pulp fiction as a form of literature, and write volumes about them, was beyond all rational belief.

Even at the time, some people wrote articles about the pulps. These articles differed sharply from our present nostalgic effusions. They were either pieces by pulp fiction authors, revealing their secrets for composing salable stories; or they were less approving articles by critics conscious of a mission. The critics attacked the pulps with gleeful ferocity, hammering at their reputed superficiality, sentimentality, sensationalism, crudity, and triteness. Critics were as difficult to satisfy then as now.

Most of these criticisms were accurate—not for all the pulps all the time; but certainly for specific magazines at a given time.

The difficulty is that "pulp" is a generic term, like "bread" or "woman." "Pulp" is shorthand for a transient, all-fiction magazine of dubious reputation. Beyond that point, confusion rages. So many magazines appeared, their range so wide, their diversity so unexpected, their quality so different, that no single appraisal serves for all. You could as easily describe a rainbow by mentioning only its red band.

The pulps' reputation for lurid, bloody excess developed mainly during the 1930s, a consequence of the Depression. At that time, the struggle for readers intensified. And as competition grew, so did a sense of social outrage and fear, as if malign forces beyond control ravaged and tore. If the First World War marked the fiction of the 'Twenties, the Depression tainted the popular fiction of the 'Thirties with blood and violence.

To that extent, the critics were correct. By the most favorable standards, some 1930s magazines published atrocious junk. Some reveled in a mire of girls and gore, others in sadistic horror; still others treated serial murder as a pleasant plot device, or projected nightmares of fascist slaughter in familiar streets.

Such subjects are not entirely unknown to our own well-adjusted age. But in the pulp era, certain of these subjects were new to a mass market. Consequent shock was strong, and critical reaction seems as tinged with outrage as cool evaluation.

The pulps brought further wrath upon themselves by their susceptibility to fad. Since they existed to sell, the magazines hotly exploited fads. Let a new subject prove popular and, immediately, the market boiled with imitators plundering that fresh ore.

A new fad exploded every few years. In the mid-1930s, a craze developed for stories about girls menaced by costumed skulkers. At once, on every side, popped up magazines with spectacular covers and ominous prose. Other fads at other times exploited crooked heroes fleecing crooks, or detectives who improved society by shooting crooks, or sun-bronzed adventurers of abnormal strength, or disguised aviators battling singular menaces in World War I skies. Each subject was mercilessly exploited until readers yawned, sales tailed off, and a new fad developed.

What strikes us now, so many years later, are not the fads but the variety of fiction routinely offered by the pulps. Each month brought forth a swarm of mystery and detective fiction, sports fiction, love stories, western stories, tales of adventure all around the world. A few magazines specialized in the series adventures of a single character. Other magazines, such as *Argosy, Short Stories,* and *Blue Book,* gracefully balanced a mixture of fiction types and proceeded triumphantly through the years, amassing hundreds of sequential issues.

Specialty magazines proliferated. The pulps could no more resist specializing than a tree can resist thrusting out leaves. And so some exquisitely limited titles appeared—*Speakeasy Stories, Submarine Stories, Prison Stories, New York Stories.* Specialized titles tended to fade quickly, but others equally narrow leaped up in their place: *Pirate Stories, North-West Romances, Scientific Detective Monthly, Greater Gangster Stories.*

It seems utterly extravagant now. But the shears of the marketplace pruned exceedingly close, and lack of sales provided immediate correction.

If you reread these pulps today, you often feel a degree of cultural shock. Since the fiction faithfully reproduced the beliefs and conventions of its time, you begin to feel that the familiar world has slipped a trifle out of focus. Over fifty years, social attitudes have changed. Such routine things as frequency of mail delivery, automobile performance, and the cost of dinner strike at you from the pages, giving you a small, hard jar—recognition that time has passed, change has come, things are no longer what they were. Because the pulps so vividly reflected their time, time has withered them lightly at the edge, even as their page edges are touched lightly by fatal crispness.

They show their age, as, Lord knows, we all must.

At any rate, the following pages are about pulp magazines—familiar, obscure, amusing and curious ones, and a few of the kind that once made critics cry out before the universe.

Unlike my *Yesterday's Faces* series, which seeks to trace the development of certain series character types, the essays in this book have no common thread. They are loosely grouped to satisfy a rudimentary impulse toward order. The first group concerns single-character magazines and the wonderful people who filled them. The second group glances at a few of those odd magazines which made every visit to the news stand an adventure. In the third section appear a few of the series characters who brightened the pages of long ago. The final section, all fluff and floss, is included because people who write about obsolete popular magazines tend to grow serious and declaim in significant voices, as if in the presence of the Supreme Court. Considering the subject, such intensity is gloriously inappropriate. The pulps were frequently serious but rarely solemn. So these final pieces gently hint that we are talking about 10 cent magazines, after all.

These subjects reflect the writer's affections, his prejudices, and his erratic excursions among thousands of magazines. If so many descriptive passages and story summaries startle you, they're included because endless abstractions about a vanished art are boring. Better to touch bone, even fossilized bone, then wander among misty generalities.

To those whose favorite magazine has been omitted, I offer apologies. There were so many magazines, the longest book would still include too few. When you write about the pulps, you are like a hiker moving through autumn woods. Occasionally you pick up a vivid leaf, a few acorns, a stone, and place these carefully away in your pack—while overhead, and from every side, thunder the brilliant transformations of Fall.

You save something. But it is never enough.

I
The World Of The
Single-Character Magazine

For some enthusiasts, the only pulp magazines were single-character magazines. To these they gave their full allegiance, their spare coins, and all of their attention. It is a curious selectivity, since the single-characters represented only a single wing in the gallery of pulps, and by no means the largest wing, or the longest enduring.

Still the single characters were hotly popular. These magazines featured a monthly (or bi weekly) novel about a continuing character, whose name graced the masthead and whose picture, variously drawn, graced the pages within. The action blazed continuously, waves of violence, as the hero, disguised to his toe nails, slugged mightily at Lords of Contemporary Crime. Although a genius, an extraordinary physical specimen, a miraculous shot, the hero, oozing wealth and culture, rarely enjoyed a blissful moment. Waves of killers shrieked toward him, plots dire and dread challenged him. Menace chilled the air. Each paragraph contained a deadly trap, and at the center of the holocaust sniggered a criminal genius, determined to shatter society for revenge or a two per-cent return on his investment.

Officially, the single-character era began with the April 1931 issue of *The Shadow Detective Magazine*. That enigmatic figure of the night, laughing weirdly, knowing all, penetrating the tightest plot, met instant success. Soon after, in 1933, a wave of character magazines foamed across the market:

—February, The Phantom Detective, a bored young millionaire and disguise master, battling crime through chapters awash in gore.

—March, Doc Savage, a bronzed superman, aided by five close friends, using scientific gadgets to defeat unique evil the world over.

—March, Nick Carter, a recycling of the dime-novel detective, become a deadly private investigator with harsh ways and a personal armament of four .45 caliber revolvers.

—September, The Lone Eagle, an Air Intelligence operative plunging to combat in the skies of Armageddon, during World War I and II.

—October—G-8 and His Battle Aces, another disguised genius and his ace wingmen, blasting away at super-scientific lunacy hurled across the Western Front by the Germans.

—October, The Spider, a suave young millionaire, soon to disguise himself as a homicidal hunchback, who was aided by his lovely fiancee and friends, as he slaughtered to the heart of maniac criminal uprisings.

And afterward, Bill Barnes, flying adventurer; Secret Agent X, face-changer with a gas pistol; Operator 5, a secret service ace, fighting plots, invasions, wars, as the world shuddered.

Others followed, from Chinese criminals and jungle men to G-men, justice figures with malleable faces, and reporters who periodically became invisible. A reeling, wonderful, sparkling world of drama and adventure that eventually closed in 1953, as economics folded up the magazines.

The phenomena of the single-character pulps was solidly rooted in the past. Before the turn of the century, series of dime novels had been built around plainsmen *(Buffalo Bill Weekly)*, adventuring ranchers *(Wild West Weekly)*, bandits *(Jesse James Stories)*, and nearly invincible detectives *(Nick Carter Weekly)*. Stories received reprint in various forms until the early 1930s. Even as late as 1927, *The Liberty Boys* dime novel was being reprinted, and paperback reprints of Nick Carter's adventures continued until 1933.

One of the earliest of the single-character publications was neither dime novel nor pulp magazine, but a paperback series, issued around 1908, which represents a transition between the forms: the series featured Jesse James, a fictional character created from a few shreds of historical fact. The later pulps would dispense with even that much realism.

Strictly speaking, a single-character magazine is named after the lead character, the giant whose adventures carries the series. In practice, matters were less formal. The Black Bat, a costumed hero with guns and wonderful eyesight, moved into *Black Book Detective* and made it his own, appearing in more than sixty novels. Dan Fowler, G-Man extraordinary, was the star of *G-Men*, although his name never appeared in the title; *Jungle Stories* (the second series beginning in 1939) featured Ki-Gor, an unabashed Tarzan clone. Such other figures as the Green Lama and the Crimson Mask moved into existing publications and dominated them. If these magazines were technically not single-character by rigid definition, they were in practice. They delighted readers then, and they still pull wonderfully at the imagination.

The following pages revisit a few of these single-character magazines. Their magic persists. If they now seem fantastic, violent, and improbable, they also remain fascinating. Their remarkable characters have long since entered the bloodstream of popular fiction, resonating years after their magazines have vanished.

Face Changer
(The Phantom Detective, 170 issues, February 1933-Summer 1953)

It was not quite our world, that world of 1933 pulp magazines.

In that world, as this, there was sunlight and automobiles. Crowds moved along city streets. Birds flew, books were read, dinners eaten, and skirts flipped as enticingly.

But there were differences. In that world, time telescoped queerly. You could accomplish a month's investigation in an hour. You could call the President of the United States direct and have the US Army attending your every whim before the phone cooled. You could step into the street and all the girls would sigh archly and begin powdering their noses, the little minxes. (But you would pay no mind to that. Not you.)

You could outdraw half a dozen gangsters with machine-guns pointed straight at your head—even when your .45s were buttoned under your coat.

And you could also disguise yourself with a stick of greasepaint.

In this tedious world, when you greasepaint your face, you continue to look just like yourself with something smeared on your face. But in a 1933 pulp, things are different. There, that touch of greasepaint erased your identity and substituted a new one—at the same time, altering the shape of your skull, the size of your body, the length of your nose, and such other changes necessary to look exactly like somebody else.

Apparently the greasepaint worked. The Phantom Detective used it constantly through 170 issues of his magazine, from February 1933 to Summer 1953. During that period, The Phantom changed identity more than a thousand times. Yes, he was often detected—but that was because he kept impersonating people lacking some part of a finger. He never got detected because he looked like a big husky young fellow who had smeared his face with greasepaint.

At the time that The Phantom Detective entered his first published case, the convention of the disguised detective penetrating the underworld was 105 years old. Still earlier figures there might have been. But the first to put the subject into a book was Francois Eugene Vidocq (1775-1857), who started off young and crooked and ended in prison. There he became a police informer. Gradually, by a combination of double-crossing, playing up to the authorities, and talking a blue streak, he worked himself into the position of the first Chief of French police. That organization he staffed with criminals and a high old time they had, indeed, enforcing the law. Eventually Vidocq got bounced for extended and spectacular corruption, and went on to other things—one being the establishment of the first private detective agency. Along the line, Vidocq published a four-volume *Memoirs* (1828-1829)—it was ghost-written— telling of his exploits. It was an engaging piece of sensational fiction, flecked lightly, here and there, with bits of actual event.

Among the less improbable accounts were his excursions in disguise through the Paris underworld. Got up as a low crook, or businessman, or a used-horse dealer, he would edge into the confidence of the criminals. At a crucial moment, he would whip off his false whiskers and shout:

"Regard! It is I—the celebrated Vidocq!"

Then all the French cops in the world would thunder in and that was, you might say, that.

These scenes got into the *Memoirs* and the *Memoirs* got read. Pretty soon it was 1886 and Nick Carter was standing in a den of cut-throats, wrenching off his false whiskers and shouting:

"I am Nick Carter! You are all apprehended!"

After which, all the New York City cops in the world would thunder in....

Nick Carter is the best known of the disguised, dime-novel detectives. But he wasn't the first, nor the last of that fine crew, which included Old Cap

Collier, Old Sleuth, Young Sleuth, and others. All were able to disguise themselves instantly, using a handful of false hair and a burnt cork.

While American detectives swarmed about, disguised from toes to hairline, over in England, other detectives were doing the same thing. Sherlock Holmes constantly slipped from one guise to another. So did Cleek, the Man of Forty Faces (1914), who could twist up his face, as you would clench your fist, and create a brand-new set of features. Cleek was likely influenced by the earlier example of Colonel Clay, a conniving swindler, who also had a flexible face, slightly coated by a plastic compound. Much later, in 1925, Edgar Wallace's Henry Arthur Milton, The Ringer, could disguise himself to look like anybody anyplace, and murdered blithely through a wonderful series of stories. Then came The Shadow. You remember him. 1931.

All these people practiced well before The Phantom Detective, but all of them look back to that swaggering French egomaniac, Vidocq, who grins at the root of the whole thing. By 1933, the disguise convention was solidly placed in fiction: A talented individual could disguise himself perfectly, obliterate his appearance, transform his features to those of another person, fooling his friends and sweetheart and Dear Old Mom. Maybe you couldn't do it in the real world, mind you. But you could in the pulps.

The Phantom Detective magazine was the first of five major single-character pulps launched in 1933. *Doc Savage* followed by one month (March 1933). Later that year came the *Lone Eagle* (September), and *The Spider* and *G-8 and His Battle Aces* (both October). All would endure ten years or longer and all but the *Lone Eagle* would amass above one hundred issues.

That sudden burst of single-character magazines resulted from the extraordinary success of *The Shadow Magazine*, which had gone to twice-a-month issuance in September 1932 (the magazine being dated October 1, 1932). A market had been demonstrated for series novels about a strong character and his violent adventures. And so the publishers moved. And so new titles came into being, one by one, like lights winking on in the night.

The earliest of those lights, *The Phantom Detective* magazine, began as a half-formed idea. Over the next twenty years, and as a dozen or more writers worked on the series, the Phantom and his world would alter out of recognition. The melodramatic frenzy would eventually soften. New supporting characters would appear. A sort of soft-boiled realism would work into the stories. And the figure of The Phantom, unstable as candleflame, would show as many personalities across the years as the facial disguises he adopted so readily.

There is little continuity in the series, and no sense of maturation and development. Too many writers ground out Phantoms. Even Norman Daniels, who wrote at least thirty-seven and probably twice as many, was not particularly consistent. His sentimental and incautious Phantom of 1953, babbling out his true identity to all comers, is not the rather hardboiled face-changer of the 1940s, or the lethal, chance-taking athlete of the mid-1930s. Daniels depicted all these different Phantoms. In the same way, Charles Green, W. T. Ballard, Ryerson Johnson, Laurence Donovan, Ralph Oppenheim, and Lord knows who else, each described a Phantom somewhat different from all the rest.

Because of these variations, you develop no consistent feel for the Phantom's personality. He is the least concrete of all the major single characters—as is appropriate to a Phantom.

Faced by such instability, let's turn to the beginning. Here, at least, are around two dozen novels in which the Phantom is as consistent as he will ever get. Most of these novels seem to be written by the same hand. They are signed G. Wayman Jones, changed to Robert Wallace with the February 1934 issue. Both Jones and Wallace were house names. While the actual writer of these novels has not been positively confirmed, D'Arcy Lyndon Champion (who also published as D. L. Champion and Jack D'Arcy) is probably right.[1]

The best information we have at present suggests that Leo Margulies thought up The Phantom, that Champion first fleshed him out using certain character elements he had developed earlier (wealthy society fellow with .45 seeks adventure), and that, according to Margulies, Champion, Daniels, and Anatole France Feldman wrote the bulk of the series.[2] Feldman's contributions have not been specifically identified, unfortunately.

At the beginning of the series, The Phantom is a figure of dramatic intensity; "From the slit in the mask (gazed) cold, hard agate eyes, slightly mocking, slightly cynical...."

The image is that popular 1920s cliche, the disillusioned sophisticate, a hard-drinking, chain-smoking fellow, weary of the world and its irrelevant masks. The Phantom is actually not in the least like this. But we are told that he is, again and again.

The Phantom is the *guerre de nom* of Richard Curtis Van Loan, a wealthy orphan, bachelor, and man-about New York City. Known for conspicious idleness, he polos, yachts, hurrahs in night clubs, surrounded by bright-lipped society girls giggling tipsily in their revealing dresses.

Once a combat flyer in World War I, Van Loan returned after the war to boredom, boredom, boredom. (The bored society lounger with a secret action identity goes back, by the way, to at least the early 1900s, when Norroy, a secret service ace, roamed the pages of *The Popular Magazine*.)

Frank Havens, wealthy newspaper publisher, persuaded Van Loan to look into a crime the police had flopped on. Van solved it with little difficulty, found his boredom eased, sought other crimes to investigate. To protect himself from a vengeful underworld, he took a new identity—that of The Phantom, an elusive figure wearing a simple black mask across his eyes. Sometimes he also wore a slouch hat, more often evening clothing. But always, the mask.

It is one of the conventions that such a mask completely obscures your identity. Perhaps so. Even when the undisguised face beneath is that of the well-known society playboy, R. C. Van Loan, whose picture keeps getting into the newspapers.

The problem is that Van Loan keeps falling into the hands of unfriendly people. Their dearest wish is to yank off that mask and look at The Phantom's real face—after which they will shoot him full of disagreeable holes.

That never quite happens. But a lot of suspense is generated during the first novels as Van struggles to remain masked, the revelation of his true identity only a gasp away.

A masked man has other problems. How is he to disclose himself to the authorities? For any rascal may wear a mask and proclaim himself The Phantom. Well, actually, it's a simple matter. The real Phantom wears a ring of "ebony onyx, cut in the form of a mask, set in platinum." The ring is known to the police of five continents.

Then change comes, as change will. By the June 1933 issue, the ring has transformed to a small gold badge. "Superimposed upon it in platinum was a delicately carved mask." In the following issue, the badge has become a small platinum affair with a gold mask superimposed on it. Other forms will be described, but the identifying badge, rather than the identifying ring, will be used throughout the series.

Apparently the police are flexible. Whatever the badge looks like, they immediately accept it as proof of The Phantom's identity.

And off we go to battle "The Emperor of Death" (February 1933, the first issue).

In this story, the Phantom takes on The Mad Red, a Communist plotter who plans to plunge Western civilization into confusion so that the Red Armies can move in and take over. The Red employs a hypnotizing cripple, an unofficial army of gunmen, a world-wide network of plotters, and many slick plans.

The Phantom has nothing but a few sticks of grease paint and the doubtful aid of a society beauty who is positively shimmering with cocaine.

The Phantom and The Red catch and lose each other about a dozen times. At each contact more shots are fired than at Gettysburg. The Phantom flips in and out of disguise: as The Red's right-hand man, as a drug addict, as The Red, as the hypnotizing cripple. He attempts to penetrate The Red's organization to learn more, but he keeps getting discovered and having to shoot his way out.

During the proceedings, Frank Havens is hypnotized twice, and Muriel Havens is kidnapped once, and The Phantom is inept, clumsy, and altogether amateurish. He keeps promising "The protection of the Phantom" to all these poor souls who get menaced by the forces. Then the poor souls get shredded by the forces of evil, just as if The Phantom hadn't been standing there; and then The Phantom raises his clenched right fist to the Heavens and swears a vow of vengeance on behalf of the slaughtered innocent. Well, dear, dear....

Fact is, The Red runs rings around The Phantom. To begin with, The Red, or some evil associate, impersonates The Phantom and deceives The President of the United States, no less. Then they kill anybody they wish whenever they wish, loot a bank to get sensitive papers in the vault, and finally capture everyone in the cast, The Phantom included.

Finally The Phantom reverses his bad luck with a miracle supplied by the author: the crooks don't search him well enough to find a hidden gun. By a childish trick (he changes the numbers on some prison cells), he confuses The Red's organization and suddenly The Red is wiped out. So is his enormous conspiracy. But that's just because the novel is long enough and had to end somewhere.

If you are looking for exciting incident, violence, and suspense, this is a pretty good story. If you're one of those strange types who's been reading Proust and Talbot Mundy and expect a novel to resemble a novel, then you're out of luck. This novel is a chain of incidents loosely linked chronologically. Hook up enough incidents and you have a novel. It could be 100 pages or 1000; you just add incidents to fill. The same thing occurs in the next novel, "The Crime of Fu Kee Wong" (April 1933).

Seems that Fu Kee Wong is out to restore the Chinese Empire. Naturally he begins this laudable enterprise in New York City, where he can steal the millions required. Murder begins at once. Disguised as a Chinese, The Phantom witnesses a killing and is taken by a hatchetman to FKW's lair. There he is taken on as that fiend's personal servant.

Yes, perhaps it is improbable. But it does keep the story moving. FKW plans to steal the gold shipment from the train. The Phantom intends to prevent it but gets outsmarted when the gang shoots electricity through the train car, frying everyone aboard and nearly frying The Phantom. He escapes by a fluke, as usual.

Thereafter it's one incident strung after another. The Phantom is in and out of disguise, being detected, fighting free. At long last, FKW captures Havens and Muriel and is going to extinguish them painfully unless The Phantom gives up that important ivory/jade trinket he has acquired, this being the symbol of authority necessary to weld together a new China, or some such thing.

At this point, the guns and knives really get going and the cast is sharply reduced.

Once again, The Phantom is foiled at every step. For a clever disguise artist and a detective who has "never known failure," he is amazingly inept. He investigates by coincidence and escapes by accident.

People go out of their way to be nice to The Phantom. Police are as obliging as if it were all a story book. And he rarely has the least trouble getting all manner of information from the various scoundrels he gets in his clutches. All he does is pretend that he is going to kill them. Points a pistol at their head and, in a slow, grim voice, says: "I will shoot at the count of ten. One, two, three...."

By then the scoundrel is gushing with information—where the gang is to strike. What is the secret password, known only to three men. How many left turns to the hideout. It is so useful to have exact information.

The Phantom is a sore trial to all these masterminds of crime. He keeps showing up at their elbows, disguised as their faithful hunchback, or inside their shirts, disguised as themselves. Once he infiltrates a group, he rarely does any lasting harm, because he is invariably discovered and chased off. But it is hard to get business accomplished when you have to waste your time shooing away The Phantom. And when you get back to the Board Room, ready to discuss your terrific plans, there he is again, disguised as the guard on the door.

Because he is such a nuisance, like a broken fingernail, certain masterminds decide early on to get The Phantom once and for all. The Mad Red, being one of the more sensible, decides to grab Havens and Muriel and use them for bait. Since Havens is the only living man who knows the Phantom's identity, and that fact is widely known, you'd think every wise guy and booster, card sharp and crap shooter would think of snatching Havens and snuffing anybody who came hunting for him. They don't though. Almost none of the big clever crooks think of doing this.

They do think to kidnap Muriel. This isn't because she knows anything. She doesn't. But it always upsets the reader when the beautiful girl is carried off and tied up and mean men look down at her helpless form, their cruel mouths gloating.

At this time, Muriel is a delicious jewel of a girl, "slim and blond. Her mouth was a crimson arch. Her eyes devastating pools." In later novels she will be a slender brunette with eyes that change color every issue. Until the 1950s, her function was to:

1) get kidnapped.
2) get saved.
3) read Richard Curtis Van Loan the riot act for being an idle loafer.
4) feel her heart flutter in the presence of The Phantom.
5) make The Phantom clench his mouth bitterly, as he gazed upon her blond/brunette loveliness, thinking of the happiness he was forced to renounce for The Phantom's life.

In "The Silent Killer," (Winter 1952), Muriel finally fingers The Phantom as being Van Loan. She loved both Van and The Phantom, you see, and her woman's heart told her that they must necessarily be the same. (Norman Daniels is the one who thought that up.) Thereafter, she more or less helped The Phantom in some parts of his cases. See 1, 2, 3, 4, and 5 above.

Back in 1933, The Phantom did not have the solace of Muriel's help. Or help from anybody else, either. The police were willing to call out the reserves and rush in and out of doors whenever he called, but the help they offered was about as useful as a bucket without a bottom. Other than the police, and the dubious assistance of Frank Havens, The Phantom was without aides.

In years to come, as all you experts know, various people would assist The Phantom, depending on whom was writing the story that month. The most long-enduring aide was Steve Huston, introduced in "Dealers In Death" (July 1937). Young, slim, wiry, keen-faced, Huston was a dead ringer for Clyde Burke of the *NY Classic*, one of the Shadow mob. Huston, however, worked for *The Clarion*, Havens' newspaper. Steve began with dark hair, but it got much redder as he went along.

Another redhead, Jim Lannigan, briefly appeared in "The Sign of the Scar" (September 1936). Formerly Chief Mechanic of Van Loan's air squadron in WWI, he was a big, tough, grinning fellow, but for some reason, he didn't take hold and vanished almost at once.

Chip Dorlan, a helpful boy, was the next major figure to enter the series. Chip arrived in "The Sampan Murders" (September 1939) and appeared many times during the early 1940s. He achieved a near impossibility for the pulp world: He grew up during the series and became an officer in Military Intelligence, occasionally giving up his relentless pursuit of the Axis to aid The Phantom during the war years, and sporadically later on. While Chip is practically the only character in pulp literature to grow up, it should be noted that he did so essentially overnight, adding ten years in a couple of months. But war matures a man fast.

Aside from various policeman—specific names indicates the presence of this writer or that one—only those few people helped The Phantom. Unlike Doc Savage or The shadow, Van Loan was pretty much a one-man operation.

As you have noticed, all these people had a tendency to change as the series progressed. So did The Phantom. It has been mentioned that he had several different personalities, depending on where in the series you're reading. In early issues, he's the traditional mixture of flippancy and toughness popularized by The Saint and some of the Edgar Wallace characters. As in "The Scarlet Menace" (May 1933), when he has captured two thugs:

"His voice held a slight bantering quality. His manner indicated that he was cajoling reluctant children."
"But beneath it all was a grim, ominous, though unspoken threat that thoroughly convinced the pair of gunmen that the man who covered them meant business...."

He seems to be a formidable character. His face "was a lean sunburned face, clean-cut and reckless from the nose to the chin. As for the upper part, it was completely covered by a black silk mask. Through twin slits in the silk a pair of mocking eyes surveyed them, like chips of crystal. About the mouth was a cool effrontery, a ruthless challenge which gave men pause. All in all, it was a handsome, provocative face."

It was a face that also belonged to Simon Templar, The Saint, whose influence on The Phantom, during this period, is considerable. During "Gamblers In Death" (November 1933), Van glares bright with Saintly glory, impeccably dressed, witty, and lethal, fierce beneath the polished surface.

At his point in the series, the author is feverishly clutching any trace of personality for his lead character. To be blunt, Van Loan has no personality; he is all traits, thoroughly conventional and uninspired ones common to all pulp magazine heroes.

That is, Van Loan is a tall, broad-shouldered young man, strong, wealthy, and good-natured. His eyes began as black and changed to brown; his hair was crisp brown, later altering to steel dark. He weighed the usual 180 pounds, that magic weight, and stood about six feet tall. And how that man ever disguised himself as a Chinese or a junkie is beyond this commentator.

However, his distinctive face can vanish with great speed. By the May 1933 issue, Van is doing something more than stroking his cheeks with greasepaint:

"...from an inner pocket of his coat he produced an elaborate cloth case somewhat similar to child's pencil and pen box.

"From this he extracted the (basic) make-up, pencils and greasepaint that he was never without...."

"Skillfully his dexterous fingers wielded the pencils over his face. Two small pieces of wax distended his nostrils ever so slightly. A plastered piece of crepe hair increased his sideburns a fraction of an inch. A stick of greasepaint turned his complexion an almost imperceptible shade lighter."

Eventually he gives up using wax. The stuff started to melt while he was being interrogated by crooks in "The Tycoon of Crime" (February 1938). Afterward he switched to a plastic material that was unmeltable, insoluble in water, and smear proof; it had to be removed by a special chemical. That basic disguise material was supplemented by rubber pads and spacers, nose inserts, invisible tape, vials of solution to change the skin color, and contact lenses in various shades.

That was formal combat disguise. Less intense preparation was needed for his casual alternate identity of Dr. Paul Bendix. A stoop-shouldered old scientist, wearing thick glasses and a straggling gray beard, Bendix was the face The Phantom used in his waterfront laboratory. It was quite an establishment, being packed with scientific gear, photographic equipment, guns, disguise items, and a tiny living quarters. The place later got moved to a loft in the Bronx, and fine pain it must have been to transport all that gear across town.

A second identity, used only a few times, was that of Gunner McGlone. He looked like a big bruiser, with flattened nose and swollen jaws and cheeks—caused by paraffin injections. How he removed the paraffin after it was injected is not stated. Perhaps a tiny slit with an X-Acto blade....

After a dozen years of coating his face with all this stuff, Van more or less quit elaborate disguises. He would fix his face just enough to eliminate R. C. Van Loan and let it go at that. In the final novels, his disguises are minimal, as often as not consisting of altered facial expressions and bodily carriage.

In the May 1933 "The Scarlet Menace," Van is sometimes disguised, sometimes masked, sometimes elusive. He takes on a gang of robed, hooded killer fiends who are terrorizing Zenia City, killing and extorting and mocking The Phantom's every effort. He gets detected and captured often and, as usual this early in the series, whenever he swears to protect someone, that someone gets killed completely dead.

"Mr. Phantom," snarls one disillusioned businessman, "you're a bungler and I don't propose to permit your inefficiency to murder me as it did all the others."

It's true that The Phantom has a tendency to trip and knock himself out, to get detected while in disguise and have to sprint off while the bullets wail, to make promises that go flop, to overlook things, or forget things, or fumble a plan or miss an opportunity because he must express his outrage when a low criminal sneers at Womanhood or the Flag. But you would hardly call that bungling, unless you are very very picky.

Since The Phantom rarely eats or sleeps while on a case, he keeps himself stimulated by chain-smoking cigarettes and absorbing vast quantities of alcohol. Let him settle down to think and before you know it, there goes another bottle of brandy. As a drinker, Van is on a par with Jules de Grandin, the ghost hunter of *Weird Tales* and another world-class toper. Unlike de Grandin, The Phantom never shows any effects—unless falling down and knocking himself out might be considered an effect.

Both "The Island of Death" (June 1933) and "The Jewels of Doom" (July) carry adventure outside the United States. In the first novel, a Japanese plotter is collecting horror weapons on an island; he intends to control the Pacific and take the Philippines for Japan. He doesn't.

In the second novel, there's a plot to steal the Rajah's jewels. The Phantom, disguised as somebody else, is carried off to India by submarine. There he meets the big shot who wears a white hood, fights a titanic prehistoric spider in a pit, operates a science-fictional machine that peels open safes, and generally enjoys himself.

Already, the endings of the novels are beginning to show a stereotyped sameness. They end in terrific battle; the mind behind the crimes is revealed; he snatches out a gun and sometimes he nicks The Phantom and occasionally he misses. In all cases, he gets gunned down. Thus:

"The two weapons spoke as one. Two steel jacketed bullets whirred through the air, passing each other in flight. One of them tore through The Phantom's left arm; the other thudded into a human breast, ripping through the flesh and ate its avid way into a black ugly heart.

"The (fiend) staggered backwards. His hands clutched his throat. His jaw fell open, his eyes were dilated, glazed. He fell to the ground, blood spurting from an ugly hole in his chest. He turned his head slightly as he lay there, and in that last moment of his life, spat a fearful curse at the man who had ended his nefarious career.

"Then his head fell back. A horrible gurgle emanated from his throat, and the (fiend) died as he had lived, with an oath upon his lips and hatred in his heart. He lay there, a still, inert corpse, a gory sacrifice to the evil he had created." (Adapted from "Thirteen Cards of Death" August 1933, p. 91.)

You don't find prose like that anymore. It booms along like a load of rocks dumped over the hill; if you have ever wondered what purple prose is, that's it.

"Thirteen Cards of Death" is about serial murder, a gang of masked murderers headed by a fellow in costume, and a lot of millionaires who get killed with commendable regularity. As you read this novel, you realize how early the Phantom series found its characteristic tone and slant. It is still as raw as new-made whiskey and the prose, as mentioned, is more enthusiastic then subtle. But it is clearly a Phantom, a frenzied melodrama no more realistic then a puppet show. and easily able to seduce your attention, like any puppet show, with its narrative drive.

These are not novels but fever dreams. They contain nothing resembling a realized character. No situation is tainted by the slightest whiff of reality. The action is unrelenting, giving no relief from the tom-tom pounding of murder and battle. Death never ceases. The Phantom, bless him, never fails.

"Cities for Ransom" (September 1933): The Black Admiral, a fierce ethnic from Haiti, has decided to dominate the world, beginning with Metropole City. He begins by killing half the police in town, then threatens all the prominent millionaires and does many naughty things before The Phantom brings him down.

"The Sinister Hand of Satan" (October 1933) is behind all those dead men sprawled here and there, a hole gaping at the base of their brains. Seems that Satan is stealing ductless glands. His mindless minions go tromping the streets and, worse, Frank Havens, tied to a chair, must tell The Phantom's name or die. He doesn't and he doesn't.

"Death's Diary" (February 1934). It's serial murder time again and nice fresh corpses thud everywhere, each wearing a white orchid. A madman is avenging himself on all those folks who were mean to him, and maybe he's recording this orgy of killing in a diary. Or maybe not. At the end of the novel, The Phantom almost gets a boy assistance but somebody in the editorial office seems to have squashed that idea, just in time.

"The Tick-Tack-Toe Murders" (March 1934). A very clever fellow has set up in the perfect murder business. It's kill, kill, kill, and no evidence to show how it was done. Only a strange tick-tack-toe symbol reveals that doom has struck again. The murder method, involving an air bubble injected into the circulatory system, had caused a lot of controversy some years before when used in a mystery novel. But in The Phantom's heated environment, it passes without notice.

"The Talking Dead" (July 1934) tell you believers how to invest your money. After which quite a lot of believers die. Quite a lot of other people die, too.

This bloody sequence of novels by D'Arcy (most likely) is now interrupted by the first of innumerable Norman A. Daniels Phantoms, according to Daniels' writing records. "Merchant of Murder" (October 1934) is about a bad guy in a costume who merrily murders and extorts and jeers at the police and the Phantom. The Merchant injects you with his doom-filled hypodermic. After that, you either pay him $100,000 to be injected with the antidote—or you die.

In "The Crime Castle" (December 1934) lurks The Crime King, who is forging state and municipal bonds by the long ton. He intends to use these bonds to wreck the financial structure of the country, after which he will clean up millions. Or so he thinks. To distribute these bonds, he pounces on all those bankers and brokers frequenting the Hi-De-Ho Club, blackmailing and doping them and cramming their pockets full of fake bonds. Distribute or die. It's a foolproof scheme until you think about it for two seconds.

"Death On Swift Wings" (January 1935) features that master spy, The Gargoyle, who looks just awful in a clay mask, and Magda, that seducing woman of sheer evil, and their terrible death ray. This is another Daniels novel, very physical. The Phantom gets punched, slugged, slammed, and shot in the shoulder. He gets shot in the shoulder so much that, in any reality but that of *The Phantom Detective* magazine, he would be permanently crippled. In his own world, such a wound rarely bothers him. It hardly bleeds and he is fist-fighting merrily shortly after being shot.

The Gargoyle and Magda get blown away near the final page. Or were you expecting that?

At this point, we have read through *The Phantom Detective*'s infancy and can pause to consider what we have read. The publication has evolved its familiar story line and is using themes and devices that will remain characteristic until the 1940s.

As we have seen, the subject is murder. Murder for money, murder for fun. Murder to fill up chapters when the writer is feeling sleepy. In addition to the routine killing, tossed in to keep the action moving

("Van pressed the trigger and a steel-jacketed bullet ate its avid way through the shrieking killer's devilish heart.")

there are three main reasons for all the immense blood-letting in these novels:

1) Innumerable murders result during a struggle for power or wealth. That is, I want your teddy bear. So I kill the clerk who sold it to you, the man next door to your house, the accomplice who helped me break in, the postman and mailman who saw me as I left, the old woman in the house across the alley who may have seen me and all her neighbors, and all their neighbors, and so until the territory is decimated. Thus "The Sign of Death," "Murder City," "Diamonds of Death."

2) Innumerable murders result as a group of secretly linked people are slaughtered: They share a secret, hold a common vow, or stand in line for the possession of something valuable. That is, I want your teddy bear, but you have willed it to your oldest brother, and he has five married children. Since I want free and clear title, I kill you, your brother, and all his children, wives, and offspring. To do this, I wear a fearful mask and, with artificial talons, claw the corpses something dreadful. Thus "The Sinister Hand of Satan" and "Death's Diary."

3) Untold thousands are slaughtered by terrorism and criminal insurrection to gain political power or establish a new empire. Wishing to be known as The Grand Teddy Bear, I organize a gang and kill all the police, all the politicians, and the millionaires. Then I loot all the banks and jewelry stores to finance more ammunition and an extra set of bear suits for my minions. Refer to "The Crime of Fu Kee Wong" and "Cities for Ransom."

Along with these main story ideas goes a snorting horde of gimmicks. Hypnotism crops up regularly—the good old-fashioned kind done by a villain with flaming eyes and steel-like will; when necessary to unravel the plot, The Phantom can also hypnotize, as in "The Scarlet Menace," when he hypnotizes a crook to believe that he is The Phantom in disguise.

Another gimmick is the use of a science-fictional device. Death rays appeared in "The Island of Death" and "Death on Swift Wings," January 1935). In "The Jewels of Doom" there is another dandy ray that pops open safes and vaults and in doing so violates only seven or eight physical laws. "The Sinister Hand of Satan" concerns the use of glands to bring back your lost youth; this was a fairly popular idea in the pulps and kept resurfacing in one series or the other well into the 1940s.

Other gimmicks include the every-popular use of costumes, the use of symbols such as orchids or playing cards to accompany each murder and make the police stagger in dismay, and the use of ethnic villains. The Phantom is closely packed with ethnic villains: Chinese (the lead villain is almost always a disguised white man), Japanese, Russian, Haitian, and Indian. All are ugly devils who hate white men and have an itch for white women. Like the BEMS of space, they can't keep their paws off a blond.

One device that does not appear in these early stories is the red light at the top of the Clarion Building. As Phantom readers know, Frank Havens switches on that light whenever The Phantom is needed and it glows or pulses, depending on the author, until the Phantom arrives. This light was apparently suggested by a real red light which shone at night from the top of the Woolworth Building in New York City. That was during the 1920s, before the Empire State Building reared up and put all single lights to shame.

The Phantom's light is much in evidence at the end of the 1930s. By then many changes and many authors had come to the series, and the rather rigid melodramas of D'Arcy had become more flexible, more intricate, and certainly more bloody.

During 1935-1936, when Norman Daniels wrote more than half the published novels, the character of The Phantom became less amateurish, more assured, and much less prone to fumbling and error. The stories, violent as ever, were less episodic, more tightly tied front and back. Many of the 1937 stories plunge roaring with large-scale sadism and mutilation, as in "The Beast-King Murders" (July) and "The Corpse Parade" (December). In spite of all this savagery, the stories published between 1937-1939 are competently, often smoothly, written, with more than usual amounts of characterization. Occasional traces of emotional life stir in the portrait of The Phantom.

After a period of highly uneven novels, 1940-1942, in which superior work cuddles against inept and uncharacteristic efforts (such as the November 1940 "The Green Glare Murders"), the Phantom series surprises us once again. The novels improve all out of expectation. From 1943 to 1949, the blood for blood's sake narrative is de-emphasized and a far more realistic world substituted. The criminals are vicious, the action violent, war themes are frequently used, but The Phantom, superbly competent, moves through a sharply described world and admirably worked out cases.

In part this may be because paper shortages caused a cut-back in the monthly printing schedule. Beginning with the April 1942 issue, the magazine went, generally, every other month, with some exceptions. Certainly the novels published were superior to those of 1940. Those novels bearing the title "The

Case of..." are particularly fine. Those who wish to collect a small run of Phantoms will find much admirable reading in the 1943-1949 issues.

The final years of the magazine, roughly 1949 into 1953, are mainly by Norman Daniels, and are smooth, tight, workmanlike jobs. Muriel and Steve Huston play an important role in many of them and The Phantom develops a distressing tendency to reveal his true identity, while his ability at disguise is somewhat played down. The final novel of the series, "The Merry Widow Murders," was announced but, as far as is now known, was not published— although some version of it may yet be discovered, more or less rewritten, in an issue of *Popular Detective* or *Thrilling Detective.*

This brief article can only suggest the complex richness of The Phantom Detective series as it evolved across twenty years. As a series, it was neither integrated nor consistent. More than any other single-character magazine, The Phantom had no past. Too many writers participated. Each brought to the magazine his own version of The Phantom's world, a view frequently unsullied by any informed knowledge of what had gone on before.

In spite of this, in spite of incoherent plots and wild variations in writing quality, in spite of a fluctuating cast, in spite of a dreary emphasis on blood and serial murder, D'Arcy's original concept holds its vitality. The undaunted young face-changer slides to the heart of criminal conspiracies and with raw courage, and a gun or so, shatters them.

Justice is done at last, after blood-soaked chapters. The menace ends for this month. Next month, it begins again. Next month, the red light of the Clarion Building flashes once more, and The Phantom, one face among many faces, moves quietly toward new slaughter under a scarlet sky.

Glory Days with the Ace of Space
(*Captain Future*, 17 issues, Winter 1940-Spring 1944;
Startling Stories, 10 issues, Spring 1945-May 1951)

Some years from now, not too far off, a simplified sun shines, Brave, bronzed heroes ride the spaceways, probe eerie worlds, shoot it out with thugs in black space helmets, The Solar System swarms with life, from the Sun's core to the frozen cliffs of Pluto. Civilization webs the planets and between them pass trade, adventure, struggle.

Weaving among the worlds on blazing jets roars a splendid hero—Captain Future, Wizard of Science. Born Curt Newton, he is (or shall be) young, lithe, red-headed—a fighting, laughing, scientific genius. From 1940 through 1951, in twenty novels and seven short stories, he stood firm as Earth's good champion and defender.

Although the details of Newton's young life seem wildly peculiar, they closely follow the myth of the popular magazine superhero. Which is to say, death of the parents, usually by murdering criminals; subsequently, mentors raise the child to become a superman and battle crime. It is a familiar story line, the details varying from magazine to magazine but normally preserving those grand universals: death, mentor, dedication to a life-long struggle.

Thus, Newton's mother and father are pursued to the Moon by an evil scientist. There they build a scientific enclave beneath the Lunar surface, assisted by Simon Wright, a genius whose body is dead, although his brain lives on in a crystal case. Together they construct Otho, a synthetic man, and Grag, a massive, slow-witted robot. The parents then die at the hands of the renegade scientist. Their son, Curt Newton, is raised by the three Futuremen. Intellectually and physically surpassing all men, Newton becomes Captain Future, dedicating his life to battle massive evil throughout the Solar System. Whenever he is needed, a signal blazes forth from the North Pole of the Earth. Future and the Futuremen will respond as swiftly to that signal as did The Phantom Detective, some centuries before, to the light flashing at the top of the Clarion Building.

Other continuing characters are associated with Newton's hyperactive life. The Girl of the series is Joan Randall, who will undoubtedly marry Newton one day, although not any time soon. And Ezra Gurney, the Good Gray Marshal of the Space Patrol. This small cast is rounded out by the inhabitants of the Solar System, selected star clusters, and various dimensions.

The tone for the magazine run is set by the first issue. In "Captain Future and the Space Emperor" (Winter 1940), a murderous hooded fiend of crime, with hordes of leering henchmen, uses super science to threaten the Solar System. Right up to the moment the Futuremen cut him down.

The action is fast, violent, simple. Terrible doom menaces. Astounding adventures follow, incredible sights. It is interplanetary cops and robbers, hot-eyed Space Opera. All told by Edmond Hamilton, an old old pro of the pulp magazines.

Three additional issues in 1940: "Calling Captain Future," "Captain Future's Challenge," and "The Triumph of Captain Future." The series rings with ghostly echoes from other magazine series. But in the rush and tumble of event, who cares if Future and his aides resonate to the Doc Savage melody, that the stories echo the structure of the Phantom Detective novels. That here floats a bit from The Shadow and there a whisper of E. E. Smith. Who could possibly care? Let the action roll on.

The following year, 1941, brings a descent into sub-atomic worlds via the code concealed in "The Seven Space Stones" (Winter). The Spring issue, "Star Trail to Glory," offers battle with the machine men of Mercury. "The Magician of Mars" (Summer) introduces an invisible citadel of crime and "The Lost World of Time" (Fall), tells how a world 100,000,000 years in the past is saved, improbable as that may seem.

By 1942, the Solar System has grown too small for Curt Newton's exploits. "Quest Beyond the Stars" leads him to the heart of the galaxy, where a machine continuously creates matter. The following issue, "Outlaws of the Moon," returns Newton to Earth, where he is promptly framed for the murder of the President. After clearing up that misunderstanding, he's off to visit to Halley's Comet (Summer: "The Comet Kings) and its electrified people. With "Planets in Peril," he again leaves the Solar System to battle for the freedom of another universe.

Wartime paper shortages reduced the 1943 magazine to three issues. In the Winter "Face of the Deep," the Futuremen and a pack of homicidal killers are wrecked upon a disintegrating world. The following novel, Spring, "Worlds to Come," is the first written by Brett Sterling (William Morrison), and sets the Futuremen against invaders from another dimension. Finally, the Summer "Star of Dread," by Hamilton, matches them against a mutation machine manufacturing multitudes of monsters.

The final issues of the *Captain Future* magazine appeared in 1944. "Magic Moon" (Winter) whizzes all around the Solar System with a motion picture company and, incidentally, brings that ringing phrase, "The Ace of Space," into the language. In Brett Sterling's Spring issue, "Days of Creation," Newton gets amnesia and experiences many difficult moments.

With that, the series moves bodily to *Startling Stories* and, in the Spring 1945 issue of that magazine, appears another Sterling novel, "Red Sun of Danger." After almost a year, a new novel, "Outlaw World" (Winter 1946) reuses the amnesia theme again, as Newton temporarily becomes a space pirate. In the Fall 1946 issue, Manley Wade Wellman contributes his only novel, "The Solar Invasion"; this brings back The Magician of Mars for his third and final appearance.

Then, for four years, silence.

Not until 1950 do we receive word of the Futuremen. Then they return in a fine series of seven short stories, published in *Startling Stories*. Immediately we plunge into a world altered significantly from earlier years. Newton has achieved a strange maturity. Become harder, grimmer, he moves through odd stories of regret, subtle loss, and sacrifice. Each story deals, in some way, with the temptations of absolute power and the pain of relinquishment. The tone is adult, full of complex motives and disillusionment.

In "The Return of Captain Future" (January 1950), Newton has returned from Andromeda with a strange creature that turns out to be the last of an elder master race. Revived, it seizes control of Joan Randall. To save her, Newton permits the thing to take over his own mind—but for a reason. The story and its emotional resonances are admirable and entirely unexpected for a series that has been, up to now, constructed of cotton candy.

In May comes the superb "Children of the Sun." Newton, seeking a lost friend, is transmuted into an energy creature and plunges into incredible freedom at the heart of the Sun.

"The Harpers of Titan" (September) belongs to Simon Wright. Surgically implanted in a dead man's body, he meets the terrible, gentle Harpers, prevents a native uprising, and encounters, once more, the equally terrible delights of living in the flesh.

At this point, the series is interrupted by a story featuring the robot, Grag. "Pardon My Iron Nerves" (November) labors to be comic but manages only low burlesque.

The sequence of highly emotional adventure stories resumes with the January 1951 "Moon of the Unforgotten." Ezra Gurney, investigating the disappearance of elderly people on Jupiter, learns the cause in a bitterly poignant story. "Earthmen No More" (March) is a cutting study of alienation—the familiar dichotomy of the hard, decent frontier and the corrupt city. It is the future seen through the eyes of a man from the past. Newton struggles to smash a rocket-fuel monopoly and is grim, implacable, full of bitter humor, rage, and sardonic outbursts, curious emotions for a pulp magazine hero. As a curious sidelight, Otho comes alive in this story, as an individual of complex and unsuspected depths, subtly alien, as is proper for an artificial man.

The final story, "Birthplace of Creation" (May) returns to the center of the galaxy, the scene of "Captain Future's Quest." A misguided scientist has stolen the secret of the matter-creating machine and is creating a torrent of new worlds. Newton is barely able to contain the damage, for he, himself, is nearly overwhelmed by the desire to wield such god-like powers. His brutal personal struggle is vividly told and the story stands as a splendid finale to the series.

So the record stands. Six years of pleasantly light-minded space opera; two years of something more. A hero who began in popular magazine perfection and ended as a flawed man, grim, alone, gripped by psychological wounds we barely understand.

Perhaps he saw too much. But it makes for fascinating reading.

Jesse James' Ferocious Exploits;
or, Piping the Terrible Outlaw in
The Adventure Series

The ghost of Jesse James still whispers at the back of the American mind. It is a national ghost, one of those terrible phantoms that will not leave us.

These are not traditional ghosts. They do not posture in the dark, their eye sockets flaring with Hell's light. Our ghosts are more circumspect. They haunt the stuff of history and, consequently, our minds.

John Henry persists, and Geronimo, Jim Bridger and fierce Mike Fink, and Jesse James. When the man died and was snugly buried away, his ghost endured in a haze of stories passed casually down the generations. Night songs sustained it. A line of doggerel continued it. Nothing as complex as a ghost fades easily, and these ghosts continue to stare out at you, unspeakably violent, from behind the tame confections of the present.

They are ghosts of the American mind, which is stiffened by the past and not nearly as tame as some believe.

Jesse James persists. He was created by the Civil War, made a household name by the newspapers. Made a legend by the story papers and dime novels.

He was born Jesse Woodson James in 1847, being three years younger than his brother, Alexander Franklin James. Both were born in Clay County, Missouri, near Kearney. There their sister, Susan, was also born in 1849.

In 1851, their father, a Baptist minister, joined the rush to the California gold fields. Three weeks after he arrived, he died of fever. His wife, Zerelda Lindsay James, had remained with the family in Missouri. She would marry twice again—first to a farmer named Simms, who swiftly died, and, in 1857, to Dr. Reuben Samuel.

The Samuels and the James children lived at a difficult time in that difficult place, the Kansas-Missouri border area. Civil War passions raged. Bands of armed men, professing allegiance to one side or the other, or no allegiance to anything, roamed and murdered. The James boys, strongly Confederate in sympathy, were drawn into the orbit of William Quantrill. They became part of that bloody guerrilla struggle that seesawed through the border lands, one atrocity capped by a worse. Madness, intolerance, hatred intermingled, a black thicket slimed with blood.

The Civil War ended. The border raids and struggles did not. Known Confederates were continually harassed. Those who had ridden with Quantrill found neither amnesty nor acceptance nor peace. Lincoln had wished to bind up the wounds. But in terrible Missouri, the wounds stank and rotted.

The James boys faced an implacable society that would not forgive or forget. Before that society, they could do little right. Why then, defy the Union sympathizers, the militia, the night riders, the gouging banks, the hated judicial paraphernalia of the conquerors.

Is it wrong to smite the oppressors?

Or perhaps these politically charged sentiments merely obscure the darker truth that armed robbery is exciting and stimulates the heart and is occasionally profitable. It is also a one-way road. But you don't learn that till later.

Whatever the cause, the legends began building in 1866. The bank at Liberty, Missouri, was robbed. Maybe Jesse and Frank were involved. Maybe not. More crimes were credited to the James boys than they ever committed. But implicated or not, their legend begins at Liberty, on Valentine's Day.

Thereafter, a long series of bank robberies. In July 1873, they began to attack trains. The Rock Island and Pacific was derailed fourteen miles out of Council Bluffs, Iowa, and the James boys got the credit, deserved or not.

Came 1874, a fateful year. Jesse married his cousin, Zerelda Mimms; the marriage would last until his death and produce five children, two of them surviving. And late in that year began the famous James struggle with the Pinkerton Detective Agency.

Allan Pinkerton had dispatched one of his top operatives, J. W. Whicher, to Missouri to capture the James boys. Whicher was speedily killed, shot in head and heart. The Pinkerton Agency reacted with violence. Only a few weeks later, January 1875, they surrounded the Samuel home and, with incredible folly, hurled an explosive 32-pound shell, wrapped in blazing rags, through the window. The shell detonated killing Jesse's young half brother, Archie, and severing Mrs. Samuel's right arm below the elbow.[1]

That explosion blasted away any possibility that the James boys would become reconciled with society. From this period on, their record is a string of robberies, culminating in the gang's bloody repulse at Northfield, Minnesota. (The three younger brothers, wounded, were captured and sentenced to life imprisonment in the Minnesota State Penitentiary.)[2]

After Northfield, the James boys rode west, dropped into Texas and Mexico. Returned, crime, by crime, through Nebraska, Missouri, Iowa, Kentucky. At length, all adventures ended. In 1882, Jesse was shot by Bob Ford in St. Joseph, Missouri. At the time of his death, he was thirty-five.

Frank lived to surrender. He was tried, eventually freed because of lack of evidence. Later he was briefly involved in Wild West shows, ranched in Oklahoma, died in 1915. His mother, tough one-armed Zerelda, died four years earlier.

Jesse James, Jr., rising above his father's legend, became a respected lawyer in Kansas City until his death in 1951.[3]

So much for the bones of the James boys legend.

Upon this rich material, the dime novelists pounced rejoicing. While Jesse still roamed about uncaught, he became a fictional character. His raging adventures burst forth in the *Wide Awake Library* and the *New York Detective Library*. He faced Old Sleuth and Old King Brady. His exploits flamed in the *Log Cabin Library* and the *James Boys Weekly* and *Jesse James Stories*.

For fifteen years, the James gang pounded through a complexity of titles. They were reprinted and again reprinted. New stories were added to old series. It was fiction almost entirely, with an occasional pin prick of fact inserted to leaven the dough.

The James Boys were ferocious killers. Or Robin Hoods, fine men driven to crime by the Pinkertons. Or merciless blackguards, thirsting for blood.

But historical accuracy was not required. Mention the Glendale train, the Northfield raid, the Gallatin murder. About the name erect a glimmering bubble of fantasy. No matter. Readers sought wild escapes and reeling action. Panting chases, the flare of guns by night. The sprawl of bodies in Missouri backwoods. These delights, readers received in abundance.

Until 1903. At that time, Street & Smith (publishers of *Jesse James Stories*) and Tousey (publisher of the *James Boys Weekly*) agreed to terminate the Jesse James adventures.[4] For about five years, as best we can tell, no new material was published. Then appeared a square little paperbacked book, "The James Boys of Old Missouri, and Their Outlaw Band of Border Bandits" (1907). This was the second volume of *The Adventure Series*, published by the Arthur Westbrook Company of Cleveland, Ohio. The author was said to be William Ward, a mellifluous name of suspect reality.

From this volume, a new Jesse James series grew—thirty-five novels, Nos. 9 through 43 in *The Adventure Series*. Five years after the James spectre had been banished, it returned, newly outfitted with flaming guns and Bowie knives, giving death death death.

The Westbrook *Adventure Series* books were pocket-sized paperbacks of about 180 pages, containing 16 to 22 chapters. They were decorated with color covers—deep muddy blues, accented by red and yellow, having large patches of white often integrated into the design. On these covers, in archaic line drawings, bearded men pistol the heads of their victims. Or they ride horses very fast. Or glower fiercely out at you. The only interior illustration was an ill-drawn frontispiece; this depicted a lesser scene from the story and rarely got all figures in the same proportion.

The novels, themselves, seem to have been written between 1908 and 1910. They were as coolly cynical an exploitation of the subject as anything seen in our own wicked times. In these pages, the bandits were manly figures, quick witted and competent. Their ways were rough, it's true, their actions lethal. But that was because they were hounded by posses and detectives and other bandit bands of reprehensible moral fiber, hateful representatives of law and order who refused to allow the James Boys to do what they wanted to.

Crime is horrible; tell us more.

In the telling, the stories used every technical narrative element developed by generations of dime novels: action beginnings, suspense hooks at chapter's end, dual story lines, methodically introduced scenes of attack and chase, capture and escape. Through the pages elbowed colorful characters, drawn one molecule deep and one trait wide. The well-seasoned devices of sensational literature were packed into the story—from secret doors and passages to mysterious caverns and chests of treasure. Narrative movement never slackened. The posse forever pursued, Winchesters cocked. The foaming horses forever strained up one more hill. It was continuous danger, continuous combat, continuous murder.

And, as an added enticement to the jaded reader, most stories included scenes of torture and mutilation, lovingly described, slice by slice.

The crimson trail began with Adventure Series #9, "Jesse James' Dash for Fortune; or, The Raid on the Kansas City Fair." The action opens at a two-story cabin in the Missouri outback. There live the James Boys' mother, their sister Susie, their half-brother Johnny, and their step-father, Dr. Samuels.[5]

Jesse and Frank have slipped in to visit their dear old mother, who is one of the tougher examples of border femininity. She suggests that they consider all that cash stacked around the Kansas City Fair.

For an elderly, respectable lady, Mrs. Samuels has a lot of unique ideas. In a later volume, she will suggest that the boys look into train robbing. She is not your average mother.

Full of plans for the Fair, the boys ride off to meet the Youngers. They ride to adventure which, in these books, is never more distant than the next page. In this instance, it is a string of eight adventures, each two or three chapters long.

Adventure 1: They discover and foil a posse led by detective Con Morley. (He will be a recurring character, lumpishly eager to catch them James Boys somehow.) Morley vows to catch Jesse single-handed, but is himself captured and humiliated.

Adventure 2: Jesse and Bob Younger go swimming and are trapped by a man with a shotgun. He gets dispatched.

Adventure 3: They are attacked by Black Riders—a sort of vigilante pack—and clean their clocks after a bitter struggle.

Adventure 4: Jesse finds a woman murdered in a field. She has been horribly mutilated. In disguise, he joins forces with Con Morley to track the killer down. Once the killer is discovered, Jesse spirits him away and buries him in an ant hill.

Adventure 5: In an old cabin, the gang discovers a hidden watcher. Is he a detective? Jesse thinks not. (This is only event that has plot strands more than two chapters long.)

Adventure 6: They evade a posse.

Adventure 7: Frank meets a pair of pretty girls and invites himself to their barbecue. There he is recognized and chased, but one of the girls helps him escape.

Adventure 8: Jesse goes to case the Fair and gets involved in a horse race with a tricky Texan. He escapes being captured through the aid of the fellow discovered in Adventure 5.

After all this activity, it is now time for the central crime. Jesse snatches the Fair's cash box as it is being transferred and gets $10,000.

This loose narrative structure, rattling like marbles in a box, will be used in most stories of the series. First, the crime that gives its title to the book will be mentioned. There follows a stream of more or less disassociated parts. The outlaws are menaced and chased and trapped. Jesse extracts his gang by a clever trick, after which the pursuers are shot to flinders. Then the whole process is repeated.

After 170 pages of random blood and death, you arrive at Chapter XX. In this, the title crime is committed. It is followed by a brief Chapter XXI: "Conclusion," in which the loot is counted and the burial details get to work.

Even so early in the series, you have the feeling that something distressing has happened to the chronology. You are correct. The bulk of the series appears built around specific crimes of the James Boys—or those credited to them, about the same thing.

No. 12: "Jesse James' Greatest Haul; or, The Daylight Robbery of the Russellville Bank"
No. 18: "Jesse James' Desperate Game; or, The Robbery of the Ste. Genevieve Bank"
No. 21: "Jesse James, Gentleman; or, The Hold-Up of the Mammoth Cave Stage"

The internal continuity of the series runs directly from No. 9 through No. 43. This is an entirely artificial continuity, imposed by art. The crimes that are so convincingly sequenced actually occurred at widely separated dates. The scrambling of the actual historical record is total.

Volume 9 combines the caught-while-swimming episode (Summer 1870) with the Kansas City Fair robbery (1873). No. 12, the Russellville Bank robbery occurred in 1868. No. 14, the hold-up of the Chicago and Alton train, was in 1879. No. 15, recounting the murder of Pinkerton Whicher, was in 1874. No 18, the robbery of the Ste. Genevieve bank in 1873, is followed by the Northfield raid (No. 19, 1876), the Mammoth Cave stage (No. 21, 1880), the Rock Island train robbery (No. 23,1873), and the Gallatin Bank robbery (No. 24, 1869).

The chronology is further addled by the liberal introduction of stories of pure fiction—as opposed to stories 96% fiction. These include a struggle against a San Francisco tong and its murderous gorilla (No. 22), some difficulty with a woman detective (No. 36), and a legacy Jesse must claim in person (No. 39).

You can read this series with pleasure. But it will force you to reset all your historical clocks.

Through all this muddle strides the glorious figure of Jesse James.

> Tall, broad-shouldered, his face was clean and well cut, his eyes were merry, his manners pleasant and attractive and there was nothing about him to suggest the awful deviltry which underlay his natural reticence, for only when his anger was roused or when the blood-lust was upon him did he display those characteristics, the scowling brow, the clinched jaw the snapping eyes, the black expression, the loud and terrible oaths that the popular mind has assigned to all outlaws.[6]

According to a WANTED poster, offering $50,000 "FOR THE BODY OF JESSE JAMES, DEAD OR ALIVE!" he has "curly black hair, smooth face, shifting eyes, large mouth, 5 feet 11 inches tall, weight about 170 pounds." The same poster described his horse, Satan, as being coal black with glossy skin, 15.5 hands high.[7]

Jesse regards his situation as a wanted criminal with considerable bitterness:

> Mine is a name both hated and feared throughout this broad country. I offer no apologies for this statement. I am simply stating a fact....And what is more, a price that some would consider was equal to a king's ransom has been placed upon my head. I am hunted like a wild beast both by day and by night. I am an outcast on the face of the earth, and if ever the impulse to be other than I am has been stirred in my breast it has been almost instantly crushed by the men who in the name of the law have sought my life.[8]

Well, it was all the fault of the posses and the Pinkertons, chasing around after poor Jesse, lusting for that $50,000. You get a bad name and you get your description on a reward poster, you and your horse, and the backwoods is thick with fellows waiting to backshoot you. Or to creep up to the Samuels' cabin and peer through the window. Or insult your mother and sister. A man could get driven to crime that way. People never let him alone.

In his book on *The Dime Novel Western*, Daryl Jones remarks:

> It is nearly impossible to overestimate the importance of conventional persecution and revenge as a means of justifying the outlaw's rebellion against established social and legal codes. Some such vindication was a vital ingredient in the outlaw's characterization. For although readers were themselves familiar enough with social and legal injustice to understand and identify with a man whom society had forced into rebellion, they could not condone unprovoked lawlessness.[9]

This justification sweetened Jesse's overly vigorous record. The customary additional justifications were briskly added: That he often righted wrongs and punished criminals; that representatives of law and order behaved even more vilely than Mr. James.

And perhaps most of these qualifications are right, in part. The only problem in matching the fictional Jesse James to the stereotype of the aggrieved hero is that, about twice a novel, he explodes in homicidal frenzy.

As in No. 13, "Jesse Jame's Revenge; or, The Hold-Up of the Train at Independence."

The story, like mismatched mittens, is in two vaguely associated parts. The first part consists of chase and escape, as if the writer had no particular direction in mind. Jesse and a few of the boys join a posse to capture themselves. When discovered, they capture the posse and use them as targets for some trick shooting.

In this instance, Jesse merely shoots off the knots of the neckerchieves. More usually, he would notch earlobes with .44 slugs. His shooting is phenomenal with either hand.

Thereafter, they get chased by another posse and hide cleverly. Soon after, they pounce upon four detectives and have a rousing hand-to-hand fight.

In the course of which, Jesse goes berserk:

> ...Jesse sprang to his feet, bounded into the air, landing with terrible force upon the prostrate man's chest, kneeing him.
>
> And as he struck, the crunching of breaking ribs was audible to every one of the wildly struggling men and so sickening was the sound that the others paused in their strife.
>
> The bandit-chieftain had become a fiend incarnate. His face black with rage, his brows beetling, cursing frightfully, he clubbed his guns and rained blow after blow upon his victim's head, disfiguring him beyond recognition. Springing to his feet, he yanked Bixby from off Cole, belaboring him into unconsciousness, then freed Clell from the embrace of his antagonist, finally turning his attention to the man who had so nearly caused his downfall, kicking him till his face resembled a piece of raw beefsteak.
>
> Even his companions were horrified at Jesse's fury and looked on in silence, not daring to interfere.[10]

These murderous frenzies are methodically inserted into the novels. As the series matures, the frenzies grow progressively more brutal. Murder is capped by torture and mutilation and dismemberment, as Jesse rages beyond control.

> So terrible was the aspect of the famous desperado as he uttered the awful threat, his ashen-hued face distorted with hatred, his eyes flashing fire making him seem more like some hideous monster than a human being of flesh and blood, that even his companions unconsciously shrank from him....[11]

These two personality elements of the Westbrook Jesse James are never reconciled. To the end they remain separate, two parallel rivers that mingle no water.

It does seem that Jesse's mood swings are extreme for light fiction.

During the second part of "Jesse James' Revenge," the outlaws make a secret hideout in a cave. They are much bothered by the White Caps (another bunch of night riders like the Black Riders and the Black Wings) and slay armies of them, gun flame bright in the bitter darkness.

Enter new recruit Lem Hawkins and his girl, Sadie Hargis. She is an undercover detective. He is a traitor. After Jesse discovers this, Lem is tortured with red hot irons until his fingers and toes are burnt away. Sadie escapes unharmed—by the code of the West or the squeamishness of dime novel publishers, the James' gang refuses to harm women. Even when they deserve punishment.

So protected by an invisible shield, Sadie steals Jesse's personal treasure. But in the next to the last chapter, he discovers her on the train he is robbing and recovers the wealth.

"Jesse James Nemesis; or, The Pinkerton's Oath," No. 15 of the series, is a pivotal novel. It introduces characters right and left, establishes two permanent plot lines, and stirs two dabs of fact into a caldron of fiction. Again the story has two distinct parts.

Part 1: Jesse is in Kansas City to see his sweetheart and hunt down a traitor. He has a lively time dodging police and Pinkertons and big city crooks. And killing with both hands. Saved from pursuit by the hideous, hunch-backed cripple, Dick the Rat, Jesse is led into the deeps of the sewer system. There he witnesses the slaughter of a traitor by Dick and his horrid crew: They cut pieces off the rascal until nothing is left but a rack of bones.

Jesse watches this interesting activity so passively that you have the sensation he has strayed into someone else's story. And perhaps he has. The sequence certainly seems to have been grafted onto the story. It's like finding a shoe in the mashed potatoes—you know it doesn't belong there, even if you don't know where it came from.

Anyhow, Dick the Rat is now established as a series character. He appears in most of the Kansas City stories. He also appears in places where such urban riff-raff rarely visit—moonshiners' mountains and deep Tennessee woods. He arrives when Jesse needs him desperately. He is filled with plot information whispered to him by William Ward. He knows all the secret doors and what the Pinkertons think and where Helen Ormsby has got to this time. Dick is the brace that keeps the whole ramshackle story from collapsing.

Who is Helen Ormsby?

Helen is Jesse's sweetheart. She is fresh, young, clever, and madly intensely in love with Jesse. No matter what they say about him, her love continues. No matter how her father snorts and rages—he is a Kansas City banker, very wealthy—she is Jesse's adored, his girly, his delight.

She may well be the most kidnapped heroine in fiction. Helen exists to be kidnapped. In one story, she gets kidnapped three times by three separate people. Whenever she is kidnapped, Jesse stops killing whomever he is killing at the moment and thunders away. His face is set. He radiates black. Helen is in danger and the world must pause.

Helen is a featured player in the series through No. 42. During all these adventures, no mention is made of Jesse's wife and their merry children. As far as Westbrook publications were concerning, Jesse lived and died a single man. One or two other girls stirred his heart during the series. But he fought temptation like the noble man he was. He remained true to Helen. And she, defying her father and friends, remained true to Jesse.

All this material is packed into the first eight chapters. The dead bleed all over Kansas City, the Pinkertons are humiliated, and Jesse has carried Helen off to visit in the Missouri backwoods.

Part 2: Pinkerton assigns his best operative, John Whicher, to track the James Boys down. The gang captures him instead. After some pages of graphic torture, Jesse shoots Whicher to death and sends a mocking note, written in the detective's blood, to Pinkerton.

Pinkerton responds with a full-scale attack against Dr. Samuels' cabin, where the James Boys are believed hiding out. They are not. The flaming shell is hurled through the window. The innocent are killed or mutilated. And Jesse gives up all plans to become engaged to Helen. He wants revenge. He wants Pinkerton blood. He will slay and slay and slay until. . . .

As a later story remarks:

> It was the greatest, in fact, the only regret that (Jesse) had in his wild life of crime that the detectives and manhunters would not spare his family in their endeavors to capture him and his brother Frank. And it was his dream that some day his gang should inflict such terrible punishment upon the guardians of law that they would fear again to molest the homestead and its inmates at Kearney.[12]

From this point on, the chronological confusion becomes incurable. In the world of history, the gang committed sundry bank and train robberies. After they encountered the determined citizens of Northfield, Jesse and Frank headed south to Mexico. There they robbed a silver train, and, the following Spring, routed a Mexican infantry brigade at Monclova in Coahuila. Still later, they shot up a local bandit, Juan Fernando Palaciois, for rustling some James cattle.

All these stirring adventures, in and around Mexico, entered *The Adventure Series*. But as dismembered chunks, wrenched out of all sequence and fictionalized from hair line to toe nails. The four volumes touching on the Mexican years are:

No. 40: "Jesse James' Silver Trail; or, The Plundering of the Mexican Muleteers" (The event occurred in 1876.)

No. 41: "Jesse James' Ring of Death; or, The Fate of the Texas Rangers" (All events fictional)

No. 20: "Jesse James' Battle for Freedom; or, The Fight at Monclava" (Occurred 1897 at Monclova, the correct spelling)

No. 16: "Jesse James' Terrible Raid; or, The Extermination of the Mexican Bandits" (Occurred 1877; Palaciois is spelled Palacio.)

The stories blast along packed with attacks, counter-attacks, traps, secret caverns, death traps, torture by fire gun knife, and a steady storm of killing as the population of Mexico is significantly reduced.

In No. 16, Jesse secures a magic salve that cures every ill from glanders to gunshot wounds. Marvelous stuff, created by a Mexican witch.

No. 20 is a complicated business in three parts.

During the first portion, it is routine chase and shoot. Jesse escapes from detectives surrounding the Samuels' house. Planning to form a new gang and try it out in Mexico, he recruits tough Sim Dirks. With Frank, they race away to the Missouri River and a series of bloody adventures. In the course of these few chapters, Jesse kills eleven detectives and possemen. A routine adventure.

Now, squarely in the center of the story, occurs a complete interpolated adventure. Jesse pretends to be Con Morley, the detective, and agrees to investigate weird events in New Orleans. Once there, he untangles a complicated case with many supernatural elements—a ghost train, yellow flowers that turn white, ghosts, watching pictures....It is all a plot to steal a million dollar inheritance through a fraudulent marriage.

In his two-part article, "The James Boys in the Saddle Again," J. Edward Leithead remarks that the Westbrook Jesse James novels have a familiar sound. "The style of writing and handling of incidents, to my mind, more resemble the work of St. George Rathborne and T. W. Hanshew, authors of the Log Cabin 'James Boys' novels...."[13] The New Orleans interpolation in *Adventure Series* No. 20 certainly sounds like Hanshew. It includes all those supernatural trappings that Hanshew liked to drag into a story, then explode casually. A familiar Hanshew device appears when Jesse sprinkles powder about to see if a supernatural creature leaves tracks—just as Cleek, the Man of Forty Faces, might have done.

At any moment, you expect Jesse to writhe his face into new features.

That Hanshew wrote the New Orleans material mentioned here is certainly possible. That the material was published elsewhere and revised for Jesse James No. 20 is also possible. Particularly since the New Orleans situation differs in style from the violence-oriented narrative of the first and third parts.

But we really don't know. Until the Westbrook editorial records are located and studied, any attribution of authorship is simply guesswork. Leithead is correct: The prose resembles the work of Rathborne and Hanshew. Beyond noting that resemblance, we should not go.[14]

The final part of "Jesse James' Battle for Freedom" takes place in a Texas border town. While there, cleaning up the final strands of the New Orleans case, Jesse meets Con Morley. Then follows a wonderful saloon fight. Morley gets his jaw broken and, before the guns cool, the James Boys have killed fifteen more.

In the now obligatory torture scene, Jesse seeks information from a prisoner. Then the boys go into action against the Mexican army, kill about twenty, and retreat to the States.

Around this time, you realize that Jesse James has become fiction's most efficient killing machine. During No. 22, "Jesse James' Bluff; or, The Escape of the Chinese Highbinders," Jesse and company commit eighty-two killings, including Black Riders, Pinkertons, and assorted detectives and Tong members.

The carnival begins when a detective discovers the James Boys' secret cave and steals their treasure. To recover the fortune, Jesse (slightly aided by Frank and others)

——fights free of a flaming cabin, slaughtering his captors
——traps a 21-man posse in the cave and kills them all

At this point, Sheriff Bud Hopkins slaps Jesse's mother and calls Jesse a coward. Before the wretch is punished, Jesse

——traps 17 Black Riders in a barn that burns to the ground
——ambushes a huge posse and guns it to pieces
——loads a captured Pinkerton with dynamite, ties him to a telephone pole, and explodes him with a rifle bullet.
——guns down Sheriff Hopkins in a public courtroom duel

After these stirring exploits, the gang heads toward St. Louis. Along the way, they

——obliterate a 4-man posse
——murder a gambler on a riverboat and hijack the riverboat

When they arrive in St. Louis, police, Pinkertons, and detectives die by the score. Between murders, Jesse finds time to

——execute a traitor to the gang
——steal a Tong treasure concealed in an opium joint, while blasting Chinese killers to their doom

How furiously the savage action rages.

The outlaws are trapped. By a clever trick, they slide away. Only to be surrounded by armies of men. As they fight free, Jesse is creased by a bullet, captured, tied up tight. Or some cowardly mutt slugs him from behind. But no one is clever enough to check Jesse's boots, each concealing a Bowie knife. In moments he is free, cursing horribly—slashing and shooting—splashed with blood—his face distorted.

No one may strike Jesse James and live.

No one may fire at Jesse James and get away with his life.

No one may strike Jesse James' mother or Jesse James' sister or steal Jesse James' sweetheart or injure Jesse James' horse. No one may sneer at Jesse James, steal his treasure, poke about his home, ride against him, talk about him, scowl or laugh near him, be a banker, be a Pinkerton.

Jesse James will not tolerate it.

The Bowie flashes and is dripping red. The heavy Colt thunders. The iron fist strikes home a terrible blow.

The James Boys never forgive or forget an insult. And anything can be an insult. Anything at all.

The death machine that is Jesse James rides killing through backwoods Missouri. Strides killing through Kansas City streets. Drifts killing down through Texas to massacre in Mexico and slaughter in Colorado. To gouge out eyes in Iowa, and split tongues in Kansas, and decapitate in Missouri. And kill, and kill again, and again kill.

All for the entertainment and pleasure of the reader.

By some miracle, the stories work. For all their shallow violence and lack of direction, in spite of melodrama and dramatic cliches, stereotypes, coincidence, lack of characterization, rabid inhumanity, they suck the reader along. Chapters hurtle past. The suspense would bend metal. Jesse James, that terrible outlaw, towers colossal. No man can trap him. If caught by bad luck, he cannot be held.

——Into the glowing bed of coals, he thrusts his bound hands
——Bloody wounds streaming, he slashes down the Bowie
——Tied hand and foot, he squirms to the cliff edge and hurls himself into space.

"Jesse James' Wild Night; or, The Wrecking of the Rock Island Train" (No. 23) tells how he seeks to save a kidnapped girl. At the end, he fails. Her death is avenged in blood.

The violent events of "Jesse James' Brutal Shot; or, The Murder in the Gallatin Bank" (No. 24) are again divided between town and country. The town is Kansas City, where Jesse comes to see Helen and ends putting holes in many citizens. The Pinkertons try but accomplish little. Pinkerton Superintendent Dillaby ends slugged and tied up in his own home, while Jesse flies down the street in Dillaby's coach with Dillaby's wife at his side, brightly interested. Helen, the cause of all this commotion, has been kidnapped again.

During the country portion of the story, a posse is repeatedly outwitted and shot to ribbons.

In No. 25, "Jesse James" Daylight Foray; or, The Looting of the Bank at Corydon, Iowa," a woman overhears Jesse's plans to rob a bank. He chases her and a posse chases him and it is eighteen chapters of hares and hounds and gory excesses.

In "Jesse James' Mistake; or, Foiled By Death" (No. 28), Helen gets kidnapped twice running. After saving her the second time, Jesse confronts Father Ormsby with a demand for Helen's hand—on the solid ground that the old man doesn't know how to protect her.

But Banker Ormsby flatly refuses. He intends to ship Helen off to Europe, where she will forget her infatuation with a common criminal. After she returns, she will wed wealthy young Dick Martin.

This admirable plan is immediately spoiled. Jesse rides to Martin's bank and shoots him dead. It is an ill-timed gesture. For only Martin knew the combination to the vault, now locked fast and invulnerable.

"Jesse James' Ruse; or, The Mystery of the Two Highwaymen" (No. 30) contains a bit of this, a bit of that. Fights with detectives and manhunters in Kearney and Kansas. Then off to meet Homely Harry in Colorado, where

Wild Bill (one of Jesse's boys) rides an unbreakable horse and everyone robs a stage coach. They get the money Indians received for a land sale.

The Indians promptly lead the bandits into an ambush. After a long chase, the Indians almost have them, but Jesse fires the prairie grass in the nick of time.

The bandits then rob another stage twice, pretending to be ghosts, and great is the hilarity. Particularly when Jesse decides to scare six prisoners by making them dig their own graves. At the last moment, troopers appear and Jesse is forced to kill all six. But at least their graves were prepared. It wasn't as if he just shot them and left them there.

Those readers who enjoy stylistic curiosities may note that, in this novel, Dr. Samuels' house is referred to as "Castle James." Another stylistic puzzle is Jesse's use of the exclamation "By Jove," a choice of words singularly inappropriate for a backwood Missouri boy. (The exclamation is also used in Nos. 20 and 28.)

One of the stranger stories of the series is No. 33, "Jesse James' Daring Joke; or, The Kidnapping of a Bank President." The bank president is almost incidental. He is banker Perkins of St. Joseph, who has had the bad judgement to hire Bud Simpkins and his White Caps to get Jesse. Discovering that enemies surround the Castle James, Mrs. Samuels dresses Jesse in a calf skin. He moves out through them, killing as he goes, and almost escapes. Except that he falls and knocks himself out. The White Caps capture and torture him and treat him mean. But he escapes, blowing up half their force. Presently he is trapped in a flaming cabin, from which he escapes by falling into a mountain.

Meanwhile, Bud carries off Mrs. Samuels. She is tortured to make her tell where Frank is. When her captors relax their guard, she uses pressure on neck nerves to subdue a tough killer, then chokes him to death with her single arm. Upset by her behavior, Bud drags her off to a cave and burns her feet with candles.

About this time, Jesse works out of the mountain into the cave and the slaughter is just splendid. Bud escapes, but not for long. Jesse has the satisfaction of smashing out the fiend's brains against a tree.

As an afterthought, he rides over to St. Joe, lures off banker Perkins. After robbing him of $10,000, Jesse lodges him in jail, telling everyone that Perkins is really Jesse James. Joke.

"Jesse James' Narrow Escape; or, Ensnared By a Woman Detective" (No. 36) is another town and country adventure. Jesse saves a banker's beautiful daughter from a flaming house and is lionized and made much over. However, a woman Pinkerton suspects his true identity and plots to expose him. The action is smoothly intricate and several of the characters, including the banker and his daughter, are nicely drawn. They are also sympathetic to Jesse, even when he reveals his true identity.

Then the story veers out into the country, where they ride and shoot and holler along the Missouri River.

Helen returns in "Jesse James' Surprise; or, The Looting of the Huntingdon Bank" (No. 38). First Jesse saves her (and her crafty father) from a train wreck. Then she is kidnapped by an old mountain boy who demands a ransom. Jesse is on her trail but is captured by Pinkertons and only escapes by tumbling over a cliff. Meanwhile Helen has been carried off to a cave. She beans her captor with a flaming lamp and escapes and is caught and escaped and falls over a cliff to land right beside Jesse. And away they wander hand in hand. Eventually Jesse gets her back to Kansas City, where he has a violent scene with old man Ormsby and departs, unsettled in mind.

Those are Chapters 1 through 20. Chapter 21 covers the robbery of the Huntingdon Bank, which seems tossed in as an afterthought to add verisimilitude to this bald and unconvincing narrative.

Even the most delightful pleasures fade at last. The Jesse James series nears its conclusion. Off stage, Bob Ford fingers his pistol and, onstage, the mysterious Man In Black spreads his ebon cape and glides, silent and terrible, from place to place, his eyes fixed on Jesse.

It is told in No. 42, "Jesse James' Mysterious Foe; or, The Pursuit of the Man in Black." This sinister figure dogs Jesse everywhere, causing him to scowl and shuffle his feet. After a series of violent adventures in St. Louis, Jesse is captured. But don't be distressed. He promptly escapes and races handcuffed through the city, blasting down police right and left.

Only to find that Helen has been, er, well, kidnapped, is what's happened to her. She writes a letter saying that she's being held in Kentucky.

Off Jesse goes, with Frank, to rescue her.

Now follows a train hold-up, a fight with the bandits, a plunge from a train traveling 60 mph, and excursions up and down the line. Is Frank dead? Is Jesse dead? Finally the boys steal a complete train and arrive in Kentucky, only to discover that Helen is not there at all.

This part of the story is so weakly inept it fairly screams revision of another story. A note from Dick the Rat calls Jesse back to St. Louis. There, in a scene stiff and contrived and touching, all at the same time, Helen breaks off with Jesse:

Helen: "...You and I must part. Believe me, Jess, it almost breaks my heart to have to say it, but our friendship is bringing us both misery."

JJ: "Friendship! You call it friendship?"

Helen: "Yes, but I know it is much more. This terrible strain is wrecking my life and sooner or later your love for me is going to bring you to an imprudence that will cost you your life...."

JJ: "You have ceased to love me."

Helen: "You know that is not the case. I love you too well. It is that love that imperils your life every time you seek to see me....It is because of your love that the authorities came to know that you were here. Please don't make it any harder for me than it is. My heart is nearly broken. Good-bye, Jess."

JJ: "And am I to see you no more?"

Helen: "No more, please, Jess. The clouds will never drift away. I feel it. The feeling oppresses me. I have the presentiment that we shall never see each other again."[16]

She leaves. Jesse collapses into a chair. And at that moment he learns that Helen was saved from the kidnappers by The Man In Black—who is Jeff Clayton. "Better known as Jeff The Inscrutable, the world's most famous detective."

"Good God!" murmurs Jesse James.

Now our revels are almost ended. Insensibly the accomplished outlaw gang has dispersed. Cole Younger has gone, and all his brothers, and tough Clell Miller. Comanche Tony and Texas Jack have melted into the western sunset. Sam Dirks has vanished, and Jim White, and wiry Wild Bill, that horse-riding terror.

Pinkerton Superintendent Dillaby will come no more. Nor Allan Pinkerton, himself, nor Con Morley. Helen Ormsby and her father face a new life, far away. Slow-moving, ineffectual Dr. Samuels is gone. John Edwards and Jack Crawford, both of the *Kansas City Times*, both staunch James supporters, have helped Jesse trick the detectives for the last time. Dick the Rat slips secretly into his favorite sewer, his eyes hot in the fetid gloom.

A new sun rises. Over the forests and cliffs, the dirt roads and drowsy backwoods towns of Jesse James country, glows the new sun of Jeff Clayton.

Golden and terrible he blazes. Already he stars in a serial tucked at the back of the *Old Sleuth Weekly*. (Chapter One appeared in the April 1, 1910, issue.) Published in innumerable parts, the serial was titled "Jeff Clayton's Strange Quest; or, The Trail of a Ghost." Presently Jeff Clayton novels will march through *The Adventure Series*, beginning with No. 44, "Jeff Clayton's Lost Clue; or, The Mystery of the Wireless Murder." By William Ward, of course.[17]

Thirty-four Jeff Clayton titles will be published, spread across perhaps four years. The Jesse James series has stopped at last—barring a scatter of *Adventure Series* reprints around 1915.[18] Or perhaps something more remains to be discovered. With the James Boys, you are never quite sure.

The final Jesse James adventure in the series was No. 43, "Jesse James' Fate; or, The End of the Crimson Trail." It is nineteen chapters, 172 pages of scraps. It consists of four separate stories, lightly mushed together, plus some miscellaneous incidents that are too short for stories and too long for vignettes.

Action begins, as usual, at Dr. Samuels' home. The Black Wings raid but fail to capture Jesse. They never learned. He kills a stack of them and, with Frank, goes thundering away.

Unfortunately, Satan pulls a tendon. The outlaws are forced to hide in a graveyard and, for several chapters, it's fun among the headstones. The posse members search the graveyard and are tricked and scared and clubbed and shot down. It's quite humorous, really it is. Particularly if you ain't read hardly no books.

Enraged by this constant pursuit, Jesse vows to leave a crimson trail across Missouri that the state will long remember. And off they go.

They arrive in Abington, a town Jesse judges to be too sleepy and too slow. For the next three chapters, he turns the place sideways. He forces them to observe Sunday as Saturday, drives the whole town to bathe in the mill pond, scares all the men into sliding down the mill flume. These merry exercises, enforced by fist and pistol, halt when the minister's sweet little innocent daughter begs Jesse to let church service begin. After which the James Boys enforce 100% attendance at church and lavish contributions to the church collection.

From Abington, they ride to more adventure. They attend a dance that ends in a gun fight. Save a girl from a pushy suitor. Get chased by a horde of howling cowboys. Trapped in a flaming field, Jesse hollows out a dead horse and hides inside until the fire passes. Next he joins a circus, steals their receipts, and escapes in a balloon. When the balloon sags into the Mississippi, he boards a passing steamboat—is almost captured by Jeff Clayton—escapes—flees to St. Joseph.

And, two days later, is shot and killed by Bob Ford.

No sooner does Jesse fall dead, than a black-clad form plunges smashing through the window. Two shots roar out. The Ford boys' guns are blown from their hands.

Jeff Clayton has arrived, only a few seconds late.

The Jesse James series is over.

The Jeff Clayton series begins.

The inexorable making of fiction continues down the years.

The Westbrook Jesse James adventures are strangely flawed, built of mud and flowers. They are primitive as Devonian rock.

The James Boys and their outlaw band, known historical characters, pillaged for fifteen years and were dispersed. That documented reality is the least part of these adventures. The Jesse James of *The Adventure Series* is no real character. He exceeds reality. He has become myth, speaking as myth speaks, to grave elements of the human experience—of love and hunger and death, revenge and fortitude.

From this basic stone, the series derives its power. As fiction, it is rudely unpolished. As myth, it is vividly strong, the proper food of ghosts, as the ghost of Jesse James might tell you.

A Bow to the Wizard
(The Wizard, 4 issues, October 1940-April 1941;
Cash Gorman, 2 issues, June and August 1941)

One pulp hero, at least, went adventuring without armament. Thomas Jefferson "Cash" Gorman managed it, moving through six 1940-41 novels armed only with a silver-dollar pocket piece and his wits.

That was plenty. Gorman's mind, astute, subtle, sharply informed, was the equal of a dozen blazing .45's. His magazine was sub-titled "Adventures in Finance." It was written by Phil R. Sheridan, a probable pseudonym, the stories are literate, taut, with action at both physical and mental levels. They feature corporate intrigue set against a realistic backdrop of state and local politics, union interactions, syndicated crime, and high-flying financial machinations.

Cash Gorman, an adventurer-financier, invests in shaky businesses to build them up, take a profit. Sounds simple. But he must proceed in the face of clever and ruthless opposition. He is always under attack. His problems are major, complex, and in the real world. He handles them through a series of brilliant and informed maneuvers.

Characterization fades before the fancy footwork. Gorman is well drawn, if shallowly. Other characters are penciled in as collections of peculiar traits. Essentially, the story is how Gorman out-brillianted the opposition.

The first issue, October 1940, was "Gild the Sword with Gold." We meet Gorman and he meets Jimmy Ranger, his aide through the series. We are also introduced to Phineas Gardiner, a bulging, red-faced caricature of a capitalist: his wealth, tapped by Gorman through various deals, provides the operating fluid for most of the stories. In "Sword," the subject is an involved swindle with worthless helium land as bait. The swindlers are had in virtually the last paragraph of the novel by some highly tricky sleight-of-Gorman's hand.

"Million Dollar Mutual," December 1940, demonstrates how to save a failing race track against intolerable pressures. The maneuvering, possibly the most complex ever put into a pulp magazine, is packed with multiple interactions between politics, law, finance, and business—all based in the real world. This is the most successful of the Wizard novels.

"Liquid Gold," February 1941, plunges Gorman into labor trouble in the dairy business. "Murder in Gold," April 1941, is set in Hollywood: the accounts have been tapped at the studio; the swindlers are very murderous; Gorman is very very slick.

With the June 1941 issue, "Sabotage" (advertised in April as "Saboteurs In High Gear") the magazine is retitled *Cash Gorman*. In this novel, Gorman takes over an axle-manufacturing plant which Nazi agents and a local traitor are reducing to rubble. "Murder In Santa Paula," August 1941, sets Gorman against an entrenched political boss, a massive real estate swindle, an old murder frame, and an exploding dam.

On that high note, the series ends, a victim of so-so sales and the wartime paper shortage. Too bad. As the only thinking man's pulp, it was a noble experiment. Although the final three novels tend as much to violent adventure as to footwork through the complications of corporate finance, all novels are worth reading. The first two issues are of particular interest. Even if you don't collect the things, you should locate copies and read them. It would be a shame to leave this life with that undone.

His Voice an Eerie Whisper

(The Whisperer, second series, 10 issues, October 1940-April 1942)

"...No figure ever had less appearance of menace. Moonlight played over an oddly shaped face. A long upper lip and a pointed chin gave the countenance a mildly saturnine appearance. Because of the gray attire, the remainder of the man's rather slight figure might have been any one.

"The eyes were so cold and so lacking in fire, they gave forth no glow."

". . .the room was filled with an awe-inspiring, sibilant whisper. . . .

No, no, no, no. That can't be right. It's from the December 1936 *Whisperer*, but yet. . . .

Let's try again.

His chin was long-pointed, and his blurred hair under a quaint, round-brimmed hat was whitish in color.

Otherwise, The Whisperer was a humble, mild-appearing man with a low, husky voice, hardly above a whisper at any time. . . .

(He was) dressed all in gray. . . .

Well, that isn't right, either. It may be from "Bullet Bait," the first Whisperer short story to appear in the December 1, 1937 *The Shadow* magazine, but something is seriously wrong. "Mild-appearing"? "Quaint, round-brimmed hat"? Whitish hair. Now, really!

Something later, perhaps. From *The Whisperer*, April 1942:

Greenish eyes glowed within the murky confines of the coupe. They seemed to have an inner fire of their own. One compact hand reached out. . .(and) as it did, an eerie, hissing whisper welled up inside the coupe. It was a weird, compelling sound that carried both warning and defiance. . . .

"There was a soft swish; then a figure as black as the small coupe, almost invisible against it, eased out. . . ."

There was just a glimpse of a long, oddly pointed chin below the weird and slanted greenish eyes. Coal-black hair capped a pale, wide-browed skull. The man was clad entirely in black. The jet hue of his apparel at first belittled the hurrying figure's size. He was, however, not a large man. But the breadth of the chest and shoulders bespoke a strength able to cope with adversaries far beyond his weight and statue.

Well, good night, what are we up against here? Greenish, slanted eyes; black clothing; black hair and an eerie whisper that warns and defies? While hunting The Whisperer, we have tumbled over a clone of The Shadow. How exceedingly annoying.

Which is what we might expect. The Whisperer, for all its merits, is a most annoying series.

To begin with, it appeared in four different magazines over a period of seven years. In addition, it was written by two different authors—and that alone should scramble the character beyond recognition.

The series began as a single-character magazine titled *The Whisperer*. Fourteen issues were published, October 1936 through December 1937. These were written by Laurence Donovan, who had also done novels for *G-Men*, *Doc Savage*, *Pete Rice*, and, likely, *The Phantom Detective*, The Whisperer of these novels was tougher than calculus. Violent, ruthless, often brutal, he slugged and shot his way through relentless encounters with gangland, leaving behind a trail of cracked heads, broken bones, and nicely shot corpses. All in the name of justice.

All this violence was part of a deep-laid plan at Street & Smith. In 1936, the national economy, which had showed faint traces of reviving during the previous year, suddenly slumped again. As the economy scowled and tightened, competition from other magazines increased—particularly those magazines published by Popular Publications. Such publications as *The Spider, Terror Tales*, and *Horror Stories* had bitten out a choice chunk of the market. Not only were they jammed with non-stop violence, like the fever dream of a homicidal maniac, but that dread subject sex stalked their pages. Sex, that is, as interpreted to mean woman in immediate danger of rape, at the mildest.

Street & Smith had always stayed far back from these scarlet fields. In their magazines, women were precious non-entities, about as sexual as plastic chips. They might get stolen away and tied up until saved by the hero and his flaming pistol, but the only immediate dangers they faced were muscle cramps and boredom.

Popular Publications' salty fiction had changed that. Which is why, during 1936 at Street & Smith, some girls grew brazen and other girls frequently lost their clothing during the action. And when they got stolen away by unshaven rowdies, there was the occasional suggestion that the poor pitiful darling, all tied and gagged, might experience something worse than missing her dinner. It never happened. But it might. It might.

At the same time, the level of hard-boiled violence increased. For such established series as Doc Savage and The Shadow, that increase didn't amount to much. But in the new series of The Whisper and The Skipper, an acid whiff of ferocity tinged the pages. Mayhem stomped to the fore and the lead characters seemed remarkably ruthless.[1] It was a remarkable concession for such a staid company as Street & Smith.

After the cancellation of *The Whisperer* and *The Skipper* with their December 1937 issues, both characters continued in short-story series. The Skipper became a series in *Doc Savage*; The Whisperer entered *The Shadow* magazine. The hard-boiled, rough-'em-up tone of the fiction moderated slightly.

And a new author took over The Whisperer.

Not that the change was immediately noticeable. That familiar house name, Clifford Goodrich, still appeared as writer of the series. But change there was. Donovan wrote the first and third short stories, and Alan Hathway did the second and from number four on.[2] All told, Hathway wrote twenty-two Whisperers for *The Shadow*, plus a single story for *Crime Busters* (June 1939). Then lightning struck, or earthquake or something forceful: The Whisperer was given a second chance as the lead in a single-character magazine. Polished, revised, and amended, the new Whisperer began with the October 1940 issue— simultaneously with a companion magazine, *The Wizard*.

So much for history, statistics, and dull dates. The question is, Now what happened? To this point, we have a mildly successful character, who has already appeared in fourteen novels and twenty-five short stories. As single-characters go, it is not a record to lift your blood pressure, but neither is it pathetic.

Clearly, The Whisperer had some appeal. Now, for the second time, he is launched in his own magazine. It is one of those handsome 1940 Street & Smith productions, the edges smooth, the cover (painted by Rogers) attractive. True, the interior illustrations by Newton Alfred made everyone look Chinese, but the pulps had seen worse. The magazine is sleek and fresh and new and bright.

So why did it last only ten issues? Why was it always a bi-monthly, never reaching monthly status?

The simplest answer is usually the best, and, in this case, the simplest answer is also the most obvious. *The Whisperer* wasn't all that popular. If readers had flocked to the title, crowding up to the news stand and demanded two or more copies, the magazine would have at least become a monthly. That it did not is clear evidence that its popularity never quite flared hotly enough. (At least it lasted ten issues; *The Wizard*, soon retitled *Cash Gorman*, was snuffed out after only six issues.) But why, we wonder, didn't The Whisperer catch on?

If the professionals at Street & Smith didn't know why—else they would have fixed the problem—it is improbable that some second-guesser, fifty years later, can diagnose the problem. Still it would be interesting to take a closer look at the magazine.

The October 1940 issue of The Whisperer, subtitled "The Long Arm of Justice," contains a novel, three short stories, and a department titled "Meet the Whisperer," 116 pages in all—providing that you count both sides of the front and back covers, as did the publisher.

"Meet the Whisperer" discusses that gentleman's motivation and thoroughly agrees with it. For The Whisperer....

"...tackles crime the only way it should be tackled—right at the base, tearing at its roots in a reckless, daring, smashing way."

The novel, "The Trail of Fear," tears along with great urgency, packing in one or more violent episodes a chapter, as if afraid that the reader would fall asleep in his chair if someone wasn't constantly getting shot or slugged.

The story tells how James "Wildcat" Gordon, young Police Commissioner of New York City, involves himself in the death of a rich anthropologist, discovers a series of linked murders, tracks the hidden mind behind it all to an island filled with concealed rooms, and finally ends up in a cage with two girls and a starved Bengal tiger. He escapes with the girls, as you could have figured out had you only stopped to think. After all, it's Volume 1, Number 1, and....[3]

Unlike any police commissioner of your acquaintance, Wildcat Gordon does all the investigating and racing around himself. Also unlike any police commissioner you ever met, he investigates in the disguise of a green-eyed, black-haired, long-jawed public enemy wanted by the police and the underworld alike for his habit of tackling crime at its base, tearing at its roots in a reckless, daring, smashing way. The Whisperer this figure is called. That is because he speaks in a husky, whispering voice and blasts away at the ungodly with silenced automatics that hiss sharply, when fired, and emit stabs of lurid blue flame.

How the automatics are silenced is never explained. But the Whisperer's voice is a by-product of a pair of special dental plates. These lengthen and sharpen his jaw. (Gordon's undisguised jaw closely resembles that of Dick Tracy.) The plates also alter his voice, so that Gordon's brusque, harsh, clipped tones, loud and commanding, soften to the menacing hiss of The Whisperer's speech.

These plates were manufactured by old Quick Trigger Traeger, retired ex-Deputy and Gordon's close friend. Traeger is the only man to know the secret of The Whisperer. He is described as a master disguise artist, although the only thing he seems to have done in that line is to have made the dental plates. In person, Quick Trigger is big, stooping, squinting, and bald, with only two gray tufts of hair above his ears. He carries two very large revolvers, which he shoots incessantly.

Quick Trigger is the father of a perfectly charming daughter, Tiny. In the original novels, he was her grand-father, but times have changed. We will return to Tiny in a moment.

Just why the Police Commissioner elects to pose as a wanted criminal is easily explained. It is explained in detail in every novel since the first of the series, way back in October 1936.

It seems that Old Bill Gordon, Wildcat's father, was also Police Commissioner. Like Wildcat, Old Bill was saddened by the Law's inefficiency. The apparatus of law and justice was constantly nullified by political influence and inept courts, just as today. Red tape knotted the police. Sly slippery lawyers saved blood-stained criminals on technicalities.

While still a beat policeman, Wildcat heard his father complain of this regrettable situation. Then criminals murdered his father. Flaming with outrage, Wildcat somehow became the youngest Police Commissioner in history. At that point, he decided to create an alter ego that would strike for justice. Pure justice. No politician or lawyer or sentimental jury could interfere with him.

Thus, The Whisperer, the terror of the underworld. At the beginning of the series, whispy and gray, he looked fairly innocuous until he started breaking important bones and shooting down the evil. When the 1940s series got underway, that figure of The Whisperer was reworked as thoroughly as his magazine's format. Black clothing replaced The Whisperer's familiar gray. Black powder now darkened his hair from its former whitish gray. And contact lenses changed his eyes to green rather than that almost colorless ice gray.

Whatever The Whisperer's physical appearance, it differs remarkably from that of Wildcat Gordon. Wildcat has bright blue eyes, blond or brown hair, depending on how the author feels, and clothing gaudy enough to knock down a mule two blocks away. For the 1940s novels, he dresses a tad more conventionally. But you could still see him through a heavy fog.

Wildcat does less administrative work than any Police Commissioner before or after. His secretary must have been astoundingly efficient. Rarely in his office, he attends no conferences, gives no public speeches, makes no budget projections, analyzes no statistics, evaluates no personnel or equipment plans, despises lawyers, quarrels with the Mayor, and entirely ignores the media.

Instead, he occupies his time dealing with crimes that should have been handled by one or more of his precincts. He is his own police force, his own undercover arm—and he is the bane of Deputy Commissioner Henry Bolton.

Bolton lusts to become Police Commissioner. He is a big, heavy-shouldered lick-spittle, with a nose like a pickle and a mouth like a fish. When in the presence of political or financial power, he fawns shamelessly, like a hungry cat. During the initial novels, he occasionally endangered Gordon and his secret identity; by 1940, however, Bolton has become a fool to be toyed with and jeered at. In the presence of Wildcat, he sputters. In the presence of Wildcat's friends and associates, he is a figure of fun. Henry's life is hard.

He hopes, you see, to capture The Whisperer. Imagine that. In that character's own magazine, no less. It is almost sad.

Nobody loves Henry Bolton. But that is hardly his fault. He fills the traditional role of the thick-witted cop who fumbles and blunders after the hero. Constantly outwitted and mocked, he fails, becomes a laughing stock, heaves up red-faced and puffing, only to be tricked again. Such oafs pursued most of the crooked heroes who pranced through early issues of *Street & Smith's Detective Story Magazine*. The character type was already a cliche in the 1920s and continues, almost unchanged, to the present day, still providing comic relief and emphasizing the excellence of the hero.

Since the second series of *Whisperer* novels was careful to use only the most conventional materials, we can also anticipate two other stock characters—the big dumb friend and the endangered heroine.

We will not be disappointed. Both are present.

Horace "Slug" Minor is the big dumb friend. A new addition to the series, he is a "bullet-headed giant with a jaw like an English bulldog." He has "hands like fielder's mitts, muscles like a dray horse, a childish devotion to Wildcat Gordon, and an opinion of Henry Bolton somewhat lower than bedrock."

At one time, Slug was a truck driver and longshoreman. Framed by criminals, he was cleared by Gordon, and now serves as the Police Commissioner's chauffeur. Since big, tough, dumb guys are fifty cents a dozen, a faint effort is made to individualize Slug. He travels with a dictionary and, when not driving very fast or beating up a roomful of people, he is memorizing all the hard words. This is to improve his vocabulary and confound Henry Bolton. Thus:

"Why don'tcha look where y'u're perambulating. I'll bust you in the cranium."

And likewise:

"That dump looks like the acme of nigresence."

And also:

"A hyperbolical evasion, if not actual pettifogging."

Such linguistic toying was a mark of Johnny Littlejohn of the Doc Savage series. It is not the only trace of Doc Savage to be found in these pages.

At the beginning of the 1940 series, Slug does not know that Gordon is often The Whisperer. Officially he never knows. But even a big dumb hulk can draw conclusions. Almost at once, Slug begins cooperating with The Whisperer, although the man is a deadly criminal wanted by the police; before the series is half over, The Whisperer need only speak and Slug will obey. Since he never mentions this to Wildcat Gordon, apparently he didn't feel that discussion was necessary.

For that matter, Tiny Traeger never openly connects Gordon and The Whisperer. Not openly. When she sees The Whisperer attempting to sneak out of the Traegar apartment, she turns away and looks elsewhere, suppressing a quiet smile. She teases Gordon unmercifully about his inability to nab that little whispering fellow. She constantly sees Old Quick Trigger taking orders from this unidentified person—when Gordon is the only living man Quick Trigger will accept orders from. She is captured with The Whisperer, tied up with The Whisperer, saved from dreadful menace by The Whisperer. He talks to her, hauls her around, gives her orders, and often visits the apartment while disguised as Dunk Smith.

Dunk Smith, a secondary disguise, is The Whisperer without the transparent tape that slants his eyes. Since he also huddles and cringes and hides that long lower jaw in his coat collar, nobody sees that Smith and The Whisperer are the same. Or so it is claimed. But you don't have to believe everything those writer fellows tell you. If you want to think that Tiny doesn't see Gordon under those disguises, that's fine. Think what you want. Tiny thinks what she wants, so there's no harm done.

In person, Tiny is small, brunette, and deliciously beautiful, with eyes that vary from blue to gray to green. At the series' beginning, Hathway attempted to show her relationship with Wildcat as being quarrelsome on the surface and loving underneath:

> She concealed a deep affection for Wildcat under an apparent dislike for most everything he did.
>
> Wildcat tried to conceal even from himself that he loved this pretty daughter of the best friend he had in the world. He believed his dual career as police commissioner and dark nemesis of the underworld was too dangerous a venture to permit the inclusion of women in his sphere of existence.
>
> The stiff, almost formal friendship of these two, fitting like a rough crust over the real affection that dwelt beneath it, was a constant source of amusement to old Richard Traegar, father of the delightful, diminutive Tiny.

That more or less paraphrases the relationship which had been established during the first series of novels. More or less, although not quite. Here, for instance, is a brief telephone exchange between the two in the February 1937 "Mansion of the Missing":

Tiny: Oh, Wildcat, how nice of you to call! Been thinking about me?

Wildcat: I couldn't say over the wire what I've been thinking about you! (He is speaking in a snappish, irritable voice.) Let me speak to Quick Trigger. I've no time to waste on children.

(Over the phone, he hears the sound of an enthusiastic kiss.)

The 1936-1937 novels depict Tiny as a twenty-year old girl with a violent crush on thirty-year old Gordon. She chases him with open joy, obviously anticipating success sooner or later. The fictional convention here is that the woman is the aggressor, while the male growls and grumps and denies his affection. And so, according to the rules of the game, Wildcat pretends indifference, until she gets into deadly danger. Then he darts around, tense and sweating, until she has been rescued, at which time he forgets himself a moment and hugs or kisses her. Then the comedy starts all over.

Hathway's 1940s novels mute the rather garish colors of this relationship. And his characterization of Tiny changes. No longer is she an impish, teasing young girl, who can intrigue and face down danger like hard-boiled middle age. Now she seems somewhat older, cooler, more self possessed, a woman, not a girl—and with a woman's wry amusement at the boyish behavior of her significant men. The Hathway Tiny lacks the daring competence that Donovan saw. Rather more gentle, far more conventional, she does a little social work to amuse herself and, in the final novel, charges unconvincingly about as a newspaper reporter.

But the essential point is that Tiny changes, under Hathway's view, from a high-spirited, charming pest, to a decorative victim.

During the 1940s novels, she spends her time captured, tied, and about to be murdered in interesting ways. No sooner is she rescued than she gets captured again.

In moderation, capture is a useful suspense device. But moderation is not characteristic of the 1940s novels. By the end of the series, the sight of thugs hauling Tiny away—or, for that matter, a mob beating The Whisperer flat—hardly tingles the reader's nerves. It has all happened before, so often.

As in the December 1940 "Chariot of Fire," a story which seems to have been invented as it was typed.

Major gem collections are being cleaned out—and almost nobody realized it—for false gems have replaced the real ones. It's the dire plot of a master criminal, who has many, not to say, innumerable, fish to fry. No only does he steal jewels and repeatedly captures everyone of consequence in the story, but he has disguised himself as The Whisperer, is blackmailing fine young society boys into lives of crime, and has likely by-passes the electric meter of the Utilities Company. He almost certainly has done that. How else could he afford to operate his electric chair device—his Chariot of Fire? Into this affair, he straps the familiar black-clad form of our hero, who is then fed some seven billion amps. Didn't hurt him at all. Or, more accurately, it didn't hurt The Whisperer, who had given up his place in the chair to an unconscious gang member dressed in black clothing.

After that clever trick, The Whisperer escapes. In later chapters, he will be captured twice more and get away each time. Finally, Wildcat Gordon steals all the jewels in an enormous public display, this saving them from thieves, and the master criminal slams a speed boat into a dock, dying soon afterward. It is a thoroughly exhausting story.

As is "Killer from Nowhere" (February 1941). This one borrows a premise from the Spider magazine: The Jackal, who plans to take control of the underworld, is blackmailing and extorting the wealthy. To show his muscle, he murders a rich fellow inside his own apartment. The shot came through the window. Outside is a sheer wall, thousands of feet up, inaccessible, and no building stands across the way. Murder—but from where? Since the police are ill-equipped to handle such a problem, Wildcat, as The Whisperer, goes ferreting among the stews of Manhattan, gliding gracefully from one gun fight to another:

...Guns barked and lead slammed across the room toward The Whisperer.... The Whisperer had dived to the floor. Bodies squirmed as snarling criminals leaped upon him. One huge scarred killer, who had escaped the electric chair on technicality, demanded that the crime foe be taken alive. He wanted some real torture done on The Whisperer.

...The Whisperer seemed possessed of the strength of a dozen men. His supersilenced pistols hissed in an almost continuous stream of flame and slugs that bit deep into the flesh of gangland.

When not shooting it out with scarred killers, The Whisperer busies himself with rescuing Tiny, who has developed an alarming tendency to get tied up in burning buildings. She never quite gets scorched, but it's always close.

Smoke was beginning to pour up through the halls and stairway of the building. The Whisperer picked up Tiny Traegar. He ran lightly back the way he had come. On the roof, he padded carefully to the edge. When he had made the ten-foot leap from the adjourning factory roof, The Whisperer had hurled a stout light line ahead of him. It was tightly tied to the other roof.

He seized that rope now and swung out from the roof of that blazing building. He landed on the sill of a factory window. Glass tinkled as he forced his way in. He set the girl down on the floor.

The compression of events in that paragraph is as remarkable as the physics of the rescue. From what we are told, The Whisperer and Tiny, together weighing about three hundred pounds, leap from a roof and swing between two buildings to land lightly on a windowsill. You would expect that three hundred pounds swinging freely on a rope would not only land on the sill, but carry sill, sash, glass, and some portion of the brick wall into the room beyond. But it doesn't happen that way. Luck, probably.

Before annoyance can twist up your pretty face, the story hoots away, yelping and leaping. A mysterious blond appears. If her identity were discovered, all problems would be solved. Before that happens, The Whisperer gets captured again. Escapes again. Stumbles into another gun fight. Escapes. Trots off to

Quick Trigger's apartment, where that gentleman and Tiny and the blond have just been tied up by the forces of evil. They grab The Whisperer, too, for about the third time, and doom clangs its ebon wings.

But not to worry. Under the rug, certain wires have been strung which, when pressed in the right combination, flash an emergency signal to Gordon's experimental radio room at Headquarters. If only Slug is standing by....

Slug is, coincidentally, standing by. Through the night he comes racing, impersonates a crook, frees The Whisperer in a titanic fist fight. Immediately The Whisperer is recaptured—or seems to be. Just as in the previous novel, he has switched clothing with an unconscious crook. While gangland gloats, Wildcat Gordon flits off to call in the police, at long last. Just in time, they save Quick Trigger and Tiny from being burnt alive in an incinerator, and gunfire reduces the criminal hordes substantially.

Off they race to a final reckoning with the Jackal. His impossible murder trick exposed, revealed as the least probable suspect, the Jackal attempts to escape and falls twenty stories. Which serves him right.

What extraordinary stuff! At first glance, you assume that Hathway is satirizing the single-character novel. The narrative line has been reduced to a string of captures and escapes, each more ridiculous than the last. No scene is credible. The characters act without foresight, move without caution, act unfettered by any realistic constraint. They pound through a savage day dream, hitting and shooting here, then driving fast to there, where again they hit and shoot.

The Whisperer, himself, is nearly as inefficient as The Phantom Detective, which is saying much. Basically his problem is simply lack of attention:

An unconscious whisper of surprise escaped The Whisperer's lips. It nearly spelled the end of his crime-fighting career.

He cannot manage to keep quiet. Whenever he should stand silent, he chuckles or whispers and all the forces of Hell pounce upon him.

Involuntarily, a soft chuckle of satisfaction escaped the lips of The Whisperer.

At that sound, hoods stopped their conversations, whirled to face the dim figure that stood in the center of the big room. One burly thug hurled a heavy seidel of beer straight at the black-clad figure. With his free hand, the crook whipped out a heavy automatic and began to blast. Red flames stabbed the gloom. Lead slammed across the room and ripped through the black clothing of The Whisperer.

The dark battler crouched, whipped out his supersilenced pistols; they hissed in deadly warning. He weaved and bobbed, dodging the slam of lead that came now form a dozen guns.

If The Whisperer forgets to make a revealing noise, trouble still finds him.

So completely absorbed in his thoughts was The Whisperer that he did not notice....

It happens constantly. There he stands, in black clothing, green slanted eyes, long jaw, right out in the open, thinking. He does not look behind. He does not check before entering a building. He examines evidence so intently that an elephant wearing cleats could clomp up behind and hit him on the head. And there he is, all tied up, waiting to have his throat cut, again, again.

Not that being tied up presents much of a problem. Were you hit powerfully on the head and tied hand and foot, with the expectation of being murdered dead in ten minutes, you might feel a certain apprehension. That's why you're in a dead-end job, while Gordon is New York City's police commissioner. Nothing phases him. Not only does he have Alan Hathway on his side, making all things easy, but he also has such concealed advantages as:

—a hidden knife blade in the dental plate.
—a secret vial of acid to melt away handcuff links.
—bulletproof undergarments worn every time he is about to be shot at close range.
—a secret door in the wall, a secret slide in the floor, whenever necessary.
—an underwater parachute which inflates whenever he is tied and thrown into the river.

Whatever is needed for the current emergency, Hathway provides. It is simple as that. If The Whisperer needs a blow torch or fifty feet of stainless steel pipe, he simply takes it from his pocket. The criminals who caught him never notice things like that. He could carry a locomotive under his shirt and they wouldn't notice.

By the third issue, the format of a Whisperer novel has become as firm as cement pie. A mysterious criminal genius, aided by gangsters, grabs for wealth. His activities draw The Whisperer, who is obligated by the gods of formula to fight two major battles, get captured three times, and save Quick Trigger and Tiny, plus other cast members, whenever the prose requires a shot of suspense.

The action, like a game of solitaire, is always the same, yet invariably different. From peril to peril, The Whisperer tracks a thin little faint lead. Finally caught and helpless (for the third time), he is carted away to the secret hideout. There he manages to bounce free, and a trick eliminates the gang.

Just as the mastermind crumples lifelessly, as The Whisperer vanishes, Wildcat Gordon bursts roaring onto the scene. Henry Bolton is confounded. Tiny is delighted. The adventure concludes with a mild joke or washed-out sentimentality.

Among these petrifications, unexpected variations are played, giving the effect of children capering among boulders. Slug sasses Henry. Gordon gets himself into disgrace. Tiny shows an occasional fleeting glimpse of good sense. The scene constantly changes—from rich apartments to police headquarters to desolate wharfs to secret rooms to gangland bars; constant movement around the city.

Soon we learn the familiar landmarks of the series:

The Police Commissioner's office at Headquarters, with the big desk and the chair in which Henry Bolton likes to sit when Wildcat is not around. Directly across the street, its windows looking into the Commissioner's office, is a dingy office rented the The Whisperer. Upstairs in Police Headquarters on the top floor, in an obscure room at the rear, is Wildcat's experimental room where he tinkers with radio communications.

This is the room linked to the carpet in the Treagers' apartment. That is a strange apartment in other ways. To begin with, it is a penthouse built on top of an abandoned warehouse on West Street. A private elevator takes you up. In addition to the usual stop-start control, there is a handle which can be set to release knock-out gas into the elevator. This never does any good; invading criminals take one glance and understand the gimmick.

In the penthouse, Tiny and Quick Trigger live fairly comfortably. For a short period, Wildcat had room there. Whether Tiny knows it or no, her home secretly supports The Whisperer's operations. Open that little used closet and a trap door leads down to a corridor containing detention cells (for those who should disappear from sight for a while) and a nicely equipped laboratory. Another secret opening in the corridor reveals a slanting tube: slide in, slide down, there you are in a boathouse on the river.

The equipment in this boathouse comes and goes. There are usually two boats and often a two-motored amphibian; they are replaced as quickly as they are destroyed, which makes you wonder what sort of expense account a Police Commissioner has.

Elsewhere, Gordon keeps a permanent hanger at an airfield; here is housed an experimental flying wing and a speed plane. Just how these aircraft are serviced, who inspects them, where the money comes from to keep them protected and ready for flight at any moment—none of that is ever revealed. Enough to say that it is there. No other details are given, other than that Dunk Smith is listed as owner.

We have not yet done with this complicated listing.

Scattered about town, in this cranny and that, are various caches where The Whisperer may find a change of clothing and a resupply of ammunition. One of these is on the waterfront. A few blocks away, is a crumbling old crazy tenement, apparently deserted. But the underworld knows that The Whisperer can sometimes be found there and those wishing to pass information to him need only hang around until he shows up. Criminals burnt the place up in "Killer from Nowhere." That didn't prevent it from reappearing in subsequent stories.

And finally, somewhere down town, is another ancient building, apparently condemned and closed. This place, a defunct police station, is still used by Wildcat and Quick Trigger to hold prisoners who have not been formally charged; they can sit among the spiders and wait, their location unknown, their lawyers unable to bail them out. Perhaps it might seem to a whining liberal that civil rights were being violated. But these people are criminals. They have no civil rights. If they weren't criminals, they wouldn't have been arrested in the first place.

Every self-respecting lead in a single-character magazine owned quantities of real estate and equipment. The Shadow, the Spider, The Phantom Detective, Doc Savage, all of them did—for the simple reason that it speeded up the story. If you needed an airplane to fly to Tibet, or a jet-powered launch in which to chase the Faceless Phantom, you went down to your secret room and there they were, all serviced, checked out, and ready to go.

Most characters who got a magazine named after them were millionaires or, at least, had access to enormous bank accounts. No wonder. Their operations cost incredible amounts. It was no game for a poor man.

Wildcat Gordon is not described as wealthy. He is described as honest, lives on salary, and if he inherited wealth, nobody bothers to mention it. None the less, he can afford flying wings, multiple laboratories, supersilenced automatics, and lots of high-technology gadgets. How he affords all this isn't explained.

It doesn't have to be explained. It is one of the conventions of the single-character magazines that the has have all the airplanes, boats, and automobiles he can smash up, and that his real estate scatters the city. These elements were carried over into *The Whisperer* magazine from *The Shadow* and *Doc Savage*. No effort was made to account for them. They were accepted, like gravitation. That such possessions were inappropriate for The Whisperer was simply ignored. It was expedient to do so.

After all, the series was selling excitement, not realism. If you want realism, read Dreiser.

High excitement, low realism continues throughout 1941. "Death's Double Cross" (April) brings extortion and lots of good healthy gangland violence. In "The Secret Menace" (June), the master spy is collecting industrial secrets—which narrow down to the secret of manufacturing U-235 in quantity. "The Dyak Murders" (August) floods the city with natives form Borneo, wonderful in white turbans, with blowguns and poison darts, all aiding the concealed boss to steal with both hands. During this novel, Wildcat adds another disguise to that of The Whisperer and Dunk Smith. It's a curious disguise, being the identity of a cigar store owner named Winky Withers. That small, drab gentleman was saved from extortionists by The Whisperer. In gratitude, he insisted that The Whisperer disguise himself as Withers whenever needed "to help combat the underworld.

That this makes no sense whatsoever is quite irrelevant. Dual identity figures, such as The Whisperer, always used multiple faces. The Shadow, that great original whose steps The Whisperer haltingly follows, had a different face for each hour of the day.

So, for a few novels, Gordon borrows the face of Winky Withers when he wishes to drift along seedy byways, listening intently. Then it is all forgotten.

"Death's Lottery" (October) features a nationwide lottery run by criminals, who carefully cook the drawings to cheat the credulous. "The Brotherhood of Death" (December), a crazy swirl of Japanese and Chinese, concerns the struggle to secure a formula that will eliminate vitamin B1 deficiency in rice-eating nations.

Many Doc Savage traces are now appearing in these stories. Hathway had published four Doc Savage novels during 1941 and glints from these stories dance across the Whisperer series. Like the bronze man, The Whisperer wears a bulletproof undergarment, uses radio directional finders, carries smoke and fog bombs, simulates destruction of his aircraft to fool the opposition, has a secret hanger on the waterfront for boats and aircraft, disables foes by jabbing their neck nerves.

The novels, themselves, show a Doc Savage tendency to whir up like a scared quail and dart away to a picturesque place for the ending: a cave hidden in the Palisades, an abandoned hotel on Fire Island, or one of the Thousand Islands in the St. Lawrence River, or within a sea cave on the Connecticut shore. Granted that Doc Savage would fly half around the world to end an adventure, while The Whisperer stayed in the backyard. But the locale change is evident in both series.

"Suicide Trail" (February 1942) begins with the premise that young, unemployed radio technicians are committing suicide as soon as they arrive in the Big Town. Wildcat Gordon suspects serial murder, somehow tied to military secrets. From that promising start, the story veers off into chase-shoot-and-capture as a disguise master attempts to get his hands on a device that will end submarine warfare. The terminal violence escalates to that of a small war, with machine guns and high explosive shredding the cast.

"Nihili, Doctor of Retribution" (April 1942) is punishing men for their former crimes. Give up your ill-got gains by selling out or face exposure. Not only does he have a tough crew working for him, but the dead come back to life to aid Nihili's good work. Before it all ends in a Connecticut sea cave, The Whisperer has died of gas and pistol bullets. Or so it seems, until he proves otherwise.

For all their galloping ferocity, multiple captures and escapes, structural formula, the 1942 novels are the best of the series. The stories flow smoothly, filled with incident. The rather flat, compressed tone of earlier novels has relaxed, and the secondary characters—Tiny, Quick Trigger, and Slug—contribute usefully to the action.

You look forward to the June issue, announced as "Heritage of Death." Unfortunately, you will have to wait a long time. After the April issue, *The Whisperer* was cancelled. There was no warning, and this time death was final. The character would not be revived again.

It was not a time for revival. Whether anyone realized it or not, the day of the single-character magazine was closing. The sustaining readership was falling away. About two dozen character magazines were issued between 1939 and 1942.[5] All but two of these had died by 1944. *The Shadow, Doc Savage, The Phantom Detective*, Ki-Gor in *Jungle Stories*, and the Black Bat in *Black Book Detective* would linger a few more years, grimly surviving as the cold wind blew.

Causes for this great extinction are still debated. Perhaps there had been, after all, too many dual-identity crime fighters. Perhaps the monthly struggle with a criminal genius and his killers no longer stirred the reader. During the 1930s, the single-character magazines had offered a wonderfully successful mixture of exciting fantasy and unashamed wish fulfillment. But in this new decade, as war gripped the nation, the fine old formulas no longer answered.

Readers, unpredictable as always, turned indifferently from heroic figures whacking away at crime.

Whatever the cause, the magazines terminated, one by one. And shortly *The Avenger, G-8 and His Battle Aces, Captain Future, The American Eagle, The Masked Detective, Captain Danger,* and the *Spider* would join *The Whisperer,* a mournful litany.

The 1940s had opened full of promise. But some deeply concealed taint, like corrosive metal buried in a flower bed, poisoned that promise. Gradually it yellowed and grew fragile, and no professional skill, however cleverly applied, sustained the magazines for long.

Perhaps other times would have been more generous to *The Whisperer.* Perhaps not. Smoothly polished as was the magazine, richly packed with action and suspense as was its narrative, the 1940s *Whisperer* was still consciously derivative, a copy reflecting the glitter of other pages. Its original voice of hard-boiled ruthlessness had not, admittedly, succeeded. But neither did the carefully repackaged product.

So the adventures of that strange little whispering avenger with the hissing guns ended at last, hopeful to the final page, almost succeeding, but not quite, not quite.

Ghost Story

(The Ghost, 4 issues, January 1940-Fall 1940;
The Green Ghost Detective, 3 issues, Winter 1941-Summer 1941;
Thrilling Mystery, 6 issues, September 1942-Winter 1944)

The personable young man stands chest-deep in skyscrapers. His chin is firm, his chiseled face determined. He is dressed black tie. Both hands grip batches of tiny wriggling crooks who blaze away frantically with pistols and a machine gun and a new hero.

A fine dramatic cover—introducing a new magazine and a new hero.

The Ghost Super-Detective

His name is George Chance, a professional magician and teacher of magic. He is accomplished equally in knife-throwing and disguise, in criminology, lock-picking, psychology, and the construction of stage illusions. He dazzles his friends, confounds his enemies. He has wealth. The beautiful girl loves him. His close friends are totally loyal and dedicated to his work.

In short, George Chance is a splendid success. And it puzzles the mind that he would put all this aside for the pleasure of inserting wire ovals in his nostrils; adding shadow to hollow his eyes; applying powder for pallor; slipping plastic shells over his teeth—so becoming The Ghost, walking among men, blankly staring, emitting a horrible gurgling chuckle.

From "Calling The Ghost," January 1940:

Some men...are born crazy. Others get that way, meaning you, Ghost. You left a nice gentlemanly profession like magic to play in a slaughter house.

It was George Chance's object to combine criminology and magic. An unlikely combination, although it had been done before in the pulps and would be done again. To prevent irate criminals from protesting his activities by gunfire, Chance chose to conduct his investigations in the character of The Ghost, a most unique figure.

In appearance, The Ghost is a walking corpse, a dead man in black. His teeth are fleshless, his eyes staring pits, his expression fixed. Later technical innovations bathed undelightful features in a dim green glow, grisly to behold.

The shock value of The Ghost's features are augmented by other devices. He carries a small throwing knife. He is as expert with this as he is a hopeless dub with the little pistol stashed up his sleeve. However, his main weapons are neither knife nor gun, but the sleights, tricks, and deceptions he has adapted from stage magic. Chance's great genius is in applying magic to real-life situations where the other fellow has the gun.

Masked behind his peculiar disguise, the mind of George Chance works with shrewd precision, its deductions to perform. If unskilled in police procedures, Chance is otherwise as astute and slick an undercover investigator as ever reveled in his own magazine.

The magazine, itself, was marvelously uneven. It lasted only seven issues—and those carry three different titles and two different authors. The text leaps from first to third person. One department uses four titles in four issues. Stories are announced that never were or never would be.

Without warning, the magazine flicks out of existence. When next seen, The Ghost is a featured player in *Thrilling Mystery*. The novels are reduced to long short stories. Then short short stories. Then, for a second time, in full cry, the series snuffs out. Silence for eight years. Followed by a sort of resurrection, the short stories being reprinted in *5 Detective Novels*.

It is peculiar track record, even for a Better Publications magazine.

After the first issue of *The Ghost Super-Detective*, George Chance never appears on the cover of his own magazine. From the second issue on, the face of The Ghost stares from the cover, teeth and jaw bones exposed, decorously wearing a black fedora. The covers, themselves, resolutely portraying violence and menace, have precious little to do with the stories. They appear to have been selected from a large file in the editorial offices marked "Cover Paintings Miscellaneous."

Inside, the novel amiably meanders along, calmly relating its load of blackmail, intimidation, and murder, the ordinary staples of our reading. Action presses action. But the tone is relaxed, casual, as among gentlemen lounging by the pool. If the prose is not gripped with a fierce tension, the matter described is. From the darkness materializes a lean figure in black, skull-faced and with a horrible gibbling laugh. Knives fly. Disembodied hands grip killer guns. Poisoned darts strike doom in darkness. Bodies tumble. Cars twist shrieking through streets flickering with gun fire. Green-lit faces grin. Oh, lovely melodrama.

But melodrama wondrously relaxed. Easy. Restrained. Even as events pulse on and on.

The flavor is certainly unique.

2-

Magic permeates the pulps. Occasionally in early magazines, it is real magic—as that used by Dr. Satan of *Weird Tales*, or the black-white magic wielded by Dr. Death and his opponent, James Holm. More frequently, the milder effects of stage magic appear, and the wonderful agilities of professional magicians become part of the pulp hero's skills. Mechanisms and misdirections of such magic often appear within the pulp story. And many a murder method, many an escape, was solidly based on those illusions you could watch, almost any afternoon through the 1930's and 1940's, on stage at the large theatres. It is understandable that pulp heroes, as a species, proved themselves as familiar with sleight-of-hand as with hand-gun techniques.

Mr. Kent Allard, The Shadow, was deeply informed in stage apparatus and magical methods. Many Shadow stories are constructed as stage illusions, misdirection being a portion of the plot. Which, of course, you could expect from Walter Gibson, himself, deeply involved in the business of magic. Both The Phantom Detective and The Spider were magnificent escape artists; they could throw their voices or vanish evidence with a supple rippling of their fingers. Norgil the Magician (another Gibson creation) was a stage professional, given to solving mysteries while on road tour, between engagements in *Crime Busters*. In *Ace G-Man*, Brian O'Reilly (also known as "The Ghost, practiced as a professional magician before he ever became a G-Man wanted for murder.

Don Diavolo, "The Scarlet Wizard," from *Red Star Mystery*, appeared five months after The Ghost in four excellent novels mingling stage magic with detection. At about the same time, The Green Lama was dealing with a succession of Mad Magi, Hollywood, Ghosts, Invisible Enemies, and other ravening menaces.

So magic and detective were familiar elements of the pulps. These, George Chance combined with other well-used ingredients—the secret identity, the tight-knit groups of aides, the concealed meeting place, the tacit support of authority. To these he added a perfect alibi to screen the secret identity and the liberal use of stage magic to get himself out of trouble during the story and snare the wicked at the end.

As a final touch, pains were taken to present the novels as autobiography, at least at the beginning of the series. The first four novels were told in first person. And there, in print on the title pages for all to see was the name George Chance. Circumstantial as this was, the actual author was G. T. Fleming-Roberts, who began signing the series with the fifth issue. Fleming-Roberts was all over the pulps of this period, writing good, solid stuff that got better and better as the years passed.

Endlessly clever as was Fleming-Roberts, he did not create George Chance is a single bolt of inspiration. Not quite. During 1937-1938 in *Popular Detective*, he had introduced an earlier version of Chance—this magician-detective named Diamondstone. Like Chance, Diamondstone was big, unruffled, and had red-yellow hair. Routinely he carried around enough magical gadgets to fill an hour at the Palace, if anyone had asked. Unlike Chance, he was a lone wolf. The complications of The Ghost series remained to be developed.

Like the Diamondstone novelettes, the Chance novels are cheerful and essentially light-hearted in spite of frequent blackjacks and blood smears. They amble busily along. The first-person narration restricts the scope of the action to what The Ghost observes and experiences. The movement tends to be continuous in time. You get three or four chapters of one thing following on another—an essentially uninterrupted stream of movement. For the first novels, Fleming-Roberts does not use the familiar pulp device of cutting back and forth between parallel action lines to generate a feeling of excitement and tension.

While these devices unify the story, they also tend to reduce that urgency that drives so many pulp magazine productions. "Calling the Ghost" is not characterized by constant outbursts of scarlet violence, one linked to another, as the hero battles toward the heart of the enemy. Chance is no Spider. Nor is he as incessantly busy as The Phantom, who is in and out of twenty death traps a day.

Like other pulp worthies, Chance has both a home for himself, (on East 54th St., New York City) and a separate establishment for his Ghost identity. The Ghost's place is in an abandoned rectory on E. 55th St., beside an old church. The rectory, "an unlovely gray brick house with boarded windows," has a reputation for being severely haunted. It is for rent—at a price no reasonable person would pay. And down the basement stairs behind that locked door, is a neat little apartment, furnished in modern, from which The Ghost operates when on a case. Or rather from which the Ghost and his associates operate.

Six people know the face behind the fixed grin of The Ghost. (Eight people, counting you and I.) Of that number, two are officials of the New York Police Department—Police Commissioner Edward Standish and the Medical Examiner, Robert Demarest.

Commissioner Standish is drawn rather broad brush. He is the typical senior male figure that appears so frequently in the pulps. Authoritative, of high rank, he sanctions the activities of the pulp hero. Elsewhere, Nick Carr had identified these as "father figures"—older males who admire and protect the heroes. And are outclassed by them, giving great satisfaction to the reader's ego. Commissioner Standish is a senior male to The Ghost. He is an old-line cop, past middle age, heavy of face and body, but still a fine shot with the .38. Standish was a major factor in bringing The Ghost to being, bless his silvered head. To summarize the story repeated in every issue:

Chance, fascinated by criminology, followed Standish's career closely. Performed at police benefit. Was invited to glance at a crime. Solved it by use of magic to his delight and Standish's pleasure. Standish suggests that Chance try it again. Swell. To protect himself from vengeful crooks, Chance thinks up the Ghost. Weird. Standish, approving this pulp solution to a simple matter, extends his protection and support—all unofficial but far-reaching— to The Ghost's activities. Warm. These involve such methods of investigation as breaking and entering, assault with deadly weapon, burglary, assault with intent to commit bodily harm, intimidation, kidnapping, blackmail, strewing the streets with chips from the Commandments, and practicing magic without a license.

As a result, Chance is given free run of Police Headquarters in the disguise of Detective-Sergeant Hammell, or as a consulting physician, Dr. Stacey. This medical masquerade is supported by Chance's close personal friend, and Police Department Medical Examiner, Dr. Robert Demarest.

Demarest is one of the more interesting characters of pulp fiction. Long-faced, heavy-lidded, with slightly protruding eyes, he slouches sardonically through The Ghost stories, casting a satiric eye over all the whooping and carrying on. His personality roughly parallels that of Curls in the B. C. comic strip. He is cooly amused by the demonstrated fact that Chance would rather bang around the city, looking like a ghoul, in constant danger of getting his head shot loose, than to enjoy himself quietly with the rewards reaped from successful magic.

One of the nicer elements of these stories is the interplay between the attitudes of various characters toward the Ghost. Standish is solid approval and parental concern. Demarest, cynical amusement. And Chance, of course, is fascinated by danger and hard action. (Many years later, the character of Lee Allyn, Captain Zero, (another Fleming-Roberts hero) will incorporate elements of both Chance and Demarest.)

The other associates of George Chance hold more orthodox opinions toward him and his Ghosting.

Merry White, a little black-haired, green-eyed smiler, doubles as special agent for The Ghost and George Chance's assistant on the stage. The two have been engaged for some unspecified time and are to be married in the unspecified future, and they are artlessly happy about this state of affairs.

Joe Harper, a most unique assistant, is a far cry from the usual second banana. To begin with, Joe is a sponge—an out-and-out freeloader. Among other things, he is also a part-time con man, a sometime sharpie, a Broadway flash, and a pitchman. He smokes incessantly, relishes whisky, whether red or brown, and is, in all ways, a terrible example for the young.

...you'll remember Joe—checkered suit, piped vest, snap-brim hat which is always offensively green.... Joe, lean and wolfish, with black-beetle eyes connected with an agile brain, thin lips and thin nose, the sort of chin that would break a fist.

Joe moved into Chance's guest room one day to sleep off a hangover and never left. His pockets are filled with Chance's money and Chance's cigars. In turn, he provides a well rounded and detailed knowledge of the seedy side of New York life. A valuable asset, considering the thugs and gunbums that show up during investigations.

A third aide, equally unlikely, is Tiny Tim Terry, one of Chance's oldest friends (met him under the Bally). Terry is a middle-aged midget with a penchant for cigars. Is it perhaps predictable that Tim spends a lot of time disguised as a baby? That he indulges in cigars at the wrong moment and gets trapped and is lashed to a board and the great saw roars toward him but, at the last second, The Ghost saves him? Would you perhaps believe that he speaks in a tough shrill voice hurling such gobbets of repartee as: "Shut up, frail.?"

Did you anticipate these things?

Well, your're right. He does them all. So there's no use repeating that stuff. Some day, there will be, in this wicked world, an author tough-minded enough to write about a midget and invest that individual with a distinctive personality. It has not happened yet. But until then, we will be content with mildly comic characters and their great humorous cigars.

A final member of the Chance group—and for severely practical reasons, the most important of the four—is Glenn Saunders. He is a young, stage-struck, magic-involved fellow, living, breathing, dreaming stage illusions. Saunders has given up his personality to Chance. Literally. An accident of heredity, plus plastic surgery, has made him a living replica of Chance. Constant practice at Chance's walk, talk, and appearance have made him a complete mirror image of the other. In only one respect do they differ: Saunders smokes cigarettes; Chance, a pipe and cigars. The purpose of the duplicate identity is two-fold: To create disappearance/appearance illusions that stun an audiences; and to take Chance's place in public when the Ghost walks. A perfect, built-in alibi, beautiful to behold.

And how does the excellent Mr. Saunders benefit from these complex arrangements? He is repaid by Mr. Chance in detailed instruction

about magic as an art and a business. It is a considerable sacrifice for a man to shuck off his identity, but Saunders thinks it is worth it.

Six people then—four aides and two police officials—circling the world of Mr. George Chance and his enigmatic doppleganger, The Ghost. As for the smiling, red-blond Mr. Chance himself:

I was born in show business. My father was an animal trainer and my mother a trapeze performer. Most of what I am today I owe to them and to my early life with the circus. I'm a fair tumbler and contortionist. I learned makeup from a clown named Ricki. Don Avigne taught me how to throw a knife. Professor Gabby patiently trained me in ventriloquism. None of this, of course, made me a magician. It was to Marko that I owed that. I have never forgotten the day he called me into his dressing tent and gave me a half-size set of multiplying billiard balls....

I still have the billiard balls Marko gave me, and the supple fingers they developed....

So the people of the Dream. Now let's look at the stories.

3-

The January 1940 (Volume 1, No. 1) issue of *The Ghost Super-Detective* is reasonably hard to get, and costs 20 dollars or more, depending on the depth of your need and the veniality of the seller.

The paper has that distressing tendency to turn light brown. Not brittle. Just off color. The covers usually retain their vivid brightness. Of the seven covers, the first is the best—the novel is "Calling The Ghost" by George Chance. In addition, the first issue featured two forgettable short stories, seven pages of ads, and an editorial on The Magician Detective which occupies a full page and has the content of a flea's sneeze. On page 17, a semi-biographical sketch of Chance is provided. This rehashes some of the information given in the story, coating it heavily with bright pink adjectives.

The build-up is all action action excitement excitement. The novel, not being infected with that fever, begins with placid leisureliness. We meet Joe Harper. We are introduced to one of the people of the story. Then Chance goes to bed. So far, this takes seven pages, profusely illustrated. As it develops, the point of going to bed is to permit Commissioner Standish to telephone and mutter those significant words: "Calling The Ghost." Without this episode, the story would have remained untitled. From the phone call on, things move more briskly.

The point of the story is a great insurance swindle. Gangsters persuade citizens, who should know better, to insure their lives, then fake their deaths. A certain percentage of the insurance is assigned to the crooks. The obvious happens. The citizens end up dead in wonderful ways—defenestration, poison, and such good things. The best clue that The Ghost has is a little tiny bit of coiled wire. There is this terrible lisping man and a nicely depicted killer-for-hire. And a sack full of teeth. (The clues you get in these stories are highly bizarre.) Merry and Joe Harper perform splendidly. Believe it or not, they do intelligent things on their own, even when their leader is not so very bright at times. The action climaxes in a house rigged by Chance and Saunders for special effects, and the murdering genius faces the ghosts of his past victims, all wavering and hollow-voiced, and scary. From this point on, the end of the novels is ordained; almost all have The Ghost explaining things from a small private stage and using a particular illusion to unmask the guilty.

The first issue advertises the second story as "The Ghost Strikes Again." However, this is published as "The Ghost Strikes Back," Spring 1940. It features a busy cover. Three people crouch by a railroad track. A man in a humorous cap is either bolting or unbolting two rails, while a lady with an automatic, and a gentleman with a pistol, blast at foes off cover. Behind them, very large, grins the awful face of The Ghost.

The described scene does not appear in the magazine. About everything else does. Chance, framed for murder, is to die in the electric chair. Only it is Glenn Saunders, waiting out the hopeless hours. A sinister leper prowls New York. On every side, people fall dead. But how? And will the magician's widow reveal the secret phrase worth $200,000? And what does the map of Mexico mean with the letters "he" circled on a mountain range. At the end of this, the Floating Light Bulb Illusion breaks the nerve of the arrogant supercrook, and The Ghost—from a private stage—reveals all.

The third novel, dated Summer 1940, is "Murder Makes a Ghost." (For those of you interested in trivia, page 5 contains full-page ad for "Tarzan and the Jungle Murders—a Brand-New Novel" appearing in the June issue of *Thrilling Adventures*.) Once again, Chance meets a whole series of nutty events. The worm at the root is a stock swindle. Before that comes out, the first murdered man vanishes. Then electrocuted people, wearing steel hats, are found sitting about, smoking slightly. Now comes a frightful man who limps—a murderer who is murdered—and Tiny Tim again views the wrong end of a gun barrel. At the end, a large bunch of feather flowers reveal the identity of the murderer.

During this novel, the first-person narration keeps slipping into the third person, a harbringer of things to come. Once again the cover illustrates nothing in the magazine. Equally as usual, the background portrait of The Ghost differs from all other cover portraits. Select your favorite Ghost and stick by him. The same nondescript kind of short stories (two) are used, plus a biographical sketch of Chance, and the Department, "Calling The Ghost," which features letters from constant readers, some of them perhaps real.

The first symptoms of doom creep stealthily over the magazine. Quite without warning, it is retitled *The Ghost Detective* on spine, cover, and title page. It is Volume 2, No. 1, Fall 1940, and the Super Detective reference is gone, except for one accidental reference in a strip across some early pages: "Murder Calls the Super-Detective to Action When Keys of Doom Unlock Doors of Crime." Wouldn't it be fine if they'd roll out the words like that today. The novel is titled "The Case of the Laughing Corpse." From now on, all the stories will be titled "The Case of...."

On the cover, two hardcase Chinese have got hold of this beautiful Occidental girl, but before their dagger is quenched in her heart's blood, a young hero-fellow has lunged in at them. (The cover is not associated with anything in the magazine.)

Well, in the story, a nasty so-and-so is dead, his face twisted by a leering smile. Six keys unlock something. Around these swirl a tempest of bloody monkey wrenches, drugs, dynamite traps, and machine guns. Joe Harper and Chance end up in an underground room paneled with dynamite, listening to a dead man explain how they are to die. They don't. The "Blue Ghost" illusion singles out the murderer and the last of Mr. Chance's first-person novels is over.

More change wracks the magazine. Winter, 1941, Volume 2, No. 2: "The Case of the Flaming Fist." For the first time, G. T. Fleming-Roberts signs a story. The third person narrative is used exclusively. Again the magazine title changes. It is now *The Green Ghost Detective*. If the readers were surprised by the change, the New York crooks were not. In the first chapter, they are plotting to kill the *Green* Ghost—so called because he appears amid a faintly glowing nimbus of green mist. (It is the product of chemical vapors and a green tie-light. However, the first time it's mentioned, the effect results from a vague "powder" vaguely explained as being somehow released.)

The crooks are particularly efficient in this story. The Fist of the title—a blazing gun-wielding hand named Simon, associated with no visible body—murders people on all sides. The Big Guy is out to get the Green Ghost and have his ectoplasm. Mr. Chance gets captured about every three chapters and does not cover himself with glory. The point of it all is a murder racket and a big wad of stock which The Big Guy wants for himself, the greedy rascal. His dreams of wealth end when The G. Ghost pulls the Bullet Catch Illusion on him.

"The Case of the Walking Skeleton," Spring 1941, features another marvelous miscellany of clues—plaster death masks, a rubber monster mask, and an agreeable number of fresh skeletons sitting about fully dressed. Terror stalks the cartoon shop, where murder is concealed in a half-drawn strip. The Ghost gets dumped into an elevator shaft. Tim, captured again, is menaced by death. But have no fear. The story isn't half over. The Ghost pulls a vanish, reviving his battered investigation. And now we meet the mechanical device that lets you to talk like a chicken. Soon afterward, we meet the clue of the three-dimensional movie cartoon projector. Somebody bad is blackmailing somebody else, using a lovely indoor swimming pool to murder...but there's no need to reveal the obvious. Turning his back incautiously, The Ghost ends a victim to a strangler's cord. But is he plunged to doom in the deadly swimming pool? Not if he employs the Rope Escape, combined with the Water-to-Fire trick, concluding this dazzling display by the Painted-Face-On-A-Balloon-Illusion. Hey, presto, the murderer stands aghast, facing the gun-wielding skeleton of The Green Ghost. And much disturbed about it, he is, too.

"Skeleton" is the first novel where The Ghost does not talk out the mystery's solution on an intimate little stage. In compensation, the final chapter is packed with explanation, providing the police (and reader) with all the details concealed by the action. This is usual procedure for the George Chance stories. They are, at their heart, rather elaborate jig-saw puzzles, whose disparate and complex pieces are methodically joined, one by one. The action is always over one chapter before the end. The final chapter, then, always an anti-climax.

So consistent a use of anti-climax is probably a main cause for The Ghost's inability to become more than a quarterly magazine. All elements for success are present. But they do not jell into that hard-action framework, blazing with energy, as if high-voltage were loose behind the paragraphs, which is characteristic of the longer-run pulps.

Unlike the Spider or Shadow stories, The Ghost novels never climax in a crescendo of blood and slaughter. In all cases, the story builds to the point where the hidden villain is revealed by magic. Following this, the story winds mildly down to an analysis of what happened. These endings are typical of hundreds of hard-backed mysteries published during the 1920's and 1930's. The hard-nosed boys from *Black Mask* eventually modified the technique. But the old style died hard, and you can find mysteries published last month where the final chapter is a group sit while the hero explains all.

In comparison with giants of the pulp world, such as The Shadow or The Spider, the Ghost is mild tonic indeed. The Spider novels climax with vast scarlet detonations of passion, beslobbered with gore, with Mr. Wentworth straining at the absolute limit of his physical capabilities. The Shadow's tone is more intellectual. Even here, once the explanations have been made and the Bad Guy identified, Armegeddon erupts, continuing until most of the characters have been shot dead.

Such homicidal frenzies rarely touch the Ghost's final pages. They remain calm. Soothing, even. It was not a formula for success. With the Summer 1941 issue, "The Case of the Black Magician," the *Green Ghost Detective* magazine had reached its end.

That issue featured the usual two short stories. The biography of The Ghost had been dropped in the last issue, leaving only one department, "Calling The Ghost." In this department, the editor made excited noises about the next issue and published letters from the faithful. As it happened, this department, this time, devoted about 1-3/4 column inches to the next novel:

To all of you we say: Wait! You haven't read *The Case of the Blind Soldier*. That's the large meaty morsel we've selected for the coming issue of *The Green Ghost Detective*. There are none so blind as will not see, and surely there will be no follower of The Green Ghost's exploits who would willingly miss the novel which will narrate, tensely and thrillingly, the *tour de force* of crime solution which *The Case of the Blind Soldier* exemplifies....

Which is a perfect example of first-draft composition on a subject about which the writer knew nothing. Apparently, the story existed only as a title. It never appeared. "The Case of the Black Magician" is the final George Chance novel.

It is quite good. An illusionist, calling himself The Black Magician, feeds a poisoned cocktail to a member of the audience, then escapes by vanishing from a moving elevator. The Anti-Crime Commission appears in danger of being murdered one by one. Enter The Ghost. He promptly ends up in the East River with a pair of fire grates tied to his ankles.

Escaping easily, he returns to the usual assortment of screwball clues: false eyelashes, hollow statues, a chunk of soapstone, grains of rouge, a steel hook. In the course of gathering these, Merry is kidnapped. But not for long. The hired shotgun killer dies, victim of Joe Harper's automatic, and the master crook is revealed—in a private home for a change—with only a few police for audience. The French Drop Sleight climaxes the action.

Then the magazine disappears into thin air, as neatly as The Ghost, himself.

4-

Certain rites must be scrupulously observed when laying a ghost. In the case of George Chance, some portion of the ritual must have been omitted. For The Ghost rose again, slightly more than a year later. No longer is he featured in his own magazine. Instead, he appears in the lead novelette of the September 1942 *Thrilling Mystery*. The title formula remains the same: "The Case of the Murderous Mermaid." By G. T. Fleming-Roberts.

Chance is investigating counterfeiting activities at a circus, as a favor to Standish and the circus owner. Immediately, he is treated to the spectacle of a 6-inch mermaid in a goldfish bowl, who shoots a man to death. From that point, matters grow heated. In rapid order, we meet a dumb ape man, a de Vinci sketch, and discover that the treasure was buried under a statue of a pterodactyl. The Ghost appears, saving the innocent, getting suspected of murder, and tracking down the gang of evil men at the last moment. They have Glenn Saunders a captive and are about to make him dead. But the Ghost comes through. In addition to these fine things, we meet the clown, Ricki, who taught George Chance the art of make-up. And speaking of things far out, we also see Joe Harper working—or rather, selling fountain pens with solid gold tips for 25 cents.

"Mermaid" is the first (and longest) of six Green Ghost stories to appear in *Thrilling Mystery*. At this time, the magazine is published bi-monthly, using a lead novel, a novelette, and four short stories. A department, "Mystery-Scopes" by Charka, provides four or five 500-word incidents presented as true stories of weird or peculiar happenings. With all this material, you would expect the magazine to be an inch thick. It isn't. As usual, the editor is playing fast and loose with the meanings of such words as "novel."

The 1940-41 Ghost novels average out at about 165 columns of type per issue. (For the statistically minded, that figure does not include column space used up by art, headings, or advertisements.) The novel, as used in *Thrilling Mystery*, is 66 columns of type—about 40% of the usual Ghost novel. The effect of that compression is interesting. Gone are the slow introductions of the novels, when the scene is carefully set and the characters wander on, one by one. Also gone are those elaborate endings where The Ghost, from a private stage, laughs ghoulishly and magic identifies the killer.

Instead, the "Mermaid," like the rest of The Ghost stories in *Thrilling Mystery*, opens on action. The prose is firm, supple. Events are compressed. Action presses on action, with more movement and a greater depth to the characters than the novels ever offered.

Some things are unfortunately lost. The unending procession of screwy clues is pretty much eliminated. So is the splendid bitterness of Robert Demarest. Commissioner Standish only appears twice. The scene of action moves from New York for four of the six adventures. But, on the whole, we gain more than we lose. The stories are neat little jewels, showing The Ghost to full advantage.

His next appearance is in the November 1942 issue: "The Case of the Astral Assassin." This rather-Phantom Detective-like story, 60 columns long, introduces an invisible ray machine and an invisible killer slaughtering away at the investors. Right off, The Ghost gets in bad with the police (he is discovered with his hand on the knife in the dead man's back). He also gets in bad with the crooks, who attempt to send him off a cliff in a radio-controlled automobile. Nothing daunted, our hero resolves such glorious anomalies as a legless man with legs, and a man whose fingers leave no finger prints. The Invisible Man Illusion concludes it all, and the crook is pumped full of Standish's bullets—but not fatally. In The Ghost tradition, no villain fails to live to pay for his sins.

"The Case of the Clumsy Cat" appears in March 1943. "Cat" is a 36-column short story in which, for the first time, Chance is identified as an amateur criminologist, as well as a magician. In this story, as others, Standish has learned of something peculiar which he can't officially touch and asks Chance to look into it. (The parallel with the Phantom Detective and Mr. Havens is interesting.) After about three pages of story, Chance ends up buried alive. But it's hard to keep a Ghost down. He is out immediately, and studying a boarding house where only blackmail victims live. Shortly after, Merry and Glenn end up in a dynamite trap, similar to that faced by Joe Harper and The Ghost in "The Laughing Corpse." The trap fails again, and the bad guy is brought down by a lot of bullets in his legs. To explain all this, The Ghost needs only 1-3/4 columns at the end.

The next issue of *Thrilling Mystery* comes out a month late, dated June 1943. It contains a very short Ghost, 28 columns long, titled "The Case of the Bachelor's Bones." Chance, on the road to break up crooked gambling resorts preying on servicemen, stumbles into three murders, a burnt mill, and a 300-pound homicidal imbecile. Bank robbery loot is at the bottom of all the killing, and burnt finger bones (The Living Dead Illusion) point out the killer.

Now, without apologies, *Thrilling Mystery* goes quarterly. The next issue is dated Fall 1943, and contains a long Ghost story of 60 columns: "The Case of the Broken Broom." This is one of the best of the series. A voice weeping from a grave and a terrified politician draw Chance from New York. The Ghost gets wanted for murder, and we, the amazed readers, learn of such wonders as grave bombs (they blow up grave robbers) and wireless record players (with output receivable through radios). Merry White comes within 1/583 of getting permanently killed. Eventually the killer, gaping with horror, is cornered in a nightmare cave under a waterfall. Nice story.

Winter 1944 gives us "The Case of the Evil Eye." Another 30-column short story, this features murder in front of all those people watching boxing at Madison Square Garden. It must have been the evil eye, right? Joe Harper finds a shadow hanging by the neck, which is kind of odd, particularly since it isn't there when he looks again. And who fixed the fight and the fighter? It is all revealed as the ghastly face of the Green Ghost appears for a little chat, even after the murderer has shot him twice in the head. You can't stop a good Talking Skull Illusion.

"Evil Eye" is the last of the Ghost stories to be published. We are promised that, in the coming issue of *Thrilling Mystery*, we will learn of "The Case of the Phantom Bridegroom." But, no. Instead, Chance and his friends disappear into that silence containing discontinued pulp heroes and their unwritten adventures. And G. T. Fleming-Roberts, perhaps with a slight shrug, goes on to other things—notably the superlative Captain Zero series in 1949-1950.

Still it remained difficult to terminate The Ghost. One more round was in order. In Fall 1949, Standard Magazines, Inc., began a new magazine composed entirely of reprints from earlier issues of such stalwarts as *Popular Detective, Thrilling Detective,* and *Thrilling Mystery.* The new magazine was titled *Five Detective Novels,* the word "novels" being used, as usual, very loosely. Among the reprints appeared five of the Ghost novelettes that had originally appeared in *Thrilling Mystery.*

After these resurrections, the series was finally over.

5-

Heroes grow old. Yesterday's excitement is strangely calm today—or, even worse, uninteresting. Heroes of the 1930s magazines, disguised and violent, fought, their battles, penetrated complex schemes, bled, sweat, ravaged the criminal hordes. Some endured through the 1940's. Most vanished early.

The 1940's were not good to pulp heroes. No successful, long-run character was established after 1939. During the 1940's, many a hero appeared, strangely formed from the heats of editorial conference: The Angel. Dr. Thaddeus Harker. The Wizard. Red Mask, Black Hood, Green Lama, Crimson Mask. Don Diavoli. Captains Future, Combat, V. One and all, they step forward, perform a few months, a year or so in the glare of publication. And then are gone, the melodrama cut short, the adventures untold.

Poor sales take some. More go the bi-monthly/quarterly route to oblivion, perishing, lamented, because paper is lacking to keep them alive. But something else works against the pulp paper adventures. Years of brainless slaughter through 10 cent pages have taken their toll. Years of cowled monsters. Years of killer hordes. Years of disguise, serial murders, fumbling police.

The public taste is dulled. There has been so much of this, such violent action against a painted-canvas world. And taste changes. Taste always changes. Even in heroes.

By 1940, the well-tested themes and attitudes of pulp fiction are beginning to break up. The Shadow seems stiff and uncertain. Thubway Tham is an anachronism. Doc Savage is more human but less competent. The unreal pulp stories shake and waver, like the shadow of moving smoke. Things change. In the next ten years, they will change still more. The next ten years will crystallize new patterns from the fragments of the old fiction. And slowly those days fade when only action ruled and no improbability was too huge to be overlooked, as guns pounded through punch paragraphs.

The new world forming is a literary convention as unreal as the old pulp world. But the new is couched in realistic terms, featuring people sharply realized, whose hard, negative attitudes suggest that they think. They don't. It is all illusion. Look closely. Under the new style, the old pulp game of murder and motion is being played. Only played more slickly, now.

Another factor struck at the hero pulps at the beginning of the 1940's. Beyond the news stands, the decade had opened to a stage of fire. The Battle of Britain had already been fought. Hitler moved in Europe. Torpedoes ran in the Atlantic. Italy and Japan marched on other soil. The sky burned and, from the next yard, came the stink of high explosive. In a year, or two, or three, battle would suck away tens of thousands of pulp readers. After that, things would never be the same.

The magazines of 1940 reflected all these influences. Because of them, the magazine altered and changed. Many of them, unable to change, merely died. And, so, all this is background to *The Ghost*, that interesting magazine. True, it is uneven as a log road, full of splendid moments, and some of the other kind. But we must approach it as it is: A child of change. A fine example of the transition from the wild, loose pulps of the 1930's to the new realism of the late 1940's and 1950's.

In George Chance, the Hero is trimmed to human dimensions. In The Ghost, for almost the last time, a fully costumed crime avenger stalks across the gun-infested jungles of New York City. He is splendid in his own way. From the darkness materializes a dead face, greenly glowing. With a chortle of horrible mirth, the Hero reaches up, takes off his head, and throws it at the crooks.

Splendid.

You seldom find a hero like that, anymore.

Sex and the Spider

(The *Spider*, 118 issues, October 1933-December 1943)

In from the cover's edge, the black-masked, black-cloaked Spider blasts his way. About him the enemy rage—screaming, savage figures splashed with blood.

The struggle boils artistically about a central figure. Call it The Girl In Terrible Danger.

She certainly is.

There she lies, helpless, hopeless, vulnerable side uppermost. She is clad in a scarlet dress not quite torn from her bust. It is a wonderful bust. The action has hiked the dress up about her waist, revealing gleaming thighs and rolled silk stockings.

All around her, the costumed fiends hunch, their mouths gaping, lust in their little eyes. They have strapped The Girl to an operating table, a waterwheel, a blazing rack. Greedy hands tear at her scarlet rags. On all sides loom gigantic fists and skeleton forms, masked surgeons and hulking creatures with meat cleavers and grisly cripples.

Not for a moment can you believe that torture and death are the whole intent of these terrors. Clearly they plan more than to tickle the pitiful prisoner with flaming irons. Dark passions scald them. See their twisted faces, their depraved glee.

On some covers, The Girl is replaced by a group of girls. Their miseries are multiplied. Their lips circle in silent screams. They dangle shrieking, stripped to foundations and bras, tied to conveyor belts grinding toward horror. Their makeup has impeccably resisted disaster.

Most 1930's *Spider* covers were by John Howitt who made an art of pandemonium. On later covers, in the 1940's, Raphael De Soto did the honors, painting girls with broad scarlet mouths and tight, chrome-yellow dresses. Numbers of these girls found themselves gripped by The Spider as he swung from danger to danger. Invariably the girls traveled upside down, their backs arced over The Spider's shoulder, the better to reveal their figures. They looked properly distressed, as if sensing grave grindings along their spines.

The covers promised stories of violent, unrestrained action, hotly seasoned by sexuality and sexual menace. The promise was kept. *The Spider* was a magazine for adult carnivores. Blood torrented across the pages. Slaughter-masters ravaged cities, decimated states, clawed at the sky, their laughter shrieking. The subway exploded. Anguish, mutilation, doom. As facades flamed. As automobiles ripped to pieces. As aircraft tumbled like rosy torches above the shattered trains, the blazing ships. Panic as the packed crowd screamed, fighting for escape.

While The Spider's guns hammered empty once, again. A dead man each shot. And this only Chapter One.

If death walked, so did sexual menace. Fear clutched at every woman. In an instant, she could be snatched away to be stripped and shackled, beaten and manhandled by sniggling brutes, hardly human. Lust snorted. Sadistic doctors sharpened their knives. Seducers of both sexes preened and gloated. Brazen women snuggled close, their painted lips shining. And hot-eyed men, their breath unsteady, grinned stiffly and reached out....

The Spider was the first single-character magazine to offer such a heady mixture of violence and sex. Other single-character publications shuddered delicately back from these matters. Nowhere in the early pages of *Doc Savage*, *The Shadow*, or *Nick Carter* would you learn that feminine clothing was removable, or that the sexes regarded each other with more than distant respect.

The Spider glared with stronger stuff. Its novels reflected the Popular Publications' editorial policy of working in a dash of sex, like tabasco in the tomato juice. With every issue, the dash grew larger. And yet, in spite of this content, *The Spider* was neither lewd nor licentious. If anything, it was so proper as to be prim—at least as far as its major characters were concerned.

The Spider magazine preached marriage, home, family. It demanded self-sacrifice, not self-indulgence. It celebrated service. It called for discipline and integrity. The pages rage with murder and casual promiscuity, a crimson glare. But what the series is about is personal excellence under stress and how the white proved stronger than the crimson, after all. Purity, virtue; call it what you will: honor and decency. These are very conservative characteristics, extremely old-fashioned. Yet there they are—the characteristics celebrated, issue after issue, in what was probably the most violent pulp magazine ever published.

And, what's more, a magazine saturated with sexual material.

How do you reconcile these extremes?

At first, it wasn't necessary to reconcile them. In 1933, *The Spider* drew largely from accepted fictional techniques for portraying sexual situations and female characters. There were several differing ways of doing this.

One popular method was to exploit feminine characteristics. Throughout the 1920's, teasing stories about women were staple stock in such magazines as *Snappy Stories, Pep, Breezy Stories, Saucy Stories*. These featured brassy fiction about girls who might, but didn't. A second method was to portray women as abstract decorations—adorable pets or dazzling Circes or sacred ikons or Bearers of Life. Symbols, not human beings. The moral delicacies of the 'Teens and 'Twenties afflicted pulp fiction with female characters who neither sweat nor thought and who became mothers by budding.

A few magazines traveled other paths. *Blue Book, Adventure, Argosy All Story,* and *Short Stories* frequently showed women as sensible, participating members of the human race. This required a certain technical skill in writing and a bold editor to publish such abrasive stuff.

During the mid-1920's, a third method inched hesitantly into fiction. This involved a cautiously limited recognition of sex interest between men and women, not limited to the spiritual. The idea edged into the pulps about ten years after popular hard-backed novels had tested the water. Some novels were realistic, some not. All seem less daring now than then. Among the magazines influenced by this new freedom was *Black Mask*. But that didn't happen until after the hard-boiled school took hold.

Black Mask neither fussed nor dwelled on sexuality and the man-woman thing. But the magazine had no more illusions about relations between the sexes than it had about honesty in politics. Sometimes these relations were honorable. Often they were less than that. Men and women experienced varieties of emotional interactions, many too complex to be worked out by the simplicities of a mattress. When a mattress was involved (carefully off stage), the *Black Mask* story accepted it, as *Black Mask* accepted so much else, with a dispassionate nod and no morals drawn.

The *Black Mask* influence is not much evident in the first two Spider novels. These were written by R. T. M. Scott, a highly popular 1920's author, whose main character, Secret Service Smith, was about as emotional as a quartz lump. Richard Wentworth, The Spider, our suffering hero, derived directly from Smith. But he is an idealized Smith, richer, younger, more emotional, more blithely casual. And certainly far more murderous.

From its initial issue, *The Spider*, a child of its time, incorporated a trace of sexuality. Only a hint. In "The Spider Strikes" (October 1933), Wentworth receives scalding looks from the resident vamp, Madame Pompe. She is a hot-blooded bad girl, mistress of that issue's fiend. Late in the story appears a neat little scene in which Wentworth offers to protect Madame P. from the fiend's vengeance. That offer she interprets as an invitation to spend a cozy night together. She is coy. He professes bafflement. The reader smirks knowingly. Volume I, No. 1.

In this instance, the sexual material is glossed over with a joke. But as the October 1933 *Spider* flirted lightly with the erotic, another Popular Publications magazine, *Dime Mystery Stories*, introduced a new fictional twist— the erotic nightmare, the weird menace story. And a new magazine type appeared.

According to publisher Harry Steeger, he got the idea for a weird menace magazine while watching performances of the Grand Guignol Theatre in Paris. They say travel is broadening. The Grand Guignol plays were epics of torture, violence, and sexual menace, the girls beset by capering hordes of the deformed and the maniac. This spirit, Popular Publications reproduced in 10 cent fiction— *Dime Mystery* being followed by *Horror Stories* and *Terror Tales*. Other publishers followed Popular's lead and the girls were in for an awful time.

When the *Spicy* titles appeared, beginning in 1934, the emphasis shifted from sexual menace to flesh. The girls were positively girls, darting about in wisps of pink silk, revealing immense expanses of snowy, gleaming skin. The stories were interlarded with inflamed, descriptive paragraphs and the action stopped cold to describe some little sweetie's perfume, her legs, her hair, her wonderful chest. Heavy panting suffused the prose. Then the action bellowed onward.

Similar material was used in *New Mystery Adventures*, although not quite so crudely, while such later atrocities as the *Scarlet Adventuress* contrived to vulgarize the *Spicy*-style story, improbable as that may seem.

Each of these influences bent the *Spider* prose at one time or another. It depended upon which editor was in charge and which writer hunched behind the typewriter. And above all, what lures and gauds fetched the paying customers. First and last, *The Spider* was a business proposition. The point was to sell issues. If customers flocked to well-crafted action fiction combining blood violence and naked girls in danger, then Popular's mills would grind that cane all day long. Perhaps a little art sneaked in. Perhaps the writer tucked a scrap of personal belief among the flying bullets. Let them go. Perfectly acceptable—as long as art and belief didn't damage sales.

One thing that never endangered sales was The Girl In Terrible Trouble. The editor, Rogers Terrill, liked the device (which after all was only a standard pulp suspense gimmick seasoned with sex) and Norvell Page was a professional writer. He provided manuscript to meet the market requirements. And he was full of grand ideas for Terrible Troubles.

Page was a newspaperman who had taken up fiction to supplement his income. His gift was to reel out action fiction by the mile. His serious pulp writing began in 1930, his markets including *Western Trails, Detective Dragnet, Ten Detective Aces, Black Mask,* and *Dime Mystery.* In 1933, he was president of the New York chapter of the American Fiction Guild and was writing more than a 100,000 words a month for the pulps.

His skill at pumping emotion into an action narrative was already evident. His emotional canvas was narrow but intense. Despair and desperation pulse, like white fire, through his stories. This made them unique. The usual pulp characters were posturing vacuums, destitute of feelings, hollow as the center of a doughnut. But Page gave his characters feelings. They projected the illusion of human warmth and you came to care about a few of them.

Not only did Page bring strong emotion to The Spider's adventures, he also brought touches of *Black Mask* toughness. Until the stories converted to fantastic melodrama, Page's Spider always included a scene of coldly unsentimental realism, precise as a steel engraving. Frequently these scenes were combined with the authentic stink of real sexual danger.

In Page's first Spider novel, "Wings of the Black Death" (December 1933), series heroine Nita van Sloan, blunders upon a pair of the killer's henchmen. Within a page she is tied up in a cave, her blouse torn. The henchmen then clump away on a mission of evil, obliquely promising themselves a high old time with her later:

...there floated back to Nita's ears, as she lay helplessly straining at her bonds, the coarse laughter of the two men. It was lewd, suggestive.

Page's work has hardly begun and already the poor girl lies helpless and alone. Rape impends. And there are 115 novels to go.

During the *Spider*'s first year of publication, sexual elements spark bright within the headlong prose. In "The Serpent of Destruction" (April 1934), a tough gangster states it clearly to his girl friend:

Damn it... I'm getting tired of all this stalling. You come across, or—

But you can sympathize with him, since the lady is not dressed to quench fires:

The golden flame of her hair was showered about her shoulders. Her gown was red and close. Its silken highlights emphasized every curve of her taut, crouched body.

But we digress.

Later in the year, Wentworth goes adventuring, saves a girl, but is trapped in her apartment by the police. To escape, he creates an interesting diversion. As the policemen burst in through the door, the girl "caught the red negligee about her, but not so rapidly that (the policeman) failed to glimpse the sheerness of the nightgown...."

In the other room, Wentworth, disguised as a milkman, stands sheepishly by the bed. He holds a shoe. He is bare chested and on his shoulder are toothmarks. They hide a small wound, but the policeman is too busy laughing to notice that.

Policeman to Girl: For Pete's sake, kid. Can'' you do no better than a milkman? Hell, I'm going to see if I can't get on this beat. ("Prince of the Red Looters," August 1934)

During these early issues, almost every novels contains a burst of suggestive material. In "Serpent of Destruction" (April 1934), party-goers full of dope clutch wantonly at each other. In "The Mad Horde" (May 1934), Wentworth ends up in a closet with a full-blown seductress:

Sybil leaned close to Wentworth. She laughed softly. "Is this a trick, sir, to get us alone?" Her shoulder pressed against his chest. Her head was tilted up and back so that he looked into the pale nearness of her face. Her lips were apart.

And in the September 1934 "Reign of the Silver Terror," US senators whoop it up at a wine and bare-girl feast, just as they do to this very day.

If these sexually-heated interludes were used only to jazz up the action and give the boys something to giggle about, there would be no particular point in drawing them back from oblivion. We have a surplus of gamy moments in current fiction. But in *The Spider,* such material was not only included to spice the wine; it was also used to heighten dramatic tension and to point up the moral excellence of the lead characters. They needed excellence, considering what faced them.

Through the novel roamed a choice selection of rapists, sex-crazed madmen, seducers of both sexes, and that popular figure from Popular Publications, the awful menace:

He was a grotesque thing, a dwarfed and twisted monstrosity of humanity with a great idiot's body and bandy limbs.... Nita could see saliva coat his lips....
The dwarf stopped before the woman. With a single, claw-like movement of his hands, he ripped off her clothing. ("King of the Fleshless Legion," May 1939)

Menace, direct and simple, if not absolutely pure.

In the April 1936, "The Cholera King," Wentworth ends up in a slowly heating iron cell. Only Nita can save him. But to do so, she must submit to the loathsome advances of The King; she must marry him, buying Wentworth's life with her sacred virginity. As a matter of fact, she doesn't have to, although the threat builds suspense for several chapters. The point is that she was willing to sacrifice herself for Dick. Real moral excellence.

Over the first dozen or so novels, both Wentworth and Nita are menaced sexually. They lose their clothing. They are tortured in strongly sexual situations. Seducers stalk them. And both are threatened with rape—special arrangements being made for Wentworth in the December 1934, "The Red Death Rain."

These are attacks against the person of our lead characters. But slowly this simple situation begins to complicate. A new factor is added. Used irregularly at first, it gradually increases in importance. By 1941 it will have reached the status of a sermon and Page will preach it, his message, with concentrated fervor.

This new factor is a concentrated attack upon the conscious decision made by Wentworth and Nita to observe continence until their marriage.

What was that again? Continence?

Continence, Chastity, Honor, and Duty are obsolete terms from the 1930's. They have since been discarded by leaders of our advanced national culture— the rock stars, film people, and novelists whose jolly lives and freedom from conventional restrictions shine as examples to us all.

In the 1930's, however, those terms were ideals, rather than jokes. And lead characters—particularly in pulp magazines—embodied those ideals. Embodied them with inhuman zeal. That is certainly the case with Richard Wentworth and Nita van Sloan. They are Puritan lovers at a Roman carnival. Their behavior contrasts violently with the casual carnality raging about them. Yes, even in the 1930's.

On every side glares sexuality. Here grin aphrodisiac women and lusting men. Here unrestrained parties roar and naked bodies twist in pleasure. Neither Wentworth nor Nita are immune from the stabs of physical need. Yet they indulge in only occasional kisses or brief embraces. Their chastity is impeccable. Living lives of violent irregularity, their sexual conduct would do credit to an 80-year old bishop.

It is admittedly a false position. R. T. M. Scott placed them there, and Norvell Page never extracted them from it.

Their love affair is a central point in every novel. They love each other intensely. They are engaged and will be married—just as soon as Wentworth gives up The Spider's work. For Wentworth will not permit himself to marry while he might be arrested and executed for The Spider's murders.

How did he get himself into this position? Well, he has taken on the pulp hero's burden. He has assigned himself responsibility for the safety of a society threatened by immense, evil forces. Against these, the usual social protections flop helplessly. Police forces, military forces, courts of law: all are powerless.

Wentworth is bound by his own sense of duty to protect "his people" at whatever personal cost. If this means destruction of his residences, his personal fortune, his reputation—so be it. Duty before personal considerations. And Duty before marriage.

With the exception of the love pulps, no magazine so consistently sang of marriage joys as *The Spider*. In no other single-character magazine was there so much marrying among the continuing characters. Marriage is a constant, if secondary theme, and, like other Spider themes, is used as a device to intensify drama and heighten tension.

As in the 1934-1936 novels. During this period, Nita gradually grows to understand emotionally that Wentworth's distorted views of Duty—and the figure of The Spider—absolutely block all possibility of marriage. The strain grows, deepens, gradually becomes intolerable.

At first, however, the problem is lightly dismissed:

Nita: We can't be married because you're so wild old boy. ("The Wheel of Death," November 1933)

The problem persists and increases. Not only is it dramatic conflict, but, by definition, Wentworth cannot marry without giving up The Spider. Among other things, that means the monthly magazine would be terminated.

So the marriage is constantly postponed. In "Hordes of the Red Butcher" (June 1935), Wentworth does determine to marry Nita at last. The ceremony will be performed at Sing-Sing, just before he is to be executed for murder. Then, at the end of "Slaves of the Murder Syndicate" (February 1936), the Wentworth wedding ceremony is actually underway, only to be interrupted by the reappearance of a terrible enemy. In the January 1937 "Dictator of the Damned," Wentworth announces that he has retired and will marry Nita next week. In the April 1937 issue, "Scourge of the Yellow Fangs," the wedding is tomorrow. By the May 1937 issue, the wedding has slipped to "next week." By May 1938, it is "in a few days." And so it goes.

The stress on Nita is severe. When she appears in public, a soft chatter rises, speculations as to the real reason their engagement is so long extended. She may wish a normal marriage, a home of her own, children. What she gets is a fiance believed to be a mass murderer, flaming gun muzzles and torture nests, and no prospect of a family.

For a brief moment, she has Elaine Robillard, a little red-headed child who becomes an orphan in "Reign of the Snake Men" (December 1936). In the following novel, Nita adopts Elaine who is then dropped from the cast of characters and never reappears. Several years later, Nita attempts to adopt a baby, only to be rejected by the adoption agency as being unsuitable—she has a police record.

These sacrifices Nita makes for love. They are not the only ones. Something always seems to intrude, to threaten this towering love affair. It is as if they were characters in a story and the writer was thrusting endless obstacles in their path.

Former sweethearts suddenly appear, seeking to woo her away from that dreadful Wentworth. At other times, Wentworth gets it into his head that he has lost her love, that she has given her heart to another. For an astute man, he makes the most absurd errors. During 1934-1935, suspicion eats him alive. He suspects Nita. He suspects the butler, Jenkyns. All have betrayed him. Every one. He is alone. Alone, alas.

It is a case study in paranoia.

So Nita must fight off suitors, Wentworth's unworthy suspicions, and other events even more dire. And Wentworth, for his part, must stand off mobs of vibrating women. They are glorious. They are seductive. Warm willing, perfumed, eager, they cuddle purring against him, their eyes adoring.

But how that man resists. In "The Red Death Rain" (December 1934), the Chinese sex-pot, Wu Ya Che, makes a mighty effort for his body. He spurns her in the back of a cab. But a few chapters later, he is captured, jabbed full of drugs, his will numbed, and in she comes shaking with lust. Providing that you read the scene three times, you find that he is not seduced, after all. But it is certainly hard to tell.

One after the other they follow. Tarsa, the oriental vamp (February 1936); Issoris, sister of The Living Pharaoh (September through December 1936); and sexy girls from the big city and the small town.

Now she was getting to her feet, flowing out of her chair, the curves of her plush-soft body close against him. Her full red lips were parted, eyes half closed, hands on his shoulders. . .and then she was in his arms, moist, eager lips closing over his in a kiss of complete yielding. . . . ("When Thousands Slept In Hell," May 1938)

It's disgraceful the things that poor Wentworth had to endure:

Her body was alive and warm and urgent and she raised herself up against him, and her lips found his with a kiss so passionately abandoned that it burned like something annealed in a white-hot oven. ("The Man From Hell," April 1940)

Not all these exquisite wantons are evil. Some are just poor girls making their way. As the lady named Mae says in the December 1941 "The Crime Laboratory":

I didn't inherit a million dollars. I got just one thing, and that's the way I look and dress, and believe me, babe, I'm cashing in on it.

Seducers riot through the *Spider*. No character, major or minor, is safe. One of the secondary women in "The Flame Master" (March 1935) is seduced by the villain and later kills him before committing suicide. She reacted more violently than usual. More than half the villains have mistresses—it's one of the ways you know they are villains. A few others are hunting mistresses. And the rest have such peculiar sexual tastes that no woman would have them.

Nita is sweet-talked by a number of glib fellows. But no one endangers her more than The Living Pharaoh in "The Devil's Death Dwarfs" (October 1936). He manages to hypnotize Nita. Then he tells her that he is Wentworth and they have just been married. A scandalous plan that goes sour at the last possible second.

In The Spider's world, spiritual love is handled roughly. Even when not directly attacked, it is mocked, parodied, and vulgarized. In "Reign of the Death Fiddler" (May 1935), the disguised Wentworth finds himself making love to a gun-moll in an effort to extract information from her. He is disgusted with himself. He could be with Nita, married; and here he is in a low dive, squeezing a low woman, on The Spider's work.

Temptation is ever at him. In "The Coming of the Terror" (September 1936), Nita gets kidnapped by the forces of evil. To get information on her whereabouts, Wentworth is strongly tempted to make love to Princess Issoris, who knows. Not for pleasure, you understand. For information. He doesn't though; he never yields.

For her part, Nita is constantly getting into compromising situations, as she works for The Spider. To come to grips with a band of blackmailers, she makes a series of searing telephone calls to a married friend in on the plan, embarrassing herself considerably ("Satan's Switchboard," December 1937). And often, she goes out in disguise on the Spider's business:

Nita van Sloan opened the (barroom) door and walked in casually. She walked with an exaggerated swing of her hips and insolence replaced her usual pride of carriage. There was too much rouge on her face, too much lip-stick on her mouth, and her chestnut curls were pulled forward about her cheeks and forehead. The cheap coat that was part of her disguise was pulled very tight.

She leaned her back against the bar and tossed an order for beer over her shoulder. She hooked a too-high heel over the brass rail and, deliberately, insolently, looked over the four men who sat in booths against the wall. ("Murder's Legionnaires," February 1942)

She is fond of this disguise, uses it frequently, and just as frequently finds trouble, if not information:

A few safety pins shortened her skirt and drew it tightly across the hips. Her hat was tilted brazenly and her lips and cheeks were bright with rouge....

The men were grinning and there was hotness in their eyes. One of them dropped an arm around her shoulders....

"Don't do that, boy friend, unless you mean it," she told him, hoarsening her voice. "It's apt to cost you." ("The Spider and His Hobo Army," November 1940)

On The Spider's work, love is vulgarized and physical sexuality emphasized. No place here for high spirituality. The contrast is sharply defined and hammered upon. Here is what Wentworth and Nita want to do. And here is what they must do: The Spider requires it. You might read into the situation that such parodies of love give them a moment's relief from their denied sexual impulses. But Norvell Page offers no light on this. It is a speculation you make at you own risk.

Psychological abstractions have their place. But in a pulp magazine, you are served more physical stuff. Dangers threaten the body; we will take up the soul some other time.

The Spider brims over with dangers, scalding floods of them. A great many are sexual dangers, the magazine being a Popular Publications' production and partial to such matters. And Nita is right there to be endangered.

She is. Constantly.

Few other heroines had such a hard time of it.

...the fiery flames...threw a weird, ruddy glow over the soft, white skin of her body which was exposed where the Russian had ripped her dress away.

...his thick fingers twisted in her glorious hair. She was just conscious enough to feel the pain of that tugging against her hair. She swayed on her feet, with her dress ripped open at the breasts. ("The Milltown Massacres," February 1937)

It happens constantly. The moment that the forces of evil capture her, they rip off all her clothing. She spends days of captivity stripped to a blush. She is hurled nude into cages, cells, dank basements, concealed caverns, hidden operating rooms, temples, tunnels, fearful old mansions. She is hung up by the hands, nude. She is chained to walls, nude. No situation is too fantastic not to include Nita, all bare skin and determination, waiting helplessly for the next terrible event.

Nor is she alone. All women captured during the course of a Spider novel experience the same thing. The first step is to strip them naked. Then they are beaten by fiends with whips; or loaded on board ships bound for South America; or inserted, drugged and chained, inside glass cages; or wrapped in transparent, flammable coverings and set afire.

Women are for demeaning. They are not characters—most usually not. They are only female bodies (nude) on display, being punished, being shamed. Sexual menace heightens the drama and sells copies.

...(he) grunted and bent toward her with marauding hands.

The menace is specific and rape impends.

(Captured still again, Nita is dragged into an underground den, past staring crooks: "The Spider and the War Emperor," May 1940)

Crook: Swell looking legs she's got there. Hey, yellow boy, stand her on her head.

(Captured once more in "Pirates From Hell," August 1940, Nita is tied in a cellar. Enter a pack of low-life Orientals:)

One of the men giggled and she heard his hoarse breathing as he bent over her. His hands were fumbling about her.

They will pay, these hoarse-breathing bummers. They all end with a hole in their forehead and a little red print of a spider on their skin. Unrestrained sexuality is punished—although rarely before the reader has a good long look at a lot of undressed girls, helpless and undefended.

Rape and the threat of rape haunt the action. In "The Red Death Rain," (December 1934), Nita is to be sexually attacked by an orangutan while Wentworth watches in horror. In "Hordes of the Red Butcher" (June 1935), waves of animal men engulf small towns, doing dreadful things. In "Slaves of the Dragon" (May 1936), a Chinese fiend—*The Spider* was strong on Chinese fiends—plans to create a master race by mating 100 kidnapped women with gigantic Mongols. In the January 1939 "Claws of the Golden Dragon," Nita is to become part of a harem. In "The Spider and the Death Piper (May 1942), she is attacked in a dive by thugs who rip her dress and attempt rape on the spot.

For every scene of sexual assault, there is one showing torture. In these scenes, also, the sexual components are emphasized.

They lifted her bodily from the floor, stretched arms and legs to the great thick spokes of the wheel and bound them there, ripped off her clothing with rough hands. Even before that task was finished, a gnout whistled through the air to lay its streaks of torn red across her white body. ("The Spider and the Eyeless Legion," October 1939)

You can hardly find a novel uncontaminated by the acrid stink of sadism. At various times, and in various issues, Nita is subjected to the Inquisition rope torture, hung by the neck, tied to a water wheel and plunged headfirst into a pool, tied to a treadmill over a pit of molten metal. Her limbs are surgically malformed. She has a terrible time.

...four other blades flicked in at her. One reached its mark, gashed her shoulder, ripping the dress and cutting a bloody furrow in her white skin. ("Scourge of the Yellow Fangs," April 1937)

Ripped dress. Blood on the white skin. Mortal danger. The poor thing.

Not all the sexual dangers met in *The Spider* are so clearly external dangers. That is the dangers represented by brute men, mad doctors with their blood-stained knives, masterminds in hoods with all sorts of torture devices, and underworld types burning with lust. Their needs are simple and can be ministered to by a bullet between the eyes. Not so easy to handle are those menaces which attack the minds and will of the victims. Which change nice people into ravening sex machines. Which blot out spirituality, cause Mother's warnings to be forgotten, make the mild horny, and generally rip the social fabric.

These are the menaces of artificial arousal. They put the conscience to sleep and stir up the body. Then all hell breaks loose. The usual agent is drugs.

Pulp magazine drugs are aphrodisiac. In that less dramatic world beyond *The Spider's* covers, the more usual drugs either put the user to sleep or reduce the sexual urge. Within those covers, it's another matter. Two or three whiffs of marijuana transform the smoker to a scarlet wanton. An inhalation of opium causes the breath to thicken and clothing fly about. And with hashish, cocaine, or heroin, the effect is even more pronounced; reticence departs in waves of mindless passion.

It's much more dramatic and effective than a glass of gin.

If you expect to find *The Spider* garish with drug parties and loose behavior, you will not be disappointed. These begin in "The Serpent of Destruction" (April 1934), where a large party gets high and all the girls are naughty with all the boys. And this scene is repeated, with dozens of variations, into the 1940's.

By then, Page has thought up some fine new ways to menace.

As in "The Spider and the Scarlet Surgeon" (August 1941). Nita has been captured and strapped to an operating table. Over her bends the Scarlet Surgeon, the scalpel glistening in his fingers.

Surgeon:...soon, I shall operate upon your brain. I shall remove your inhibitions. As a completely liberated woman, as uninhibited as any savage, I shall set you free, my dear.

As a form of woman's liberation it is thoroughly novel. But not a success. He does operate. As far as we can tell nothing happens. Perhaps his blade was dull.

Other novels; other victims. In "The Spider and the Death Piper" (May 1942), the device is a sonic beam. It numbs self-restraint. It sends people wild. Girls, especially:

...there was something feral and animalistic in her every movement.
Her head swayed slightly, slumberously from side to side, as if she heard slow and languorous music.
...She sauntered up to the bar.
She tossed off a drink and turned her back to the bar, cocked a heel over the rail, leaned back.

The device of artificial arousal is taken to its limits in "The Gentleman From Hell," March 1942. In this rather complicated story, women are lured into a sort of plush bordello, The Temple of Beauty:

Nita: All women who enter here drink from a golden chalice that contains a fiery wine. I think it anesthetizes the spirit....
They become all body, all flesh....There is only one way they can be saved. I shall prove to them that they can conquer this flesh'....
...I made a deliberate choice, in order to help the women here....To prove to them that they are stronger than their flesh, even though their spirit is drugged.

After drinking the wine, the women are maddened by desire. They do terrible things and crime and are blackmailed and pile up vast revenues for the fiends in charge.

Nita is filled with reformer's zeal. At the Temple, she drinks the wine, is inflamed by the drug—but resists. She intends to prove to the other women that the naked will can overcome the body's most urgent demands, drug induced or not.

This she manages to do—after scenes of high purple drama, during which cataracts of glad tears splash. It is all highly emotional and Nita emotes high grand thoughts until the sky rings:

Nita: I have my work to do for womankind. As you (Dick) have yours to do for all mankind....I made a deliberate choice, in order to help the women here. To prove to them that they are stronger than their flesh, even though their spirit is drugged.

This is grand stuff. It booms with self-sacrifice and nobility. The thunders are so impassioned that it's hard to make out exactly what is being talked about. It seems that the wine has such violent effects, that after drinking it, the women bed everything that moves. When the effects wear off, they are then sorry and ashamed and are given to suicide and such dramatic gestures.

But Nita understands, she does. Faced by a crazed, kill-mad drug victim, she says:

I am a woman, too. What you have felt, I have felt.... What you are, I am. There is no
difference between us....
Therefore, it is not I you wish to kill at all. You wish to destroy the woman who has committed
all these crimes against your conscience. That is myself. As it is yourself, as it is every woman
in this room. As it is the *body* of every woman in this room....
You have my permission to kill me, and I forgive you for it. For you see, you are not killing
me at all. You are killing that part of yourself which your conscience condemns....You
hate the things you body has done. But you are stronger than you body. You are stronger
than death. You are strong....
We were drugged into doing what we did. I, the real I in each of us, never consented for
a moment. Let us forgive ourselves...

All this emoting might easily be dismissed with a brisk cynicism about
the quality of Page's preaching. (And several readers did just that, drawing
a contrite promise from Grant Stockbridge that he would tone the sermons
down.) But to dismiss the scene is to dismiss Page's central point. And he
plays that point back at us through so many different novels, you feel it must
have personal meaning to him.

There is no power (Page says) as invincible as the power of the will. The
will shapes destiny. It is his unfaltering will that makes Wentworth The Spider.
It is the will that continues battle in the face of defeat. It is will that drives
the body on. The will wins victories, defines fate, defeats death.

By exercise of the will, such inflammatory drives as sex can be controlled.
That message is built into the 1930's Spider novels. The sermonizing that breaks
loose in the 1941-1942 novels only beats upon a point long made.

The civilized mind sets standards to live by; the will achieves these standards.
If the goal is service to humanity, the will achieves that service, even when
it is highly unpleasant to do so.

When the standard set is continence until marriage, your will enables you
to face all temptations, no matter how deliciously perfumed. And then thrust
them to one side, unsampled.

Given this point of view, Page uses sexual elements rather differently than
his fellow novelists. It's true that he dramatizes the action with sexual menace,
The Girl In Terrible Trouble, The Woman Demeaned, The Exquisite Seductress.
All these are standard devices; they spice the pages pleasantly and heighten
those dangers faced by the lead characters.

But in addition to this conventional usage, Page takes an additional step.
The sexual menaces faced by Wentworth and Nita are as often directed toward
their moral characters as against their bodies. The attack is against their wills.
If their wills falter, sex rages in and Hell prevails.

Down under all this solemn stuff glows the gold of folk myth. The
immaculate hero is a figure of folk lore, things having not always been as
they are now. If the hero is to slay dragons and shatter evil spells, he must
be of absolute purity. Just as virgins, and only virgins, could call unicorns,
retain fairy gold, and resist the goblins of Eden.

To these high occupations, any form of carnal knowledge is fatal. The immaculate man, the virginal woman, are set apart from their fellows. They may be wise in all ways but one. Chastity is their armor, their magical protection, and their divine ignorance.

Let the hero marry and his armor is gone. He enters normal human life, a hero no longer. His high calling of public defender is set aside. The magic that made him unkillable is dispersed. He becomes merely a husband.

Thus, sexual activity represents a deadly danger to such as Wentworth. *The Spider* magazine leaves no doubt about this. Sex is equated with aggression and frenzy. It represents danger, shame, punishment. In its wake comes death.

Selfless love is one thing, but carnal activity is quite another. The hero of a single-character pulp magazine has a lot going for him. But he carries crushing burdens, as well. And one of the heaviest is his inability to share completely the full range of human experience—at least as long as his series continues.

II
Some Rather Odd Magazines

The short-run magazines shine with their own peculiar charm. By definition, a short-run magazine never quite solved the riddle of public taste. For two or three issues, perhaps a dozen or a few more, it would float at the verge of success, like a chip in the shallows just beyond the main current. For months, sales might teeter tantalizingly above the break-even point. Optimism would flare and dwindle in the editorial offices.

But at last nothing happened. And the hard economics of magazine publishing would prevail, adding another title to that great discard heap of splendid ideas that did not, for this reason or that, catch the fickle public's love.

It was not for lack of trying. Some of the short-run magazines are miracles of ingenuity, put together with cunning professionalism and an eye for the unexploited niche. Which unfortunately was not quite enough to save *Indian Stories*, or *Comet Stories*, or *A. A. Merritt's Fantasy Magazine*. Or *Wu Fang* and *Doctor Death*, two magazines devoted to the series exploits of magnificent villains, often foiled but never entirely suppressed.

Whatever its premise, every magazine showed a definite personality. Some may have been a trifle schizophrenic as they attempted to appeal to all readers at once. Others positively glowed with subdued violence, optimism, or manly courage, or the kind of sentimentality that seems to hope the world is really, after all, made of pink candy.

Even the short-run magazines projected a distinct personality. One of the joys of reading through a sequence of pulps is to observe how that personality develops across the years—how it changes from the original idea, thrusts into new areas, learns to speak in its own distinctive voice. It is possible not to care for the fiction but to be entranced by the changing face of the magazine. Like rings in a tree trunk, long forgotten decisions permanently mark the pages. The shadowy images of crises and hope seem to speak in a language we cannot quite understand. We see only change, and speculate as to the causes. It is one of the more interesting by-products of reading.

The following articles touch one or two titles from the immense treasury of the pulp magazines. Two of these pieces, on *Scotland Yard* and *Five Detective Novels*, attempt to catch the personality of a magazine as it changed during its brief life. Other articles attempt to conjure up the essence of a series magazine at a specific time. This is like attempting to capture the essence of Spring in a small glass bottle. Often enough, what you capture is nothing more than your own reaction. The essence of a season or a magazine is elusive and not easily preserved.

Still, the magazines speak in their own voices. We only have to listen. The following represents what one reader heard.

Yes, I Know Exactly What It Is, But What Is It?

Down here in Alabama, the land of cotton and grits, many things have different names. Down here *toboggan* is not a sled but a long woolen knit hat. A *pone* is a hunk of corn bread. A group of sleazy scoundrels is the legislature.

Among these obscure etymologies, I've never found the word to describe pulp magazines.

"Pulp magazines," you say. "You know—fiction—10 cents—action covers...." But that intelligent Southern face has gone as blank as a *hawg*, which is a big diesel tractor trailer.

Show them a pulp and their faces brighten. "Oh, that," they say. "They used to sell those down to the old candy store." And if pressed, your informant might also recall reading *Argosy*, a magazine which seems to have been only slightly less widely distributed than nitrogen.

But exactly what you call *Argosy* is a word missing from the regional patios. "That" is about the best word I've found, as in "Oh, that." The pulps are recognized, if unnamed.

You find a similar shakiness at the national level. Even *The New Yorker* seems a trifle imprecise. Curious. For *The New Yorker* is as acute and perceptive a commentator on popular arts as is published in this country. Occasionally, in its moving picture reviews, the magazine uses the word "pulp." As "This film is pulp...." In this context, *pulp* means exciting, shallow, action-oriented material. The connotations are not entirely unfavorable. Not altogether.

What we have here is a change of word meaning induced by the obsolescence of the pulp magazine. *Webster's Dictionary* still remembers. The Dictionary gives seven definitions for *pulp*. The seventh is "A magazine using rough-surfaced paper made of wood pulp;—often with derogatory implication of tawdry writing or sensational tone." That meaning has now detached itself from a magazine and got hooked to a style of writing. Not a particularly admirable style of writing, either.

This seems manifestly unfair. Those of us who have to do with the pulps recognize that "tawdry writing" and "sensational tone" were not their invariable characteristics.

Admittedly, we are in the minority. We represent only a tiny fraction of the population. Most people have never seen a pulp. Even fewer have knowingly read one.

Hard to believe, isn't it, that only thirty years ago, you could buy a real, live, fresh-minted pulp off the news stand. Or at the candy store. The magazines were still available as late as 1958. And until the mid-1960s, stacks of them sat forlornly in second-hand stores, shedding bits of cover and looking very uncomfortable in the new, paperback-oriented world.

That was years ago and generations past. Time enough for the pulp magazine to become—dear God—a collectible, that noisome word.

Well, yesterday departs and here it is, tomorrow, already.

It is mighty disagreeable to talk to yesterday's children, become today's literary critics, as you try to convince them that the pulps were not always tawdry, not always sensational, and sometimes not even violent. They know better. How they know puzzles the heart. They have drawn their information out of the air, apparently. Perhaps they've seen a reproduction of a cover from a 1935 *Terror Tales* or a 1937 *Spicy Detective*. One glance at a cover tells all. After that glance, the mind closes and the smile hardens to ceramic inflexibility, faintly derisive.

It is even more disagreeable to explain what a pulp magazine is—or was—when you know for a fact that, for every example you dredge up, there was an exception.

The problem is partially of our own making. We use "pulp magazine" as a generic term designating a kind of publication. Within the narrow pulp magazine world— which is composed of a few dealers and a few collectors wrapped in symbiotic embrace—there is reasonable agreement as to what one of these publications is. Usually it is a 128-page, all-fiction magazine, costing 10 cents. It has an illustrated cover, periodic issuance, and a habit of appearing a month before the cover date. The paper is coarse, the fiction extroverted.

Fine characteristics, all. Every single one of them has an exception.

The pulp magazine can be large or small, slim or thick, cost 5 cents or 25 cents. It can look like a tabloid insert or a slick magazine. At the same time, magazines that are not pulps can look like pulps, even from two feet away.

As an example, a 1933 *Weird Tales* is flat out a pulp magazine. But what then is a 1923 *Weird Tales*, a large thin thing that looks like an advertising flyer from the Sunday paper? Well, yes, that is a pulp magazine. Isn't it?

Consider the September 1935 *Flying Aces*, another big flat magazine. This one measures 8-½ x 11-½, contains 80 pages, cost 15¢. It included not only fiction but a "Model Makers" section, plus 19 departments and features. A pulp? Sure it is. Or is it?

What is your opinion of this August 1926 *Everybody's Magazine*? It contains articles on national affairs, a "Personalities" section, an inserted page of photographs, and fiction. Half the paper is slick, the other half high-class pulp. The cover is illustrated but not enough to scare you.

With *Everybody's*, we step delicately to the fringe of the quality magazines. Better paper, better pay for the writers. Maybe better fiction, although, if you mixed the fiction up with that of *The Popular Magazine* or *The Argosy*, you wouldn't find a hair of difference.

The quality magazines of the early 'Teens resemble the true pulps because the same printing machinery produced them both—together with the same impulse to produce for 8¢ what could be sold for a quarter.

There were many quality magazines. *Short Stories* was one, until it converted to pulp paper and action fiction. Another was *Lippincott's Monthly Magazine*. This issue, dated September 1912, contains a couple of articles, a few poems, a whole lot of fiction. All on book-grade paper. Writers include Chekhov and Sara Teasdale. Also John Kendrick Bangs and Hulbert Footner. Although this issue looks like a pulp, it is definitely a quality magazine. Quality magazines published Chekhov and Teasdale. On book paper.

Back to the real pulps and more variations of the genre.

Mystery Magazine, April 15, 1923. It cost 10¢, has 64 pages. It is a little thin thing with two staples and an illustrated cover. Has fiction and articles. Pulp paper. No interior illustrations. It looks like an overgrown dime novel. But it's a pulp.

So is *Detective Fiction Weekly*, November 29, 1941. Can you question that *DFW* was not a pulp? This particular issue measures 8 x 11-¼, has 68 pages (including covers), and has been saddle-stitched. That is, all pages have been folded over and staples inserted through the spine. Or where the spine should be, since there is nothing but a fold. The magazine contains three true crime articles and three departments, as well as a serial and three short stories. But it's still a pulp, right? Sure. It even contains a Lester Leith story.

Now here is an *Argosy*, July 19, 1941. Also 68 pulp-paper pages, including covers. It's in the same format as the *DFW* cited above. It is packed with *Argosy* writers and *Argosy* fiction. It almost—not quite—looks like a general-circulation slick magazine, full of he loves she but loses her till the last page. Only the violent cover gives it away.

And here we have some *Blue Books*. *Blue Book* was a pulp since 1905, when it was called *The Monthly Story Magazine* and offered pictures of actresses. Around 1931-1932, *Blue Book* got fancy and expanded to bedsheet size, around 8-½ x 11-½. It did the same thing again in 1942, when it not only went oversized, but had a wraparound cover illustration and 144 pages for 25¢. And so it continued into the 1950s. Same writers. Same kind of stories. By January 1954, it had become a saddle-stitched magazine, with a cover that might have been used on *Sports Afield*; that issue contained six articles, five short stories, and a novel.

Is the November 1954 *Blue Book* a pulp? Well, no; it's a slick magazine. More or less; the paper is better than pulp, although not as good coated stock. So when did *Blue Book* quit being a pulp?

Blamed if I know. I look squarely at a running set of them and I don't know. Probably the magic moment was with the February 1952 issue, when the cover illustration became glossy and superficial. However, the format didn't change. Nor the writers. Nor the contents.

And are the contents tawdry and sensational? Not in 1954. Nor in 1942, either. Go all the way back to 1905 and all the tawdry, sensational fiction you find in *Blue Book* (Tarzan adventures included) wouldn't make a meal for a termite.

Blue Book was a pulp magazine though, as were *Dime Western* and *The Shadow*.

Which leaves us, dear friends, with pulp magazines that look like dime novels, *Liberty*, and *Redbook*, and quality magazines that look like pulps. This worries me a little and I think about it sometimes, when I'm supposed to be doing something else.

It seems strange that so simple a form as a pulp magazine should prove so slippery to get hold of. There it stacks on the shelf, a solid, specific thing. Only when you try and explain it to *The New Yorker* or that friendly Southern fellow down the street, do you experience any doubts. Then, in an instant, the solid, specific thing glides away. There are exceptions. There are contradictions.

But there should not be exceptions and contradictions.

"Pulp Magazine" is one of those useful portmanteau descriptions, concentrating much in a few syllables. It generalizes. It gives an overall view without focusing much on the hazy edges. Just a couple of words generally describing a type of popular magazine. It is foolish to worry at it like this.

Yet I continue to wonder.

It is as if I walked in the dark down that familiar path from the porch to the cars and somehow found myself, against all probability, in the garden or tangled in the flower beds. As if the familiar had turned underfoot and become another path, going to another place, not quite as familiar, not quite as friendly, as the parking area.

If, with all our experience, we cannot quite tell what a pulp magazine is, then what other strangeness waits for us in the familiar dark.

What other understandings do I have in my head that aren't quite so? That lead somewhere else. What other well-understood words mean something more or something less?

It is darker than we think, and the path is more deceptive.

Fourteen Issues

Caught in the flashlight glow, the safecracker crouches. Behind him gaps a wall safe. From his fingers drips a pearl necklace. His expression is shocked.

The painting, by Sidney Reisenberg, appears as the March 1930 cover of that new magazine, *Scotland Yard*: bi-monthly, 20¢, Dell Publishing Company.

Inside, the first story is

The absorbing story of a suave international crook...by a former *London Times* reporter. On the veranda of Beauville's white, moon-drenched casino, Larry Kent paused to peer swiftly over his shoulder....

So began yet another magazine of mystery fiction—a magazine intended

...*not* to give you stories of a feverish imagination all dressed up in flowery language but...true stories of some of the most famous crimes ever committed.
They are all told by someone intimately connected with the case and come from all the capitals of the world....

Scotland Yard is the only magazine of its kind printed that insists that its stories be true and told by a participant in the arrest. It takes you to strange places in the world, paints a picture of the crime and how it was solved, detail by detail; how police officers and scientists matched their wits against the cunning of criminals all over the world. It is said that the truth is stranger than fiction and we believe that after reading this first issue you will agree.

So the premise. In *Scotland Yard*, truth would reign. What if the editor were occasionally deceived? What if authors concocted unscrupulous fictions? What if the fact in the magazine occasionally represented only a jot of cream in a very black coffee? There's only a narrow separation, after all, between fact and fiction. And writers are congenitally unable to distinguish between imagination and the real world. The artistic blood, you know. A pity.

Truth or fiction or both, *Scotland Yard* is a fine example of a magazine making that delicate transition between two eras—the 1920s and the 1930s. The process is agonizing. The magazine quivers indecisively. It longs to stay with the old safe fiction formulas. Yet hot winds blow. The sniff of change is everywhere.

In his book, *Pulps*, Tony Goodstone remarks that the publisher of *Scotland Yard* bought English pulp stories cheaply and rewrote them for American readers. That would account for much. In the first issues, the stories brim with loveable crooks and heroes of rich sentiment but no instinct for self-preservation. Womanhood is sacred. So is honor. Gentlemen have Codes. And police officers, gruff Irish soft hearts that they are, know instinctively that good breeding and personal integrity equate with innocence, regardless of the evidence.

Close at hand, in the next rack of the newsstand, burn the astringent angularities of *Black Mask*. Carroll John Daly's tough guys blast and stomp. The Nebel miracle has begun. The Chandler miracle will soon begin. The era of hero pulps is hardly a year away.

But at *Scotland Yard*, expediency is the policy. The editors seem unable to select a prose tone for their publication. They fumble, tinker incessantly with the format. The front cover and title page change, issue on issue. Spine colors fluctuate. A gaggle of artists appear, none for long. The magazine boils a strange gruel of true crime, fiction disguised as true crime, verse, games, departments. It is a mad diversity. Everything is tried—except quality.

The first issue (March 1930) features the novel, "A Modern Robin Hood." ("Novel", as usual, being a euphemism for a long short story.) It is written in self-conscious 1920's prose, tarnished to a gray glistening. The young crook, a disguise artist, outwits the Paris police. Pitifully they blunder while he glitters all around them.

The lead serial, "Charity Sheen, Gentleman," features another dashing crook who robs from the rich to give poor. (Yes, even that.) "Charity Sheen" is six parts long. And so, from the beginning, the magazine saddles itself with an immense iron weight. For six issues, the serial wallows tediously along, gobbling up its 25 pages an issue, a blight from the 1920's, verbose, stale, improbable.

You find more vigor in the short stories, whose titles, at least, ("The Rat Killer," "The Shake Down") reflect contemporary usage. As fiction, they are blighted by sentimentality of the Fuming Pink variety. Elsewhere in the issue, appears the first of a long series of fact articles—"Tales of a Prison Doctor." Later retitled "Leave It to the Doctor," the series was full of real inside stuff, some of it possibly true.

The first issue is rounded off by the usual obligatory department, "The Laboratory." This is operated by an anonymous someone named The Inspector to whom readers address questions. Gene Malone of Boston, Mass., heard about the new magazine and wrote in a question on fingerprints at precisely the right time for his letter to be included in that first issue. Sheer luck.

In the fine old tradition of pre-war magazines, *Scotland Yard* contained no internal illustrations. It was 126 pages long, including 14 pages of ads inserted in the front of the magazine and 16 in the rear.

The second issue, May 1930, repeats the glories of the first. "Death Diamonds" continues the adventures of The Modern Robin Hood. Again he fools police and crooks alike and has a generally good time.

In "Sealed Lips," we meet a

> ...vulture who lived on the weaknesses of other men. His red trail led through broken lives of countless derelicts to come to halt in a mission of charity. Told by a man who lifted himself from the depths...."

How those editor fellows do go on.

The issue contains three short stories. Their titles evoke Nick Carter (or Sexton Blake) adventures of long days past: "The Wire of Fear," "Black Shadows," "Poison Law." You may expect that they aren't very good, and a lot of them aren't. But you can get used to junk—or even cultivate a taste of it. The great difficulty is that whoever wrote them has experienced most of what he knows about human passion and the life of crime through reading. He hasn't been reading stuff that is much good.

The short stories sound like every piece of fiction published in the back pages of *Popular Magazine*, *S & S Detective Story Magazine*, *Triple X*, and *Top Notch*. Neither wit nor artistry brightens the prose. Theft is committed, murder done. But who cares? The evil are captured. The wronged are avenged. Oh yes. All written in first-draft haste:

> ...the rooming house smelled to heaven of cooking cabbages, onions, stale meat, and what not....
> In making this gift...Detective Duggin had a sinister purpose....
> Once she had the wild idea of going to the money-lender's room to plea on bended knee for his mercy. And then had come to her a clear vision of that man with his loose mouth, his heavy jowl, his beady eyes.

This dilapidated prose litters short stories that characteristically end with ironic twists:

——A young man is consumed with fear that Japanese are going to strangle him with their choking wires—but they weren't.
——The crooked cop falls victim to his own frame-up.
——The crook, having eluded a cop for years, is finally trapped by that officer's corpse.

Irony, after a fashion. All stories ingenious. All wooden. The situations are worn to the nap. The characters were stereotypes in 1900. No discernable human emotion interrupts endless pages of attitudinizing.

Comes issue number 3, July 1930. The magazine becomes a monthly. Clearly readers came to buy again, seeing a spark of merit that, today, escapes our less acute eyes. On the cover, a beefy crook, his automatic spitting flame. Behind him, across a mustard-colored background, writhes the hindquarters of a dragon. The story, "Whispering Shadows," is a "Smashing Gangland Novel":

The inside story of a real mob. They planned their raids like generals but in the end they turned their guns on each other.

Thirty-three pages. The "real mob" is not convincing. On the final page, the hero cop is locked in a death struggle with a great huge burly crook:

Through dilating nostrils, his breath came in a maddening trickle, then ceased to come at all. He was choking; his head seemed to burst with the terrific pressure. . . .
In spite of his furious efforts to free himself, the plain-clothes man felt life slipping—slipping off an abyss, into a world of shadows. Faces peered at him, the faces of his friends, of his old mother, dead these twenty years. . . .

But he gets out of it, thank goodness, by a superhuman effort.
In "As the Clock Strikes," a convict's revenge is foiled. In "Peril's Pause," we meet a fellow who looks just like the hero, thus causing complex problems; we meet a good girl and a couple of bad girls and pistol shots and all manner of excitement. They get married in the last paragraph.

For there could be no woman in all the world who would make me a finer, truer wife then Nanette.

The Laboratory, in this issue, advances some minority opinions on crime. And incidentally, it throws a brilliant glare on certain ideas advanced in the *Doc Savage Magazine*, three or four years later. The article states:

. . .For years many of the country's greatest specialists have held theories that criminals differ from law-abiding citizens only by some slight abnormality. Many of them have claimed that criminals could be cured; not by long years in a prison, but by an operation on the abnormal part.
It has remained for Dr. Reynolds, former President of the American Medical Society, to bring forth statistics and back them up by proof. . . .
. . .Dr. Reynolds states that every murderer exhibited an over-secretion of the thyroid gland. This little gland, located near the pharynx, controls certain growths of the brain. . . .Every forger examined showed under-secretion of the pituitary glands. Many

operations on the men convinced the physician and the authorities that many forms of crime can be eradicated by the physician's knife. It was further stated that every criminal of any sort examined showed a mal-secretion of some gland in the body, and that in nearly all cases they were curable....

From here, it is barely a step to the surgical treatment of crime favored by Clark Savage Jr. Inevitably there follows his secret hospital in upper New York state and the medicine practiced there. Many jeers and hard words have been lavished on Mr. Dent since he worked the "crime gland" concept into the Doc Savage series. True, he soon dropped most of it. But the brain operation remained, sourly scoffed at by generations of unbelievers—all unknowing that the whole idea was blessed by a former President of the American Medical Society....

The August 1930 issue begins Volume 2 (Whole No. 4), the contents presenting the mixture as before. The lead novel, "Crystals of Fire," is a "Smashing Mystery of New York Life."

Into the whirlpool of night club life came a strange figure to weave one of the greatest mysteries that ever blackened the Great White Way.

The novel is apparently one of those English imports. The first page mentions a gentleman's "corporation" (of which Sir Henry Merrivale had one) and a sister living in Kew Hills. The action includes a mysterious gypsy and gas flames that sing and a mysterious detective and events that are mysterious. At the very end, the villain is disclosed by a trick that would have fooled your little sister, providing that she is unworldly. Then the villain sneers out a detailed confession while the cast stand about the drawing room murmuring "Jolly Rotten Show Poor Bloke Ripping Doncerknow," as New Yorkers do in times of stress.

Elsewhere in the issue appear stories about a clever dog, about a soulless killer trapped by a mirror, about a pick-pocket.

Guff. Endless plains of guff.

Just as you are positive that the magazine can no longer continue publication, that suspension is inevitable with the next issue, change arrives.

At this time, the significant staff people of *Scotland Yard* were Editor Richard A. Martinsen, Managing Editor George T. Delacorte, Jr., and Business Manager Helen Honig. One or more of these decides to jazz up the magazine.

September 1930. Interior illustrations appear for the first time: Frank Tinsley (later to receive wide acclaim for his aircraft illustrations) provides a pencil drawing to open each story. He also contributes a masthead drawing showing a Bobby peering across the type toward a Policeman.

The cover, by H. C. Murphy, shows a young lady in rather limited clothing restraining a man with a gun. He has obviously gone kill crazy and only her slender strength etc. etc. etc.

The front cover carries the words *Scotland Yard Detective Stories*. The spine remains unchanged—white with blue lettering.

The emotional content of the story titles is hyped up. Those cool 1920's titles are replaced by ones of the shock and stomp variety, ringing with the authentic feel of the 1930's:

Tomb of Dread

Prince of Evil

Crazy to Die

The cover also lists "Voice of Nemesis," although this is an error; that story does not appear until the following issue. A second error occurs on the title page, where the issue is identified as Whole No. 4, rather than Whole No. 5.

Inside, the stories continue in the same old style. In "Behind the Bars," a sympathetic crook escapes from prison, decides he erred, escapes back in. Easy. "Tomb of Dread" is a sort of 1920's Gothic. The hero's inheritance, a grim old house, is haunted by a black-cowled monk. A murderous bed canopy descends to smother the incautious sleeper—just as Robert Louis Stevenson described. Traps open in the floors. Secret doors gap. Malignant secrets choke the paragraphs. The heroine bears up wonderfully under it all, being:

Fair and slim, with eyes of cobalt and a mouth made for laughter.

If you want to know, the whole thing is about this Black Mass Cult.

"The Prince of Evil" is a crook story set in modern surroundings, featuring a hero newspaper man. All the characters appear to have escaped from a Tom Swift novel. "Crazy to Die" is another "ironic-type" story, this one ending happily—it's about a young man who hires a crook to kill him and then meets The Girl Who Sets His Heart A-dancing. Well, can't you imagine the suspense as....

"Traitor's Claws" shows how a shrewd young attorney outfoxes a crazy crimemaster and his murdering minions. As in the other stories, the sentences are short, the crooks unreal, the hero a fumbler.

October 1930. On the cover, a grim fellow holds a gun in one hand and with the other supports a particularly delicious young lady in red dress who has fainted bow upward, so to speak. Inside, Tinsley does all but two of the drawings. And "Charity Sheen" drags listlessly to the ultimate yawn, ending on a tide of sugar water. The final words are:

Kiss me!

Other contents include a fact article on the practice of Thuggery in India and a long story, "Five—for Revenge"—which is (according to the cover announcement) a "Book Length True Thriller." It fails to qualify on any one of those terms.

In this issue, a new department is added. Unfortunately titled "Bafflegram," it is designed to lure eager hordes of readers. All you have to do is read the two-page mystery, adorned with clues and misdirections, then submit a brief solution. Cash prizes! The first Bafflegram bore the stimulating title of "The Bride of Death."

To accommodate all this change, the magazine is increased to 128 pages, 20 of which are ad pages—ten fore and ten aft. The price remains 20¢, unless you are unlucky enough to live in Canada, for which you pay the penalty of an additional nickel.

The spine is reworked and gussied up. On either side of the words Scotland Yard appears a blue box within which shines (at left) a yellow revolver and (at right) a yellow mask.

With the following issue, November 1930, the spine goes all scarlet. The pistol and mask appear as white outlines against the red. On the cover, a flapper in a blue cloche blasts an automatic with her right hand, steers a coupe with her left. Her escort slumps over the wheel. If we can judge from the bullet-hole in the windshield, he has met a dreadful surprise.

Most of the inside art is unsigned but appears to be by Tinsley—except that of the Bafflegram. The three short stories waddle ironically. The novel, however, is of great interest. Titled "Blood on Broadway," it is the first of the *Scotland Yard* pieces to have a distinctively modern tone. Its flavor is close to that of *Dime Detective*, some five years later. As usual, the story is unsigned. Certain word usages suggest that it may have been written by Hugh Austin, one of the early specialists in police procedural mystery.

The characters in "Blood on Broadway" are, at first glance, the usual stereotypes: The stodgy cop, the drunk reporter, the bright secretary. The great amateur investigator is also featured, together with his Boswell. All familiar faces. But, here, all are different. With unexpected art, the people of the story are permitted real emotion. The language they speak is American. They respond not only to the plot line but the necessities of their inner experience. In doing so, they expand beyond the stereotype in which they are cast and resonate vitality peculiarly their own. If the cop is stogy, he is also competent. The secretary is not only ornamental fluff but has a clever mind and a predilection for doomed men. The drunk reporter is a man of ability, not quite in control of any single part of his life.

Even the amateur detective possesses a chilly life. Not quite Holmes, not quite Philo Vance, he deducts with icy precision. He does not deduct the murderer. The story is probably obscure enough to report that the blackmailing scoundrel is the investigator's Watson, a lovely twist.

The other long fiction of this issue is titled "Doom Thursday." The writing style suggests G. Wayman Jones, being mannered and talky. The murderer confesses for nearly a page before escaping from the butterfingers who have him in charge.

It should be confessed, right now, that G. Wayman Jones is a house name, used rather like a public umbrella. It is surpassingly hard to determine who is concealed by the name. The first eleven *Phantom Detective* novels were attributed to the pseudonym, and it is liberally sprinkled over short stories in subsequent issues of that magazine. G. Wayman Jones was used extensively in the Standard Publications magazines and also adorned the Black Bat series in *Black Book Detective*. Among those using the pseudonym were Norman Daniels, Anatole France Feldman, Edwin Burkhilder, and Jack D'Arcy.

Unfortunately hard evidence is lacking as to specific authors of specific stories. From behind this tangle of double and triple pseudonyms peer living faces. But it is only occasionally possible to associate actual writers with a given work.

It is reasonably sure that the same man who wrote the first eleven *Phantom Detective* novels, also wrote quantities of prose for *Scotland Yard*. Stylistically, the *Scotland Yard* and *Phantom Detective* prose are sliced from the same haunch. For that reason, when necessary to identify this author, he will be called G. Wayman Jones, whether that means Jack D'Arcy (or D. L. Champion, his more usual pseudonym), or the Shah of Tush.

The December issue reflects more diddling with spine color, which becomes white with black lettering. The pistol/mask spots show white within blocks of scarlet. Tinsley's art vanishes forever. All interiors, done in nicely delineated line, are initled RR, the left letter being reversed. An almost identical symbol appears on the cover of the February 1931 issue, which is credited to William Reusswig.

December titles include "Blood Whirl," "Devil's Mask," "Poison Web"— names a lot more stimulating than titles six issues prior. The stories occasionally flash with vigor, although the prose is littered with sentences gone all funny:

The ravishing beauty yawned affectedly behind a white hand.
The blackness of primeval forest closed around them, beating upon them with a physical force. It was uncanny, gruesome, sinister, there in the woods. (G. Wayman Jones in full cry.)
The plan sounded feasible, providing the Texan was willing to give Scalvi the works.

The next issue skips a month, being dated February 1931, Whole No. 9. The magazine continues to call itself a monthly. The cover, by William Reusswig, is very fine—perhaps the most successful of the run: a bare-back woman in scarlet dress throws out a restraining hand as a villain smirks leanly toward her from between black hangings. The spine changes color again, reaching its ultimate transmutation as scarlet. It will be scarlet to the end.

The title page sports several innovations. The locale of each story is now specified—Australia, London, New York, Chicago, and other foreign climes. Each story is identified as being by a Newspaperman, an Ex-Secretary, a County Coroner—an anonymous glory at best.

Beneath these tags lurk the same authors whose intellectual effusions have stimulated and regaled us through past issues. Their styles, familiar now, glow with predictable light. With few exceptions, the authors remain unidentified.

The illusion that all is true, all factual, in the wonderful world of *Scotland Yard* is further advanced, in this issue, by photographs illustrating the true crime articles. Each article contains not only a double-page line drawing but two or more photographs. From the pulp paper pages peer out the stolid faces of the 1920's, looking clenched inside their clothing.

The title of one article, "The Horror in the Crypt" by James Martindale, rings with authentic Lovecraftian tones. The text is less inspired:

With a finger that shook, the attorney pointed downward. From the low end of the mound protruded a moldy tennis shoe—encasing a human foot!"

Whoever James Martindale was, the bets are that he wrote most of the fact articles. They all have the same quality of prose—which may be a tribute to the editing but probably is not.

The Bafflegram is omitted from the February issue, apparently squeezed out by all those fact articles and a very long novel. Titled "Czar Sinister," the novel was written by "A Newspaperman." He is our old friend G. Wayman Jones, writing at full shout. His paragraphs leap with purple flame, peppered by words frequently close to the meaning intended:

She inhaled on a cigarette.
Diana felt the terrified shriek go down her spine like a chill.
Where he went on the many mysterious journeys he made when he dropped from sight as if he were dead, none could say.
The form stirred uneasily, twitched like a man in most dreadful agony. Hideous dark pools splotched the sidewalk, gathered into a stream and coursed down the incline to the gutter.

For interested collectors, "Czar Sinister" is rich in elements later to reappear in the *Phantom Detective* novels: the bronzed young millionaire, bored and competent, mysteriously affiliated with a major newspaper; he commands the worshipful assistance of the police, carries a heavy automatic, and, if he doesn't disguise himself, he is at least as adroit as Richard Curtis Van Loan in getting out of lethal situations. He battles a shrewd master-criminal who has organized gangland into a corporation "like General Electric."

So, this early, most elements of that super-hero saga lie waiting, like protein chains in the primeval soup, to bond into a series. It will happen in 1933 for The Phantom....

The March 1931 issue of *Scotland Yard* features a sneering masked punk, splendid in a top hat, tux. A cigarette lolls from his lips. He menaces the reader with a pair of uncocked automatics. Across the top of the cover, white script announces "Man-Hunts in All Nations!" Beneath the word Scotland Yard, a line of red type shouts "International Detective Stories." The issue is Volume 4, Whole No. 10. Interiors are divided between RR (it is his last issue), a newcomer named Hewitt, and someone else who remains unidentified, justly enough.

All manner of material crams the issue. John H. Thompson regales us with light verse, "The Bump-Off," ending merrily:

And now Tim sits for death to gloat
    He's doomed to hang tonight—
The poor boob framed a farewell note

For a guy who couldn't write.

The "Leave It to the Doctor" article is signed, for the first time, by Dr. Edward Podolsky: apparently he has been writing it all along. Three other true articles are included, all sounding as if birthed by the same typewriter, all illustrated by line drawings and photographs. Several of the photos appear to have been selected from a file marked "Miscellaneous."

Short stories by G. Wayman Jones and, very possibly, by Martinsen, or equally possibly, by some lost English pulpster.

"That's where you're barking up a wrong tree", (the Scotland Yard inspector) confided with an assurance that sent a creepy chill down my back.

But forget these small ills. They dwindle away in the red glare and snort of the lead novel, a spectacular eruption titled "Wildcat," by a "Tulsa Newspaperman." As best is known, this is the first appearance in print of private detective Curt Flagg.

It is the authentic voice of Lester Dent, narrating a merry holocaust of automatic weapons fire, explosion, murder, maniacal swoops in elevator and airplane to the chasm of death. Slaughter begins with the first words. Blood gutters among the paragraphs. The story races onward, an unrelenting fury.

Curt Flagg is a semi-intelligent, 240-pound mastodon, with hands immense as those of Renny Renwick, one of the Doc Savage aides. Flagg pounds, bellows, bleeds, stomps, and mashes through slobbering hordes of killers, treacherous women, and danger, incessant and dire. He evades scores of murder traps to bring vengeance to those deserving it.

For all its violence, the story shines with that particular playfulness that is Dent's special gift. Nothing at all serious (he says): hardly more than a mild case of berserk blood lust.

Dent's early fiction is packed with amiable savagery. At the beginning of his career, he rarely presented a character more substantial than a cartoon. His people thump around, vividly outsized, not particularly intelligent. Their adventures are cut for the likes of Paul Bunyan. The story drives furiously, a prose locomotive gone mad, leaping the rails to hurtle overland, smashing up cities, forests, whole mountain ranges.

Behind all this wonderful excitement glimmers Race Williams, the *Black Mask* private investigator who punched and shot his way through four decades of pulp magazine fiction. First of the hard boiled detectives, Race was big, tough, eager to use his .45 to blot out those needing blotting out. Dent's early detectives derive from the Williams' school. Which is not to say that he copies Race—only that he is working in the convention of the big, tough wildman, loose with a gun against corrupt society.

Comes now the April 1931 issue, Whole No. 11. Another Reusswig cover— a policeman in ripped uniform supports a sagging girl at the corner of 11th Ave and someplace. The illustration, placed on the lower right of the cover, is hemmed in by masses of type, brown, red, yellow type, crushing in, pressing. It is not a cover for claustrophobics.

Inside the magazine is another Irish stew.

Inazel Foster (Inazel Foster?) contributes a light verse, "Stop Thief," which will not be quoted here so that your eyes will not overflow and force you to stop reading.

Two true features appear, each wondrously illustrated. One article is by Mr. Martindale; the other by Francisco Jose. We may suppose that Jose is alternate spelling for Martingale, since the writing style is identical.

The magazine contains six short stories and a complete novel. The novel, a very very long production, is by a "Consular Agent," who titled it "One Day To Live," and placed it in

Alexanderia, where a Yank engages in a "lone-handed struggle against the sinister magic and grim regime of the mystic East."

The hero is enthusiastic, the heroine amiable, the villain aided by hordes of knife-throwing, skulking, foreign sneaks. The murder weapon is a living chair. Also featured are catacombs, a stolen gold casket, and knives that whiz in the dark, narrowly missing your throat. All by G. W. Jones.

"Answered By Gats" either is or is not a Lester Dent. It's hard to tell. No characteristic words or phrases, but the action goes like a steam hammer and there are plenty of Race Williams echoes. The hero is an ex-prizefighter who has been framed out of his profession. He is marvelously lethal. The story is improbable but busy, down around the Mexican border.

"Grim House" is in England, a country where a building may be constructed with the roof at ground level and the foundations up in the air. The story is not as peculiar as the house. A retired Chief of the French Secret Service solves the mystery in two-and-a-half columns, after pages of plodding preparation.

"Gun Girl" thinks he's a smuggler and shoots him. And he thinks she's a crook and doesn't shoot her. The Immigration Service saves both of them for matrimony. "Jungle Claws" fetches a US detective to face down a Mafia-type crime lord fled to the heart of the jungle, his criminal career to improve. From there the story progresses, by natural stages, through an elephant stampede to a sleeting of poisoned darts.

Finally, The Laboratory announces a contest. A Great Contest! A $500 Gold Contest!! Beginning in the next issue. You can win.

And sure enough, there in the May issue (Whole No. 12) is a prose explosion:

Solve This Cover
$500 In Gold!

The cover of this issue is a picture depicting a dramatic incident in real life. Simply write a letter of not more than 500 words describing the circumstances which led up to the situation, what is happening, and what is going to happen to the man and the woman on the cover.

The man and woman on the cover are intricately involved with a telephone. Either he has snatched the telephone from her, or the telephone is alive and strangling him. It's hard to tell. He wears a tuxedo, about the only costume allowed on Scotland Yard covers. Her dress is the same red as the words "Scotland Yard," immediately above.

(Closing date for the contest was July 1, 1931, so you are too late to submit an entry. The $500 gold prize was, by the way, to be divided unequally among five winners. More of this later.)

Interior illustrations are by Hewitt. His art, stylish, deft, tasteful, is wholly satisfactory. Inside are featured the usual departments and articles, five short stories, and a long novel. Inspector Gobbelin (G. Wayman Jones again) signs one of the stories; he has been featured as a leading actor in one or two epics of past issues. The novel "Doom Ship" is another Curt Flagg romp—men in rubber suits hijack ships and it's blood blood blood, a roaring joy.

Apparently, Lester Dent at one time remarked that he wrote complete issues of *Scotland Yard*. Considering the length of some of the Flagg novels, this isn't too far from the truth. But the literal mind does not find the legend to be supported after the issues are closely examined. It is possible to identify three novels and three short stories that Dent wrote. There is reasonable doubt as to whether he wrote one other novel and, perhaps, three short stories. It is deeply regretted that you will find here no resolution to that problem. An educated guess is that Mr. Dent wrote only those pieces specifically identified as his in this article.[1]

Most certainly Dent did not write complete issues, as he once remarked in a moment of casual exaggeration, but there were times when he came close. Over the life of the magazine, the author who came closest to writing complete issues was our man of mystery, G. Wayman Jones. Certainly there are occasions when Jones provided more than half the fiction; the pages are dense with his stylistic infelicities.

The May 1931 issue divides honors rather closely between Dent and Jones. Dent provides the novel and the short story, "Teeth of Revenge." Jones does the novelette, "Serpent's Tomb," and two additional short stories. Martindale does two articles, Dr. Podolsky one. That leaves two articles and the Bafflegram unaccounted for, although Martindale may have handled some of those.

The June 1931 issue (Whole No. 13) features a third glorious Curt Flagg novel, "One Billion—Gold." It is dense with that diction later adorning the Doc Savage novels and half a hundred short stories:

The operator...had a big head, big hands, big feet, and a big stomach, and the remainder of him was little more than strings of bone and flesh hooking these parts together.
The pavement shuddered and leaped under his big frame. The huge plate-glass window in the front of Giffian's, Inc., puffed outward. Shattered glass showered his prostrate form. A terrific concussion plastered the gas mask to his head. The explosion was inside.... It was cataclysmic, deafening.
The waiter possessed a thick neck, one cauliflower ear, and looked determined.

While he was in the air, two sub-machine guns and an automatic shotgun erupted from inside the tan Buick. Curt lost his balance when he hit the bottom of the pit and fell on his back with the young woman on top of him. Brick dust and strings of splashed lead showered them.

It is possible that Mr. Dent also contributed "Out China Way," a short story featuring a very very tough hero who blackjacks his enemies and appears angry at virtually everybody.

Other non-Dent short stories are laid in such diverse areas as:

Morocco—"A fighting Yank vs desert treachery—and a woman"

Glass cracked; a bullet shattered the gas gauge; another cut through the windshield. There was nothing for it but to stand and fight.

London—"Murder—and a Yard Inspector's Code":

See what you make of it, Boyce. Hold your torch..., constable. This gas-light's vile. The door was locked from the inside, Superintendent. You'll observe, sir, that the bolt's still shot.

and a couple of stories from Washington and New York.

Three fact articles appear this month, plus the Bafflegram, plus The Laboratory. Also included is a new feature by Major George F. Eliot: "An Exclusive *Scotland Yard* Feature" titled "Police—Cops of All Nations." First of a projected series, this discusses the Spanish police and is brief, tight, well written. It is both the first and last of the series. The second article never appears.

Format change again grips the magazine. (Like Baron Frankenstein's celebrated experiment, *Scotland Yard* never found physical peace.) The title page is again revised, this time listing contents under three separate headings:
"A Full Length Action Novel"
"Five Vivid International Yarns"
"Five Absorbing Features"

Hewitt draws most of the interiors, signing some by initial, some by name, some not at all. His work continues superb.

The cover is another of those $500 gold things. A bare-backed lady before a vanity mirror is undergoing a spasm of fright and has dropped her stag-handled knife with 10-inch blade. Reflected in the mirror is a masked gentleman, finger to lips, soliciting silence.

Now, with neither warning nor explanation, Scotland Yard again skips a month. As is well known, skips in a pulp magazine schedule are equivalent to heart attacks. They are indicative of disorders, deep and deadly, for which miracles are the best cure. Worse, you have to wait for the next issue to see if the magazine survived.

In this case, *Scotland Yard's* next issue is dated August 1931, Whole No. 14. On the cover, a green-eyed badkin, wearing a black hood, purposefully squeezes the throat of a plump-cheeked young lady. Her features express concern. But help may be close. Four male fingers grip the hooded monster's shoulder, and we deduce the presence of a lithe young man, tough as hickory, with dancing blue eyes and hard fists.

In small print at the bottom of the title page is a statement that the magazine is now bi-monthly. In much larger type, above, the Table of Contents announces Three Full-Length Action Novelettes, Four Vivid International Yarns, Five Absorbing Features. Such as:

Kidnapped! by a Foreign Correspondent. The Apache of Paris were not safe playmates for Abby Deep, beautiful American heiress.
Framed! by a Newspaperman. Lashed to a frame of lies, he watched her drink the bitter cup of vengeance to the dregs.
Diamond Death (South Africa) by a C. I. D. Official. Red flame lanced out of the black patch and the grounds quaked with the explosion of a heavy-caliber pistol. Doak Shea flopped on his stomach and rolled for the shelter of a bush, tearing at the Webley slung under his arm. He got the weapon out and shot four times into the darkness under the tree. (Lester Dent, again, in a story filled with characteristic phrases.)
Blood of Buddah (Burma) by a Far East Traveler. A lean brown hand split through the bamboo drape. The hand gripped the haft of a long, curve-bladed kris. As the gleaming blade flashed to the horizontal the fingers relaxed. The weapon hissed across the room....
Red Mantle (Spain) by a Consular Agent. On the tiles near the fountain lay a great blotch of startling color—scarlet—a scarlet cloak. From beneath it projected a human arm, dreadfully contorted. A dark stain, creeping from beneath the edge of the outspread garment, fouled the polished marble in a blackened pool above which flies buzzed like hovering ghouls. (G. W. Jones in full cry.)

John H. Thompson contributes five stanzas of light verse titled "How to Nab 'Em," which concludes:

For the iron-clad rule that never fails—
It's in the books in a million tales—
Shows the guilty one who's to be detected
Is always the guy the least suspected.

This, while elsewhere, 1931 intellectuals grumbled of the death of the American muse.

And in The Laboratory, the kindly old Inspector announced the winners of the May Bafflegram: Jules J. Siekman of Harvey, Ill. won first prize—the original oil of the cover. Helen Allwork of New York City won second prize—a $5 gold piece and a year's subscription to the magazine. P. J. McDonald of Halifax, Nova Scotia, also won a year's subscription as third prize.

Having put forth these lavish gestures, the magazine expires.

No death rattle. No warning. Just gone.

What happened to the "Solve This Cover" contest or the bags of gold, we don't know. That was long long ago, and now we shall never discover why the man snatched the telephone (or was eaten by it) or why the girl had that immense knife at her vanity table.

So the magazine ends. Fourteen issues to oblivion, leaving behind a few good stories, a number of excellent illustrations, and at least two subscriptions which, we hope, were switched to some companion pulp—*War Birds*, perhaps, or *Cupid's Diary*, or *Film Fun*.

1931, that black abyss, was, in many ways, an inopportune time for a magazine to die. Already, brave new ideas stirred at the news stand. *The Shadow* magazine, issued in early 1931, revived for full-scale treatment, the single-character tradition of the dime novel. By 1933, a deluge of hero-oriented magazines would foam over the market. But immediately before that revival, whole classes and sub-groups of pulps met extinction. Well-proven formats, familiar fictional forms long crystallized, shattered beneath the Depression's stress. Down came a sad tumble of literary styles, publishers, titles, *Scotland Yard* among them.

The magazine is uncommonly uneven and presents problems both to the commentator and the collector. Its personality is as difficult to capture as sun glints on a river. This month it is one thing. Next month, it rejects its former self and, in altered covers and spine, bravely faces the future. Only to change again.

Remember that the magazine was published during bad times. Its constant inconsistency certainly reflects the commitment of its editors to earn some sort of profit, while, on every hand, the magazine business plunged straight down the chute. The fact that *Scotland Yard* survived fourteen issues is, in itself, a tribute to the improvisional brilliance of the editors, continuously fine tuning their publication to public buying tastes.

The peculiar flavor of *Scotland Yard* results from this incessant search for a viable formula. The end product was interesting, if inadvertent. The magazine concentrates about thirty years of popular fiction styles into its fourteen issues: It is a cross-section of detective fiction as it evolved from 1915 pseudo-gentility to the 1930s blood and action—although, oddly enough, the *Black Mask* tough realism is hardly represented.

Scotland Yard is so extremely erratic that its influence was negligible—save as a training ground for Lester Dent. Its chief interest is as a sort of fossilized history, a unique artifact in which you can trace the disparate literary conventions melting one into the other, fascinating to those who relish the oddities of change.

Pretend Not To See Her, She's A Scarlet Adventuress

How could you possibly have forgotten the names of Lady Nora O'Neil, or Kara Vania, or Nila Rand? It seems impossible. Is there something the matter with your circulation?

Nila, that charming exotic, was not merely a woman, but a creature of "warm flesh, rounded limbs and mysterious allure." Oh, you remember now? She had "the features of an angel—and a body that the Devil had fashioned to ensnare mankind."

Yes, that Nila Rand:

Her face was a creamy oval framed by dusky hair—her lips a carmine allure. A tiny, uptilted nose....And beneath their long lashes, her eyes were tawny-amber pools that were inscrutable, mysterious—and infinitely alluring.

That's three "alluring" in as many paragraphs. But who is bothering to count adjectives. The game is afoot and she's taking her clothing off. In a moment, someone will get shot or robbed or almost seduced or give up the secret of Singapore's defenses to whiff perfumed tresses. The only thing certain is that there is going to be a great to-do about warm flesh and silk underwear. For we have come by accident to *The Scarlet Adventuress*, a magazine of fitful fires. You may prepare for the flesh-pots.

From *The Writer's Market*, November 1936: *Scarlet Adventuress*:

Here the woman adventuress must be sophisticated, charming, and quick-witted....The story must be told from the woman's angle and she must be of the sort who has a definite goal—love, money, power, or revenge—toward which she steadily forges, using the allure of her body and her ready wit to carry her through perilous situations, but never actually losing her virtue. The sex angle can be played up..., with frequent hits of intimacy between the two sexes, through never beyond the limits of decency. We want the glamorous type of woman who takes all and gives nothing.

So the editorial requirements for the magazine's fiction. Or that's what they said that they wanted. In practice, other material was included which the editor forgot to mention. Such absent-mindedness comes from dipping into too many tawny-amber pools.

The magazine seems to have begun around 1935 and may have first been titled *Modern Adventuress*. There is a great lack of volume and issue numbers, and the title page information is uncommonly reticent about frequency of issue. For at least part of its life, the magazine seems to have been a quarterly. In early 1937, the title briefly reverted to *Modern Adventuress*—or it appears to have done so. That change brought forth mildly reduced editorial requirements—the editor now wanted "sophisticated short stories of female adventuresses, involving sex without licentiousness."

Well, they could hope. And they were paying ½¢ a word, too.

Presumably the magazine melted into a perfumed haze soon afterward. The final issues have not been traced. The magazine had a rather short life but while it was underway, it certainly threw up gaudy sparks.

The name "Scarlet" is the overall adjective attached to some products of this particular magazine group, which included *Scarlet Confessions*, and (as advertised) *Scarlet Murderess*, in addition to *True Gang Life*, and *Detective and Murder Mysteries*. These were put out in Philadelphia by Associated Authors, Inc.

Whatever the other magazines were, *The Scarlet Adventuress* was not quite a confessions magazine and not quite a pulp. It was large, about 8 x 11 inches, and flat. It looked as if the editors had ripped about one-third of the pages out of a standard pulp magazine, then squeezed it very hard in a press. The residue was juiced up by ads for black lace underthings and virility improvers.

Just how many authors wrote the contents is unknown. Two or three, at least, although up to ten names appeared in the Table of Contents. Among them were Thelma Ellis, Edmund O. Kyle, Franz LeBaron, Roberta Dean, and Robert Leslie Bellem—so we know that at least one name was not a pseudonym.

The story was, usually, told from what passed as the woman's point of view. That's so the male reader could understand how the poor girl felt when all those gross men gripped her pulsating flesh and ripped off her finery.

The prose reminds you irresistibly of a wet diaper. The word "exotic" appears about six times a page, never correctly used. The story lines, such as they are, support descriptions of feminine undressing and sly mention of those various mysteries attendant to that sex in an area bounded by the chin and heels.

Through it all, adventuresses came and went, all approximately the same. All with the identical dehumanized air of scented bait about them.

Lady Nora O'Neil, for example. She was an iron-willed Irish fighter for liberty, and wore a pistol holstered in the top of her silk stocking and didn't care who she shot in the stomach.

In "The Red Hand Blanches" (January 1936) by Clive Stewart, Lady Nora is assisting the IRA. She vamps an English Colonel until he nigh breaks in half. Only an opportune telephone call saves her from becoming a woman of shame. And after she tried so hard. The IRA then shoots the English and vice versa, and a respectable quantity of bodies accumulate. The survivors agree to a prisoner exchange. Lady Nora, shining with honor, leaves the English and goes to spend the night with her lover.

That's reasonably typical of Lady Nora's accomplishments and you can figure out whether she's a villainess or heroine yourself.

You have a lesser problem with red-headed Kara Vania, Secret Agent XW9, the Lady of Doom, the Tiger Woman, the World's Most Glamorous Spy. She had a terrible time staying dressed.

As in "Lady of Destiny" (July 1936). She has been falsely accused of murdering the Marquis and stealing the secret documents. Someone else very bad did those dire deeds. She escapes from Old Bailey dressed in brassiere, panties, and one stocking. Can she recover the documents and prevent the communistic invaders from murdering 100,000,000 peaceful Orientals?

Sure.

The chase goes all the way to Shanghai. Kara loses her clothing twice more, is sold as a slave to an opium house, escapes from there dressed as a Russian officer. Then steals back the papers and flies back to friendly lines. During her flight, she loses all her clothing and arrives as naked as only a sensuous spy can get who has ripped it all off to dazzle the enemy's mind.

Admirable as these exploits are, they dwindle away before the glory that was Nila Rand—"that strange exotic creature who turned the blood of all men into molten fire—yet always forced her head to rule her heart until—"

Nila has risen from the chorus line to the higher notoriety of Broadway, the Riviera, Paris, Frisco, London, and Shanghai. She mixed only with gents who were class—and with a few underworld figures—dabbling here in the market, there in blackmail. An adventuress, you see.

To savor the heady musk of Nila adventures, consider "The Devil's Mistress" (July 1935) by Beech Allen.

She is in her bath. In the bedroom, Jeff Harwood, a rival adventurer, impatiently shifts feet among piles of her lace garments. Eventually she comes glowing out, clad mainly in a pair of filmy panties.

For a full column of type they talk plot—who has what valuables that need stealing. Then Jeff, now raised to volcano heat, seizes her in "a long abandoned kiss."

Her heart is strangely stirred but she refuses to become his partner, whatever that means. At that moment a knock on the door. Jeff hides, just as in a French farce. In staggers Carter Willoughby, licking his lips meaningfully. He has a problem—rather, another problem. His sister, Joan, is even now cavorting about the apartment of that ancient rotter, Lester Bondy.

Scenting quick cash profit, Nila offers to extract Joan—for a fee. And to close the bargain she sways forward (still in her panties), "her lips parted in scarlet invitation."

At Bondy's apartment, matters are sticky. Joan is hopped out of her head with drugs and drink. Bondy is busy taking art photos. Gliding in, Nila gives him a glance that makes him flame all over.

She suggests sending the amateur competition home. While he is scraping Joan up, Nila steals one of the photo plates but can't get the others.

So, as soon as she dumps Joan into a taxi, Nila slithers back to the apartment—and there is Bondy knocked cold. The art treasure plates are stolen.

At once, Nila rushes back to Jeff's apartment, where he has spent the evening writhing on the bed and gasping *Nila, Nila* in a smothered voice. In the following scene, he gets his hands on her twice, looks down the barrel of her pistol once, and has a generally unsatisfactory time. He doesn't know anything about plates—and she won't play.

Later that night—having stripped off all her clothing—Nila admires herself in the mirror. This goes on for quite a while. "Her fingers were liquid fire as they traced a path down her side....She was passion incarnate—and all the while, she was thinking of Joan Willoughby."

Next day she meets with Joan and Carter Willoughby and offers to get back the plates for $20,000. The sum makes them lose faith in altruism. Leaving the club, she is abducted by Jeff. He carries her back to his apartment, questions her for twelve seconds, and then they get a good grip on each other.

Which is interrupted by a fierce coarse fellow who comes in from the fire escape and abducts them away to a gangster's hideout. Instantly they get the drop on the crooks, tie them up, rush away to beard the Big Boss—Ace Morgan, Public Enemy #1—in his den at the Silver Bubble Club.

Even at that moment, in a flashy room, Ace is leering at Joan. He has the plates. She can have them for 50 grand and a few private poses. His hands clutch her. Just as a "thin stream of saliva runs from the corners of his mouth," enter Nila and .45.

Away goes Joan with Jeff. Nila stays to negotiate with Ace. She gets fifty percent of the blackmail. He gets the other plate—and her.

They pick up the plate and head for his apartment. She spends about a column taking off her clothes and locating his safe. Then in she undulates, glowing with exotic perfume, whispering:

"I'm much better after a few drinks."

Suddenly she is back on the bed and he is kissing the "beating flesh of her throat." Before he can do more than kiss, she has lifted the pistol from his hip holster—he's the kind who makes love while wearing a gun. Now it's child's play to force him to open the safe, knock him cold, and exit.

Just at dawn, Nila returns the plates. Brother smashes them at once, and Joan gives Nila the nicest kiss, pressing her rosebud lips to Nila's carmine ones..."For a moment the whole room faded away into nothingless. Darting green flecks danced in the amber irises of her eyes. Then she...gave herself up to a moment of heavy, exotic intoxication."

And so another adventure ends in the exotic haze of lesbianism, seasoned liberally with voyeurism, symbolic castration, aggravated assault, pornography, rape, near rape, and off-color thinking.

But the story is told from the woman's point of view.

And does this stuff keep on so?

Apparently. In the September 1935 "Rogues In Paradise" it's more of the same. Nila is attempting to secure a munitions order from the King of Livno. To get the order, she must make love to selected men, discover who murdered the boy, smile on the King, outfox the King's French hussy and his aging strumpet, remove all her clothing, have all her clothing removed, offer herself to the King's lust.

Ultimately, with a $75,000 check concealed in her stocking, she glides off with Jeff for an exotic weekend alone in Tangier.

At this point, we will leave them. Enough's enough.

Nila was the chief cream puff among those feminine pastries displayed in the *Scarlet Adventuress/Modern Adventuress*. There were others, six-seven-eight an issue, who made one-time appearances, clad only in a spraying of exotic perfume, their wonders to perform.

Call them villainesses, if you wish. Or heroines. Or sporting girls, ready for fun, frolic, and quick cash. All were something apart from the more usual feminine fiend who prowled pulp pages, flaming with sensuous sadism and thrusting her attributes about.

Nila and the other adventuresses are a different breed. They go their own way through the magazine's inflammatory dribble. They radiate lust and swoony passion. They live forever aroused, constantly concentrating upon themselves in the act of sensation.

All else is secondary—adventure, money, action. Fine in their place. But sensation is first.

So it must have seemed to those male readers, turning pages with unsteady finger. This is how it is to be a woman. If I was a woman—not a virile masterful solid masculine man, but a woman—this is how I'd feel in silk and perfume and carmine lips and all. If I was a woman, this is what I'd do. Yes, sir. Boy, now. You bet.

What woman readers thought is another matter. But after all, were there woman readers? Of the *Scarlet Adventuress*? Do you really think so?

Well, maybe. The trouble with these sophisticated stories is that they muddle your judgment. Read a couple of issues and you forget where sex stops and licentiousness begins. Everything starts getting exotic. And alluring. Haven't you noticed?

The Second Time Around

Five Detective Novels, that handsome magazine, was born in 1949 amid aftershock and stress. Not many months before, Street & Smith had terminated its pulp magazine line. That abrupt defection froze professional hearts, sent apprehension chittering along professional nerves.

It was a year of unease. The whole pulp magazine business was unsettled. The Second World War was over, but its malign effects lingered like a spider bite. As production costs increased. As distribution problems multiplied. As sales lurched and faltered and slowly slowly contracted—or sometimes not so slowly. As the first unclear signs appeared of that wave of extinction which, in 1953, would rise to black climax.

Or so we know now. In 1949, the future seemed less bleak, although, God knows, times were competitive and tough.

Such times had been met more than once in the pulp business. To survive, you cut costs, improved the product, experimented timidly, held on, waiting for the advertiser and the reader. In 1920 and 1932, and 1936, those dreadful years, readers and advertisers alike had fallen away. But they had always returned. Always.

And so, in preparation for that happy return, the magazines of 1949 burnished their format and prepared to meet prosperity more than half way. As it turned out, prosperity had other ideas. But at least the magazines tried.

Five Detective Novels was a child of the period. It was intended to produce revenue at minimum cost by reprinting older fiction from the Standard Magazine files. That included fiction originally published in *Thrilling Detective, Popular Detective*, and *Thrilling Mystery*, for the most part, although other magazines crept in later. Whether authors received a pittance or merely a warm glow at seeing their names in print is not known. We may suspect the worst. For, in those dark days, some publishers were known to purchase all rights and a sale was forever. (The subject of unreimbursed reprints generated much flame within professional writers' groups of the late 1930s.)

Although the fiction was reprint, the cover was fresh, modern, handsome. The most usual cover assembled such standard ingredients as menace, gun, and girl—this last ingredient being shown with exquisite mouth and a frontal development that should have made walking impossible.

The covers of 1952-1953 are rather darker than the covers of 1950-1951. The invariable subject, the girl in peril, floats against a background of shadows. Her limbs are pale, her face distorted by fear. She peers toward some dreadful event occurring past the other side of the cover—out where the reader stands peering in.

On earlier covers, backgrounds are lighter, colors richer, and the girls are not always helpless victims. In all cases, they are refreshingly female. In almost all cases, they wear red dresses.

The initial issues of *Five Detective Novels* offered 146 pages—148 pages, if you included both sides of the front cover, as did the formal page count. For 25 cents, you received five longish short stories, the "novels" of the magazine's title. Each ran about 20 pages. Stirred in among these were two, sometimes three, honest-to-God short stories.

This dose of fiction did not quite use all the available space. So the blank areas were filled by other means, rather as an unprincipled restaurant will artistically pad a plate with lettuce to conceal the modest dimensions of the meat.

Padding in the magazine consisted of a pair of articles, themselves brief enough, and a mass of filler material, grandly described as "Features." This stuff took various forms: a verse, a cartoon, or diminutive paragraphs offering a joke, an anecdote, or a small wad of facts. It was the trivia of yesterday.

Each issue also offered an extended department in which the editor waxed lyrical about the contents of the next issue. Plot summaries of coming attractions, often in great detail, sopped up the remaining blank space. Infrequently, letters from readers appeared.

As in any well-organized magazine, the ads paid the freight. Full-page ads filled most cover space and a few interior pages. In the back of the book, ads were much smaller, each about 1 x 2-¾ inch. They marched in columns down the page, shouting at you: Become a Famous Artist, stop gas pains with garlic tablets, mount birds at home, metalize baby shoes, stop Tobacco use, and write for the free catalog illustrating television sets with Giant 16" pictures.

Thus, in general terms, the physical plant of *Five Detective Novels*, "A Thrilling Publication," issued by Standard Magazines, Inc., N. L. Pines, President.

Either seventeen or eighteen quarterly issues were published from late 1949 to late 1953. (Although a final issue dated Winter 1954 has been reported, its existence has never been confirmed.) The run contained six volumes, each of three issues—Volume Six being incomplete. Or maybe not.

Behind these passionless statistics is another story. That tells how the magazine began as a superior reprint, its future luminous and its heart quick. And how the future became something else altogether, something grayer and thinner, so that the magazine changed in little ways no one would have anticipated at the start. The years slipped away, and the magazine began turning this way and that, seeking the way back to that first promise. But it was not a time for finding the way back.

This search gives a faint, sad overtone to later issues of the magazine. But an overtone only. We ought not to read tragedy into what, in truth, were routine editorial adjustments. *Five Detective Novels* was a sound professional magazine attempting to make some sort of profit by recycling the past. As all magazines, it adjusted to the problems of the moment. It shows what professional skill and workmanship could do in the early 1950s, and its changes are almost as interesting as the prose.

The magazine began ambitiously. The first issue, dated November 1949, was planned for every-other-month publication. It was in the fine old tradition— a thick-bodied pulp measuring about 7 x 9-¾. The editorship was credited to Harvey Burns, apparently a house name.

An admirable selection of mystery-action fiction was offered: "The Murder Bridge" (reprinted from 1934) by George Harmon Coxe; "Too Tough To Die" (from 1935 and featuring the hard-boiled detective, Red Lacey) by George Bruce; "Murder In Mexico" (1938) by Steve Fisher; "The Hooded Killer" (1934) by Paul Ernst, the story opening with dire thunders:

Nicholas James shuddered with dread premonition as he fitted the key into the lock of his door. Something deadly seemed to be hovering over his house.

And, finally, Richard Sale's "Death On an Ocean Liner" (1940), tough, fast, slick.

It is a curious prose mixture. Hooded killers had been passe for nearly a decade, and tough detectives, Red Lacey not withstanding, had quietly changed their shirts and drinking habits. Sale's galloping contemporary fiction, stressing character, mixes oddly with the other novelettes of brutal action.

But if the fiction appealed to incompatible tastes, the writers appealed to everybody. They were proven performers, each with his cadre of admirers. Most would appear again. Some, like Bruce's Lacey, would appear repeatedly.

In addition to the five novels, that first issue contained an article by Ray Cummings ("A Portrait of Alexander Hamilton") and a thin little true fact article by S. M. Ritter. The editor's department, "On The Docket," was an extended puff for the next issue. A little space was squandered to welcome readers and to state, in breathless self-admiration, the wonder of the new magazine:

If the year 1949 is remembered for any particularly outstanding event in the publishing field it will be the advent of the remarkable new magazine entitled Five Detective Novels. You are now holding in your hands a copy of the inaugural issue which contains five dramatic, thrill-packed novels by the world's top-ranking mystery writers all for the amazing low price of 25 cents. Just think of it!...

This—our first number—will probably become a collector's item, so we advise you to hold onto it. Don't give it away. If your friends want to read it, lend it to them but be sure to get it back.

This euphoric tone was carried over to the second issue (Winter 1950), the editor remarking:

Let's begin by expressing our thanks to you hundreds of thousands of readers who, with overwhelming response, welcomed our first issue....

It was almost certainly to the bitter disappointment of those hundreds of thousands of readers that the second issue had quietly become a quarterly. The story selection remained interesting. Another Red Lacey adventure from 1936 ("The Claim of the Fleshless Corpse") by George Bruce, together with stories by Frederick C. Painton, Norman Daniels, and Westmoreland Gray. A welcome addition was a G. T. Fleming-Roberts novelette about George Chance, The Ghost Detective—one of the superior magician-detectives of the pulps. The story, "The Case of the Astral Assassin," had been originally published in the November 1942 *Thrilling Mystery*, and was the first of four Ghost adventures to be reprinted.

(Chance had originally appeared in seven issues of his own magazine, variously titled *The Ghost* and *The Green Ghost Detective*, during 1940-1941. After the magazine terminated with the Summer 1941 issue, Chance moved to a 6-novelette series in the 1942-1943 *Thrilling Mystery*. The novelettes are probably better than the novels, although any Ghost Detective adventure is fine reading.)

While Chance did not appear in the Spring 1950 issue of *Five Detective Novels*, Red Lacey did: "Murder Money" (1935). Sam Merwin, Jr., was represented by a smooth, non-stop action piece, "Talent for Trouble" (1941) that had a New York City jazz background. And one of the short stories was by Arthur J. Burks, a neat little piece of jungle violence, "Kill-Dog Kill," that does not seem to be a reprint.

The last of the large-sized issues of *Five Detective Novels* was dated Winter 1951. It was a particularly fine issue. It contained another Ghost novelette ("The Case of the Clumsy Cat" from the March 1943 *Thrilling Mystery*). There were also three hard-boiled novelettes by H. H. Stinson, W. T. Ballard, and Nelson S. Bond—this last being a Red Drake case, "Murder for a Million," originally published in the Winter 1941 *Exciting Detective*. Also included was Fredric Brown's "The Jabberwocky Murders" (*Thrilling Mystery*, Summer 1944), the first of four Brown stories reprinted.

Two short stories were also used, one of them being Seabury Quinn's "Dead Man's Shoes," which is not identified as a reprint.

The "On the Docket" department rather casually summarizes what is to come in the next issue. Equal space is devoted to a puff for *Giant Detective* and *Popular Detective*; all the stories described sound exactly alike.

One thing not mentioned in "On the Docket" is that the magazine is about to drop fourteen pages and ⅝s of an inch height. Such distressing information might frighten the reader, a notoriously spooky quarry. As a result, not even a whisper of change leaks out.

However, change comes. The Spring 1951 issue is decidedly smaller, decidedly thinner. By some arcane magic, there seems to be the same amount of fiction.

The other visible change is that "On the Docket" was replaced by "The Lowdown." This temporarily contracted to a single page, most of which was spent discussing current slang.

The novels offered include "The Case of the Broken Broom," the last Ghost reprint (from the Fall 1943 *Thrilling Mystery*). Also "Murder Music" by Robert Wallace—which sounds as if it should be a Phantom Detective novel but isn't—that was originally published in the October 1938 *Popular Detective*; "Must This Man Burn?" by Frederick C. Painton (August 1939 *Thrilling Detective*). And two other novelettes by Westmoreland Gray and John Hawkins.

For those who keep track of such things, it may be noted that, for this issue only, the Volume number is given as "XX," rather than "3."

From this point on, the magazine glides smoothly out, issue after issue. It has reached its height of excellence and continues to hold fast. Major features include novelettes by such highly popular writers as G. T. Fleming-Roberts (not about The Ghost), W. T. Ballard, Talmage Powell, Fredric Brown.

And now, softly, softly, like mice dancing in the night, the editorial policy is modified. Standard Magazines are no longer the only source for the fiction.

Two stories are reprinted from *The American Magazine,* a major slick publication, and four stories are drawn from *Black Mask.* Original novelettes begin to appear and more first-run short stories. These unexpected changes will continue for about a year.

To the Fall 1951 issue is added a new department, "Cryptogram Corner." This continued for five issues, through Fall 1952, bringing satisfaction to those eager for mental anguish. During the same period, the number of "Features" ballooned madly, eight, ten, eleven items. All were cited on the Table of Contents, so that a cursory glance suggested the magazine contained an immense amount of reading material.

These changes are more or less correlated with the editorship of David X. Manners. His name is cited as editor in the Fall 1951 issue. His selections are increasingly modern, increasingly smooth, with characterization, some psychological insight, and an occasional whiff of the supernatural. He reprints Paul Chadwick's "Angels Die Hard" (Winter 1952), "The Ghost Breakers" (Summer 1952), and "The Cat from Siam" (Spring 1953).

These stories are intermixed by the *Black Mask* reprints, the first by Dale Clark ("This Will Slay You," 1941) in the Summer 1952 issue. It was followed by Frederick C. Davis' "This Way To the Morgue" (1938) and Stewart Sterling's "Kindly Omit Flowers" (1942). (Both appeared in the Fall 1952 issue of *Five Detective Novels.*)

After little more than a year, Manners was replaced as editor by Morris Ogden Jones, whose name first appears in the Winter 1953 issue. With the coming of Jones, a number of editorial readjustments take place. Reprints are soon limited to material published in the Standard magazines. The "Features" are pared back. "The Lowdown" is farmed out to such visiting writers as Stewart Sterling and Harold Gluck. (Gluck had been steadily contributing non-fiction articles to every issue of the Columbia Publications' *Famous Detective.*)

In spite of these changes, the magazine continued to offer the authentic old wine in glossy bottles, lean and attractive. Usually.

The Winter 1953 issue has a dreary dark cover, but it contains crackling stories by Powell, Ballard, Roan, and Frederick C. Davis—whose "Stop The Presses" is from the December 1938 *Black Mask*. Both the Roan and Powell stories seem to be originals.

As a bonus, there is also a Hildgarde Withers/John J. Malone adventure, "Once Upon A Train" (1950), by Craig Rice and Stuart Palmer.

Stewart Sterling again wrote "The Lowdown" for the Spring 1953 issue, plus a new story, "Model for Murder." In addition to a strong selection of writers—Fredric Brown, Merle Constiner, and Wyatt Blassingame—there was a story by Louis L'Amour, "With Death In His Corner," reprinted from the December 1948 *Thrilling Detective*.

The following issue, Summer 1953, contained reprints from *Popular Detective, G-Men Detective, Detective Novel Magazine, Thrilling Mystery*, and the E. Hoffmann Price "Murder In Florida" from the December 1940 *Thrilling Detective*. There was enough variety to please the most picky, and writers included such old pros as W. T. Ballard and Norman Daniels.

But competent writers, interesting stories, appealing covers were not enough. By then, excellence no longer made much difference. One—or possibly two—issues later, the magazine ended.

Over the course of its life, *Five Detective Novels* had published ninety long short stories, or novelettes, or call them what you will. Almost incidentally, it had also published about forty short stories. This imposing mass of fiction, generally of superior quality, provides a fascinating view of the longer pulp fiction mystery during the late 1930s and 1940s.

Few magazines approached the sustained quality of *Five Detective Novels*. It was, almost certainly, one of the finest of the reprint magazines, rivaled only by Street & Smith's *Detective Story Annual*.

And it was, even for those not drawn by mystery stories, a shining example of the art of the pulp magazine.

Selections From A Magazine Library

The magazines all differed from one another. Superficially they shared certain characteristics, as children from the same family may share red hair, musical talent, and short toes. Like children, each magazine developed its own personality, its own unique shine, red hair or not.

This section is devoted not so much to odd magazines as substantial ones—titles that still rear up out of the past and are remembered. Each offers a distinctive twist, a strong different voice. Some lived only briefly; others seemed to continue to the end of time. All were distinct personalities. No timid compromising here. They were what they were and that's what they were.

Most magazines reviewed in this section are somehow associated with the mystery field, but so great is the variation between them that they hardly seem of the same species. Between 1915 and 1957, about six hundred different mystery titles appeared. While differences were occasionally microscopic, most managed, in some way, to be different. It was needful. The marketplace was a harsh arena, and a magazine that offered only more of the same enjoyed no long life.

To please those unfortunate enough not to revel in mysteries, two other magazine forms have been included. *Sea Stories* is an early adventure magazine which followed the lead of *Railroad Stories* to specialize in a single form of fiction. *Weird Tales*, which lived up to its reputation as "The Unique Magazine," is caught here as it entered the 1930s, full of hope, horror adventure, and its own curious version of the science-fantasy.

1—*The Shadow Magazine*, August 1, 1934, Vol. X, No. 5,
published twice-a-month by Street & Smith, 10¢, 128 pages.

Superlatives being an indication that enthusiasm has paralyzed the judgement, this piece will restrain superlatives about *The Shadow Magazine*. It is tempting, but discipline will be observed, cost what it will.

The magazine deserves superlatives. It arches across the bright red world of 1930s pulp magazine fiction, an extended series of danger, death, and detection. Its central figure, The Shadow, was enthusiastically acclaimed at the time and has since hardened to a sort of national ikon, symbolizing mystery—although precious few remember what the ikon represents.

The magazine, itself, revived the single-character publication, dormant since dime novel days. First issued in 1931, *The Shadow* continued until 1949, amassing 325 consecutive issues, nearly twice that of *Doc Savage*, its nearest competitor. For years, the covers were admirable and the interior illustrations utterly superb. Even the magazine's short stories were, more often than not, models of the art.

Through this delightful magazine glided the dangerous figure of The Shadow. He was a gun-fighting investigator who battled gangsters, weird crime, and criminal geniuses, deducted like a battery of computers, disguised himself effortlessly, employed enough agents to staff a small corporation. The Shadow was entirely marvelous. In him, the pulps found the stuff of myth and this they exploited for nearly twenty years.

The image of The Shadow, his laugh, his black costume, his guns, his equipment, his disguises, his agents and associates, even his enemies, got into the bloodstream of the pulps like some form of benign virus, bursting out when least expected. Even his arch-rival, The Spider, went through a period in 1937 when he became a close copy of The Shadow.

In the 1930s, as today, success meant commercial exploitation. As intensely exploited as Tarzan, The Shadow sold wrist watches, coloring books, disguise and fingerprint kits, sheet music, Better Little Books, comic books, and a succession of nearly worthless moving pictures. A long-enduring radio series spun from the character, its rudimentary simplicities nearly obscuring the original concept. Forty years after the magazine died, recordings of the radio program are still available. The character has been revived in books and paperbacks, as well as graphic novels—a fancy name for comic books—some of which are not contemptible. The exploitation continues. It is a remarkable record for a character created in 1931.

Success came quite accidentally.

The Shadow began as a disembodied voice introducing the "Street & Smith Detective Story Hour." The program was intended to whip up interest in the *S&S Detective Story Magazine*. Public response to the voice and its sinister laughter was strong. Scenting opportunity, Street & Smith moved to copyright the name, The Shadow, by publishing an issue or so of *The Shadow, A Detective Magazine*. From that casual decision, an industry grew.

Newspaperman, publicist, amateur magician Walter B. Gibson was selected to write the novels, using the house name Maxwell Grant. Gibson had written several non-fiction books relating to magicians and magic, a few short stories, and no recorded novels. As it turned out, he had the flare for fiction. When he sat before a typewriter, words poured forth, a hyperactive stream of words that swiftly translated to successful magazines.

Unexpectedly, sales boomed. Gibson found himself a professional novelist, settled to the production of a 70,000-word novel every two weeks, a torrent of prose whose composition would have disintegrated any lesser mortal.

Over the years, two other writers, Theodore Tinsley and Bruce Elliott, would contribute to the series; and Lester Dent would write one story, later revised by Gibson. But the bulk of the series was by Gibson—112 consecutive novels in five-and-a-half years, before Tinsley's first story; 282 novels over the entire series.

By 1934, Gibson had warmed to his astounding labors and was writing at heights he would not soon equal. It was a vintage year, 1934. The rather nebulous image of The Shadow, "That Weird Creature of the Night," as the editorial puffs called him, had developed to a firmly detailed personality, sustained by an elaborately detailed background.

At the beginning, Gibson had nothing more to work with than that sinister radio voice, that hollow, sneering, weirdly laughing voice that was a stage melodrama cliche. The demands of fiction required that Gibson create a character consistent with the voice. He did so by combining the cliche voice with that equally venerable cliche, the mystery figure—the black-clad, white-faced, blazing-eyed, sinister lurker and follower, which had peopled sensational fiction for more than 100 years.

From this unpromising union of material, an oddly appealing figure rose. That this happened is a tribute to Gibson's imaginative force. His mind disliked generalities. Always he turned to the specific and the concrete, a clear image, a firmly rendered character. These images and characters are not subtle and rarely are they surprising. They have little depth but surprising vitality. Gibson rarely viewed more than the surface, but what he observed was rendered in strong line. His forte was not complexity but complication. And in the figure of The Shadow he produced a simplicity that was tangled beyond comprehension by complications.

The Shadow was an amazement buried within overlapping mysteries. Seldom directly visible, conducting his investigations (at first) through the services of various incompetents constantly requiring saving, The Shadow dazzled and baffled. He was everyone and no one. He slipped effortlessly among multiple identities. He was a World War I flying ace. He was a former spy, a master of codes and ciphers, with a pronounced bent for obscure chemicals and the gadgets of stage magic.

He wore a distinctive ring, a fire opal. Perhaps he owned two of these. He communicated in disappearing ink with a growing legion of agents. He communed with himself in a darkened room, laughing as if demented. His funds seemed unlimited. And early in the series, he began using hand guns against criminal plotters and gangsters.

At the beginning, the plotters were rather small scale, bad men who disguised themselves and kept strongholds filled with secret panels and concealed their malignancy behind a smile. The gangsters were the same sweatered ruffins that filled the pages of Nick Carter dime novels and Frank Packard magazine serials. Gibson's version of the underworld was, in fact, based on the New York street gangs of 1900, rather than the more sophisticated, Mafia-based organizations that rose during the 1920s.

Obsolete and hackneyed as were these materials, they grew molten at Gibson's touch. If his fiction did not resemble any recognizable reality, it still possessed inner coherence. The melodrama, dark with violence and danger and death, gripped with startling force. And it flowed intensely.

By 1934, The Shadow had materialized firmly, an intricate character. No longer lurking at the fringes of action, he stood at the center of the shooting and screaming, fully controlling the situation. His agile mind was always four chapters ahead of everyone else.

At this point in the series, we turn to *The Shadow Magazine*, August 1, 1934, the fifty-ninth issue of the series.

The magazine contained a novel, three short stories, and three continuing departments. Of the three departments (to take the last first):

"The Third Degree" was a brief crime puzzle, so written that readers of agile wit could guess the solution before the answer was printed in the next issue.

"The Shadow Club" was a rallying place for faithful readers. Members pledged themselves to give their "moral, and when called upon, actual support to uphold law and order and down crooks." For ten cents (stamps or cash), they received an admirable round pin showing a profile of The Shadow. For an additional dime, members could also buy a rubber stamp, reading "Shadow Club Member"; the ink pad was not included.

Readers not fortunate enough to be Club members were encouraged to write to *The Shadow Magazine* and receive "a special message from The Shadow, written in one of his many secret ink compounds."

In addition to these enchantments, the Club offered four pages of bland articles. This issue, the articles addressed Youthful Offenders, a London clinic for evaluating criminals, and emergency police communications—suitable discussion fare for the weekly club meeting in the basement, with all the lights turned low.

The final department, "The Pulse of the Nation," fifteen letters from high school students, a sailor, a detective, an ex-secret service man, and an enthusiast in England. All expressed admiration for The Shadow Club, the great work accomplished by the magazine, and, to a man, they supported Law and Order:

I always do my best to thwart crime.

From these inspirational notes, we turn to this issue's main novel, "The Crime Master." And there he sits glaring from the cover of the magazine, an aged fiend, white haired and with only two teeth showing in his upper jaw. He sits at a transparent grid overlaying a map of the city. That transforms the city into a game board on which the Crime Master manipulates wooden pieces representing frustrated good and triumphant evil. At the other side of the board sits The Shadow. He holds a black piece and has clearly loused up the old devil's plans.

The novel symbolized by the cover, it is now time to plunge into the action. Which is quick, violent, and exciting.

That dread invisible criminal genius, the Crime Master, has embarked on a career of robbery with violence. Hordes of gangsters wait for his call, fingering their machine guns. The police drift helplessly. Even Detective Joe Cardona, a key figure of the series, is all at sea. So is Ralph Weston, Police Commissioner, prig, snob, and pain in the neck. But glory be, Cardona has found a clue in a dead thug's pocket. It was placed there by The Shadow and its discovery urged by Clyde Burke, newspaperman who secretly works for The Shadow. Cardona, however, thinks he has discovered it himself. And so led by gentle hands, he squeezes an informant, startlingly named Squawky.

Squawky sneaks off to the Pink Rat, a sordid dive, and is spotted by The Shadow in disguise. But The Shadow is after larger prey. He pursues Trigger Maddock, confronts that deadly gunman in his room. Then in bursts the whole mob, pistol first, their puffy faces snarling. And the guns begin:

(The thug) saw a twisting mass of blackness. He fired—a split second late. His bullet pounded the wall on the near side of The Shadow. A booming report came in answer. The Shadow, in his whirl, has loosed a shot straight for the door.

(The thug) crumpled. Above him, the other mobsters aimed to kill. But that one shot was but the first blast of The Shadow's rapid fire. Zimming bullets came with bursting flame as The Shadow spat quick shots to the source of danger.

One mobster toppled forward; the other dropped back, with a cry of anguish. Five bullets, drilling in quick succession, had found human marks within the space of a single second.

The exchange leaves Trigger about 94% dead. As he fades away, The Shadow forces him to write a note sketching out the next crime planned. This note Cardona finds and prepares a trap. When the Crime Master next strikes at the Trust Company, the police and The Shadow are waiting. During the fight, Cardona is severely wounded and the crooks partially escape, shot all to rags.

Thereafter, both the Crime Master and The Shadow plot and plan. The Crime Master needs a new lieutenant; The Shadow must figure out who it will be. As usual, The Shadow has returned to his sanctum:

A light was burning in a black-walled room. Bluish rays shone on the polished surface of a table. White hands, living things that extended from blackness, were at work. A glimmering gem—The Shadow's girasol—sparkled from a tapering finger. Its iridescent hues, changing in constant procession, seemed to reflect the mystery of The Shadow himself.

Accurately deducting that gang boss Eagle Tabrick will be recruited, The Shadow slips into Eagle's apartment. Eagle has just shot the Crime Master's emissary dead, and a minion of the Crime Master has just shot Eagle dead. The Shadow leaves another note for the police and depart. But now the Crime Master has learned that The Shadow was responsible for the failure at the Trust Company and takes action.

He lays a trap, using two full mobs. In the ensuing fight, The Shadow is seriously wounded, barely escapes. While he is recovering in the private rooms of his favorite physician, Dr. Rupert Sayre, his agent, Cliff Marsland takes up the trail.

Cliff manages to tip the police off to one planned crime. But the second time he attempts to pass on such information, he is trapped, hauled in front of the Crime Master, and pumped so full of drugs his hair floats. As a result, he gives bad information to Burbank, The Shadow's contact man, and The Shadow ends up trapped in a steel-lined cellar, waiting for the Crime Master's men to come and blast his series to a sudden end.

Meanwhile, back at the transparent map, the Crime Master feels strong enough to take over the city. To begin with, he decides to reveal himself, capture Commissioner Weston, and otherwise do a lot of things which make no particular sense, except that it is getting close to the end of the novel, and master minds do a lot of silly things toward the end of novels.

At the moment, the situation is black. There sit Weston and Marsland, dizzy with drugs. There cackles the Crime Master, self revealed as Ganford Dagron, retired financier. There deploy the forces of crime, out to loot the platinum bars from the vault.

And, behold, Commissioner Weston appears at Headquarters. Incisive, commanding, confident, the antithesis of his normal self, he barks out instructions, sets a gigantic police trap. Then vanishes.

He is, or course, The Shadow, escaped from the steel-lined trap and wonderfully disguised.

The army of criminals are promptly obliterated. The Shadow then materializes in the Crime Master's personal warroom and, in half a page, blasts old man Dagron and his two close aides from this life.

A throbbing, outlandish laugh broke through the Crime Master's lair. It rose to a pitch of strident mockery. Sardonic echoes answered. The Shadow's triumph!"

Well, this is all completely delightful. It is, perhaps, not quite at a level with "King Lear" or "The Divine Comedy," but it has its own merits. The action, transparent and intense, flows from one sharply visualized scene to the next. Cause and effect link the major scenes. Suspense draws you ever onward. The Shadow, although clearly superhuman, is not altogether invulnerable, and that ability to bleed like the rest of us, softens the otherwise rather austere edges of his character.

It is probably unnecessary to report that delicate levels of spiritual experience remain unexamined by this adventure. Nor do any concerns about mass murder by a self-appointed justice figure disturb the serene surface of the story. It is all action. Impelling, hot, gun-rich action expressing that familiar point of view: The bad guys asked for it, and they got it.

Essentially the same thing happens in each of the three short stories included in this issue:

"Poisoned Cattle" by George Allan Moffatt describes the defeat of an extortion scheme—Pay or the cattle in the stockyards die *en masse*. Detective Lody traps the three-man gang at the top of a 50-foot water tank and stops them, at terrible personal risk.

"Scoop" is by Roswell Brown, a pseudonym for the admirable Jean Francis Webb. This is the first story of the Grace Culver series. It is steeped in danger and violence. Grace, a reporter for the *Banner*, investigates the murder of a nice old rich lady, finds that single clue the police overlooked, and confronts the murderer. With the result that she nearly gets shot through that cute red head. But she doesn't. And, as the story ends, she is about to join a private detective firm. (For further details, refer to "Grace Note" in Chapter III of this volume.)

"Murder on a Rainy Night," by Milton Burns, concerns murder by accident. The two gunmen have shot the wrong man in a yellow rain coat. Tough cop Gorman tracks them down to a final vicious gun fight in a blond's apartment.

So *The Shadow Magazine* during its finest year. It was a beautifully balanced mechanism that offered, as Editor John Nanovic once remarked, "Not art but excitement." It did that. And, almost incidentally, it added what may yet be a permanent figure to our national folk heroes—a lethal figure gliding from the darkness to punish crime. The guns are silent now, but echoes of The Shadow's laughter continue. His image lingers after his adventures have been forgotten, and the magazines have crumbled away.

2—*Sea Stories*, November 1926, Vol. XIII, No. 3,
published monthly by Street & Smith, 25¢, 192 pages.

Sea Stories is one of those massively beautiful magazines that the 1920s did so well. It is one of the earliest of the specialized adventure magazines, beginning in 1922.

The cover is attractive enough for framing. Painted by Richard V. Schluter, it shows the U.S.S. Constitution, its gun ports agape, "carrying all sail that will draw before a bright following breeze." Which is a fair sample of the magazine's prose style.

Inside, each story is illustrated by a single line drawing of no particular distinction placed at the beginning of the text. The Table of Contents has more character. It is ornamented by sea horses and mermaids gripping discretely placed anchors. Each story title is spiced up by a brief descriptive line:

> *Out of the Tides*—"From the shipping office to the sea"
> *The Horse on Seaward*-"A diabolical scheme on shore."
> Then forward into an endless swamp of ads:

Follow This Man! Secret Service Operator 38 is on the job. (SS Op. #38 is apparently a lab technician in evening dress who analyzes fingerprints and drags down $2500 to $10000 a year. He wears clean clothes. His days are brightened by excitement. His ad is brightened by red ink.)

As is:

> Don't Pay Me A Cent If I Can't Give You A Magnetic Personality
> and
> Three Electrical Lessons Actually Free

The 21-jewel Studebaker watch ad (Send $1.00 Down) is tastefully tinted yellow. Gold, even. And, elsewhere, Prest-o-Lite, we learn, still serves Marmon, and shows photographs of that machine in 1906 and 1926. The Baby Ruth candy bar was 5¢. Cowboys use Mennen shave—there's a testimonial. And "Good Reading" by Charles Houston—which is a fake book review—plugs four brilliant novels published by Chelsea House, a pseudonym for Street & Smith when reprinting novels from its pulp magazines.

The ads, all on coated stock, are split between the front and back of the book. When you come to the fiction, however, alchemy transmutes the paper back to dross.

The stories in *Sea Stories* are—how can it best be put?—vigorous manly adventures out on big waters. Which is to say that the ghosts of Joseph Conrad and William McFee waft transparently among the pages, watching lesser artists sweat blood to give their fiction the proper salty tang.

The magazine is filled (or, perhaps, awash) with dramatic situations. Clean vigorous action. The sniff of salt air. Strong men in conflict. The stories favor tall ships (i.e., those with sails rising tier on tier), but there are sufficient gunboats, coal-fueled merchant vessels, and steam launches to satisfy all itches. The ships appear in a variety of settings—from Hudson Bay to mermaid rocks off the coast of somewhere. Freedom is what you pay for in *Sea Stories* and what you get.

The lead novel, "Out of the Tides" by Gustaf Olander, contains 29 chapters and 103 pages. If reading the story won't ennoble you, you're beyond hope.

Grayson, an ex-mate, has spent 20 years in a city office. Gave up the sea to take care of his mother. But she dies. He then buys a passenger ticket for an around-the-Cape voyage in the Flying Cloud, a ship of many masts and

ropes. It comes fully equipped with a bad sneaking Captain who is guilty
of barratry. (Nothing to do with sex; he deliberately wrecked a former ship
for the insurance.) His officers are no better than he is.

Pretty soon, the Captain gets arrogant with the passengers. They show
him the hollow end of a pistol, which unsets his mind. Everybody speedily
hates everybody else. Except that Grayson is growing to love Agnes, who is
lovely and gentle and the first woman who smiled on him (other than his
mother) in twenty years. Then the Captain strikes by abandoning them on
a derelict full of scorpions.

It was a Spanish derelict, if that explains matters.

At this point, chance steps in. The derelict is also full of gold and fur
coats. Then a US Navy sloop-of-war happens alongside and kills off the
scorpions. Then it turns out that the ship is in swell shape, just a bit dusty.
Grayson marries Agnes and off they sail.

Only to collide with the Flying Cloud. It seems improbable but, of course,
the Cloud is now painted black. The Graysons spend some time in a lifeboat.
With their luck, they barely get thirsty before rescue comes. Shortly afterward,
they arrive on dry land, the Flying Cloud is captured, and the captain dies
of drink. Such luck hasn't been jammed into twenty nine chapters since *Swiss
Family Robinson*.

"The Fore Peak Ladder," a short story by Eugene Cunningham, tells how
a low-down skunk accuses a clean-cut young fellow of murder. But it was
really accidental death, the victim having fallen down the fore peak ladder
while carrying a shears in his pocket. The plot fails. Evil is punished.

The "Star of Hope" (short story by John T. Rowland) is a junker that
runs out of coal in Hudson Bay. All hands abandon ship, except the Chief
Engineer. He stays to rig up an ingenious kerosene-burning rig to keep up
steam, while Lester Dent and William McFee nod approvingly from the wings.
Single-handed, he steams the ship to shore, is saved from the rocks by a sweet
Eskimo girl. She does not anticipate the storm which arrives on the next page.
The Star, blown here and there, rams the ship of a crook, pirate, and Eskimo
molester. This villain has picked up the Star's crew and is treating them without
respect. But he gets his—an Eskimo shivs him in the back. Another happy
ending.

Then, for a change of pace, "A Wet Tale" (short story by Arthur Mason)
tells how a crusty old hard-nosed stringy sea captain becomes pliable as a jello
sandwich when he learns to love a kitten.

"Command," short story by L. Paul, tries mightily to conjure up the weird
of Conrad. A cowardly sea captain, afraid to make decisions, elects to go down
with his ship during a storm. During the final 3-⅛ minutes of his life, he
learns to be a commander and sinks beneath the raging billows with a sense
of accomplishment.

Now for the serial. It was a well-known fact that no pulp magazine could
survive without a serial to draw readers panting from issue to issue. The
installment this month is Part III, "The Unattainable," by Carrington Phelps.
In this, the spoiled son of Bidwell Shipping wakes (with an incredible hangover)

to discover that he's been shanghaied aboard one of his father's ships. Imagine the irony.

Being a self-indulgent snit, he instantly mouths off, instantly gets punched in the teeth, is forced to work, forced to keep clean, forced to become a man, etc. etc. etc.

Just as sea air is reshaping his soul, some mysterious figure cracks him on the head, tries to flip him overboard. No luck. He survives. Who did it? Grim mystery. Down on his bunk, he holds his head, muses glumly:

All men were liars and cheats. Women didn't count because they were negligible....

To be continued in Part IV.

"Mermaid,' short story by George Allan England, is broad-gauge comedy. Captain Leonidas T. Tripp, a miserably hen-pecked skipper (retired) comes straight from Lord Dunsany's stories of Jorkins. Or even from "The Rime of the Ancient Mariner," since the Captain locks in on a visitor to recount at vast length how he once fell in with a batch of mermaids. Later, through involved bad luck, he ends disguised as a mermaid in a flea bag side-show. While at this shameful occupation, he is detected by his life-long enemy, Captain McWhirt. That precipitates one of those silent movie fights that reduces the area to shambles. The story is the best in this issue. But then, England was always competent.

The final short story is "The Horse on Seaward" by Nicholas Brigg. Captain Joshua Thaxter, president and owner of the Red T line, has seen three of his ships lost in four months—all in the same area. He thinks this odd. And now, Tom Whidden—Tom, who'd been like a son to him—to whom "in a few short months he was to have given him his daughter Margaret—his Peggy—the apple of his eye.

"And now Tom Whidden was gone—gone—gone."

Have you guessed that it's a devilish plot to ruin Old Man Thaxter? Well, it is. "Crazy" Totten, once Thaxton's rival in love, has rigged a phoney light on an island and when the ships pass by on foggy nights....

But Old Crazy dies for his sins, hurled "headlong onto a granite boulder and cracking the evil skull like a rotten egg."

The Captain finds poor Tom Whidden tied up in Crazy's cellar, so the apple of his eye will get her husband after all—after all—after all.

At the rear of the magazine is tucked that mandatory department, "The Log Book." Most magazines included a department from which the pulp editor murmured secrets into the reader's ear. His language was adjusted to the format of the magazine. In *Sea Stories*, the editor is densely nautical. In other publications, he would be woodsey, or cowboyish, or self-consciously man-to-man.

In turn, the readers spoke to the editor. Judging by the letters in "The Log Book," some authentic sailors read *Sea Stories*. What they thought of the fiction isn't clear. But they provided considerable hard information about ship types and yarns of voyages in bitter weather. These letters fill the back columns with shocks of reality. The real world feels suddenly close—that is so grayly described in the fiction. The letters are bare statements by men whose work was done between the sky and the water. But they live. The correspondents wrote in gold, whether they knew it or not.

If the letters are real, the fiction classifies as genuine synthetic. This is in the proud tradition of the pulps, where ignorance never interfered with the story. In general, this issue of *Sea Stories* is filled with sound, minor fiction, slanted to a specialized market. It draws heavily on the short prose tradition of Kipling, Doyle, Conrad, and McFee—also characters and scenes from the same source.

The prose is the color of a gray day. Sentimentality and bathos rear up in queer places. Coincidence clomps heavily about. The ideas are slight, the characters flat as a pressed butterfly.

Defects, certainly. Typical of the time and the medium.

However, "Mermaid" deserves reprinting. It is funny and too saucy fresh to stay locked in the files. For the rest of the stories, if they aren't good, they are interesting. They keep you with them. Somehow, they manage to recreate wide spaces, movement, violent conflict, the living presence of the ships. They are paste diamonds. But such a pretty shine.

Anyway, the ads are worth the price of the issue.

      3—The Black Mask, A Magazine of Mystery, Thrills, and Surprises, November 1921, Vol. IV, No. 2, published monthly by Pro-Distributors Publishing Co., Inc., 20¢; 128 pages.

Black Mask in childhood.

H. L. Mencken founded the magazine early in 1920 and sold it in November of that year. It had been a swift success, and he needed cash to support *The Smart Set*, then afflicted with the falling sickness.

Black Mask was the second major magazine to specialize in detective and mystery fiction. The first had been Street & Smith's *Detective Story Magazine*, which leaped to popular attention in 1915, when it swallowed up the *Nick Carter Stories* dime novel like a bass striking a fly.

Black Mask also began fast, public hunger for mysteries being acute. But the *Black Mask* of those early days differed radically from the magazine of the late Twenties and Thirties. As yet, no glimmer of greatness warmed its pages. Far from it.

In late 1921, *The Black Mask* still carried deep marks of its origins among manuscripts rejected by *The Smart Set*. With all its heart, *The Black Mask* also yearned to be smart. It limped hopefully in *The Smart Set*'s shadow, straining for worldly elan and viewing its own fiction with condescending distaste. For, really, no intelligent person could take a mystery story seriously.

Which may partly explain the fiction of the November 1921 issue.

On the cover, a fast-looking girl, her red hair bobbed, slips a key to an oily male in evening clothes. Both glance queasily about, the naughty things.

Inside the front cover are ads for two other magazines—*The Follies*, its lead story being "A Fool On The String," and *Saucy Stories* (Mencken's pastiche of *Snappy Stories*), featuring "In The Face Of Scandal."

At the rear of the book, pages 127 and 128 are riddled with small ads, strongly woman-oriented, puffing no-smear mascara, facial remedies, an inexpensive ring with a stone Just Like A Diamond, free dress designing lessons, and a chance to complete high school in two years.

YOU CAN BE BOBBED
Without Cutting Your Hair,
send a strand of your hair and $10.00

or

$1.00 DOWN gets you A ROOM FULL OF FURNITURE
(6-piece Set of Fumed Oak)

And on the back cover:

110-piece Gold Decorated MARTHA WASHINGTON
DINNER SET
Your Initial In Two Places On Every Piece
ALL HANDLES COVERED WITH GOLD

Excluding the ads, the magazine contains 126 pages, most of them fiction. For 20¢, you received a novelette, ten short stories, and a department of book reviews. Thus the fiction costs less than 2¢ a story. This explains a good deal.

The Table of Contents is headed *The Black Mask* in bold black type and includes a small sketch of a black half-mask. Behind this are crossed a flint-lock pistol and dagger. This symbol appears at the end of each story, enlarged or reduced to fill available space.

Down the Table of Contents parade the usual unfamiliar 1920's names. All sound vaguely spurious, and some openly suggest wry editorial jests. Boxed at the bottom of the page are the names of those dignitaries associated with the magazine: F(lorence) M. Osburne, Editor; Executives of the PRO-DISTRIBUTORS PUBLISHING COMPANY, Inc.-A. W. Sutton, President; P. C. Cody, Vice-President and Circulation Director; F. W. Westlake, Secretary and Treasurer.

Now begins the fiction. The first story offered is "The Dead Man's Letter," a complete Mystery Novelette by Victor Lauriston. Since the story is 22 pages long, "novelette" is a most fulsome description. But let that pass.

The story is illustrated by two full-page sketches, done by hand by Archie Gunn. Mr. Gunn specialized in drawing the faces of bobbed-hair women. When he had to draw the rest of them, his technique wavered slightly. To avoid technical difficulties, he swathed his women in sheets of dangling material, and pictured all his men as standing rather straight on short, little legs. All his characters stare point peer but without expression, and they bend stiffly at joints not usually found in the conventional skeleton.

"The Dead Man's Letter," being inept drivel, shifts point of view three times during the twenty two pages. We begin with the doctor, who discovers that the rich old sourball has been dosed with arsenic; then we shift to the sourball's business partner; then to the deliberations of the smart city dick.

The story progresses by that fine old technique of accusing a different character on every page. That saves the author the boredom of constructing a coherent plot. Eventually, the nurse (suspected) points out a CLUE to the investigating detective—a feminine fingerprint under the sealed flap of The Dead Man's Letter.

And is the detective grateful. Say!

The next story, by Bessie Dudley, is titled "The Blond Shadow," an ironic yarn of crime and punishment. Thus:

Kerrigan, the cop, has never been able to arrest Summers, the clever bank robber. After the 9th National Bank is cleaned out, Summers vanishes and Kerrigan suspects the worst. So he goes to work on Summers' wife, Molly, and flames her with jealously by whispering that Summers is having a Hey-Hey time with a blond sweetsie.

Livid with jealousy, Molly bombards Summers with messages in code. Finally he comes home to confront her in a scene strikingly illustrated by that subtle master, Archie Gunn.

At this point, Kerrigan leaps out and arrests Summers. For what is not explained, unless suspicion is proof. But, for this story, it is essential that Summers be arrested. And so he is arrested and loaded down with chains.

But as he is led off, Summers whispers to Molly that the blond was the new wife of Molly's brother, who really robbed the bank, but he, Summers, is ready to take the rap for the lad because he wished "to see the young folks happy."

This high tone of ethical merit among the lawless now gives way to a story of violence and adventure. "The Hand of Destiny," by Harold Ward, opens at a ruined house in the woods.

It is night. Icy rain pours down. Inside the house lies a crook, stabbed twelve times. Someone bad has also cut off his hand.

Enter the brave Secret Service men, tracking a gold ship. In the dark, they grapple with the killer, who escapes, leaving behind the severed hand.

In that hand is clutched a cypher!

At their hotel, the Secret Service men work on the cypher, undaunted by the jeers of a seedy private detective. Just as the solution is found, telling the location of the stolen gold, a hand slicks through the window and snatches away the deciphered message.

But the Secret Service sets a clever trap and, in an exciting climax, the gold is recovered, and the sneering masked fiend is trapped.

The next story is titled "The Man Who Died Twice"—which is possibly the favorite title in all pulp literature. This one is by J. Frederic Thorne. It is not really a story but one of those monologues that were so popular in 1920's amateur theatricals. This monologue is delivered by a lawyer to the jury. Seems that his client is innocent, although accused of murdering his partner in Seattle, although the partner really seems to have died by accident in Hong-Kong.

Dorothy Parker shaped the short story monologue into an art form. J. Frederic Thorne does not.

"The Silver Lining," by John Baer, is all decked out in synthetic *Smart Set* style:

> Most stories start in one of two ways. The hero is either in love or in debt. Often he is both. So is our hero, and in this respect he is therefore not in the least original.
>
> Meet him. At this particular moment he is in his bedroom, and in no mood to be introduced to strangers. Take a look, anyway.
>
> He is standing before his dressing-mirror, fitting on a mask. The mask is black and covers his entire face; there is a slit only for the eyes. On the dresser is a revolver. Oh, yes; it is loaded.
>
> Now, putting two and two together, as the saying goes, we arrive at the total four. The young man anticipates a lively evening. He needs money and he's going to get it. . . .

Enough of this self-conscious simpering. In brief, the young man attempts to rob the heavy winner at a gambling joint. In the scuffle, he is injured, flees, finds that he has exchanged hats with the victim. Since the lost hat bears his initials, he must re-rob the victim and exchange hats. So he does—only later learning that the winnings were concealed in the lining of the returned hat.

It is sorry work to plod among these pages. Over the stories hangs the gray taint of inability. Not only are the authors pretty condescending about mystery fiction, but they are unaware that they do not know how to write the stuff. Outside, in the big world, tower early giants of detective and mystery fiction, from Sherlock Holmes to Madame Storey. But *Black Mask*, insulated from mainstream, lolls in solitary appreciation of its own cleverness.

In the next story, the title tips off the device. "The Whip of Death," by Ward Sterling, presents a murdered man sprawled out there in the swamp. Only his footprints cross the mud, yet the knife has been plucked from the wound. Puzzling.

"The Bamboozler," by J. R. Ward, begins by torturing the English language to death:

> Out of the underworld, like a groundhog fearing his shadow, came, on a night when the moon was hidden by heavy clouds, Sleepy Norton, bad man.

This sort of play, a hesitation waltz in prose, is entertaining when you're funning around; the balance of the story, however, suggests that Mr. Ward thought he was being eloquent. It tells how a crooked lawyer is caught in his own web. The story has a serious structural problem caused by split point-of-view.

Both "The Sheriff Takes The Stand" (H. W. Starr) and "When Two Plus Two Equals Five" (Grover Fayerweather) are framed stories. That is, they are told by the principal character to an audience within the story. The technique had been popular in English fiction at the turn of the century but had become obsolete, died and went to Heaven. Its resurrection is unfortunate. So is the name, Fayerweather.

"The Death Warrant" is the last of a two-part serial by J. Frederic Thorne, fresh from his triumph with "The Man Who Died Twice." After a 300-word synopsis in wee tiny type, Part II opens with a chapter consisting entirely of questions about Part I. Seems that intolerable complexities abound. The Admiral (you see) was murdered as described in a mystery novel. But the slick killer is caught anyhow.

"The Emperor of Blunderland" is a second story by J. R. Ward. It describes how a Keystone cop deduces that the jewels were stolen by an infant in arms. And, in the final story, "The Talking Wall," by Walter Deffenbaugh, a Secret Service ace uses an unconventionally hooked-up Dictaphone to snare a bad apple.

These stories are followed by the only department in the magazine—"The New Mystery Books" by Captain Frank Cunningham. He reviews seven new books, among them the new Lone Wolf novel, *Red Masquerade*; H. Rider Haggard's *She and Allan*; a Hopalong Cassidy adventure, *The Bar-20 Three*; and Arthur Somers Rouche's *Find the Woman*.

Captain Cunningham despises all these and savages them good in about 100 words each. He does like a couple of books which have vanished forever. But then criticism is a slippery art.

This, then, is *Black Mask* before Race Williams, or the Continental Op, or Joseph Shaw. The magazine became great by a series of improbable coincidences and accidents. Its early form was sterile. It existed without conviction, without direction, without self-respect.

Others have commented on the English detective story influence in these early issues. It appears, however, that this influence was very small. The English tradition was that of the problem story, a formal narrative, disciplined and tightly structured. These characteristics are obviously lacking in early *Black Mask* fiction. Rather, the stories are feeble imitations of the crook and police detective stories appearing in *Detective Story Magazine*.

What ailed *Black Mask* was the baleful influence of *The Smart Set*. The lesser magazine still aped the attitudes of the greater—and so, *The Black Mask* distained its own fiction, smirked at reader tastes, and remained haughtily aloof from the field in which, ten years later and with a fresh point of view, it would stand pre-eminent.

4—*Crime Busters*, November 1937, Vol. 1, No. 1, published monthly
by Street & Smith, 10¢, 128 pages

The charm of *Crime Busters* glows undiminished, even after fifty years. It had presence. It had style. It radiated a glorious nuttiness. *Crime Busters* was always a little giddy in the head, and the pages glitter with delicate self-parody, as if the whole cult of magazine heroes, in all their excellence, is being kidded by friends.

The editorial idea was simple—a monthly short story magazine featuring popular Street & Smith writers—usually—and illustrators, presenting bright new series characters in bright new adventures. The whole was garnished by a photographic cover showing some girl in a suspenseful predicament.

The photographic cover vanished rather swiftly. Just as well. The girls looked stuffed, rather than fearful. You were less interested in their plight than in their rolled stockings and modestly hiked-up skirts.

Strictly speaking, *Crime Busters* was not planned as a new magazine, but as a continuation of that venerable title, *Best Detective Magazine*. In the final issue of that publication, dated September 1937, appears an announcement of its replacement. *Best Detective* had begun, November 1929, as a reprint vehicle of fiction originally published in *Street & Smith's Detective Story Magazine*. But fresh winds blew. In the September 1937 issue appeared extracts from original stories by Lester Dent ("Talking Toad") and Theodore Tinsley ("White Elephant"), which would be presented in full in the initial issue, November 1937, of *Crime Busters*. It was first intended that the *Best Detective* volume numbering be continued for the new magazine, so that the first issue of *Crime Busters* would have been Volume 16, Number 6. But at the last second, it was decided to make a clean new start—Volume 1, Number 1.

Readers picking up *Crime Busters* learned that the magazine was their toy:

You have a chance to edit your own magazine.

Meaning that you could vote for stories you liked and against stories you hated. If you did so, you received a free copy of either *The Whisperer, The Skipper*, or *The Feds*, three titles whose sales must have been very sick.

Just why *Crime Busters* leaves such a good impression is a circumstance the angels will have to explain. It is hardly an angel's dish. From front cover to back, it is marinated in the sort of violence they yank off television these days. Gun-wielding hordes blaze and shout. Battered corpses litter the landscape. The pages resound with the smack of fist on chin, gun butt on skull, the shriek of women in mortal danger.

Story probability is traded for extreme action. Struggle is incessant, murder continuous. You can forget realistic stories or social messages or even the laws of physics. It's action only—and a crisis every two pages.

Yet how nicely it works. Lean back, brush the real world from your mind, and enjoy yourself.

The Table of Contents glitters with familiar names. (If you like their novels, you'll love their short stories.)

White Elephant by Theodore Tinsley (Illustrator: Earl Mayan)

Talking Toad by Lester Dent (Illustrator: Albert Migale)
Death's Ruby by Norvell W. Page (Illustrator: Edd Cartier)
Mail-Order Busters by Clifford Goodrich (Illustrator: ?)
Norgil by Maxwell Grant (Illustrator: R. Doremus)
Odds On Murder by Steve Fisher (Illustrator: Edd Cartier)
Boxcar Wrecks 'Em by Laurence Donovan (Illustrator: L. Bjorklund)
One For The Book by James Perley Hughes (Illustrator: Earl Mayan)

Each story is introduced by a single, double-page line drawing, three-quarters of a page deep. For reasons that puzzle the heart, the stories are divided into three to five chapters.

The first story instantly establishes the tone of the magazine. "White Elephant," by Theodore Tinsley, is packed with cheerfully lunatic goings-on. Because it is the first story, we will linger over a few details. They are arresting.

"White Elephant" introduces Carrie Cashin, the glamorous detective, a slender little brown-eyed stainless-steel sweetie. She wears a small automatic strapped to her left thigh and carries a brown leather handbag with a secret compartment. Formerly a department store detective, she has opened the CASH AND CARRY DETECTIVE AGENCY, run on the sound American principle of pay in advance: "You Pay, We Deliver."

Since clients are ignorantly biased against girl detectives, Carrie has hired "Handsome Aleck" Burton to be her front man. He is a big blond good-looker with a competent smile, although he "doesn't know a clue when he sees one."

Carrie, herself, spends a whole lot of time disguised as Daisy Snaggers, the office girl. As Daisy, her complexion is pallid; she has freckles, hair in a bun, glasses, a cud of chewing gum, and a black dress from Schottenstein's.

When not filing, Carrie occupies the back office. This is separated from Aleck's desk by a sheet of Argus glass, likely supplied by the Moon-Man Helmet Company. Thus she can observe clients and direct Aleck. This is done by typing instructions on a device that projects words across a concealed panel set into his desk.

The Agency is on the 10th floor. Immediately below it, one floor down, is a bare room containing two locked closets. One of these is a miniature dressing room and shower where the Carrie/Daisy identities are exchanged. The other room contains a secret elevator to Carrie's 10th floor office. There is likely some good reason for all this play-toying around.

So to the story. We join Carrie on the ledge outside the 15th floor hotel room of Bert Hanley, jewel thief. She has been retained by Professor Drebber to recover a stolen prehistoric Aztec elephant amulet. Stealing the amulet back, she returns to her room, next window down, to discover the Professor dead, stuck with her nail file. Outside, the hotel detective pounds on her door.

Thru the window. Up and over the roof, followed by Hanley and gun. To evade him, she plunges into the subway and across the tracks, having a marvelous adventure with a train, and flees triumphant to her office.

As Daisy, she enters the office to discover Professor Drebber, somehow alive, interviewing Aleck. Suddenly suspicious, she checks the elephant, finds it conceals a huge diamond.

Now enters Hanley, with pistol waving. Easily overpowering him, she instructs Aleck—via his desk communications system—to handcuff the Professor, who is really the hotel dick in disguise. Hanley turns out to be an insurance investigator.

So it all ends with smiles. Aleck gets the credit. Carrie keeps her identity secret and gets the cash.

How do you like the magazine so far?

"Talking Toad," the second story, is by Lester Dent and is another gloriously peculiar adventure. It starts that wonderful series about Clickell Rush, the Gadget Man, who has invented 1000 gadgets to help police catch crooks—only the police think his inventions ridiculous.

At the opening of the story, he has about $3 cash, a rented office packed with gadgets, and a dead man on the floor. Rush has never seen him—nor has he seen the statue of a huge toad that is now sitting on half a $10,000 bill and some instructions. For the toad is a radio transceiver. At the other end is a mysterious who calls himself "...Bufa. I feed on snails, slugs, *et. cetra*—of the human variety."

Bufa offers Rush the other half of the $10,000 bill if he will investigate some stolen frogs. Rush strongly objects. Tough. Bufa has already involved him in the action. Which begins instantly.

And consists of a beautiful Irish girl with no toes, one thousand stainless-steel frogs, and a hi-jacked gold cache. The action is breathlessly violent. To stay alive, Rush uses innumerable tear-gas cigarettes, exploding matches, hypodermic needles strapped to his arm, and both fists.

The first story sets the format for the series: Bufa will drag the protesting Rush into a long series of unholy murderous messes, with gadgets spilling marvelously through the pages. The stories are gloriously goofy, full of comic touches. Our civilization will not reach its Golden Age until all eighteen Gadget Man stories are reprinted.

"Death's Ruby," by Norvell Page, features Dick Barrett, a former cop so efficient that five insurance companies have set him up in the stolen-jewel recovery business. Barrett is a Richard Wentworth type, blasting crooks through the skull with his .45's, and getting himself hammered on so badly that he can barely stagger.

He is assisted by Miss Fay, an old-maid sort, who owns an enormous collection of detective stories and affects a Bowery accent in moments of high emotion. This pair attempt to recover a stolen ruby from a treacherous woman, assorted gunmen, a guy with turban and knife. There follows gun fights, car wrecks, daring leaps, sluggings, kidnappings, and a cobra death trap—all in the pulsating Spider tradition.

"Mail-Order Busters," by Clifford Goodrich (in this case Laurence Donovan), is a vicious brainless business. It features two postal inspectors: Howdy Hawks, tall, emaciated, clever; and Bimbo Bimbozo, short, fat, dull, immensely strong, and with an Italian accent lifted from Joe Miller's Joke Book. They are battling a gang that has robbed the mails of $100,000. At the end, Bimbo kills nine crooks in less than a minute, smashing them with a tree limb, a stove, and other devil's tools.

"Norgil-Magician" is"...suave to the tips of the pointed mustache that adorned his sophisticated, oval-chinned face." So the bugles blow and Mr. Gibson is off on another tear. Norgil is a professional magician traveling with his own show and stopping crime wherever it rears its head. In this story, he takes on a theatre extortion racket, slickly out-maneuvers the murderous minions, and reveals the identity of the Big Shot as the climax of his evening's performance. Norgil is forethoughted as The Shadow and tricky as original sin.

In "Odds on Murder," by Steve Fisher, a poor fellow accidentally photographs a murder and ends up slaughtered. Plain clothesman Arlen Canfield, "The Spinner," investigates with the subtlety of a berserk sledge-hammer. Canfield's a college-looking dude, a "superior wrestler" who gives killers a throwing twist that whirls them spinning slam into the wall. Thus his nickname. "The Spinner" doesn't use a gun. Odds mean nothing. He gets wounded in the hip and side during this adventure, but cleans up three separate packs of crooks in four chapters.

"Boxcar Wrecks 'Em," by Laurence Donovan, features still another fighting pair—this time, railroad men. So it says. Red-headed Conductor "Boxcar" Reilly and brakeman "Hoppy" Sims (who looks like a limping corpse) battle crooks to recover boxes of antimony stolen from a locked, guarded shed. Before the action subsides, Boxcar and Hoppy have spent the night charging about in a coupe with a dead man riding in the rumble seat and have been shot at, hit on the head, kidnapped, and suspended from duty. Eventually, the master plotter is revealed. Boxcar is promoted to the police division of the railroad, with the clear understanding that he must have numerous adventures.

"One for the Book." by James Perley Hughes, features one Charles Q. Logan (formerly of *Detective Fiction Weekly*). Logan is a trouble-shooter for the motion picture industry. They need him badly. Consider the problem. The crew is out on the slopes of a volcano shooting a movie. Suddenly this huge bear appears. Before they realize what's happened, the bear has kidnapped a fellow and left a $50,000 ransom note. Soon after, the bear returns to kill the director.

All is consternation. The story is told first-person in hyped-up press agent jargon, so that the proceedings sound even screwier than they are. If possible. It's an admirable piece.

So much for the first eight stories in *Crime Busters*. For the maiden issue, it's astonishingly good, and the magazine managed to retain that high standard almost to the end, even after it had been retitled *Mystery*.

In 1937, the hero-oriented formula was still far from exhausted. But it had been used hard and the well was low. From 1931 to about 1937, the hero action story, featuring avengers and adventurers who were larger than life, swarmed over the news stand. In a few years, a combination of war events, an increasingly realistic trend in fiction, and readers' saturation with the omnipotent hero image, would cause pulp fiction to alter beyond recall.

Crime Busters is one of the key transitional publications of the time—a remark which would probably surprise its editor. Nonetheless, it mixes elements of the older single-character tradition with foreshadowing of the stories ten years off. Its warmly lunatic heroes race from death to death through a world almost—not quite—in focus.

The faults of *Crime Busters* are the faults of the time and, at the time, were not considered faults at all—conventions of the period, merely. Reading the stories with that reservation, they spring to life, exuberant, glittering, breathless, entirely satisfying in their own giddy-headed way.

5—*Scientific Detective Monthly*, January 1930,
Vol. 1, No. 1, published monthly by
Techni-Craft Publishing Co., 25¢, 96 pages.

In the firm belief that science in its various application will become one of the greatest deterrents to crime, the SCIENTIFIC DETECTIVE MONTHLY will be launched.

So Mr. Hugo Gernsback, Editorial Chief, in the editorial that announced his new magazine.

The time is about ten months after Gernsback's bankruptcy with *Amazing Stories*, and not quite two months after the stock market crash. Optimism is needed. And the *Scientific Detective Monthly* is one bright shout of optimism: Science is magnificent. Science will soon eliminate crime. Science will soon re-educate criminals. Beware of criminals using science for crime. Through science, and the *Scientific Detective Monthly*, police will be helped, readers enlightened, and a new creative force turned loose.

The editorial is surrounded by an ornate printed design topped by an eagle, hunched over fiercely.

"SCIENTIFIC DETECTIVE MONTHLY will publish no stories," promises Mr. Gernsback, "unless science in some way enters their make-up."

Seems only proper.

The magazine is in usual Gernsback format—a large, thick publication on soft pulp paper. The cover is brightly colored, much red and yellow, and decorated with exuberant type. Inside you find five short stories, a serial part, two articles said to be non-fiction, and six short departments. The stories are each illustrated by a single line drawing, with results ranging from good to dreadful.

The title page is bordered by a frieze of tiny significant drawings. To the left, a skeleton key, bomb, poison, and such other devices as are used by crooks and fiends. To the right, the implements of society's saviors: a microscope, test tube, magnifying glass, and wire tap.

At top center, lending a quasi-official status, appears a large police badge. Down either side of the badge roars an avalanche of consultants:

Arthur B. Reeve, Editorial Commissioner

Edwin J. Cooley, Assistant Editorial Deputy (Professor of Criminology, Fordham University)

Henry A. Higgins, Assistant Editorial Deputy (Department of Criminology, Massachusetts Prison Association)

These dignitaries are aided by editorial associates, whose duties peek, with sly eyes, through the gaudy splendor of their titles:

Hector G. Grey, Editorial Deputy

A. L. Fierst, Editorial Inspector

C. P. Mason, Scientific Criminologist

Captain Lucien Fournier, Continental Deputy Inspector (Paris)

Dr. Alfred Gradenwitz, PhD (Correspondent-Inspector Detective, (Berlin)

N. J. Stone, Mechanical Deputy

Forego those cynical smiles. The profundities of the title page clearly reveal Gernsback's intent. The *Scientific Detective Monthly* will be a powerful tool to strengthen right. These Commissioners and Deputies have pledged their trust to crush the worm of crime, to stand for good, to refresh and invigorate the national spirit, to reaffirm still once again those principles of justice and order, sacrifice and social zeal, a dedication at once comprehensive and exultant.

The magazine spine is yellow with white ends.

Flashlight beams illuminate the red letters of the title. At spine top and bottom, green type on white specifies volume number and date.

Inside, following Gernsback's editorial, appears an article by Arthur B. Reeve, once known as "The American Conan Doyle." His reputation later slipped. Back there, from 1910 on, he boiled forth smothering quantities of scientific detective stories and became permanently identified with the school, its acknowledged leader.

Reeve's article, "What Are the Great Detective Stories and Why," does not tell why. Nor does it have much to do with scientific detection. It is an intensely condensed discussion of early detective fiction greats, beginning with the Bible and striding forward, a la the Dorothy Sayers introduction to her 1929 *Omnibus of Crime*. Up to about 1922, Reeve is reasonably sound. After that, he begins missing such major figures as Sayers and Christie, and you gather that he never heard of the *Street & Smith Detective Story Magazine* or *Black Mask*.

Aside from this, the article is written in a prose gone scarily wrong. The sentences grate together. The paragraphs slew this way and that. You get the impression that Reeve dictated the piece while fleeing down twisting corridors.

Following Mr. Reeve's article is a story by Arthur B. Reeve, (Editorial Commissioner). The story features Craig Kennedy ("The American Sherlock Holmes") and is titled "The Mystery of the Bulawayo Diamond."

Kennedy, a Professor of Criminology at Columbia University, and his friend, Walter Jameson, a dim-witted newspaper man, investigate the theft of a large diamond. This vanishes during a party at a Long Island mansion—or, correctly, an "Automatic House," meaning that it was heated by a thermostatically-controlled stoker and had indoor plumbing.

The action is mainly conversation. After talking in short, significant sentences for many pages, Kennedy learns all. Not that he tells Walter. Instead, he unveils the obligatory scientific device, in this case, a bolometer. That seems to be a form of thermocouple. It measures imperceptible changes in heat, even to the blush on the maid's dark cheek.

In a way not intelligible to this reader, measurement of her blush proves that she swiped the diamond, hid it in the furnace ashes, sent it outside to her husband, who sewed it into his vest. If he had dug a hole and buried it, the case would still be open. But there it is, in his vest, and Kennedy's science triumphs.

If this seems feeble fare for a magazine devoted to scientific detection, have patience.

The next story, "The Campus Murder Mystery," by Ralph W. Wilkins, introduces Professor Armand Macklin. He is Professor of Police Practices and Crime Investigation at Roger Williams College and will appear in two subsequent issues of the magazine.

A tremendous explosion at the center of campus. Crowds rush in to find pieces of a Professor Kapek littered amid stacks of glass fragments. Also at the scene, a peculiar dampness that weirdly vanishes, and a cat, stark and cold, that suddenly returns to life.

Following these clues, Professor Macklin deduces that Professor Kapek has been slipped into a bottle of liquid air, transported by balloon to campus center, and dropped. With police in tow, he confronts the jeering fiend responsible. Since no hard evidence is presented, the fiend takes mercy on the author and commits suicide:

I have already squeezed a little needle into one of my veins, that releases me from any terrors your clumsy law might have for me.

Patience, please, patience.

True science appears in the next story by Edwin Bulmer and William Macharg. Titled "The Fast Watch," this is the only scientific detective story in the magazine, assuming that a scientific detective must detect using real science and real scientific equipment.

The story features Luther Trant, the first American scientific detective, who appeared in *Hampton's Magazine* during 1909-1910. This story, the second of the series, appeared in the June 1909 issue.

Trant's problem is to identify the murderer from among sixteen suspects. Hard for you and me. But Trant is a trained psychologist from a Chicago University and applies the equipment and testing techniques of the psychological laboratory to criminal cases. The equipment is real. The testing methods are real, although the testing situation is less than controlled. In this case, the murderer is identified by his reactions while attached to a galvanometer—hold an electrode and, providing that you sweat in fear at a significant word or smell, your response registers on a dial.

The murderer's palm does sweat, and his alibi, built about an altered watch setting, falls apart.

After Trant, authentic science in the *Scientific Detective Monthly* sort of melts away. The next story, "The Perfect Counterfeit," by Captain S. P. Meek, USA, features Dr. Bird, who detects a matter duplicator being used to create $20 bills. Dr. Bird also appears in the June 1930 issue, and he would show up in issues of *Astounding Stories*.

Unabashed science fiction immediately discredits the magazine's elaborately developed verisimilitude. This didn't seem to bother Gernsback or Reeve. It certainly didn't bother the readers. Nothing seemed to bother the readers.

"The Eye of Pometheus," by R. F. Starzl, contains a faint element of science. The principle involved is that a thin platinum wire glows hotly when exposed to alcohol fumes and oxygen. Seems that this rich fellow goes down into his wine cellar and is instantly engulfed in flame. Investigating are Chief of Detectives Klise (middle-aged, small, unimpressive, effective) and a newspaper friend, Heinie Lanther. The author neatly plants the murder device in the first two pages and writes a straightforward story. The death trap seems improbable, but you can't expect perfection in every single detail.

"A Message From the Ultra-Violet" purports to be a true crime, written up by H. Aston-Wolfe of the French Surete, formerly an assistant of the great Bertillon. The story, told in good round American dialogue, is salted by the more assessable French expressions, *n'est ce pas? Oui? Bien!*

The case involves an evil scientist who marries a rich but innocent girl, then murders her with his sinister ultra-violet machine:

Long spiral tubes glowed and flashed fantastically, and a huge lamp of complicated shape rotated slowly, sending out whirling beams of green light which produced a numbing thrill when they touched the skin.

To demonstrate how closely life imitates art, two separate elements of this article appeared in former Craig Kennedy stories: murdering your wife by artificially-induced cancer was the theme of "The Deadly Tube" (March 1911), and blinding by gross exposure to ultra-violet light may be found in "The Invisible Ray" (October 1912)—*Cosmopolitan* in both instances.

To conclude his fiction, Gernsback offers the first of three installments of "The Bishop Murder Case," published in book form the previous year. In this story, The Bishop, a highly effective madman, slaughters almost all the characters; only when he has killed everyone in sight is Philo Vance able to expose him. Vance uses no visible science. According to Gernsback however, S. S. Van Dine's "observations on the higher sciences are tremendous in breadth and clear thinking."

The magazine departments are numerous and odd. "How Good of a Detective Are You?" tests your powers of observation. First, examine an illustrated crime scene; then turn to page 86 and answer questions about it. On that page you also find "The Readers' Verdict"—12 letters from readers and Gernsback's replies.

Following that are reviews of two detective plays—both very good, both utterly forgotten. Then half a column titled "Science-Crime Notes," describing how a motion picture camera recorded a murderer confessing. Finally, five book reviews.

If nothing else fascinates, the back cover tells about INKOGRAPH, The Perfect Writing Instrument. You can also learn how your Grasshopper Mind may be cured, or apply to become a Real Estate Specialist, learning at home in your spare time. The Rasco Radio Parts Company offers a free catalog. You may join the Literary Guild or learn to play the tenor banjo or get the facts on Modern Eugenics, including a Chapter on How To Be A Vamp, only $2.98, sealed in a plain wrapper.

The gentle innocence of the *Scientific Detective Monthly* is touching. It is a charming magazine. It strives so sincerely. Its goals are so magnificent. Its dedication is so complete. Over the pages hovers that wonderful Gernsback mist, the same pale, transparent blue that Autumn pours into distant valleys, and which, in magazines equates with an enthusiastic amateurishness—the dimness of policies not quite formulated, intentions not fully thought out; the haze of a guiding mind too filled by vague competing enthusiasms to bother tracing out the consequences of its whims.

The magazine remained the *Scientific Detective Monthly* until the June issue, when it was suddenly retitled *Amazing Detective Tales*. Under this title, it continued through October 1930.

Whatever the title, it stayed the same magazine to the ultimate page. It ended as it began—an awkward, striving, young wonder mumbling eagerly over Fourier transform functions, while fixing a broken cup with adhesive tape.

6—*Weird Tales*, The Unique Magazine, September 1931, Vol. XVIII, No. 2, published monthly by Popular Fiction Publishing Co., 25¢, 154 pages.

Weird Tales, The Unique Magazine, died four times and was revived each time, rising from the grave rather like one of its own vampires. It began with the March 1923 issue, a large, flat, badly illustrated pulp. For thirty-one years it continued, finally terminating as a digest-sized magazine dated September 1954, issue number 279.

Thereafter it was revived once in the 1970s and three times in the 1980s, as magazine and paperback. In 1988 it was an extraordinary revenant from the past, the last living example of those fine old pulp titles. No longer on pulp paper, polished to a dazzling shine and filled with polished contemporary fantasy fiction, it resembled the rough old *Weird Tales* of yesterday as a newly painted and refurbished Victorian house suggests its former self.

Throughout the first phase of its career, 1923-1954, the magazine customarily tettered along the edge of oblivion. Strong commercial success eluded it. While *Weird Tales* developed a following that was devoted and articulate, it was a following only large enough to sustain life.

Although chronically malnourished by meager funds and audience, *Weird Tales* left deep, and possible permanent marks, on American fantasy fiction. It was the first magazine devoted exclusively to the genre. It introduced readers to a wide variety of traditional and not-so-traditional fantasy forms, emphasizing pseudo science and horror-tinged adventures in far places. It emphasized physical conflict, intense narrative movement, and free use of monstrous life forms. And it nurtured a long succession of writers whose subject matter, themes, and techniques became touchstones—models to be imitated and followed.

No matter how admirable, touchstones limit. While the stories of H. P. Lovecraft, Clark Ashton Smith, and Robert E. Howard (among the many) satisfy on their own terms, other terms are possible. Eventually such other magazines as *Unknown, Fantasy & Science Fiction*, and *Beyond* would react against the *Weird Tales* models and explore alternate approaches to fantasy.

Whatever complexities of influence and reaction that were to come, the September 1931 *Weird Tales* is an interesting example of a magazine in full stride, still youthful, still crackling with brash energy and enthusiasm, testing its own limits.

For this issue, Editor Farnsworth Wright selected five short stories, two short short stories, a novelette, and two serials. Also included were a short poem and a department, The Eyrie, which announced the next issue's wonders and printed letters from ecstatic readers:

Having traveled extensively and seen many odd, weird and unbelievable things, I find your magazine extremely interesting....Your authors are experts in producing stories that are the quintessence of all that is outré, macabre and soul-chilling.

The cover of this issue was outre, macabre, and soul-chilling enough. Painted by C. C. Senf, it illustrated a moment of high excitement from the lead serial, "Tam, Son of the Tiger." From his seat on an enormous beast, resembling a tapir, a leering four-armed giant thrusts a trident toward Tam, a slender, half naked youth. Tam clutches a sword and looks ineffectual. One of the giant's arms grips a girl in form-fitting golden armor. Her left arm seeks to restrain the trident, a pitiful gesture. Your heart goes out to her.

Inside, the magazine begins with a full page ad for the Johnson & Smith novelty company. That is page 145, since page 1 was used only for the start of each new volume.

The first story, by Robert E. Howard, is "The Footfalls Within," one of the Solomon Kane series. Kane is described as "a dour Puritan" and strides across the world having savage adventures. For a Puritan he is uncommonly prone to violence. He customarily carries a sword and a pair of horse pistols, minimum equipment against the ghouls, monsters, and unnatural terribles that snarl from the pages.

In this story, Kane has wandered into Africa and got himself captured by an evil, leering Sheik. As the Sheik's party trudges toward the slave market, where Kane is to be sold, they come across a ruined mausoleum brooding in the jungle. Scenting treasure, the Sheik orders it opened. He ignores its stench, ignores the whisper of footsteps from inside, ignores the obvious fact that in *Weird Tales*, you do not rip open mausoleums with impunity.

He does and he does not. Out rages a gigantic slobbering red Thing without shape. Promptly it shreds the Sheik. As it turns on Kane, he stabs it to death with a long staff. This seems to have belonged to Solomon the Wise, who sealed away the demon in the jungle some eons back. So the abnatural horror is destroyed by physical means, which happens a lot in *Weird Tales*. The story is effective, if not coldly realistic; but who expects realism in a Robert Howard adventure?

Paul Ernst's "The Golden Elixir" tells of an anti-social chemist who blends this fluid in his laboratory. When drunk, it separates the body and the soul. In this way, the chemist's body can attend all those annoying social functions, while his intelligent essence remains at home, reading good books. Or so he tells the narrator of the story, a weak sister who would be improved by kicking.

Shortly, disaster. While the intelligence is explaining all this to that boob narrator, the body is out at a party proposing to a pretty girl. And is accepted. Since a gentleman honors his commitments, the chemist marries her, making both miserable. It ends in divorce, after the new wife destroys the elixir formula, on advice of the narrator.

"The Message" by Clinton Dangerfield tells of singular events in the death cell. The young man has been framed to die. The pardon is on the way but may not arrive. From the cell radio comes the voice of the prisoner's beloved. She speaks to him in the Glowing and Elevated Language of Mystical Profundity. The pardon doesn't arrive in time, and the young man goes to his death, joyous. And what's this about? The final line reveals that the girl has just been killed in a railroad wreck. That is supposed to be a surprise, but isn't, since the story makes no sense unless she's already dead. You'd have to be dead to blather on as she did.

"Satan's Stepson" is another of Seabury Quinn's stories about Jules de Grandin, who battled the supernatural through *Weird Tales* for years. Most de Grandin stories are suspenseful adventures, violent and amusing. This one seems overlong and involves combat with an unkillable Russian demon. As usual, the girl ends stripped absolutely bare, about to be devoured by the forces of evil. However, de Grandin finds a way to slay the demon and cover the girl's luscious bareness and it all ends merrily.

Everil Worrell's "Deadlock" features an inventive explorer, his inadvertently bigamous wife, his wife's current husband, a cowardly sneak, and his wife's manipulative and murderous mother. This dismaying group end all together in an airplane flying across the Solar System at the speed of light to meet their destiny. The situation is huffing melodrama, the characters names on the page, and the science invented for the occasion—although there is mention of using planetary gravitational fields to modify a trajectory.

"The Immeasurable Horror" is another of Clark Ashton Smith's excursions into adventure horror. In the steaming swamps of Venus, the expedition discovers blobs of protoplasm the size of small towns, and investigate, at terrible cost. Smith's stories are curiously cold and hard, as if meticulously carved from a glacier. Curiosity or the love of power energizes his characters. Unprotected by kind fate, they blunder into the presence of forces too vast for man to deal with, and routinely they are destroyed or maimed. It is as impersonal and implacable as mathematics. Often, as in this story, Smith expresses these indifferent forces as monsters, and so they are. They lurk in dark caverns or creep across mountains, but they are not malevolent. They are simply dreadful dangerous, as lightning or earthquake are dangerous. You simply dare not get too close to raw force of this magnitude. His characters do, and their mortality rate is extremely high.

With "Tam, Son of the Tiger" (Part 3 of 6), you come to the main serial. This, by Otis Adelbert Kline, borrows brazenly from the works of Edgar Rice Burroughs, mixing Tarzan, John Carter, Pellucidar, and that favorite Burroughs' situation of a lost world in which two opposing city states hack at each other. The whole is salted by liberal doses of Hindu gods.

Seems that a white tiger has carried off two-year old Tam Evans and reared him in an abandoned pagoda at the heart of the Burmese jungle. Naturally the boy grows up acting like a tiger and making friends with the jungle animals.

He is discovered by a friendly lama, who educates the boy and teaches him the use of weapons. When he is twenty, Tam goes wandering in the jungle, meets Nina, a beautiful girl in golden armor from the subterranean world of Iramatri. She has come to warn the outer world of a planned invasion by evil forces.

Immediately they are attacked by four-armed white giants serving Siva. The girl is snatched away and Tam must trail the abductors back to the concealed world, filled with prehistoric carnivores and such.

From that point on, it is capture, battle, and escape. Each chapter ends on a cliff-hanger, switching back and forth among the characters as they bash and whack through Iramatri, facing white four-armed giants and blue four-armed giants and stalk-eyed terrors, and coiling monsters, and lumbering monsters. It is intense, active narrative, shallow and mindless, just the thing to read while you're waiting for a bus.

In the final paragraphs of this serial part, a tree cat pounces on Tam, who is balanced on a branch, one hundred feet above the ground.

> Thrown off his balance by the impact of the heavy body, he toppled and fell headlong.

You surmise that nothing permanent happened to him, since there are three more serial parts, and, after that, later adventures.

After all that raw excitement it is soothing to turn to the musical strains of "Moors of Wrann," a poem by A. Lloyd Bayne. Among other valuable observations, Mr. Bayne notes that:

Terror shall strike while the night is young
And the souls of the lost that in space are hung
Tonight toward Earth will be awfully flung
    And the shrieks of the Damned will quiver.

Makes you come funny all over.

Two short-short stories follow. The first, by August W. Derleth, "The Bridge of Sighs," is about a plot to assassinate the Doge of Venice. To make absolutely sure, the conspirators enlist the aid of a magician. Their mistake. "His Brother's Keeper" by George Fielding Eliot, tells how one brother does in another, plus a faithless woman, using an iron maiden.

And finally we come to the "Weird Story Reprint," a usually interesting feature of the magazine, which reaches into the past for lost masterpieces. In this case, the masterpiece is an eight-part serial by Alexander Dumas, "The Wolf Leader" (Part 2). In this segment, a poor shoemaker strikes a deal with a huge black wolf, walking on two legs, to have certain wishes come true. The fee is a single hair for the first wish, two for the second, four for the third, and so to baldness. Only the hairs don't vanish: they turn bright red and are indestructible. And the wishes have all manner of painful consequences unforeseen. It is interesting but slow.

And this, you cry incredulously, this is the famous *Weird Tales*, the Unique Magazine, whose value is expressed in gold bars, the magazine loved and revered and revived, which generated swarms of influential writers and stands, like a volcano, glaring across American fantastic writing?

Well, yes.

But this is drivel, you cry. Most of these stories are inept, obvious, muddled, derivative, written so incompetently that they suffer even when compared to Congressional speeches or television comedy series. How can anyone take seriously this tedious drizzle of monsters and menaces; this parade of cliches and stereotypes masquerading as characters; these blatantly incredible situations where atmosphere is created by ponderous purple successions of adjectives and tricks of narrative suspense that were ancient when silent movies were young? More than half the prose is as dead as salt ham. The rest sweats like a laborer in the sun to jazz up excitement.

Well, yes. Much of what you say is true. Time has got at many of these stories and pitilessly exposed their hollowness. But don't be so eager to consign them to the boneyard. They may be minor commercial fictions, now horridly obsolete, but there's a reason why they're like that. There's always a reason for things being the way they are.

Much of *Weird Tale*'s fiction shares a close family resemblance to that published by such related magazines as *Amazing Stories, Astounding Stories,* and *Wonder Stories*. In all these magazines, we find the identical bent toward simplistic characters, strong action, and a studied indifference to scientific rigor. The stories are wildly speculative. They favor the extraordinary, the unusual, the novel. They revel in other dimensions, malicious aliens, cities at the far edge of space and time, weird consequences of excursions into regions strange and fantastic. They frisk among novelties beyond all human experience.

In brief, these magazines offer non-realistic fiction that emphasize wonder. They make no attempt to reflect reality. What is important is the portrayal of the marvelous.

On their own terms, these stories were not failures but highly specialized, if highly limited, literary forms. Today that form is obsolete, and the stories appear strange and inept. But no wonder. Tastes change and fictional styles change with them. Presently, we require fiction to speak to us from realistic settings, and demand that characters display some of the psychological ambiguities we find within ourselves. That is our present convention. It is no more and no less valid than that *Weird Tales* fiction which neatly satisfied the rather different conventions of its time.

It neatly satisfied the readers of the time, too. But those readers, it's sad to report, are long gone; they are watchers, now, sitting transfixed before the television's glow and absorbing a gussied up version of pulp fiction that has all the defects of a *Weird Tales'* story and few of its virtues.

Photos

Fantastic Adventures, June 1950. Toffee, the red-headed dream girl, materialized from the unconscious of an inhibited young man and pranced through pastiches of Thorne Smith novels.

Captain Future, Spring 1943. The magazine was unabashed space opera; the science was piffle; but the action raged as Captain Future and the Futuremen fought evil galaxy wide.

Doc Savage, March 1933. First issue of the magazine, the cover by Walter Baumhofer, the novel by Lester Dent. The splendid figure of Clark Savage Jr., The Man of Bronze, realized every young man's dream of physical, financial, and mental superiority.

Action Stories, Spring 1944. On the cover, Senorita Scorpion was depicted as a female mystery, striking without mercy. But the cover had little to do with the story contained inside, which featured a lovely young lady, endlessly put upon, who used a gun only occasionally and a mask not at all.

The Whisperer, February 1941. Impatient of rules coddling criminals, Police Commissioner Wildcat Gordon fought crime in the guise of The Whisperer, a long-chinned justice figure wanted equally by the police and underworld.

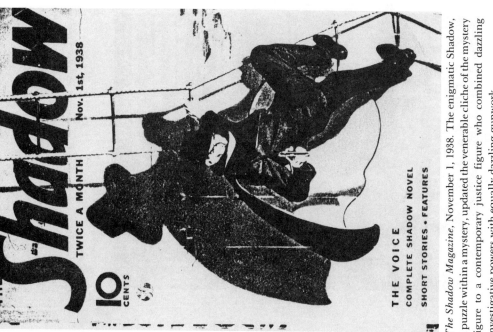

The Shadow Magazine, November 1, 1938. The enigmatic Shadow, a puzzle within a mystery, updated the venerable cliche of the mystery figure to a contemporary justice figure who combined dazzling investigative powers with equally dazzling gunwork.

The Spider, August 1938. Most violent of the pulp magazines, *The Spider* celebrated decency, self-sacrifice, responsibility, and service in stories blistered by emotionalism, incredible melodrama, and massacre.

Five Detective Novels, Spring 1951. Almost entirely a reprint magazine, *Five Detective Novels* was a jewel of the editor's art, offering superior mystery fiction and frequently admirable covers.

The Ghost, January 1940. The admirable George Chance, a professional magician, combined magic and detection as he investigated bizarre cases in the guise of an ambulant dead man.

The Phantom Detective, November 1934. Continuous, savage, improbable action as The Phantom, a wealthy young disguise master, fumbled his way bullet by bullet through the plots of lunatic crime masters.

III
Mayhem, Confusion, and Disorder

Series characters made the pulp magazines a continuing joy. As we have seen, some characters became stars. Their names blazed at the mastheads of their own magazines. Their fame reached outward to moving pictures, radio series, comic books, Big Little Books, and wrist-watch faces. They were widely popular and the fame of some persists. But these stars represented only a few of the many continuing characters whose rambunctious adventures packed the pulps.

Through the magazine pages passed a constant flow of lesser known, continuing characters. Almost every title offered them. Readers enthused over them. Covers illustrated molten moments in their adventures. For a few issues, they shone fiercely.

Then, for this reason or that they dimmed. And other names and other adventures replaced them.

Some appeared in novels or novelettes. But for the most part, you found them in short stories, a particularly specialized literary form. The short story is a dagger, stripped and lean. It is made for a single swift stroke, and, when it is successful, it strikes with force. It demands economy and concentration. As Poe said long ago, it requires the writer to focus his technical skill on a single point.

Many people published short fiction in the pulps. Among them were masters, story tellers of power. Whatever faults we find in them, sixty years later, we never doubt their narrative skill. Once begun, they catch the reader in a grip that never relents. If their characters seem sometimes transparent and their sentences unduly brief, if danger and difficulty arrived with mathematical precision and violence flashed on every page, still the story never faltered. The narrative flow overrode every improbability.

It is a tribute to the durability of the series characters that they survived that frantic atmosphere. For months or years, they survived repeatedly. It was a harsh life, although interesting.

In this part, we glimpse a few of these lesser-known series characters coping with life in the pulps. They include a fraudulent swami who is a practical amateur detective, a tough tall sailor who appeared in two masterpieces of hard-boiled detection, a pair of masked justice figures, a Sherlock Holmes clone, and two delightful girls who could never keep out of trouble—bad trouble.

And to prove that not all series were grim, we'll meet Toffee The Dream Girl and the lunatic cowboys of Pipe Rock County, both series unrepentant farces.

These are interesting people. Granted that their lives were spent in a whirl of mayhem, confusion, and disorder, which would drive less robust types mad. But it did make for fascinating reading.

Pandemonium In Yellow Rock County

In the deeps of Yellow Rock County, Montana, three tiny towns glower at each other. One town is central to our story; from Piperock we can glare fixedly toward the other towns, Yellow Horse and Paradise. At once, we can see that they

...are a couple of villages of vice, harboring the finest collection of penitentiary bait you ever seen. There ain't an ounce of brains in the two towns and they don't know it. It's sure a sad state of affairs, but where ignorance is bliss, it's a hell of a good place to stay away from.

Piperock is different. Containing nearly 350 citizens, it provides all the amenities of rich communal living. Which includes such conveniences as a general store, a school, a church run by that ferocious shepherd, Old Testament Tilton, a blacksmith's shop, a post office, a livery stable, and a saloon operated by Buck Masterson.

The time is in the middle 'Teens of the century. The magazine publishing the Piperock saga is *Adventure*. The writer is Wilbur C(oleman) Tuttle.

Son of an honest-to-God western sheriff, Tuttle was born in the family quarters over the county jail, while a major blizzard roared outside— November 11, 1883, Glendive, Montana Territory. He grew up in a cowtown, was casually educated in a school where, as he said: "You didn't graduate. You quit."

After quitting, he held such low-pay, labor-intensive jobs as cowboy, railroad hand, salesman, and professional baseball player. On the side he began to write.

At this period, two native art forms were crystallizing from the American air. One of these, the all-fiction, pulp-paper magazine was spreading vigorously; the other, the silent moving-picture comedy, had come to gaudy flower. In 1910 Mack Sennett began making comedies in Hollywood; in 1912 he organized the Keystone Company and, that year, filmed one hundred and forty silent comedies, mingling reality and fantasy in joyous partnership.

Now both the pulps and silent movie comedy enter our story.

In 1915 Tuttle began contributing humorous short fiction to *Adventure*. His stories caught some of the eccentrics and characters he had met in Montana—always allowing leeway for writer's exaggeration.

His fiction was broadly humorous, farces told with a serious face. The stories began reasonably, became more and more outrageous, ultimately ascended into fantastic, falling-apart confusion. Every part was narrated in a cool factual voice, giving exact detail.

Tuttle quickly sopped up all that he could learn from silent movie comedy—multiplying complexities and disasters, the dangers and escapes, and particularly the pandemonium of the all-out chase, with its trail of destruction and debris. His characters, done in modified dialect, faced adventures incredible in a reeling world.

The longer Tuttle wrote Piperock stories, the more completely they resembled silent comedy shorts. At length the circle closed. During the early 1920s, while working for the movies in Los Angeles, he transformed many of the Piperock stories into silent films.

Most of the stories were published between 1915 and 1922 and appeared in *Adventure*. A thin sprinkling of stories continued over the following thirty years, cropping up unexpectedly in a 1933 *Adventure* or a 1950 *Short Stories*. In 1963, Avalon Books, a publisher of westerns, issued *Piperock Tales*, an eight-story collection; there was editorial pruning and the beginning of each story was lightly reworked to provide a spurious sort of continuity, so that very dull readers might believe they were reading a novel.

At the beginning of the series—say from 1915 through 1917—each story contained a dab of plot. An initial problem is proposed: Capture of a bank robber for the reward ("Fate and the Fool," March 1917) or capture of a rustling band ("Cows is Cows," Mid-November 1917). At story's end, the robbers or rustlers are caught. The plot, such as it is, and its resolution, are only incidental to the telling of a comic series of mishaps. These progress through multiplying disasters to an ending of total confusion.

"Cows Is Cows" is typical. Piperock's sheriff, Magpie Simpkins, and his sometime aide, Ike Harper, have been unable to stop an epidemic of rustling. Four ranchers band together to hire a detective, Spade Wilson. The detective speedily discovers evidence that each rancher is stealing from the others and arrests them one by one. At the end, the detective is exposed as the rustler posing as a detective; the real detective was there on the scene posing as a religious nut.

But the plot is the least part of these stories. The pleasure lies in the humor of the characters, their conversation and observations and behavior as the comic situation sweeps over them.

Collectively and individually, the characters are concentrated lunacy.

Series narrator is Ike Harper—Isacc Beiling Harper—a short, heavy, mustached cowboy, part-time deputy, sometime miner. The others regard him as slow witted, although he tries to resist entanglement in confusion characteristic of Piperock social functions.

In early stories, Ike's partner is long-nosed Magpie Simpkins, who is thin "as a whisper for help." Nearly seven feet tall, Magpie is filled brimful with impractical ideas. Until 1922, he holds the job of Piperock sheriff; after that he becomes President of the Chamber of Commerce.

Dirty Shirt Jones later becomes Ike's partner. A miner along Plenty Stone Creek, Jones wore the same shirt for six years. Eventually it became nothing but patches. He is a "measly little devil," skinny, crooked nosed, with hair that "stands around on his head as though it just does not give a damn." His left eye wanders jauntily about, independent of his right eye, never managing to line up. Any mention of that eye causes Dirty Shirt to pull his gun.

These primary characters are supported by an immense cast of zanies. These include:

Mighty Jones, "as big as a bar of soap after month of laundering."

Trailer Johnson, who slouches along in the middle of a 50-dog pack of curs, mongrels, and mutts.

Mrs. Dulin, six feet six inches tall and "weighs just short of a hundred and ten. She could take a bath in a shotgun barrel."

There are such hard guys as Yuma Yates, Tombstone Todd, and Dog Rib Davidson, who are so tough "that they ache without any pain at all."

Through the action wander such other marvels as Hip Shot Harris, Hair Oil Heppner, Telescope Tolliver, Jay Bird Tolliver (who owns the Cross J ranch), Hassayampa Harris, and two dozen others. Each is a caricature, each drawn about a single trait. Each is a bright fleck in the rolling farce.

By the 1920s, Tuttle no longer bothered to organize his stories around a continuing plot element. He had discovered that the stories pranced as joyously along when he headed the narrative toward a terminal event, involved the disenchanted Ike in the festivities, and let the whole thing fly away. This is the reason so many stories record holiday celebrations in Piperock. In each case the town plans a celebration that includes Yellow Horse and Paradise, and in every case, the festivity comes unglued.

"Peace on Earth" (*Piperock Tales*) is reasonably representative. Scenery Sims goes on a spree in Butte and returns with a camel he bought. His mining partner, Dirty Shirt, stomps furiously off to Butte, tastes the liquor when it is red, and returns with an automobile. They decide to auction off the automobile to help build a new church. On Christmas Eve there will be a grand drawing, complete with a Nativity Scene, Three Wise Men, the camel, and a long-horned steer.

Sounds simple. But Paradise wants to get that automobile and, to make sure, buys up all the raffle tickets. All but one lost in Ike's pocket. Before the drawing, the three towns spend the day emptying bottles as fast as they can be opened. Which is why, when the pageant begins, Ike finds himself dressed as Santa Claus and perched on a ladder high above the stage. Believing that Ike has won the car, the boys from Paradise open fire on him. He falls on top of the steer. Which leaves.

My nose and chin knocked the front out of that fireplace. I saw one horn hook into Dirty Shirt's...robe and he seemed to open up like a newspaper in the wind....

"Hookum cow!" yelped somebody in the audience and the willing steer started sunfishing right across the stage, heading for the audience—kicking at everything in sight. It is about eight feet from the stage to the floor and I've got both feet locked behind the steer's horns when the drop started.

All I know about it is the yelling, crashing of chairs, and all that as Yellow Rock County tried to make an exodus in the dark. I am in what you might mildly term a daze, but when a Harper gets his hands on something he never lets loose....

Then the steer said, "Well, damn you, hold my arms if you want to, but get your hair out of my mouth."

A light stopped beside us and I looked up at Dirty Shirt. He has a lantern in his hand, but he is almost as naked as the day he was born. I am sitting on Dog Rib and he looked as though he had been mistreated.

Tombstone Todd has won the automobile and is trying to get it started. At this point, the steer charges the group, knocking Ike into the automobile, just as the automobile explodes into motion and sweeps them all away.

...I hit something so hard that all the big and little stars clustered around me. It was a sight worth seeing, but it got monotonous after a while....

(The automobile) shot off the top of those steps, crashed onto the sidewalk and roared out into the street. We make a left-hand turn just in time to knock every post out from under Buck Masterson's saloon porch....Everybody is yelling and running, trying to get away from that flaming juggernaut. One didn't. He came over the front end and landed in my lap....

Then I was conscious of a dull crash—and perfect peace. After a while I heard someone moving around and a lamp is lighted. There is Testament Tilton, trying to stand against his pulpit. He hasn't hardly any clothes on. One eye is swelled shut and his nose looks like a pickled beet.

"We will open services with a prayer," he said.

Silent Movie.

Whatever the occasion, it ends in uniform disaster. "Ike Harper's Historic Holiday" (Mid-January 1920) describes a Fourth of July celebration in which Ike must play the role of Pokyhontas saving Custer from Her Paw. On another Fourth of July, Piperock arranges a bull fight—with three bulls and three volunteers to fight them; on this occasion, "Throwing the Bull for Piperock" (February 15, 1933), most of the town is demolished.

"The Peace Ride of Paul Revere" (*Short Stories*, December 1950) sets off to celebrate a peace conference between Piperock, Yellow Horse, and Paradise on Christmas Eve. But the pageant again gets out of hand and you can't hear the peace for the shooting and screaming.

As Ike elsewhere remarks, "Celebrating any holiday in Piperock is like thawing dynamite in the oven."

Part of the problems come from excess lubrication with whisky. They spend a lot of time leaning over a bar in the swallowing position:

> ...says Dirty Shirt, "Dig out that nitric acid, which you call whisky." Well, we had a couple of burning sensations....

And a couple more. And before, during, and after calamity, they have still more. Sobriety and straight walking are unique conditions. In "Throwing the Bull for Piperock," Ike sees that he is going to be forced to serve as a matador for the bull fight. So he elects to put himself out of nomination:

> ...I went behind the bar and helped myself to a bottle of whisky. I filled eight glasses, lined 'em out on the bar, and then went around and started down the line. I'd jist eliminated number seven when I finds the room fillin' up behind me. I manages to get my gun loose, but they took it away from me. Dirty took that last drink of mine while about seven fellers shook me all to once....
>
> Them seven drinks of whisky hit me about that time, and I've got another blank period; but someone held my head under water, dang near drownin' me and I commences to git what Magpie calls lucid periods....

In Piperock, chaos is apt to come, even without the blessings of whisky and festival. "Tippecanoe and Cougers Two" (Mid-May 1921, *Adventure*) described how a group of Englishmen came west to photograph the wild life, only to face a pack of hounds, a grizzly bear, and a pair of mountain lions roped in a cabin. In "Local Color in Locoland" (First August 1921), two eastern writers come west for local color—most of the story is told by one of these—and get misunderstood, stepped on, and mauled while trying to understand the odd Piperock ways.

But enough already. No need for further discussion.

The Piperock stories are clearly formula fiction, playing truly amazing variations on familiar materials. To describe additional stories—such as the ineptly titled "Between Pike's Peak and a Pickle" (Mid-April 1920)—would be merely repetitive.

Certainly, each story takes off at a slightly different angle. In "Pike's Peak," for instance, Yuma Yates bets that he can ride anything. So the Piperock boys take bets, set him up with a motorized two-wheel cycle.

It's a different twist. But you've probably guessed how things will develop and I doubt that you'd be interested in reading all the details. Such as how the machine starts up in a cabin and demolishes it, and Ike with it.

...I got knocked under the bunk with part of the cook stove in my lap and the pantry on my head. When I got out and looked around I can't see Dirty Shirt or Magpie. The (cycle) is in the middle of the floor, the stove is upside down, and our one window ain't got neither frame nor pane left.

But what's the point of describing all this joyous nonsense to you sophisticated readers who are anxious to get back to your books of economic theory. Very likely you think that the bet will now get involved with a local celebration. And so it does. Just as you suspected, there is a brass band and a bunch of animals. And so there are—including a mean horse, a grizzly bear, and a pack of coyotes.

But I don't mean to bore you with still another story summary. Heavens, no. By this time you understand how things go in Piperock. Formula stories, of course, heavy on the slapstick. I understand that sophisticated readers demand....

Did I mention that all the animals get loose inside the saloon? Or that the two-wheeler whirls Yuma Yates through the parade, flinging bandsmen and horns in all directions and flipping Yuma away ?

...through the saloon window comes Yuma Yates.

He turns plumb over, ricochets off a cardtable and lands in behind the old pool table, flat on his back, with both feet up the wall. Glass and busted window frame spills all over everything....Behind the bar, kinda wedged in, is Dog Rib's bronc; on the bar is the grizzly and under the stove is two coyotes trying to dig a hole in the floor.

"My_____," gasps Magpie. "This is awful...."

There is no reason to bore you by recounting familiar material. It isn't even necessary to point out that Ike is stumbling around in the saloon just as the animals panic and try to escape:

I'm only a few feet from the bar, but somehow I ain't got the ambition to look out or stop anything, and when the fool bronc switched ends in there and upset the bar I didn't have energy to do anything except sit there and watch bar and bear fall right on top of me, but I did have sense enough to grab a handy rope and that bear yanked me out from under the bar, leaving both my boots beneath.

I seen Magpie fall backwards out of the window and then me and the bear knocked Buck's feet from under him and all three of us went under the old pool-table.

At this point, Ike, Buck, and the bear get tangled in the rope. Then the bear bolts away through the window. The main action now begins.

But enough, enough. No need to repeat all this. Nor is it necessary to mention the usual confusion, yelling, falling down, flying up. No need to tell of the female parachute jumper or how a run-away balloon swept away Ike, tangled at the end of a rope or the disastrous descent into a cattle stampede.

No point into going in that detail. The Piperock stories settled to formula, the same in 1950 as in 1920, more or less. After 1922, Tuttle turned from Piperock to longer, more serious fiction about Hashknife and Sleepy and other western characters.

Still you may find it pleasant to read a Piperock story every so often. An occasional taste of farce is healing. They aren't filming silent comedy these days. So it's nice to know that the old form still lives on in Piperock, where life continues frantic and glorious nonsense is still as bright as the morning sun.

Guy's Ghost

It is 1909 in New York City, home of Nick Carter and Felix Boyd.

Horse-drawn traffic rumbles over brick streets. Overhead interlace webs of telephone lines. Gaslight glows in saloons where ragtime stutters and the free lunch spreads in salty stacks beside the shining bar. Swaggering toughs cluster Lower East side streets but on Long Island, the rich man has his mansion so fine.

And out on Forty-Second Street, near the Broadway lights, stands a modest little house. Beside the front door gleams a small, black, gilt-lettered sign:

GUY and GHOST
Psychic Detectives
Materializations at any hour of the day or night.
a specialty

Above the house looms a new electric billboard—the very latest mode of advertising. Alternately it flashes a pair of messages:

DO YOUR FEAR EVIL?	CRIME PUNISHED
GUY and GHOST	The Malefactor Fears
WILL PROTECT YOU	GUY and GHOST
	Psychic Detectives

It is 1909 and in the pages of *The Popular Magazine* stirs that brief series, "Guy and Ghost, Psychic Detectives." Written by Lester Griswold, the series ran from August through November 1, 1909.

The premise was simple. According to the magazine's editor, "The spiritualistic Medium, the clairvoyant, and so-called 'fortune tellers' generally obtain from their clients, in the course of business, much information that is really of value. Not a few charlatans have made use of information so obtained for their own nefarious uses; but there is no recorded instance of a man with the instincts of a detective taking up this line of work and using it as a means to the detection of crime."

But it can be done.

Enter the house at Forty-Second Street. The Russian servant, Vladimir, leads you silently to a room of dark red walls. A droplight of crimson glass spills its bloody glow on red leather chairs. Here, in somber glory, sits Guy. He is wrapped in a red velvet robe and a diamond star is bound to his forehead. His face is disciplined. His eyes, shaped like those of an Oriental, are of a peculiar tawny hue, cold, direct, unsentimental.

By mystic arts, undisclosed, he has gained influence over a former French prefect of police, Monsieur Guillaume. Bored by life after the grave, M. Guillaume has agreed to assist Guy in unknotting cases of interest.

You follow Guy into a rear room. There extends a mighty table flanked by twenty heavy chairs. Overhead hangs a vast gilt chandelier. Heavy curtains veil the walls. At one end of the room is a slightly elevated dais. Here Guy seats himself, bowing his head as the room blackens.

From somewhere whispers the faint rasp of wood sliding against wood. Then a brittle rustling. A luminous figure glides forth. It is faceless, moaning, terrible. As it vanishes, a giant figure rears hugely up within a pillar of light. Its words boom in this fearful place.

And, yes, your throat closes. Your blood shivers. Your hands knot themselves in dread. In this black room, horror walks and—mercy, mercy—the dead speak.

After you have stated your problem and the spirits have answered (promising clarification later), you pay the fee and you depart. When you return later, the spirits, terrible as ever, will reveal the solution to your problem.

So much for the surface of the business.

Under the surface is quite another reality.

After you leave, the lights go up. A wall panel slides open. Through it steps a muscular young man draped in pale gauze. His name is Cornelius Wraye. He handles details of ghostly manifestations, creating ectoplasm and materializations with a craftsman's skill. He is front man, research staff, leg man, and full partner in the business.

On the dais, Guy removes the paste star from his forehead. His full name is Guy Keels, "a farmer by training," come to the big city to make his fortune. As we presently learn, he has earned that fortune.

Both Guy and "Corny" are cheerful young men, perhaps undistinguished in their appearance, but with wits and tongues that glitter like real diamonds. Under the gaudy front of their business, they run a successful and entirely honest detective agency.

(Guy) undertook nothing that was not perfectly honest. If he failed, there was no charge. Who can blame him for using methods that gave him free advertisement—methods which he regarded as a competent theatrical manager would his stage accessories?

The methods seem effective enough. In three years, Guy and Ghost have earned $172,000. Even when split between the partners, that's a rosy sum.

Behind such earnings must be more than a show biz facade. And there is. Guy is not only a first-class showman but a natural detective.

Although he is quite unlike the usual detective in 1909 fiction. He refuses to sit, eccentric and solitary, weaving logical webs. Nor does he lunge forth, disguised and armed, darting among death traps until the criminal fiend is captured.

Instead, Guy investigates as if he thought the date were 1989.

First, that spectacular interview with the client.

Then he plunges into a search for background information. Like every detective who ever lived, except those in story books, he routinely checks all available public documents: Newspaper morgues, the social register, Bradstreet's, maps, building plans.

Then a torrent of small bribes spills from his fingers. Scraps of information flow from elevator starters and messenger boys, switchboard operators, servants, clerks, doormen and cabbies. As every detective and fake medium knows, these modest investments yield a priceless dusting of facts.

Since a medium or a detective is only as good as his contacts, Guy has carefully established contacts all over town. He knows bartenders, reformed crooks, and a good number unreformed. He has personal lines to bankers and bums. The night editor of *The Messenger*, that influential newspaper, is a close friend. Each such contact can furnish certain specialized information. Each is carefully cultivated. Guy is liberal with his cash and quick to do a favor—piling up points against future need.

These coldly practical methods sound more like the Continental Op than a psychic detective. Except that Guy (unlike the Op) gets along badly with the police—the Central Office as they are called.

In the first story, "The Perfume of the Poppy" (August 1909), he refuses to pay graft to a police detective. As a result, the agency is in danger of being shut down. To protect "Guy and Ghost," Guy must solve a case that the police have flopped on—and solve it spectacularly. Which he does by materializing a wanted man into police custody, while newspaper men watch. Very effective.

As usual in this casual fiction, the police are incompetent. They are also corrupt and malevolent. Popular mystery fiction of this period hammers at police corruption. Memories were still fresh of the police graft scandals a few years earlier.

But not only the police are corrupt. In this series, corruption shows everywhere. Politics and crime are tightly tied. How little things change. The political boss manipulates his sluggers and bagmen and is immune from either arrest or investigation. The rich man chats at the Astor, while his hireling thugs slouch in infested saloons. A dollar buys immunity. Only the poor man is not safe. It's like reading *Black Mask* or today's newspaper.

Where it differs from *Black Mask* is in the picture of the underworld. This is the old-style underworld, organized around street gangs. It is savage enough, brutal enough, vicious enough. But it has not reached the heights of organization achieved fifteen years later, after Prohibition had poured millions into the hands of illiterate killers.

This old-style underworld is familiar to readers of Nick Carter and Jimmie Dale—filth and shadows, stinking air in crazy wooden buildings, gaslight, men dirt-caked and reeking of old sweat in sweaters and caps. The same scene appeared in the early *Shadow Magazine*, an anachronism by then, a revenant of the 1900 underworld long gone. But the image lingered, like the sun's after image in the eye.

In the November 1, 1909, "The Inevitable Woman," Guy's investigations carry him into the fetid heart of this underworld. "The door swung open and admitted them into a kerosene-laden atmosphere. Chains rattled back into place and several bolts were shot."

" 'G'wan upstairs' directed the guardian of the door, whose features were impossible to make out in the dim light, which came from a small oil lamp fastened in a bracket, halfway up a flight of rickety steps."

Guy is carrying an unaccustomed automatic in this Jimmie Dale environment. He needs a weapon. In this episode, he ends up shot in the side, having slugged a political boss into permanent imbecility just before a fight with knives and guns.

But that is the way of this series. The stories begin in the spooky world of the seance and end in underworld darkness. The actual problem investigated is usually rather trivial. Olive oil is disappearing from a bottle on the windowsill or a girl is seen stealing a necklace, although she denies it. Minor problems. Yet nothing is as simple or trivial as it appears. Guy's investigations resemble a man following a string through dim rooms. At last he traces the string to a simple little wall ornament. But when he tugs down the ornament, the wall collapses and sewage gushes out.

This curious dark undertone sounds throughout the series. You feel the presence of something hunched and stealthy snuffing behind the old-fashioned prose. A ghost, perhaps. Not Guy's ghost, a construct of cheesecloth and light. But a more ambiguous ghost of silent emotion or fear.

The stories contain much fear, lightly treated. As in the Prologue to the series. In this, two housebreakers are terrified by one Guy's seances. Humorous. He kicks them down the front steps. Still, they carried a chunk of lead pipe to crack interfering skulls, casually ready for murder. Behind the obvious humor, darkness moves.

Scared crooks are stereotypes, as are other characters of the series—fine young men, corrupt detectives, silly old women. Yet human quirkiness touches each. You feel they live more broadly than the story permits.

For instance, during the final story, "The Inevitable Women," Guy falls instantly in love with a girl accused of theft. He clears her, the gimmick being that a long lost brother, a twin, committed the crime. It is a well-worn device, as is love at first sight and ending a series with the prospect of marriage.

But Guy tells her an odd thing: "I love you. It is the first time I have either loved or trusted. For God's sake, don't let me make a mistake."

The stereotype of the fine young man, the brilliant natural detective, cracks at this point. Deep inside the crack, you glimpse a strange darkness. It has not been hinted at before.

But the series is riddled with such cracks. Each opens to a blackness murmurous with ghosts. Corny's skillful hands did not create these. They are concealed inside the series. Only briefly, during the hoop-la and small excitements, do they reveal themselves. They leave fleeting touches of cold along the edge of your heart. And, momentarily, a routine detective series, with a peculiar premise, becomes touched with fear and darkness.

The Murder Cases Of Pinklin West

Success isn't nearly as easy as it looks.

The 1920s mystery magazines glitter with series characters who are smiling, popular, successful, adored by readers, sought by editors. Most characters have since faded to footnotes. But in their day, the wonder was in them, their light brilliant.

The wonder and the brilliance conceal a few gray facts. For every successful series character, a dozen or more others appeared and plodded and vanished. Their series were brief. Their lights burned low, even with the wick turned up.

We remember Race Williams and maybe Madame Storey. But few among us can recall Reverend Brace, who would have been a detective if the ministry hadn't called. Who remembers the ghost of Diogenes, a 2000-year old sorehead who became the chief investigator for a private detective agency? Or Nan Russell, a chorus girl become the dearest sweetest darling investigatrix you ever met, the adorable thing.

Or, for that matter, who recalls the bland Pinklin West?

West was one of those players who strutted and fretted his hour on the stage of *Detective Story Magazine*, and then was heard no more. A brief candle, you might say. Six stories published during 1922-1923. Then gone.

Six stories was the usual length of a series showing promise but which, for various reasons, failed to catch on. *Detective Story* was packed with such short runs, among them Tiptoe Tatterton, Rev. Brace, Initiating Noggins, Boston Betty, Old Windmills. They came. And very soon they went. Mostly they went.

Whatever cut them short, it did not seem to be the lack of an interested readership. In 1922, detective stories twined through many of the slick magazines and most of the general pulps. If you were an insatiable reader, you could also turn to the specialized mystery magazines, four of them available that year—*Black Mask, Detective Tales, Mystery,* and *Detective Story Magazine.*

Of these, *Detective Story* was still the major magazine. Founded in 1915, it had finally shaken off its dime novel origins. Now, a 144-page, double-columned pulp, it offered an ever-changing mixture of detectives, criminal heroes, plain crooks, and costumed bent heroes—in serial, short story, and novelette, offered each week, every week of the year, 15¢ a copy. Nine or ten pieces of fiction were provided each issue. This in addition to two articles, five departments, and a gang of short paragraphs about crime, detectives, and criminals used as filler in the magazine. Each paragraph was listed on the magazine's contents page, giving the impression of unbearable reading riches.

So much for the 1922 environment in which Mr. West appeared.

Mr. West, himself, is a criminologist, that favored profession of the early 1920s. Exactly what a criminologist did back then is not clear. There seems no difference between a criminologist and a private investigator. Except that the criminologist wears clean underwear.

West performs his miracles in Chicago. He and his assistant live in an apartment house in a fourth-floor suite used impartially as living quarters, office, and laboratory. At this period, all criminologists operated personal laboratories. It was because of the benign example of Craig Kennedy, who still towered high, inspiring detective story writers—as did the word rates Arthur B. Reeve received for the Kennedy adventures.

As in the Kennedy series, West's cases are told by a first-person narrator. And, like the Kennedy series, the narrator is an eager boob who could overlook a mouse in his milk.

Thorne Miller is his name. All stories are signed Thorne Miller, adding still another pseudonym to those swarming on the *Detective Story* contents page.

Miller's fictional function is to answer the telephone in the first paragraph, saying "Pinklin West's assistant speaking." He also speculates about stray facts, draws foolish conclusions, and gives the reader someone to feel superior to. Why West would associate with such a dolt is never explained; Miller must be a poor relation.

As a curious—and likely inadvertent—consequence, Miller becomes the most vivid character of the series. Even when self-pictured as an inane babbler, he makes West look transparent.

Not that West would throw much shadow in full sun light. You never saw such a self-effacing fellow.

Pinklin West's impassive face, his colorless, blinking eyes, certainly give no hint of his tremendous brain power, his almost uncanny ability to see things which remain hidden from the average eyes.

He also has the uncanny ability to listen. Through most of a case, he merely stands there, mild, blank faced, eyes blinking. If his eyes blink rapidly, that signals he has heard an interesting fact.

I will say that (West) is the most accomplished listener I have ever known; I have seen him listen for more than an hour without being tempted to utter so much as one syllable. Which does not mean, however, that he is an uninteresting talker when he is moved to speech, for he is fluently versed on many subjects.

You modern readers, in all your smug righteousness, may not be impressed by West. But the Chicago police certainly were. When they are stumped, West is the first man they call in. That happens less than twice a day, most days.

Which brings us to "The Silent Shot" (June 10, 1922), the first story of the series. Inspector Landers is stumped. There sprawls the body of District Attorney Robinson, dead of a .32 bullet to the temple. He lies in a soft chair in the smoking room of the exclusive Dearborn Club, his newspaper fallen beside his chair. The chair faces the window. The window overlooks Michigan Avenue, along which a parade just passed. The noise of the parade must have covered the sound of the shot, for none of the six prominent men in the room heard a thing. Or saw a thing. And the gun is missing.

Kincaid, the DA's bodyguard, is carrying an unfired .45, but you can't suspect so obvious a suspect. With great post-disaster efficiency, Kincaid has detained the six prominent men until the police arrive.

They arrive to be baffled.

It is an impossible crime

How glad Inspector Landers is when West enters. "For the present, Mr. West, the investigation is in your hands." It is not the customary police routine, but those were unsettled times, and the story is only 8-½ pages long. Impossible crime or not, it must be solved in this issue. And it will be.

For, as West points out, "There is always something, you know, Mr. Inspector; the inexorable law of clews is the best ally that we have."

They look all around the room, Miller spewing out a torrent of obvious observations. Then West questions all the suspects, which the police have forgotten to do. Obviously, the next step is to have them reenact their movements. By this time, West observed a smudge of powder stains on the newspapers by the DA's chair. The police haven't noticed this because the police have been shuffling their feet and clearing their throats.

The six prominent men move to their original positions. And one of them is carrying a cane—obviously a gun cane. You could tell from the smudge where the powder-stained tip touched the newspaper. And thus and so and....

"Through The Air" (July 29, 1922), another West triumph, succeeds because the police are blind, numb, and stupid. Particularly Detective Sergeant Burley, who is so ill-informed as to sneer at West and his new-fangled methods.

He, Burley, has already snared the murderer—rather, the murderess. She has obviously shot her employer, Travis Whitson. Shot him right square in the head, right square in his electrical lab. This ungracious act followed a violent quarrel.

Heavens knows what she did with the gun. It has vanished away, as guns have a tendency to do in a Pinklin West case.

The girl, Norma Benson, claims she was leaving the lab when the shot came. And she didn't do it, didn't do it, didn't do it.

Thorne Miller: "A hunch tells me that this girl didn't kill him."
Pinklin West: "Guessing! How many times have I warned about that, Thorne?"

For once Miller is right. Norma didn't do it. As can be demonstrated by examining the dead man's ear, which is smeared with burnt powder. Then examining the telephone, which contains a pistol built into the receiver.

Burley never got around to examining the receiver, since this is a story in which the police must appear in the worst possible light, enabling Mr. West to glare and glitter all the more. But as soon as West saw that ear....

The shot was fired by a radio signal sent, as one might say, "Through The Air." Since the murderer had to know when Whitson had the receiver to his ear, the murderer was obviously the other man on the telephone.

As the deduction is made, the murderer (who has been eavesdropping on the investigation by radio), laughs wildly, confesses in a great voice, and shoots himself. Nicely confirming West's analysis.

"Too Clever" (August 21, 1922) concerns a doctor found dead in his garage. It is obviously death by accidental carbon monoxide poisoning. You can tell. The fresh snow around the garage is marred only by prints of the dead man's shoes going in, and his housekeeper's tracks to and from the garage. These tracks are paralleled by a line of holes in the snow, as if someone had jabbed a broomstick down every forty inches. But holes mean nothing. How could they?

So why does West suspect murder? He listens blinking to the housekeeper; he listens blank-faced to the doctor's brother (who longed for the dead man's fiancee). No clues at all.

Now West inspects the doctor's room. Discovers the open window and the clue of the partially snow-covered window sill. Discovers the clue of the gas jet. Looks under the bed and discovers the clue of the dead dog.

No clue is shared with the reader. You might think that West would comment on the phenomena of the dog under the bed:

"Say, Thorne, you'd never guess what I just saw under the bed...."

Not West. He says not a word. Just dusts off his knees and blinks. Oh, he's close, West is.

All these clues are held back till the end of the story. Then out they blaze, confounding the reader and the murderer, whose identity (since it wasn't the housekeeper) is tolerably easy to guess.

Miller nearly has a spasm explaining how clever West is. How astute. A wonder man, don't you agree, dear reader?

Dear reader can hardly respond, since he is choking on the explanation of the holes in the snow. Seems that the murdering brother carried the doctor dead from his gas-filled bedroom across the snow to the garage. Then he recrossed the snow on a pogo stick. This device never appears in the story. However, it must have left those holes, and that's proof enough for a Chicago criminologist.

After this horrendous swindle on the reader, West returns to his apartment house. He is inventing things up there in his lab. He has invented a new way to transmit fingerprints by telegraph. He is now working out a new system of criminal identification, ten times more effective than fingerprinting. Craig Kennedy would be proud to boil a beaker with him.

Before West invents himself out of a job, new case arrives, "In His Own Hand" (November 4, 1922). Wealthy young Hulbert Chalmers has mailed his fiancee, Patricia Thayer, a hand-written, special-delivery suicide note. Too late she enlists West's help. When they reach Chalmers' apartment, they find him shot dead behind a locked door.

West promptly calls for Detective Sergeant Burley, that hard-nosed scoffer of "Through The Air."

The veteran headquarters man had begun his association by sneering at Pinklin West's methods of crime deduction, and had wound up by being both his admirer and warm personal friend.

Burley is not convinced that the Chalmers matter is a case for Homicide.

Burley: The trouble with you, West, is that you always want to make a mystery out of every case you get on.

West must be wrong. The building attendant testifies that Chalmers gave him a special delivery letter to mail the previous evening. His story is confirmed by playwright Fleming Bruce, who was visiting Chalmers at the time. Bruce remarks that Chalmers was nervous and distracted and sad. Ready for suicide, maybe.

No soap. West deduces murder, reasoning from such clues as the special watermarked paper in Bruce's rooms, an opened and resealed envelope, the serene handwriting of the suicide note, and significant cut marks along the note's upper edge.

These clues are not provided the reader, who would only misunderstand them.

Your intuition is correct. Bruce did it. He loved Patricia and could not endure losing her to Chalmers. Pretending a sprained hand, he dictated a page of play script to Chalmers, who kindly wrote it down. Part of the dictation included a suicide note—and there you are.

"And Then A Game of Golf" (December 2, 1922) occupies a few brisk hours one rainy morning. Burley calls West, urgent, urgent, to investigate a bank robbery. Just happened. $50,000 gone. Teller shot down. The police are all doing something else important, which is why Burley calls on a criminologist for help.

The dying teller has identified his killer as Roger Fenley, the confidential secretary to the bank president. Seems impossible. At the time, Fenley was in a taxi cab, far away, riding to an appointment with the president.

The taxi driver is unshakable; the alibi is not. West exposes a complicated meshwork of impersonation, substitution, conspiracy, embezzlement, and secret marriage. The detection requires only a few hours. After that, the criminals are marched away and the rain stops. Now Thorne Miller can get in a round of golf.

One final case appeared—"Deadly Safety," March 3, 1923. With that the endless silence fell, inexorable as the stroke of a cleaver. Although a few readers wrote, urging more stories, none seem to have been published. Pinklin West's history was complete.

All this happened sixty-odd years ago in the flaming youth of the detective story.

What was acceptable then, in 1922, in the more casual popular magazines, is stylistic criminality today. Our present literary convention requires fair play with clues, realistically motivated characters, touches of psychological insight, a musky dab of sex. Good things all. But not immutable. These are the conventions of our time, the style that shapes our writing and guides our reading.

If these conventions now seem permanent, so did the rather different conventions of the past. As will the much different conventions of future detective fiction. Our present beliefs about literary merit did not trouble Thorne Miller, writing sixty years, ago. How cheerfully he concealed clues. How irrational his police and their procedures. How repetitive his devices and motives.

To the last, he worked in the convention of his time, blithely indifferent to the real relationship between policemen and private investigator in the world of 1922. He seemed unconcerned that Pinklin West was as colorless a figure as ever melted into the page. He followed uncritically the tradition of Sherlock Holmes and Craig Kennedy.

But even the brightest sun sets at last, the most adept imitator fades. Today Pinklin West is interesting mainly as an example of a minor magazine detective series at the opening of the Twenties.

That the series was so brief is suggestive. Perhaps those distant readers and editors were less easily charmed than we believe. Perhaps a series so flawed could sustain itself only briefly. Perhaps Miller, whoever he was, tired of Pinklin West. Perhaps.

Only the very confident venture to explain why a series ended. We only know that success isn't as easy as it looks. That West, like so many others, vanished after six stories, leaving behind a few questions inconvenient to answer, and an ambiguous footnote to the history of the detective story.

Rings Of Death

The story of the White Rings begins with a crashing misstatement:

"Miss Marchard never knew why she snipped the clippings from the newspaper.

When Erle Stanley Gardner wrote that line in 1934, he clearly had no idea what Miss Marchard knew or didn't know. It hardly mattered. He provided her with essentials—a fabulous memory, scissors, and employment with a mysterious millionaire. Given these points, the story raced forward to airspeed. And change. Even Miss Marchard, who began as an industrious, highly-paid blank, changed. But a lot of Gardner's details kept changing.

Gardner tended to plunge into a new short story series without knowing all that much about it. In the instance of the White Rings, he had certainly tasted the central idea—two masked men battle criminals that the law can't catch—and found it good. Why not? In 1934, lots of people costumed themselves to battle untouchable criminals. The premise was as familiar as rain in April. Granted that Gardner did not foresee how quickly Miss Marchard would discover the secret of the White Rings—by the second story, no less. But these things happen when you whang out fiction every day of your life. What does count is that he had a solid grip on the series premise. That man knew what a series was all about.

Between 1921 and 1934, Gardner had published more than 450 pieces of fiction. That was, of course, a long time ago, when the pulp magazines, ragged of edge and giddy of cover, gulped fiction with the zeal of a black hole sucking up suns.

Gardner was nicely tuned to the needs of this market. A writer of ferocious energy, he explosively ejected quantities of fiction for such titles as *Breezy Stories, Black Mask, Short Stories, West, Top Notch, Three Star, Ace High, Clues, Detective Fiction Weekly, Gang World, Western Stories, Dime Detective*, and *Argosy*. His example should stimulate us all.

Perhaps three-quarters of these stories featured series characters. The pulps and their readers doted on series characters—individuals whose sassy competence solved every complication lavished upon them, story after story, to the limit of the writer's ingenuity. If a spark leaped, if a character drew fire from the writer and admiration from the reader, the series rolled irresistibly through the years, piling up colossal archives of adventures.

By mid-1934, Gardener had created 32 separate and reasonably distinct series characters. These included such long-enduring figures as Perry Mason, who lives on to this day in television and reprints; and Lester Leith, who blithely robbed thieves and is warmly remembered. But Gardner also gave us extended story sequences featuring Sidney Zoom; Ed Jenkins the Phantom Crook; Senor Lobo; Bob Zane of the the Whispering Sands series; the Patent Leather Kid; Paul Pry; and the urgently named Speed Dash.

Not all Gardner's series characters flourished. About half of them appeared in only two or three stories—assuming that two stories represent a series. For an instant, they flared brightly. Then heaven knows what happened. Maybe Gardner lost interest. Or he dropped the character because it lacked an individual voice. Or he stopped writing for the magazine in which the character appeared. Or more urgent work interceded and, in the unrelenting blizzard of pages, the character accidentally got misplaced. All or none of these.

For whatever reason, Go Get 'Em Garver and Yee Dooney Wah appeared only to disappear. As did Rex Kane, Buck Riley, Dred Bart, and the wonderfully named Fish-Mouth McGinnis.

As did the White Rings.

It's a shame about the White Rings. They should have lasted more than three stories. Gardner went to elaborate lengths to devise their background and operations, sharpening their characters, planting conflicts and emotional entanglements. It's as if he laid out the foundations for a 100-room palace, built three closets, and then left town. But we must be thankful for what we have.

The White Rings, themselves, were terrors.

...a mysterious organization composed of at least two individuals is making a secret war on crime. The members of this organization wear black masks covering the upper portion of their faces. Around the eyes are large rings of white, giving to the faces a peculiar weird appearance and making recognition almost impossible. (They) seem to possess most accurate information concerning the big shots of crime. They do not bother with the small criminals, but rather pick on a criminal who has shown an ability to elude the police and who has become a hero to the underworld. The members of this mysterious organization ask no quarter and give none; they confront the criminals suddenly and dramatically, when they are engaged in the perpetration of crime. They always give the criminals an even break, always shoot it out, and invariably place their shots with such uncanny accuracy that the criminals are wiped out, then the men disappear.

From this, we conclude that the White Rings are part Wild West hero, part justice figure, and part costumed menace. Each of these parts was a convention in the fiction of the mid-1930s and each convention was exploited by various characters in various magazines until it seemed hardly possible that one more variation could be squeezed out. To the 1988 eye, the White Rings seem bizarre; to the reader of 1934, they seemed merely routine, a sub-type so common as to be accepted without comment.

Most of the lethal crime-fighters used, as justification, that they attended to matters normal law enforcement channels couldn't touch. That convention was established at the turn of the century, when Edgar Wallace's Just Men set up in business. Some thirty years later, Judson P. Philips' Park Avenue Hunt Club continued the tradition. The Hunt Club—four men and a whole lot of guns—took on concealed crime bosses, Nazi sympathizers, and deadly disguise masters, and shot fool out of them. Their activities began with the January 27, 1934, issue of *Detective Fiction Weekly*, and continued for ten years thereafter. They did not normally use masks. Didn't need to. They left no survivors.

On the whole, the costumed crime-fighter was a lot less deadly than the justice figure. The costumed figure, wonderfully garbed and cowled, rose from the dime novels. You can dig out earlier roots if you have a mind to. Then Johnston McCulley took hold of the idea, creating Zorro, a bunch of non-lethal costumed criminals from Black Star to the Crimson Clown, and a couple of costumed heroes who did illegal things while striking at entrenched white-collar crooks.

While McCulley's characters meticulously avoided bloodshed, others did not. By the end of the 1920s, costumed criminals reveled through the magazines, slaughtering casually while scooping up somebody else's money.

If criminals could, heroes ought to. And so, in 1931, the first costumed justice figure, The Shadow, got loose in fiction. By 1932, The Shadow and his .45 automatics had established mass homicide as a corrective for criminal behavior. Afterward came the ferocious Spider and all the rest, men against crime, demonstrating that honesty grew from the muzzle of an automatic.

And why costumes at all? Why Masks?

There was something peculiar in the psychological reactions engendered by the black masks with the large white rings around the eyes—a something which had a tendency to strike momentary terror.

Fear—terror. Those are reasons enough. Startle a gangster by your peculiar appearance. Before he realizes that he is clutching a machine-gun, you pot him right between the eyes.

As Jax Bowman, creator of the White Rings, pointed out:

It's the psychology of the thing. The criminal mind is afraid of the unknown and it's afraid of the bizarre. They know too much about the politicians who can control police organizations, about the shyster lawyers and jury-bribing detectives, to feel any fear of ordinary justice. But this mask idea gets on their nerves. The fact that they can't find out anything about this new enemy is a powerful psychological factor in adding to their fear.

For those of you who came in late, Jax Bowman, hero of our series, is a sun-bronzed millionaire in his early thirties. For reasons having to do with the economics of crime-fighting, large numbers of dual-identity avengers were millionaires. That meant they had lots of free time and ample funds for cartridges, masks, and carfare. Large wealth also meant that they were superior men. If Guy the Gun elects to shoot a few of his sleazy friends, he's a murderer; if Guy Van Townsend, bronzed young millionaire, shoots a few criminals, he's a justice figure.

Bowman was in the early thirties. His skin was bronzed from exposure to sunlight. There was a disconcerting deadliness about his eyes, a keen appraisal which seemed to strip aside all subterfuge and penetrated to the very soul. His motions were as quick and swiftly efficient as those of a bird hopping about on the ground, picking up insects. He radiated power and vitality...as dazzlingly concentrated as the spot of sunlight which is gathered by a big reading glass.

No one knew the extent of his fortune. Perhaps Bowman himself didn't know. His money matters were delegated to subordinates who occupied several floors in a skyscraper office building....

Jax's partner in the White Ring enterprise is Big Jim Grood. An ex-cop, Big Jim is thick-necked, broad shouldered, built big. He has a cauliflower ear, fists like cement clubs, and a cigar permanently jammed into his face.

Big Jim Grood...was a two-fisted cop of the old school. He firmly believed that there was more law in a night stick than in a court room; that fear was the only deterrent to crime; and that the hue and cry about police brutality, which had brought about something of a revolution in police methods, was responsible for the increase of crime and the systematic racketeering which corrupted the larger cities.

Things are so simple when you understand the situation.

This unlikely pair met when Big Jim came to Jax with a proposal—How about financing a central bureau of crime detection. Exactly what that meant is never explained, but no matter. They would set up to solve mysteries. And Jax, always the sportsman, decides they will also punish criminals.

"It ain't the detection you get a thrill out of," Grood tells him, "it's the action."

Leave small criminals to the police. The White Rings would specialize in the master criminal, the secret mind striking invisibly throughout the country, backed by gangland guns. In 1934 action fiction, hundreds of such groups ravaged, each headed by a criminal genius, each destined for obliteration by an equally secret justice figure.

So far we have a wealthy young sportsman, and ex-cop, a pair of odd masks, and a case of .45 automatics. To focus these fragments, we must now re-introduce Miss Rhoda Marchand.

No crime-fighting organization, real or imaginary, exists without information sources. It is a long-standing mystery fiction convention. Archer calls on a friend in Homicide. Holmes has an elaborate series of scrapbooks. The Shadow is supported by innumerable agents listening at rat holes. Each series has its own technique. But all rely on someone to collect information. It speeds up the story wonderfully.

And so, in the beginning, the White Rings hire a girl to clip and file newspaper stories.

> Miss Marchard had a photographic memory. She had a remarkably quick eye, could scan the columns of a newspaper, and get the gist of the news with such speed that it seemed impossible that she had done more than merely glance at the paper. She could, moreover, remember a similarity in method, so that clipping could be filed in the 'mode of operation' file with unerring accuracy.
>
> Every day the postman brought a great bundle of newspapers, papers from all the larger cities in the United States. Miss Marchand pounced upon these newspapers with quick, eager eyes, and sniping shears.
>
> ...When enough clippings were gathered under one particular mode of operation to make it seem that some astute criminal was consistently getting the better of the police, the clippings were fastened together and brought to Bowman's attention.

In the beginning ("White Rings," *Argosy*, June 30, 1934), Miss Marchand reads all those newspapers, herself. She works alone in an one-room office, no name on the door, the telephone unlisted. Soon enough, the operation grows. By the third story the single room has expanded to an office suite. A permanent staff has been hired and bundles of clippings arrive daily from clipping services. Although weighted by responsibilities, Miss Marchard reads and indexes and sifts records for dim intimations of crime.

The first batch of intimations she turns up in our presence are about the White Rings, themselves. Rumors of their activities have made the newspapers; the stories have been clipped; and Miss Marchard, in her old-maidish innocence, presents these to Mr. Jax Bowman and Mr. Big Jim Grood.

Scoffing gently at such foolishness as masked avengers, they pass on to the next case, the first recorded by Gardner.

Since all the White Rings cases have a strong family resemblence, it wouldn't hurt to summarize their general features:

1) The Rings review Miss Marchard's work and decide to investigate.

2) Either Jax or Big Jim pretends to be crooked and contacts the criminals.

3) They meet a very beautiful girl, somehow wound in the criminals' tolls. Taken by her charms....

4)...Jax gets captured and tied up very tightly.

5) He escapes, usually with Big Jim's help.

6) Together, they shoot down everything in sight.

7) They discover that the beautiful girl is innocent.

"White Rings" creates these data points which the other stories faithfully follow. A gang is holding up particularly large social functions, stripping away jewelry, wads of bank notes, and similar gauds of wealth. To date, these outrages have occurred in Denver, Kansas City, and San Francisco. In each case, the butler has bolted, leaving behind evidence that he is an ex-con using forged credentials.

If you or I were asked to develop a lead from this material, we would chuckle nervously and start adjusting the air conditioner. But Big Jim is far more competent. He knows all about that last fleeing butler, an ex-convict named Silver Smith. He knows, for example, that Smith has a penchant for El Paso. That he is likely on the Mexican side of the border. In a certain cantina. Big Jim is as well informed as a character in an Edgar Wallace novel.

And so, with that blithe disregard for expense typical of fictional characters, they fly to El Paso, cross the border, enter the cantina, and there sits Silver Smith, nervously pushing at a beer.

Under no great pressure, Smith claims he was set up as a fall guy. He interviewed for a job in answer to an ad that discreetly offered employment to "persons who have erred against society." Cons, that is. A beautiful woman took his application, sent him off to this swell society place —and now look what happened. Never trust no broad.

The Rings check out the ad that snared Smith. Research (that is, the valuable Miss Marchand) locates a similar ad in a New Orleans newspaper. With pulses tingling, the Rings race away to that city. Jax applies for a job and is accepted by a 28-year old lovely with silver-gray eyes.

Beautiful. Simply beautiful. And unaware that she is serving criminals. Obviously.

How can an innocent beautiful 28-year old girl with silver eyes be a criminal?

Easy, says Big Jim,. He has recognized her a Rita Coleman, a frivolous society girl who once got full of champagne and cracked up her automobile, killing a child. Never trust no society skirt.

Jax disagrees. At his next meeting with Rita, overwhelmed by those silver eyes, he mutters obscurely that she ought to leave this crooked business.

And off he goes to butler at the society affair, where a string orchestra plays languid minuets by Ferdinand Morton and jeweled belles drawl in their warm Coco-Cola accents. Before Jax can do ten cents worth of butlering, Rita Coleman slips in through a back door and sticks a pistol in his face.

No sooner does she tie him up than in stride three masked men, very tough. Instantly they recognize that she tied up Jax so the police wouldn't think he was with the robbers. Never trust a double-crossing moll.

They smack Rita down, tie her, and exit to rob and steal.

At this moment of high drama, when all seems lost, Big Jim steps from a closet, where he has been watching the proceedings. He frees Jax and they revive Rita, who then pours out her story. As you may have suspected, she had been duped by the mob and only now realizes how crooked it all was, although she was only trying to do good in atonement for her past errors.

But perhaps you anticipated this. In *Argosy*, beautiful, silver-eyed girls are usually innocent. If the Continental Op found out otherwise, that was in *Black Mask*, an altogether different magazine.

It is now action time. The Rings mask up in Rita's presence, casually blowing their carefully concealed cover. Into the hall they step, guns in hand, to confront the three thieves, who are wandering around out there, armed to the teeth, waiting for the shoot-out.

> The man in the lead swung his gun and fired—fired with nervous rapidity, a hysterical yell on his lips as he pulled the trigger.
> Big Jim Grood's weapon roared once. The man jerked forward as though an elastic band had suddenly tightened about his head and heels, snapping them together.
> A bullet clipped plaster from behind Jax Bowman's head. Another bullet ripped the shoulder of his coat. The gun in his hand thundered twice.

That the criminals fire first is another highly respected convention of these stories. By doing so, they force the heroes to shoot in self defense, which is quite different from murder, isn't it. About the only gun-using hero of the 1930s to fire first was the Spider, although The Shadow did it occasionally. Both those gentleman were death on wheels and you expected it of them. All the other heroes preferred to defend themselves, which they did with relish, corpse after corpse.

Now back to the festival:

> Big Jim Grood's gun...roared almost in Bowman's ear. The man on the window ledge spun half around, flung up his hands, pitched out into the night, falling head first.

After this highly satisfactory conclusion, the Rings look around for Rita. But she has fled the story and we will never see her again. Not that she entirely left the series, for she is a distinct off-stage presence in the second story, "No Quarter" (September 22, 1934).

In deference to your patience, the action of "No Quarter" will not be detailed, since you already have a good grasp on the plot and there is no reason to infuriate you by counting those marbles again. This story concerns a murderous con man and his deadly gang. Aided by a girl, Evelyn Mayer, who is moderately naughty but not really wicked, the con man swindles wealthy fools, then kills, them. The action starts in Mexico, leaps briefly to Hollywood, races headlong into the desert. Where Jax and Big Jim expose a confidence game involving lead bars painted gold and wipe out a fierce gang that simply snorts with blood lust.

During these agreeable proceedings, the girl, Evelyn, gets badly shot. She was, at the time, engaged in shooting down two thugs who were attempting to bushwhack the Rings. Seems that Evelyn had a girl friend named Rita— yes, indeed, the very same one—in whom she confided. Rita told her that the con men were really a pack of killers. The information so shocks Evelyn that she reforms completely. Since she also gets shot, her redemption is complete; in light fiction, nothing so completely absolves you from sin as a slight wound.

In gratitude to the girls, the Rings send them on a round-the-world cruise, and the series ends before they return. So those of you who were calculating that two girls and two Rings equal romance are going to be disappointed.

But where Gardner closes one door, he opens another. In this story, Miss Marchand reveals that she has guessed the secret of the Rings. Not only has she become slender and hazel-eyed but sharply intelligent, as well. She has noticed things: That when her employers fly off to some obscure place, the newspapers report that the Rings have gunned down a gang in the very place. She has wondered about the unmarked offices. She has puzzled over the relationship between wealthy Bowman and hardboiled Grood. She has, in fact, figured it all out. And one day, she appears in Jax's office to tell him what she has noticed.

Bowman: I presume that you're about to tell me that you wish to resign, is that it?
Miss M: No. I was about to tell you that if you ever wanted to use me for any activities outside of the office, I too could wear a mask with white rings about the eyeholes. . . . Some day. . .I think you'll need a girl who can think straight and who can shoot straight. When you do, please remember that I put in my application for the job.

You couldn't ask for a more solid piece of plot development than that. Nor can you easily find one that is more completely dropped.

Because nothing happens. Nothing at all.

The third story, "Bunched Knuckles" (September 21, 1935) was published a year later and nothing at all has changed. Miss Marchard continues to sort clippings. Rita and Evelyn continue to sail around the world. And the Rings take on a gang of swindlers who are into serial murder. Just why isn't clear until Bowman turns his full resources into investigation.

The mysterious offices occupied by Jax Bowman and Big Jim Grood clattered with feverish activity. Messages streamed in and out over the wires. Private detective agencies in different cities flung all available men into hurried investigations. . . .

Rhoda Marchand worked frantically, tabulating and classifying the various information received. . . .

It was the type of service which only a multi-millionaire could have commanded. Within a space of hours, trained investigators had covered the entire country with swift activity. From information which they had been able to furnish, cablegrams had been sent to foreign countries. In some instances, there had been trans-oceanic telephone conversations. Then, as suddenly as they had started, the investigation had ceased...because, from the information which had been received, Bowman was able to make several logical deductions.

Somebody is killing the heirs to the Proctor estate in England. Only three heirs are left: Sidney Proctor, who is exploring up the Amazon; Phyllis Proctor, who is young and beautiful; and Harry Cutting, who has vanished.

When you don't know what to do, stir things up. Big Jim passes himself off as Sidney, back from the Amazon. Immediately Phyllis appears, eyes glittering. A couple of pages later, Jax has been hit on the head and flown to an isolated cabin in the desert, where he is imprisoned with a girl—the real Phyllis Proctor.

Both are slated to be murdered. Phyllis is more valuable to the criminals dead. And a White Rings mask has been discovered in Jax's luggage.

As it happens, Jax doesn't die. He gets loose. He fights. He is almost shot, would have been shot. Except the Big Jim, in full, mask, comes blasting through the door at just the right time.

And how in the world did Big Jim locate his fellow mask? Well, he recognized the fake Phyllis, hunted up her lover, and pounded him (title of the story is, after all, "Bunched Knuckles") until he gave the address of the hideway.

Now free, Jax races after the escaping crooks in a airplane. After several paragraphs of acrobatics, he forces them to crash. So the White Rings' real identities are still secret—known only to Phyllis and Evelyn and Rita and Rhoda. But not one of them would ever let slip the least whisper of a hint of the secret she holds locked in her heart.

At this point, the White Rings series simply evaporates into the blue sky, leaving not a whisper behind, as far as this commentator can find out. Nor do they seem to have left any descendents. A pair of hooded crime-fighters (the Red Hood and The Black Hood) cropped up in two 1941 magazine series, but these were singles. They owed no allegiance to the White Rings or the Just Men convention.

By the time the White Rings appeared, years of fictional murder for excitement had dulled those delicate ethical filaments which are usually found in the Just Men stories. Although the Men tamed a little toward the last, they were ruthless and their self-appointed function was to remove surgically untouchable human cancers from society. At that, they warned three times before they killed.

Such an operation was fine for Edgar Wallace's audience. But Gardner's audience wanted dizzier stuff—more action, more suspense, more lovely tricky girls. The rushing narratives of the 1930s discarded many earlier fiction conventions. Particularly, they discarded the ethical justification for all this vigilante violence. Curiously enough, the ethical component was retained in the Spider novels, the most violent and bloody of all pulp magazine series. But such minor stuff as White Rings didn't bother with dull stuff, ethical justification and such, to excuse all those deaths.

The Rings were adventuring executioners. Their approach was touching in its simplicity: By some preposterous error of nature, criminals appear to be human. They are not. They are no more human that those sticky creatures oozing through Lovecraftian attics. Criminals are criminals by intent. They want to be criminals. Like the sooty minions of Hell, they cannot be rehabilitated. They can only be shot, cancelled by bullets.

The assumption becomes thoroughly ambivalent at this point. Presumably, criminals are shot to scare other criminals into being good. But, by definition, criminals cannot be deterred from criminality....

Well, well. Away with dreary thought. These stories were offered as casual entertainments, never intended to carry the weight of consistency. Accept the White Rings as they are— admirable men whose delight it is to hunt down criminals and shoot them dead and save the sweet girl from shame. They do that very well. We should delight in their dedication. And their stories do bounce merrily along.

Grace Note

She was a dainty diminutive girl for such violent life. We can suppose that her red hair had nothing to do with that. The genes of small, red-headed ladies with sherry-colored eyes are not intrinsically violent. Still, for Grace Culver, killing savagery came at least once a month.

She was slender, rather undistinguished of face. Possibly her nose was a bit long. But she was rather a beauty when she smiled. Her father, a policeman, died with five bullets in him from gangster guns. Perhaps this set the latent fury behind her eyes. We really can't tell. But the fury is obvious. It bursts out all through the stories of her adventures, in all manner of odd forms, subtly disguised, by circumstances, as necessity.

Necessity excuses much. Admittedly, Grace's occupation—a sort of associate private detective—required a degree of latent fury. Else how could she survive her cases? Even as the heroine of her own short story series in the mid-1930's *Shadow Magazine*, the odds against her seem excessive. At the end of her simplest investigations, homicidal menace stood slobbering. A bit of fury on her part was obligatory. She died, otherwise.

Come join Grace in the final minutes of any case. They are brutal minutes. You have been kicked, hit, tied. Beaten to the floor of a sordid den, you stare up into a thug's leveled hand cannon. You are bloody mouthed, nauseated. The world blears at the edges. Now the pistol hammer lifts back. Who cares now about your red hair, your sherry-colored eyes? Your dead father? If you have a gun, got God knows how, you use it.

The thug staggers. He tumbles down. And so it has happened again. From story to story, the situation repeats compulsively. The filthy room. The beaten girl. Pain. Gunfire. The repetitive death.

It is strike hit shoot in the underside of the pulp magazine world—back in folio 5, immediately after the main novel. Things are simple, back there in folio 5. The thug dies. You live. Another case completed in a drift of powder fumes. Culver, of the Noonan Detective Agency, squeaks through again.

Never count the dead. Never ask why this situation has happened again.

Her smile was rare but extraordinarily sweet.

Grace Culver appeared in 20 short stories in *The Shadow Magazine* from 1934-1937. She was, in fact, the first of the magazine's series characters, aside from The Shadow, himself. Her first appearance, titled "Scoop," was published August 1, 1934. The author was Roswell Brown, a house name used by Jean Francis Webb.

At the time, *The Shadow Magazine* was published twice a month, dated the 1st and the 15th. Beginning with "Scoop, Grace appeared in six consecutive first-of-the month issues. In the beginning, she was a reporter for *The Banner*— a reporter in the old Chicago style: Get your hands on the story. Put it under your arm. Run.

It helped that she knew the inspector in charge of that first recorded murder. Tim Noonan: Even then, his resignation from the police department was written. A detective agency glimmered behind his eyes. Well, a big knobby old giant of an Irishman should have ambition. And Grace is the same as a daughter to him, since her father, you understand, was killed. But a woman shouldn't mess in murder cases.

The sherry-colored eyes flicker at that. The undistinguished face flashes with momentary rage. Run along, Grace; buy a double chocolate soda. Keep safe. There's murder and a jewel robbery and Big Tim Noonan must clear it and get to organizing his agency.

But feminine smiles do wonders to police officers, particularly in 1934 pulp magazines. So, after all, Grace is allowed to see the murder scene. And she has this hunch, the first of many. However, Big Tim out-weighs her by 150 pounds and 18 inches. His murder theory is, therefore, correct. As for Grace, her stocking is snagged: She mutters in "truly feminine rage."

Still she follows her hunch, checks the room of the suspect. Sure enough, the stolen jewels are in his drawer. At this point, he appears silently from the background. And it's close. Terribly close. If she hadn't pulled the rug from under his feet, the Culver series would have ended right there, back in the fifth folio. But he falls, loses his gun. She gets it first, and so Big Tim gets the murder and his completed case. It's agency bound for him, then, taking with him young Jerry Riker to help with the detection. And Grace, too, who gives up her newspaper work to perform light typing for them.

The formula pulp detective story was an art form, as limited and vigorous as a boogie-woogie chorus. The stories throbbed with action, violence, movement peaking to the blood bath. What passed for character development was, most frequently, the iteration of mannerisms. The character was a named shell whose simple idiosyncrasies enlivened any paragraph unmarked by death and fire. Thus Grace was red-headed and curious. She reveled in double-chocolate sodas. She was bedecked with symbols for femininity—beads, high heels, lipstick— most wonderful to ranks of male readers. And, since women are widely understood not to reason, she specialized in hunches and acted upon these, madly indifferent to personal risk.

Customarily, the Culver stories, are compressed into 12-13 double column pages, containing perhaps 6,500 words. The length imposed certain rigidities on the narrative. Action occurred in well-defined surges of formula: Introduction and problem. First hard action; first desperate danger. Then trapped. The beating. The holocaust.

The stories roar along under vast internal pressure. Furs are hijacked. Unprotected laundries explode. The heir vanishes, leaving only a blood-sodden bed. The crooks have it all their own way, down in their fetid lanes. How can they realize that the painted dance-hall girl, the dumb secretary, the babbling society deb (all of these redheaded) is Grace Nemesis, fixed by coincidence on their trails.

Tim cannot shunt her to less dangerous activities. "You're a secretary, Carrots. Not a detective." He is never successful. Fortunately for him. Big solid Tim, he is too slow for this frenzied environment. Away after the wily snipe, he rushes, sack in hand, .38 in the other. He will reappear in the final pages, there to be shot in the face or shoulder. But he will do merciless execution on the hordes, menacing his girl.

It is hard, being the head of a detective agency when you are so often wrong. No matter. Grace will always lead. She is the mind of the Noonan Agency. What is opaque to Tim is transparent to her. Faced with the typewriter and twelve uninteresting letters to transcribe, her heart rises on wings. She has this hunch, this new angle on the case, drawing her off to violence. Her plain face brightens. She seizes purse and is gone. From sunny 1930's streets fades the sound of an automobile, driven hard.

Her investigations are sensible and direct. Yet they lead at once to situations of appalling personal danger. She plunges into a vortex of brutality, instantly to be trapped and helpless in the clutches of criminals scarcely human.

You have met these criminals before: the evil woman of powerful personality and cryogenic emotions. The businessman, lost to greed, his self satisfaction screening homicidal frenzy. And the gangland minions, perverted and dreadful, slouching through filthy black halls, hunching in fetid rooms, amid a hard metallic stink.

They are massive brutes. They glow with undirected anger, mindless, terrible. They are not human, really. So they can be killed individually or collectively without blame. No one is held accountable for their deaths. It is not murder. Merely extermination.

Against these stands Grace, Jeanne de Arc in high heels. Alone. From the beginning, her cases always pit her alone against the gangs.

9/1/34. "Dumb Blond" involves the hijacking of cosmetics. The gang is tough as all get out. It takes Grace fully 13 pages to put an end to the ghastly activities of the killer moll and her cohorts. In "War Paint," 10/1/34, the evil sister traps the good sister and wealthy husband aboard their yacht. To save them Grace moves against a crew of roughs and. . . .

Flame coughs red in the night. A red fountain spurts from the thug's maimed hand. Struck by a steel bar, Grace sees red tortured haze. The shot thug totters, clutching his stomach. A froth of bloody bubbles. . .But now the pirate crew rushes from below decks. Desperately, she smashes a pistol into a snarling face. Red gore. He plunges back into the hatchway. Furiously struggling, Grace locks shut the hatch, her rapidly numbing arms in an ecstasy of pain. As the villain darts up the boarding ladder, her pistol levels. As he falters, Noonan and the harbor guards arrive. Crime crushed. Thirteen pages.

Through 1934, into 1935, one continuous storm of violence. Counterfeiting. Arson. Extortion. Bullets and brutality. Tim is shot in the face once, twice. Jerry is shot all over. Grace, more fragile, is shot in the shoulder, the most neutral part of the feminine anatomy.

But the head is the usual target. Blows to the jaw, the mouth. Chairs crash skull. Ink wells batter. Or paperweights. Acid sears eyes. Boiling grease scalds snarling faces. In a hot red stream, blood spurts. Shot in the stomach, a killer crashes dead. And another. Her father, the policeman, taught Grace to shoot when she was a little quiet girl.

Through 1935, disguised as a cheap woman, vividly lipsticked, in red-flowered dress and mascara, she prowls crime's musty corridors. From the darkness, arms clutch her in a steely grip. She is beaten. Take that, you little hell cat. Tied. But she escapes. Bullets flail the wicked. Justice triumphs.

Perhaps, in the strictest sense, her associate, Jerry Riker, does not receive justice. As the young male lead of the series, we expect great things of him. But these are not to be. In the early days of the Noonan Agency, he gallantly offers his strength for Grace's protection. Momentarily, wan warmth glimmers between them. But the role of passive beloved is not for Grace. She fumes impatiently. Beyond the door lie clues, excitement. Dismissing their dinner date, away she darts, hot on a lead. You may come, too, Jerry. But his luck is always bad. If he follows he will promptly be shot and tied up and will languish, an ignominious prisoner, while the action rages. Other heroes sweep the pliant lady from the gape of doom. Jerry's fate is otherwise. He is forever the rescued. It is little Grace, bloody and triumphant, who strikes his manacles and leads him stumbling forth.

His status thus diluted, he diminishes from month to month. Remember our dinner date, Grace. Remember our theatre party, Grace. You need a cozy little home, Grace....

How badly he misjudges. The potential husband of 1934 is the warm friend of 1935, is the valued associate of 1936. He finds it sad. She offers him a thin red smile and pats his arm, a soothing reflex, gracefully extricating her from more complex emotions.

Her room is plain, a little bare. A frilly lamp. A tautly-made bed. The photograph of her martyred father peers sharply from the mantel. Perhaps she has other friends, a close girl friend, perhaps, with whom she can field-strip the Colt .25 auto, or demonstrate those odd heirlooms her father left, like artifacts from Doc Savage's workshop: The lipstick case that squirts acid. The cigarette case with a hollow back. The necklace, intricately wrought, that folds amazingly into a skeleton key, formidable to all locks.

We meet none of her woman friends. Her personal life is smooth and blank, an ivory ball. What key, intricately wrought, opens her secret heart, we are not to know. Her professional friends—the police, the newspaper crowd —she greets with friendly impersonality. All casual she is with them, with off-hand tongue.

"You're the well-known pal in need. I'll love you till I'm old and gray, I will."

There will be little enough love.

1935 closes on a yammer of machine guns. The sherry-colored eyes glint with excitement. There follows airliner hijacking. A murder case in a Long Island movie studio. The gambling ship is heisted. The case of the kidnapped editor and the disappearing room. Slaughter at the amusement park. Seven cases in 1936. Some are mystery puzzles. Others race across the countryside, chasing or chased, the night enlivened by gunfire. There are new locales. Fewer gangland dens. Fewer ravening mobs for a 110-pound girl to crush, thug by thug—violence to violence. In one mad leap, she seizes the loose pistol. No longer does she hesitate or wound. Gunfire shocks the room and Grace, unmoved, stands over the new dead. Locked in the noisome cellar, hunted through the sound studio by the killer, alone in waist-deep water with a killer in the shadows. Unconscious in the gas-filled room. Caught by arsonists in the gasoline-saturated house, her broken ankle blazing with pain, Jerry tied, unconscious....

Sill, a resourceful woman will find a way.

Her sharp, raspberry-colored nails gouge in....

Her spike heel digs the instep of the clutching crook....

Her pistol snuggles against a silk-sheathed leg....

Her curls, her compact, her garter holster. The trick necklace that is a key. The trick belt that is a picklock. The chiffon collar and Indian flint charm bracelet. Her skirts. The necklace. The accouterments of femininity that dazzle the reader and lure him from issue to issue. Accent the woman. Play up the female angle. The little girl against the gorillas and she wins out.

The thoughts "linked together in her brain like bangles on a goodluck bracelet."

Was she ever, you wonder, troubled by retrospection? Did the pulse of action totally fill her life, denying memory of brutality in darkness and men limp in smoke-choked rooms. She was not one for the rhetoric of remembrance. Facts she understood. Fact discrepancies she reacted to with a sensitivity surprising in a nature so lacking in shadows.

Pedants have described ladies whose emotions twist in hidden flame. Beneath their waking minds, some wish themselves helpless, battered by brutal males. Struck in the face, the mouth. That splendid pain. (Even in the foulest den, they are never struck lower than the hips, even when helpless, unconscious, even then.) But the pulp story relies on no such dark psychology. Its meaning remains in the sunshine. A cool light glows through the story. It illuminates all corners. The simple people discharge themselves in violence. They feel rage and fear but no complicated passion. Action, action. All is lucid. There are no complexities. None at all. She was a dainty girl of violent life.

It ends in 1937. Three Culver stories appear. An auto racing episode, with a climactic gunfight on track at the height of the race. Then, another arson case (fire was often met in Grace's life). And finally, a wild struggle to save a crusading judge from murder. Using a flashlight to bluff two killers, she saves the judge, saves Jerry, saves herself. But not the series The Redsie Culver stories vanish from *The Shadow Magazine*.

1937 was a strong year for series characters in the shadow. Sheridan Doome, special investigator for the Navy, and Danny Garrett, the Shoeshine Boy detective, were in the first flowering of their long careers. Hook McGuire, the bowling detective, appeared in seven issues that year. And in December, the Whisperer series would begin. Perhaps the competition was too intense. Or perhaps stories of lethal red-haired secretary-detectives no longer drew the dimes as once they did.

So the silence came to Grace. As it would come to Hook, to Danny, and, ultimately, to The Shadow, himself. But in fiction, as in nature, nothing is wasted. So the themes of Grace's fiction, brushed and refurbished, set forth other tables: That the jungle is just outside the door, in the sunshine around the corner. That you are on your own. The police, impotent, arrive too late. If there is to be law and justice, you must administer it yourself. And good shall win out, though beaten helpless, through the final great exertion, at the very last gasp.

Although the stories stopped, her career must obviously have continued. You might have seen her during the late 1930's, a slight redhaired girl with rather a long nose. At lunchtime in Liggett's, she bends over a double chocolate soda. Her sharp raspberry nails tap the counter. She contemplates the deeps of the glass, not seeing the liquid, but motives, actions. A formless intuition runs along her nerves. The feeling is familiar, a rise of knowledge she did not know she had, hidden behind the soft plain face, the assessing eyes, from the secret places no key has yet unlocked.

Neat powder conceals the small white scars around her mouth. Hidden by her dress, the pale shoulder skin is puckered by bullet wounds. Other scars are less obvious. Her face shows neither rage nor remorse nor solitude nor regret.

The soda glass gurgles empty. She leaves the store, moving through the crowd, with the profound skill of the New Yorker. The air smells of exhaust, frying food, soot. A hint of April cuts through it all, a cool thin smell of ripening, against the gray concrete. As she walks, her eyes probe and test. In the glass of a window, she sees her face reflected, pale and plain. She does not recognize herself. Who stares into her eyes? Once her father said: "Watch all the time. Listen and watch." Perhaps he said that. The memory is vaguely unpleasant.

Her nerves pulse. Consider the current cases. Something is false and hidden there. It is, it is....Off through the crowd she hurries, pressed by knowledge and time. Her red hair gleams within the crowd. Gone. To find her own ripening, or not, within the gray concrete of the 1930's.

The Tall Man

Biscayne Bay, mid-1930's. Behind the dock lies Miami, smaller then. Offshore, salt water glistens. The air smells hotly of tar and salt, fish, creosoted wood.

The tall man ambles along the dock. He is dressed solidly in black: black tennis shoes, trousers, polo shirt. Himself, he is very brown. At the end of the dock, he swings long legs aboard a 45-foot boat—technically, a Chesapeake Bay five-log bugeye. It is also black hull, sails, sail covers, masts. The tall man disappears off inside it. The fat blue revolver in his pocket doesn't show at all.

His name is Oscar Sail, and he is tall, extremely tall. Shockingly tall. People, seeing him, are impelled to poetry:

> They sure left the faucet on too long when they poured you...
> You're about two men tall and half a man wide, aren't you?

Of him, Lester Dent, writer of the story, said:

Sail would have been all right if he had been a foot or two shorter. His face would never wear a serious look successfully. Too much mouth. Sun and salt water was on its way to ruining his hair....Bare feet had long toes. Weather had gotten to all of the man a lot."

Only two Sail stories appeared, both in *Black Mask*, that intense magazine. They are splendid. Critical recognition of them continues to climb as they appear and reappear, like splash rings, through the anthologies.

The first story, "Sail," was published in the October 1936 issue. The editor's preface reads:

A lot of costly baubles get lost, and a whole lot of people get hurt trying to find them.

Yes, it's sort of a treasure hunt. It's night. A Miami dock. Silence after a scream. Sail frantically hacking up a fish, using its blood to conceal a human blood spill. Finished barely in time, he bluffs a policeman, investigating. Under the dock is a corpse. Sail hauls this to a nearby island, searches it, carries off clues, returns to his boat. In rapid succession, a woman attempts to trick him (he drugs her), a man tries to kidnap him (he escapes), the police arrive to check him out (he is uncommunicative). Next day, using the information removed from the corpse, he hunts out a charter captain named Andopolis, slugs this wild fellow unconscious, hauls him to an isolated place for questioning. It is a mistake. The captain wakes, raving, breaks a goodly number of Sail's ribs. Obviously it was the wrong way to investigate.

Representing himself as a shady type, Sail summarizes the background for Andopolis (and, of course, the eager reader).

Andopolis, you see, has located the hulk of a private yacht that went glittering down, with the jewels of the owner's wife. Andopolis decides to salvage it secretly with the aid of a friend, the friend's wife, and her brother. The friend decides to learn the location of the wreck, then eliminate Andopolis. The plan, while promising, is marred in execution. The friend ends up, dead, under Sail's dock. So much for background.

Andopolis and Sail uneasily agree to cooperate, head back for Miami. On the way their car is shot off the road into a canal. Wife and brother did it. They capture the captain, take him off. Sail, eventually, returns to his boat. There, the police force him to disclose that he represents the company which insured the jewels. Disgruntled, the police leave. Sail locates the house boat where sister and brother are torturing Andopolis. They were torturing him; now he is loose and running amok, and is stopped only after a climax of some considerable violence. Sail finally learns the location of the wreck, which he wanted, and a term in the hospital, which he didn't.

So, boldly, the first story.

It is a beauty. The sentences, exact as a knife slash, crackle with precisely observed detail:

> The fish shook its tail as the knife cut off its head.
> Two stubborn crabs and some seaweed hung to the Greek...
> Blick had his lips rolled in till he seemed to have no lips.
> The wrist and arm were more flexible than that much rubber would have been.

The sentences drive furiously along. Adjectives are few. Verbs carry the load.

The car broke most of its windows going down the canal bank. The canal must have been six feet deep. Its tea-colored water filled the machine at once. Sail's middle hurt, and he had lost his air, and had to breathe in, and there was nothing but water.

Or...

The man began big at the top and tapered. His small hands were callused, dirt was ground into the calluses, the nails broken. His face was darker than his hair.

Or...

Sail stumbled through the handiest door. Waves of pain jumped from his ribs to his toes, from ribs to hair. The bandages turned red, and it was not from mercurochrome.

If descriptions are laconic, spoken dialogue is downright sparse. Initially, Sail speaks in two to four word sentences. When he finally speaks at length, it is to snow an investigating officer. Later in the story, he permits himself a second burst of words, again for a purpose—to persuade Andopolis to trust him.

The more words, the more deceit. A dependable equation. The same purpose lurks behind the freshets of language pouring from Police Captain Cripp. His splendid oral meanderings conceal an impassive intelligence, waiting patiently as a trap under water.

These bursts of dialogue are mortised neatly into the story. They break up the staccato of one and two sentence paragraphs, all busy with verbs. Aside from the informational content of the dialogue, its longer rhythms and sound clusters periodically slow the narrative pace. It is just sufficient to avoid the monotony of the monotone.

The story moves along a chain of encounters, each involving strong personal tension or action. Sail, constantly on stage, meets successive waves of crises. His personal danger steadily increases. As this develops, he becomes progressively weaker. (Remember, he is rushing about with a chest full of broken ribs.) With terrible speed, the story converges on that point where his weakness will fall below his ability to cope with the ballooning violence.

Personality driving action? You bet. Sail's personal responsibility drives him through the final pages. If you commit to a course of action, you are responsible—you are ethically required—to conclude it. Familiar words, these. They underpin much of the 1930's hardboiled detective fiction, which was heavy on ethical positions, in its day.

The second Sail story contains an even stronger statement of personal responsibility. This, titled "Angelfish," was published in December 1936. Ellery Queen quotes Dent as saying that it is "an example of the word savagery 'Black Mask' brought out in its writers."

"Angelfish" opens with a young lady, Nan Moberly, stretched out under the Florida sun. She is pretending to have been shot and robbed to confuse some people who, at least, want to rob her. Sail, hired to help, thinks "...this stunt takes the goofy prize." But the fake robbery begins as planned. Sail, seizing a mysterious box from her purse, flees, pursued and shot at by two men, Saunders and Caesar, who seem to know Nan. Sail returns to Miami in a taxi driven by a one-legged man named John Silver—an obvious nautical. From a hotel, he calls Nan. She sounds strange. She assures him that the scheme worked fine. Someone will go to his boat, pick up the box. Sail immediately opens the box, finds it filled with aerial photographs—apparently of an undeveloped oil field.

From Nan's intonation, Sail concludes that she is in trouble. When the messenger arrives—a fat young osteopath names Sonny—Sail tussels briefly (and painfully) with him in a locker, leaves for Nan's hotel. There he discovers her tied hand and foot in bed. Under the bed is the corpse of the doctor who backed her story of being wounded. At this point, two large, fat men, Doll and Tom, emerge gun-first from a closet. They get the film, Sail, Nan. All adjourn to a nearby boathouse. There Sail escapes, capturing and nearly drowning Doll. But Tom gets away with Nan in a speed boat. Returning to his boat with prisoner, Sail finds Sonny gone. Tied up in his place is the taxi driver, John Silver.

By now, the hurricane, which has been developing since paragraph four, is ripe to break. Sail learns that Tom has taken Nan to Angelfish Creek. The leader of the bunch has a cabin cruiser moored there. Sail elects to go after Nan, since Angelfish offers no protection from the hurricane. With him goes Doll, tied up, and John Silver, who it develops, is an oil company detective.

At Angelfish, the cabin cruiser is already in storm trouble. Boarding her, Sail fights through the gang, one at a time. The ending is of extended viciousness. Nan is saved. The villain dies out of sight in a scene of repellant power.

"Angelfish" is a superlative piece of work, emotional, coherent, intense. Its effect is grandly magnifies by the device of coupling the development of the investigation and the development of the hurricane. They ripen together. As Sail's investigation reaches its conclusion, the hurricane (actually its fringe) reaches climactic ferocity. Prose counterpoint.

The characters are as violent as the hurricane. Each is vulnerable; each makes mistakes. But not one is a push-over. Five bad men appear in "Angelfish." Each one is hard, efficient, authentically vicious. It is no coincidence that four out of the five are overweight. The parallel between fatness and evil, fatness and perversion, is a recurring symbol in Dent. But whatever fatness means, it does not stand for inefficiency. The bad men are marvelously efficient. They do considerable damage to Sail. He amply returns the favor.

Both "Sail" and "Angelfish" are technical triumphs of the hard-boiled detective school. The prose glitters with images from reality:

—Seagulls fly up, startled by gunshots.
—Puffy gray blisters cluster around the tortured man's eyelids.
—Sail stumbles over coconuts littered under a palm tree.
—Hurricane swells slather the beach under acres of foam.

Clinically selected detail establishes a sense of physical presence.

She was a long, blue-eyed girl who lay squarely on her back with sun shining in her mouth. Her teeth were small and her tongue was flat, not pointed, and there was about two whiskey glassfuls of scarlet liquid in her mouth.

Beautiful exact stuff. The illusion of realism is maintained through both stories. The descriptions are polished like oriental lacquer. The lovely lean narrative line is graceful as ballet.

And it is all illusion. Under the shining surface, the prose is dense with melodrama, powered by romance. That is Romance in the traditional sense. The Quest-Grail kind. Out there, wait oceans of oil, masses of diamonds. Out there, distant as the Emerald City, glimmers wealth. Out there. Out there. The melodramatic action, loaded with events unexpected, matters harsh, presses on toward the oil, toward the diamonds.

It is a curiously effective combination: the romantic goal; the unremitting action; the realistic world enclosing these. It is all beautifully balanced. Your critical sense suspends itself. First you accept the precisely observed details. Then you slip, unwitting, into acceptance of the compressed time frame. Finally the growing savagery of the participants seems almost normal as the paragraphs rush toward the ultimate killing.

In subtle ways, the illusion of reality is sustained. All the characters make mistakes. They misjudge situations. They leap too quickly to conclusions. Their clever stratagems curdle or fail outright. They inhabit, in fact, the same imperfect world as we do, and suffer our measure of confusion and error:

—The two fat killers get stuck coming from the closet.

—In the climactic fight aboard the cruiser, Sail falls over a body, loses his gun, and lets the leader escape.

—Police, trying to chase a stolen automobile, forget to turn on the ignition switch and can't get their motor started.

—Sail, attempting to escape from a sunken car, can't get either the doors or windows open.

—As the big cabin cruiser sinks, "Mattresses, folding chairs, canned goods, and (the unconscious osteopath) sloshed around on the floor."

Dent specializes in these little flashes of observation, the touch of nature. He sees, with delighted eye, the petty malfunction, the minor accident, the unplanned confusion. He observes that action is not neat, but cluttered, confused, full of uncoordinated frenzy. These incidents, the small change of living, seem coupled in his mind with the stuff of reality. He will use them, through the years, with increased care. But they remain a distinctive element of his writing, appearing in all contexts, at all times, as if, here, he had a finger on a fundamental life chord, from which a person might reconstruct reality, if he were so inclined.

Lester Dent's writing career opened about 1931, closed with his death in 1959. In 1936, when Sail appears, Dent had already published extensively in the pulps. Thirty-six of his Doc Savage novels had appeared. A Shadow novel had been purchased (but was not yet released). Several serials were about to appear in *Argosy*. And his short stories were broadcast, like dandelion seed, throughout the pulp field.

In most of this published work, there is no such thing as a developed character. Instead, there are mobs of people who may be described as Extraordinary Peculiars—individuals of curious traits and odd personal characteristics. They are bizarre and fascinating. Each possesses one large peculiarity and at least a couple of minor ones. This fixes them in the reader's eye and instantly identifies them whenever they appear in the story. Such tags are most useful to an author, particularly one whose characters do not so much generate the action, as ride upon it, like kites in the wind.

These are the characters of Dent's formula writing. They exist without family, without beliefs or taste or background. They exist brilliantly in one dimension. They are painted cardboard, devised to support the narrative as it boils along. For twenty minutes you marvel with them. Then you lay aside the shallow story and you, yourself, go out into the swarming series of contacts, subtle, intense, continuous, that is the reality of your personal life. You live in a seethe of silent meanings. You read an attitude in the emphasis of a word, in the movement of a head. You compute your own position in others' minds by a complexly continuous sensing of the words and emotions, spoken or otherwise as these flow from human interaction. This interaction, so intricate and personal, is rarely depicted in literature. But it forms the stuff of our lives and we are immersed in it from our first human touch.

The pulp story made no effort to reflect this complexity. Its purpose was amusement, another form of reality. Through the magazines, simplified people competed violently for something of value. Lester Dent was very, very skillful at constructing these antic stories. He was a master of narrative movement, and his busy little amusements please us still.

At length, they did not please him.

By which we recognize that sensitivity, in Mr. Dent, that lies in us, ourselves, with which we compare our inner lives to the world outside. So, Mr. Dent, listening to the flow of language around him. Listening to men speak. Watching how people conduct their lives and commit themselves to what they feel is of value. So Mr. Dent, examining the look of sunlight, comparing this with his words. Finding how they lacked. He examined his characters as they struggled and bled across the paragraphs of *Doc Savage* and *Ten Detective Aces* and *Scotland Yard* and *Popular Magazine*. He is very sensitive, is Mr. Dent. Very perceptive. He knows that the question is not what a man feels, given thus-and-so violent circumstances: he knows what the man feels. His problem is to get that feeling into saleable sentences in magazines that rarely publish anything truly reflecting how man feels and acts under stress. His next problem is to load that information into sentences that do not sacrifice the pace of the paragraph. The third problem is to allow real emotion into the story in such a way that it contributes significantly to story development. Anyone can slop emotion into a piece of fiction. It is the selection of significant feeling that matters. It is the selection that makes art.

At *Black Mask*, certain of the writers were practicing selection. They had been devising complex contemporary characters whose choice and decisions drove stripped-down, hard-action narratives.

At its best, Black Mask published the sparest prose of any magazine in the country. Joe Shaw used to admonish his new writers, 'Prune and cut, don't use a single word that you can do without...'

Character and situation interacted. It was art. Perhaps no one but Raymond Chandler knew it then. Words like "art" are applied fifty years later, after the scholars have squared their private inclinations with their public positions.

Many of the Black Mask technical solutions, while specialized, addressed problems that concerned Dent. The results of his personal contact with that body of work, and with editor Joseph T. Shaw, were immediate.

The *Black Mask* experience split his work into two primary branches. The commercial branch—*Doc Savage, Argosy,* the short stories for pulp markets—proceeded essentially unchanged. The second branch, beginning with the Sail stories, set off in another direction, forming a body of work significantly different from his commercial writing and one that caused him a lot of pain and personal trouble.

Lester was an extremely facile writer and craftsman but was dissatisfied with his Doc Savage writing and tried to do better things. I believe that he contributed only two stories to Black Mask...which he wrote and rewrote. He spent at least two years trying to crash the slick paper magazines and I believe he wrote twenty stories and finally sold one.

In general terms, Dent used reality as a matrix for his story. Sharply drawn people, realistically described in a detailed setting, worked with problems deriving as much from their attitudes to each other as from their wants. The ultimate evolution of this branch of work was not publication in the slicks, but that fine series of "Lady" mystery novels (five of them using the work "Lady" in the title) which began appearing in 1946. By a strange quirk, some of the new writing techniques merged with the Doc Savage 1947-48 novels, and Doc rose again, marvelously enlivened, in a fresh series of novelettes.

All this first began in 1936. Not that Sail suddenly materialized from the air. Nothing so simple. Sail lies in the mainstream of Dent heroes. He shares familiar characteristics with them. True, he is presented in richer detail. He is drawn with deeper shadows, more revealing highlights. But he is of the Dent brotherhood. Know other Dent heroes and you have insight into Sail, himself.

To begin with, most of these heroes evolved from the same genetic pool. They were physically powerful men. Fast on their feet, faster of mind. Each was gifted with certain wonderful peculiarities.

As a class, most of them were tinkerers, gadgeteers. Few of them traveled armed. Rather, they festooned themselves with equipment—electrical, mechanical, chemical. This they applied to the dismay of the lawless. Sail is atypical, here. Devices play no large part of his style. He uses few—a mirror on a pole is about his speed. Or tear gas shells in his revolver. Of ID papers in a trick beer can. These classify less as gadgets than forethought.

Dent's people are all long on forethought. Some few (Clark Savage, Jr., for example) are exceptionally sensitive to the immediate situation. Extrapolating from a possibility, they erect complex chains of plans. They provide for contingencies at ten removes, grandmasters of living chess.

They are exceptionally sensitive to interpersonal nuances, mainly between men. With women, their competence level tumbles. They know it. It makes them uneasy. Even as you; even as I.

One common characteristic was the ability to learn rapidly. Their minds, flexible and bright, instantly gulped a situation. If occasionally, they lacked experience, they could always handle problems by sheer mental competence. Inexperience does not mean impotence. Not in the least.

These heroes and their multi-colored adventures are cheerfully cockeyed. Their world is rich with shades and tones. Adventure capers before them. Any moment, a splendid girl may cry for help. Singular men will appear, each an enigma. Away they will all hurrah, breathless, through wondrous danger and exertion.

Sheer joy. Fun. If the hero is often scared—sometimes hunted by the police—if he has only 5¢ and a two-day hunger—bear with it. Soon, the girl—Adventure—Glittering Events. Life is strenuous. Good. A magnificent 86-page golden ball.

Dent's early crime fiction reveals a somewhat darker mood. More violence, more death. Master criminals and their minions aspire to massive loot, massive crimes. Against these, Dent's investigators traverse the warrens of their cities with acrid efficiency. Each man (tall, strong, astute) accomplishes amazing feats of competence to crush the lawless hordes.

Matters differ in Sail's world. Exaggerated virtue and exaggerated criminality are not primary factors here. Sail's experience is less vividly colored. His world resonates to more complex keys. Fundamental differences separate Oscal Sail of *Black Mask* from Click Rush or Doc Savage or the others. If Sail developed from Dent's prior work, he is still his own man. He is realized in dimension—a hard-boiled competent who has not lost his humanity.

In both stories, the tone is tough. It is a calculated effect. It comes from the terse, bright prose and from the violence that suddenly bursts, like nightmare, from out of ordinary surroundings. It is horror by daylight, the shock of dislocation as the familiar comes apart.

Sail enters a hotel room It is quiet, pleasant, overlooking a sunny beach and ocean. A woman lies in bed. All familiar. Comforting. False. The sunshine is brassy, the ocean calm because a hurricane is only hours away. The woman in bed is tied hand and foot. Under the bed is a man with a broken neck. Inside a closet, waiting, listen two killers with guns.

Surface reality is utterly flimsy. It will disintegrate without warning, plunging you into howling savagery.

—That pleasant, plump young man, blundering landlubberishly on deck, killed a man not two hours ago.
—That big fellow with the comical toothache, avoiding sweets, will explode without warning into berserk frenzy.
—That car, bumping along a rough coral back road toward Miami, is about to get shot to pieces and plunge into a canal.

The reality you see is sham. Killing violence is a breath away. Such major social elements as the police or big business are tainted with self interest. No stability in this world.

It is the familiar hardboiled world of movies, books, short stories. Hemingway, West, Caine, O'Hara worked here. Hammett, Chandler, Daley, Gardner worked here. Here moral constraints have collapsed. Ethical constraints do not exist. A man's behavioral guides are imposed by himself, on himself, to stabilize himself against surrounding chaos. Beyond the window, sunshine; under the bed, a dead face.

Rely only on yourself. Expect from others lies and half-truths. In both stories only two characters do not lie to Sail. Both are minor. In turn, he deals enthusiastically in half truths and deception as he works through a grisly haze of evasion and lies.

For all this, Sail is not particularly hardboiled, in the sense of being emotionally callused. He can assume the attitude—but it is for effect. Otherwise, his emotions are unfettered. He feels. He reacts. It puts him in human terms. He gets scared enough for hand tremors. Fumbling over a corpse nauseates him. A strange girl in his boat surprises him to headbumping speechlessness— although her presence doesn't slow down his mind a bit. The immediate threat of being shot makes him sweat; again, it doesn't slow his mind. He is, shortly, one tough, astute fellow, full of recognizable human emotions.

Now *Black Mask* was dense with hardboiled investigators. Some used one gun, some two. Characteristically, they are steeped in knowledge of that dim social interface where politics, crime, and money meet. Corruption is no new thing to them. Nor is integrity. Although they see a lot less of that.

Some chill sense of waste hangs about them, some terrible hint of abilities wasted and years lost down in the unlit social deeps where the predators hunt. So the investigators frequently show stress. They handle weapons with too great facility. They are too expert at handling people. They have large fondness for the great warmer, bourbon. Or they are that fraction too remote, too cool, marks of a man watching from his personal abyss.

Some of these characteristics appear in Sail. But not many. You won't make much sense out of Sail by thrusting him into the private investigator's mold. He won't fit. Long ago, he reached some personal compromise with his internal tensions. In consequence, he withdrew from the city to salt water. In Dent's private shorthand, that equals salvation of a sort. In the city, a man fester. But salt water purifies him, if he can be purified at all.

Like Travis McGee, twenty years later, Sail finds that life on the ocean edge cleanses. Salt water provides him with a moral base, sharpening his perception of individual freedom and individual responsibility. These are the classic attributes of the individual who holds himself removed from society. The assumption, here, is that society naturally corrupts. If you are a part of it, you are corrupt, wittingly or not.

So far Sail has escaped this. He is not self-destructive, not warped by obscure psychological wounds. The constant gibes at his height slide by him. He chooses to live alone in the monastic neatness of his boat. He regards that boat with controlled passion. Other human contacts may be restrained, but for the boat, "Sail," that black surrogate, he has pride and care.

Pride does not imply softness. He uses the bugeye as he uses himself, to the limits of endurance and beyond. But only in a service of importance. As he drives himself, rib-shattered and agonized, from violence to violence in "Sail," so he drives the bugeye, in "Angelfish," to the bursting of its sails.

He has a particular awareness of what is needful and what is not. This knowledge makes Sail unique among the Dent's characters. Knowing that there are limits natural to man or craft, he knows, also, when it is necessary to exceed those limits, whatever the cost in canvas and bone.

Which argues a value system of some sensitivity. A curious thing to find in a pulp magazine. (And not at all the type thing our parents thought we would find.) Well, sure, Sail is hardboiled enough, when he has to be. But that is not a permanent attitude. It is only one way of handling a problem.

Sail, grabbing a fistfull of fat lips, held most of the sound back. Sail twisted the lips cruelly, ground them against the teeth, pounded the man's head on the floor.
Sail was set. He had his belt strapped tight around his fist. The man got down on all fours to mew his pain. Sail hit again, then unwrapped the belt, blew on his fist, worked the fingers.
Sail thought of the doctor with the broken neck, and of his own arm which still hurt, and he kicked hard, permanently altering the young man's dentistry and driving him back to land in the water-filled cabin.

None of this brutality is for pleasure. It is only pragmatism in action— the way of least complication and greatest effect.

Complexity, he distrusts. Nan Moberly's scheme—bullet holes, blood in the mouth—is too elaborate. He instinctively dislikes it. He has the realist's feel for directness. When a girl appears in his boat, claiming marriage to him, his instinct is not to fence with words but to feed her truth serum and proceed to questions. When his activities reach a point violent enough to engage police attention, he obligingly reports to the police first—although the amount of truth he passes on wouldn't choke a butterfly.

In common with other private investigators from the pulps, his relations with the police are more cool than cordial. They constrain that independence he has carefully treasured up. He resents the police captain's artful maneuvering and reduces his cooperation accordingly.

...If you hadn't tried to fancy pants around last night, I'd have showed you something then.

The "something" are his credentials as a private investigator. The police have just advised that they are going to arrest him and sit on him till they find out a little more about what he's doing in Miami. At this point, Sail, who has carried reasoned defiance, bluff, and evasion as far as is safe, now shows his papers. The police clear out. They ignore the fact that he probably concealed a crime, a matter on which you'd think they'd make it warm for him. On the other hand, it would hold up the story if they did.

The episode is instructive. Sail has no interest in posturing and attitudes. They waste energy. When he sees that a position will become insupportable, he leaves it. But only some positions. Only some of the time. He is a total pragmatist. That doesn't mean that he will bend forever. Only that he understands what is important. He is disciplined enough not to let his personal feelings interfere with his maneuverings.

Self-knowledge. Well, you have to understand a lot of yourself to be perceptive about others. He sees through John Silver almost at once. He is acutely sensitive to voice nuances; immediately he knows that something is wrong by the tone of Nan Moberly's voice on the telephone. He has observed that people don't really hear and will accept any bold statement, as long as it is spoken with assurance.

—Holding a man he has just knocked out in a hotel, he rings for the elevator and carries him on, with the explanation: "Quick! I gotta rush my friend to a place for a treatment."

He's very competent as a character reader, Sail is. He may have partially disengaged from society. But he is highly informed about the people it it, and how you operate in it. It's unlikely sophistication. But again typical of a Dent hero.

His reading of people is fast and to the point. He estimates to a nicety the extent Police Captain Cripps can be bluffed. He identifies, almost at once, the man Saunders as the head of the group attempting to hijack Nan Moberly's film. And, in spite of her insistence on melodrama, he has a good opinion of Nan:

I like that girl. She does cookoo things, and I wouldn't want her around as a fixture, because she'd probably get me killed in no time. But I like her, even if she is funny....

This could be classed as knight-errant stuff. But it isn't. Call it, more accurately, professional integrity. She's his client; he's responsible for her, as you are responsible for any job you take on. Perhaps his feelings aren't that cold. There is much left out of the sentences. You have to listen to them, not as dialogue spoken by pulp fiction characters, but words spoken by men— which is the way they were written. Doing it this way, you may hear something more than detective-client relationship behind Sail's words. Maybe not. Anyhow, she's his client and he's responsible for her.

There is, throughout the stories of Lester Dent, a sort of phantom situation to which, in one way or another, his more realized characters usually fit. Generally, the situation is this: here is an individual who, because of his unique background, is able to operate at one remove from society. This is mainly because he has not accepted society's goals and motives as his own. Essentially, he is an informed outsider. Therefore, he sees that bit more clearly and reacts that bit more rapidly. Sometimes his unique background is, like Doc Savage, a factor of extensive and isolated training. For others, the chief component appears to be a rural background, so that the prose always seems to be about the countryman putting it over on the cityman. Dent, himself, was a Missouri countryboy. The marks, in one way or another, remained with him. Someplace in the years far back, his distrust of the cities began. His characters continuously reflect it.

Whatever happened to Sail after 1936, we have no notion. The stories give us not much past and almost no inkling of future. Sail's future, as a fictional character, is much clearer. He inaugurated the line of rounded characters which fill Dent's realistic fiction all the way down to "Lady in Peril" in 1959. Sail was the first of these. Later, others would be developed in elaborate dimension, psychologically rounded, described with precision and depth. A few would be as physically outstanding. None would be tougher or more competent.

It all happened, as you know, a long time ago. Sail is better than 90 now, give or take some. The detective story has got older too. It has changed, like everything else. The *Black Mask* school has done its work and gone. Even in 1936, it was in its final stages. Mr. Dent arrived only just in time. After that, writing in the style continued, but it no longer grew. It had said what it was going to say.

But beautiful once, beautiful still. You can overlook the few imperfections in the stories. So Sail gets around with smashed ribs just a fraction too well. He's a trifle too fast with the truth serum. The Police Captain backs off just that little bit too quickly. Minor matters. The stories are solid, internally consistent. They are full of light and clarity. And through them, permanently, in that far off time, the tall man, silent, clothed in black, ambles through Florida morning toward violence

About Senorita Scorpion

Action Stories was no magazine for softies. Not a bit. If your idea of bliss is lolling lazily with liliaceous blonds, you don't need *Action Stories*. But if you're for the less languid life, pick up a copy of the magazine. Strap on your pistols. Fork your cayuse. Grab a lungfull of alkali dust and bash a friend in the face. This is he-man fiction.

It is a peculiar magazine to feature a series about a woman.

It did and she was. Senorita Scorpion she was called, a name of great promise. On the magazine covers, she appears in a riot of action. Most of the time, she is blond. Much of the time, she is masked.

Down she storms on her Palomino. Her gun flames. The unrighteous die. And in the extreme left-hand corner of the cover beams the happy cowpoke she has rescued. He is all tied up and bleeds slightly from the mouth.

Even if he hadn't been saved at the last moment, he'd die beaming. For Senorita Scorpion is spectacular. She wears a red blouse, yellow sash, and riding pants tight enough to seal off her pores. Down the pant seams runs intricate red-black-yellow embroidery. The stories describe the design as roses but the cover paintings ignore that refinement.

The covers ignore a lot. They clearly portray Senorita Scorpion as a dual-identity heroine, beautiful, masked, violent. Regrettably, the covers seem to have been some cynical ploy, taking advantage of those hungering to read about female Zorros and feminine Lone Rangers. That is not what the Senorita Scorpion series is about.

What it is about is about beautiful blond Elgera Douglas and her exhausting life. But she does not wear a mask. She has no dual identity. She rarely saves anyone. And, although she is occasionally called The Scorpion, the exciting sobriquet is hardly more than a nickname.

The eight (or more) stories of the series ran in *Action Stories* from Spring 1944 to about Winter 1949. The writer is identified as Les Savage, Jr., a name we should regard with the deepest suspicion. At least one story was contributed by Emmett McDowell. This story is included in the series, although it should not be, and will be discussed later.

In keeping with the editorial requirements of *Action Stories*, the series is physical. Violently physical. Brutally so. Not that many people get killed. But a lot of people get mauled, get beaten to a pulp, get chased, kicked, pounded, slammed, hammered, bloodied. Half the characters stagger around with concussion. The other half are way too busted up to stagger.

About twice a story, an extended fist fight is described. Not just a quick swing and it's over. These are *fist fights*—about a page and half long, every blow described. Every crushed mouth, swollen eye, smashed nose lovingly pointed out.

As in this aftermath of a fight between two of the main male leads, both good guys:

Hager...lay there with his shirt almost ripped off, blood leaking from one corner of his split lips, one eye closed and beginning to swell already. There were big beefy spots on his lean torso as if he had been slapped with the flat of a board....He didn't move.

(Chisos's) face was even worse than Hager's. His brow was laid open from one temple to the other, bleeding profusely, and his cheeks were lacerated and torn till they looked like fresh hamburger. He was bleeding at the mouth, too; he spat out a tooth, and kept dabbling feebly at his eyes that way and walking in circles. Elgera realized that he couldn't see.... ("Secret of Santiago," Winter 1944)

The two of them are terribly battered. But they will rise and get terribly battered again.

Johnny Hager is sheriff of Brewster County, the toughest part of Texas. He left the Army after Geronimo was defeated and drifted down south, taking up sheriffing as a challenge. He has eyes for Elgera.

So does Chisos Owens, "a square, heavy man who was neither graceful nor awkward in his movements, whose every deliberate step seemed to hold an intrinsic purpose within itself." He is taller than average, heavy-shouldered, and his big hands are scarred and cut by years with ropes and horses and such Western things. Chisos is not at all the fast gunman, as is Hager. Chisos is a bull-headed, iron-fisted, straight-ahead slugger. He adores Elgera.

And Elgera Douglas, herself? She is young, tall, blond, her eyes luminous blue. Her ripe underlip looks as sweet as a berry. Drives men mad, let me tell you. She wears a sombrero, those tight pants mentioned earlier, and her boots have spike heels, since she does more riding than walking.

She rides a big Palomino named La Rubia (The Blond) on which she dashes here and there. She is one stunning woman, which explains why all the characters slump like over-heated marshmallows in her presence. Under that glow of supercharged femininity lies a rather harder person. She has disciplined a rather quick temper. If necessary, she will slug a man down or ambush him with a rock. She is hard to ruffle and she won't be pushed.

For these reasons, perhaps, the Mexicans call her The Scorpion. The why of the nickname isn't quite clear. The implication is that if you fool around with her, you're going to get stung. The sting, in Elgera's case, is carried in an Army Colt.

She carries one all the time—one of those big single-six jobs. She is nearly the fastest thing in the world with this unwieldy chunk of ordnance:

> She didn't know she'd drawn until the gun bucked in her hand. Gato's left-hand weapon slipped back into its holster as he let go to claw at his right shoulder and his other six-gun dropped to the ground from the spasmodically stiffening fingers of his right hand, and he reeled back with more surprise on his face than pain. ("Secret of Santiago")

Not a woman to go fooling around with. But the danger only fascinates men. As one of her admirers remarks, in "The Sting of the Scorpion" (Winter 1949):

> You're beautiful when you're excited. Your lips glisten like they're wet. You looked that way when you shot the beaker from Cora's hand last night. Wild. Like a cat or something. I like that. I guess you've never been tamed, have you?

Wild and untamed. The stories hammer away at that.

> Senorita Scorpion threw back her head and there was something wild in her laugh, and the three men looked at each other as if they knew how long it would be before any of them ever tamed a girl like that.

It sounds as if Les Savage, Jr. had been reading from the works of Max Brand or Edgar Rice Burroughs or both. Elgera's feral touch crops up only occasionally. She can also be seductive, especially when charming lawmen. And frequently she is exhausted and scared. Considering the trouble she sees, it's no wonder.

The series begins with an enormously complicated background. To compress.

Elgera Douglas is mistress of the Circle S, a ranch isolated in the inaccessible Santiago Valley. The Valley lies within the Dead Horse Mountains in the Big Bend country of Texas. Back in 1681, Simeon Santiago and George Douglas discovered the valley and its fabulously rich gold mine. No sooner had they begun working the mine, than the Comanches raided the valley. They killed everyone but Douglas and a woman, both somehow remaining hidden.

When the Comanches left, they collapsed the mine tunnel—the only way out of the valley. Douglas was sealed inside and there he stayed. His descendents begat descendents. It was a small enough gene pool.

After about two hundred years of incest, Elgera's father was able to cut through the collapsed mine tunnel and open the valley to the outside world. That was about fifteen years before the series opens. So Elgera has had time to get a smattering of education, and learn to handle an Army Colt and walk on spike heels. When we first meet her, she is about twenty years old.

That's the background story, although details keep shifting. You wonder if a lot of details haven't shifted. Elgera and her brothers, Natividad and Johnny, certainly show no signs of inbreeding. But these scientific niceties are overlooked in the raging howl of adventure after the Douglases enter that big mean world beyond the mountains.

"Senorita Scorpion" (Spring 1944) tells how the half-wild Elgera goes out to look around and is followed back to the valley by the entranced Chisos Owens. He was the first outsider in 200 years to see the valley and very helpful he proved to be. For once word leaked out that the fabled Lost Santiago Mine really existed, every sharp-shooter in Texas came crowding down. The next two stories tell how crooks attempted to grab the gold.

In "The Brand of Senorita Scorpion" (Summer 1944), Elgera has sought help to work the mine. Her main assistant is mining engineer Ignacio Avarillo, "a pudgy barrel of a Mexican with big sad blood shot eyes." He is massively fat, cheerful, and the most intelligent character of the series. Very very bright. And amazingly he is on Elgera's side. Loves her, of course, although he knows that she is not for him.

Trouble comes thick and deep.

First, Father Douglas gets sick and has to be carried to a hospital. There he dies, becoming an indispensable plot element.

Next, Elgera and brothers are swindled out of their property title by Hawkman and his very wicked associates. These take possession of the valley and turn all the good characters into slaves, digging for gold.

The story now splits into two lines and begins dodging back and forth between them, just as the Tarzan stories used to do. In one line, Elgera escapes into the mountains, is hunted by Hawkman and a pack of killers. In the second line, Chisos blunders into Hawkman's men as he enters the valley, is chased, trapped in a collapsing mine section, escapes with a couple of reliable men, takes off to save Elgera.

He finds her alone, standing off the Hawkman crowd. Then it's a bloody, fumbling, smashing, blundering, murderous hand-to-hand fight. Hawkman and company are wiped out one by one in an ending of intense savagery and suspense.

"Secret of Santiago" (Winter 1944) is more of the same.

Elgera is visited by a fellow named Bruce-Douglas. He claims to be a direct descendent of Douglas, from the family left behind in England when he went prospecting for gold in the New World. Bruce-Douglas is, therefore, the legal owner of the Lost Santiago, the only direct-line inheritor.

Elgera and Avarillo doubt this story. For reasons of his own, Avarillo takes the claimant off to a distant mission to review some original documents. And once again, the story splits into two separate lines.

While Avarillo and Bruce-Douglas travel, Elgera and Chisos ride into town. There Chisos meets with Hawkman's former lawyer, a crooked snake fearing for his life. He has (he says) one-third of a map showing the Secret of the Santiago. The Secret is.... At this point, a shot through the window kills him.

Amid a wild convulsion of plot threads, Chisos is accused of murder. He is almost arrested by Sheriff Johnny Hager. Not quite. Hager gets slugged by Elgera. She and Chisos thunder out of town.

They escape to a hot, harsh ride, Hager trailing grimly behind. At last, by a singular coincidence, they take refuge at the very monastery where Avarillo is studying those old records.

According to these documents, the Santiago Mine was about worked out. The bulk of the gold was actually coming from another, even more secret, location.

During these revelations, Hager pounds up. It is time for a bloody fist fight to refresh the weary reader, sick of talk. For about a page and a half, Hager and Chisos slug each other to paste. All for the love of Elgera, who thinks the whole thing foolish.

While they sprawl helpless, fought out, weltering in gore, she allows that she likes both of them as friends. It is an emotional commitment somewhat less than they had anticipated.

But they patch up a temporary truce. For they discover that Avarillo and Bruce-Douglas have slipped quietly away, headed off through the desolation toward the sinister Haunted Swamp.

Elgera and her battered friends follow. At this point, according to *Action Stories* formula, they should be captured and tied up and treated badly. And that's exactly what happens. Bruce-Douglas and his tough pal, Gato, capture the whole bunch.

It is now torture time.

Bruce-Douglas admits that he is a fake—a con man, not a true Douglas. He is after the third piece of the map which, when assembled, will show the location of the secret mine. He will have it—if he must burn off Avarillo's feet—if he must sear away the beauty of Elgera's face.

At that threat, Chisos lumbers into action. Although he's tied up tighter than a spider's dinner, he goes after the crooks. Confusion. Action. Fury. Avarillo uses a cigar to burn Elgera free. By then, Chisos has ripped out of his bonds. Grabbing a gun, in a blind, white-eyed fury, he stomps toward Gato:

The first bullet caught his arm from wrist to elbow, jerking it up, and he still didn't fire. The second one took a hunk from his neck and he felt the hot pump of blood out over his collar. He was almost running when the third one burned through his side and threw him halfway around. He lurched on forward, twisted like that, almost falling until he finally squared himself. And still he didn't fire. And his boots made that inexorable pound against the ground.

At a range of about three inches, Chisos blows Gato full of .45 holes. While he is blasting away, Elgera has jumped Bruce-Douglas and they are having a merry time:

> She beat at his pale thin face with the dueling pistol. She caught his gun and twisted it away as they both fell in the mud. The strength in her grasp must have surprised him; for in that instant there was no resistance in his wrist as she twisted it. Then his arm stiffened and his body arced against her. The gun exploded between them.

That gets rid of him.

Quiet descends.

As the blood soaks peacefully into the sand, Senorita Scorpion and friends find the final piece of the map. Putting it together, they locate the hidden gold mine—as well as a new entrance to the Lost Valley.

It's share and share alike. All will be millionaires. And Elgera is still not tamed.

You can squeeze a lot of fiction out of one plot idea. But even the juiciest idea eventually dries up and must be replaced. Perhaps that explains why the 1947-1949 stories turn from Lost Valley gold mines to the compromised innocence of Senorita Scorpion.

Now I don't mean that at all. Shame on you.

She has to keep proving her innocence. And sometimes it is hard, hard.

As in "Lash of the Six-Gun Queen" (Winter 1947). Chisos sees Senorita Scorpion empty her gun into a U. S. senator. The morality of that act is suspect even in our own troubled times. Back then, it was considered murder, not political protest.

Without further discussion, Elgera becomes a wanted woman. Marshall Powder Welles (the first-person narrator of the story) is on her trail. She is alone. Hunted. Every single one of her friends believes her guilty.

There follows enough plot to make a novel, and enough fist fighting and violence to make a comic book.

Senorita Scorpion struggles to prove her innocence against eyewitness testimony.

Marshall Welles struggles to investigate with a broken arm, while having life half beaten out of him every second chapter.

Chisos struggles to stay alive after infiltrating a gang of hard-rock rustlers and getting shot, arrested, tricked, bashed, and held prisoner for his trouble.

All this hurrah turns out to be the crafty plot of Striker, a human devil. He is mixed up in rustling, illegal horse dealing, corruption of the US Army, and various revenge schemes against the dead senator and Elgera Douglas.

The trick turns on an exact double of Elgera. The toothsome wench is finally confronted by Elgera, two Senorita Scorpions face to face. The imitation just doesn't have that magic touch with the six gun. And the big Palomino knows the difference between them, if Chisos does not.

"Gun-Witch of Hoodoo Range" (Winter 1948) is a freak story, an anomaly. It was written by Emmett McDowell. Once again two Senorita Scorpions appear. Neither of them is Elgera Douglas. In fact, Elgera does not appear, nor does anyone else from the series.

Seems that greedy rancher Rafflock is out to drive off the small ranchers and ingest their spreads. He does will, secretly bossing a gang of rustling, house-burning toughs.

That isn't enough trouble for the region. The Mexican rustler, Cahrera, is also stealing away at the herds. Riding with his gang is the flamboyant Senorita Scorpion. She is a dance-hall girl from the Mexican section of Tombstone, and always wears a fitted green mask to hide her scarred face. Got cut by a broken beer bottle in the hands of a jealous hussy...

When out rustling cattle, she wears a green hood covering her face and shoulders.

It happens that the Cahrera and the Rafflock gangs blunder into each other one night. Cahrera is chased down and killed at Old Tom Hunter's place—a small spread he works with his wife and daughter, Meg.

First the Rafflock men try to hang Old Tom. When this is prevented, they haul him off to stand trial in Tombstone. But Senorita Scorpion shows up during the night and frees him.

From that point on, it's war between the Scorpion and Rafflock, with Jesse Morgan, another rancher, mixing his gun into it. Jesse cannot quite understand what's going on. Could it be that Meg Hunter is Senorita Scorpion? Impossible. The Scorpion is known to be that Mexican spitfire in Tombstone. Yet all the evidence seems to point to lithe, young, slender, blond, adorable Meg, whose laughing blue eyes mock him....

The truth comes after a raging gun fight, which eliminates the Rafflock problem. The Mexican Senorita Scorpion died, without anybody knowing it on about the fourth page, and under the green silk hood shows the delicate golden hair of....

Oh, you guessed it, did you?

"Hoodoo Range" is a pleasant enough story, although Heaven knows why it was included in the Senorita Scorpion series. It's like entering a goldfish at the terrier show. With "Sting of the Scorpion" (Winter 1949), however, Les Savage, Jr., returns—and so does Elgera. All other supporting characters have vanished.

You don't miss them. It is the same familiar story, gussied up with some new plot variations.

In this one, Elgera is being hunted by Marshall Terry Dexter. He thinks she knifed dead his brother, a government surveyor seeking water for the region.

Dexter has lots of trouble catching Elgera. That little slip of a girl ambushes him, knocks him out, steals his horse. As an encore, she disarms a posse and rescues a good-natured rustler.

Her credentials in crime established, the pair head for the rustlers Secret Hideout. Beginning a long sequence of knives in the dark, gun flame in the light, double crosses, traps, and tricks.

These stirring activities are interrupted, if briefly, by glimmers of romance. Purple romance, like those nuggets which used to be inserted between gun shots in *Spicy Detective*:

She felt his body grow rigid. Then slowly (his) gun muzzle dropped. His arm went around her and he was holding her so tightly she could not breathe. There was a great roaring in her head, a deep pound of pulse shaking her body. When (he) pulled his lips away from hers, they were both trembling.

In each of these later stories, Elgera finds a new man. Their chemistry flares. It looks as if He's the one. But He never is. Next issue, He's forgotten and another He cuddles her lithesome curves and kisses those berry-rich lips. So to speak.

Well, there never was any emotional continuity in these stories. Can't be. If you tie Senorita Scorpion down to a single man, the romance leaks out of the series. Is her darting mind to be chained to one of these lumbering male lumps? Is her energy and courage to be blunted by housekeeping? Is Les Savage, Jr. going to louse up his sales by marrying off his exciting heroine?

Very likely not. ·

Back at the rustlers' hideout, Elgera has messed up their raid on a nearby town. When they find her out, all Hell breaks loose. Death, confusion, and death. From which Elgera escapes in the company of a deaf-mute Indian.

She has saved his life, and he reciprocates by showing her the hidden water source discovered by the murdered surveyor. At this point, the real murderer bounds from the cholla, confesses, attacks, dies. All with the hearing of the Marshall. Senorita Scorpion's innocence is proven. What could be more satisfactory than that?

On which pleasing note, let's leave the series.

All those dead people, shot, stabbed, strangled, lie peacefully, heads on their boots.

All the series men lie thinking of Elgera Douglas and their hearts pulse peacefully.

La Rubina snorts peacefully in the velvet Texas night.

Elgera hugs her new fellow—maybe for life, maybe for five minutes.

Tomorrow, the bloody turmoil erupts again, savage, brutal, violent. But the final sentences of an *Action Stories* adventure are always peaceful. We end in silence. For a while.

You Red-Headed Girl of My Dreams

Soothing quiet in the Valley of Marc's Mind. Among trees oddly feathery hangs a fragile blue mist. The sky is without sun, yet the sky shines. The odd trees circle a little clearing, coolly carpeted with moss. And on the moss, relaxed, happy, sprawls Marcus George Pillsworth.

He is unconscious.

Well, you must understand, he is awake in the Valley of his own mind. But to get to that valley—if the concept is not too difficult—he must first be unconscious. Knocked cold or asleep in our stormy world.

In the Elyrian deeps of his own mind, however, he stretches upon the moss, calmly smiling.

At which point....

...two cool hands pressed down gently over his eyes and two lips closed simultaneously over his mouth. The lips were not nearly so cool or so gentle as the hands, and they went directly to the business of kissing him with an air of abandon and authority.

The authoritative kisser is a girl named Toffee. In this quiet place, down in Marc Pillsworth's subconscious, she waits for him. She is formed from his wishes and thoughts and she glows warmly.

To put matters exactly, she is a buxom, red-headed wench. Since the weather of the mind is mild, she wears only a filmy, fragile, transparent scrap of emerald-colored stuff. It keeps the dew off. In spite of this diaphanous wisp, you can see that she is extraordinarily beautiful, a full-bodied delight. Uninhibited. Pleasure-loving, you might say. Even shameless. Eager to kiss and hug and tickle....

The general idea is that she is not a feminist. And Marc is her special darling. As indeed he should be, since he thought her up.

Toffee: "All that I am I owe to you and, judging by the mirror, I'd say that was plenty. Up until now, I've existed only in your subconscious, but last night, while you were dreaming, you released me, gave me physical dimensions and a personality. Now that works both ways; it was the first chance I'd had to see you too. Well, it seemed that you were a nice enough guy, but a little mixed up about a lot of important things, so I decided to materialize myself and help you out."

Which is kind of her. But why she bothers with that inhibited stick, Marc, is hard to explain.

He recoils from her kisses. He shrinks from her hugs. He chatters vapidly of her nakedness. Yet the poor simp dreamed up this girlish glory. Surely he could think of something other than flight.

And no doubt he could, given a slight change of environment. But unfortunately, Marc and Toffee are stuck in a humorous fantasy series that began in the pulps. And most pulps got a little edgy when the heroine appeared dressed in a light mist and began nibbling the hero's neck.

Fantastic Adventures was quite careful about such scenes. The magazine's covers delighted in under-clothed, over-developed young ladies who never appeared to feel a draft. But it was a rare story that carried the cover's promise into words.

The Toffee series, written by Charles F. Myers, was no exception. The series includes seven stories published in *Fantastic Adventures* between 1947 and 1950. Later, Toffee moved to *Imagination, Stories of Science and Fantasy*, a digest-sized publication, during the early 1950s. Still later, a pair of stories were reprinted in *Imaginative Tales*, 1954.

In 1947, when Toffee first appeared, *Fantastic Adventures* was a big, solid pulp of 178 pages (including the front cover). It cost 25¢ and was issued bi-monthly by Ziff-Davis. The Managing Editor, Raymond A. Palmer, was also responsible for *Amazing Stories*, and had created *Fantastic Adventures* as a "sister" magazine, stressing fantasy. It began with a bias toward the muscleman hack and slash adventure, but before the mid-1940s it was drifting into the humorous, often cock-eyed fantasy. These were vigorous farces told in the vernacular, slangy and full of superficial characters and non-stop movement.

The Toffee series fit right in.

The first appearance was the short story, "I'll Dream of You" (January 1947). It opens in Marc's mind, and away we go:

Toffee: (Hugging Marc's neck): "You seem fascinated by beauty, almost starved for it."
Marc: (Looking dreamily off into the distance, nods).
Toffee: "Then get fascinated, you dope....I'm beautiful too and twice as much fun. Kiss me."
Marc: "Haven't you any restraint?"
Toffee: "With everything else I have, you ask for restraint."
Marc: "You're shameless."
Toffee: "Naturally."

At this point, more or less, Marc wakes from a sound sleep, finds himself in his bedroom, the alarm clock jangling. A day beginning like all other days. Except that Toffee has followed him out of his dreams, dressed in her transparent fragment, and stands in his bedroom. She is warmly friendly.

A bachelor finding an uninhibited, unclothed young lady in his bedroom promptly thinks of ways to get her dressed. This explains how Toffee, in a dressing gown, and Marc, in icy sweat, end at a ladies Ready-To-Wear store. There, Toffee climbs into a display window to insert herself into a black evening gown—to the fascination of those outside the window. Marc lunges into the window, tries to shield her from the public gaze, and make her give up the evening dress.

Girl (Observing from the sidewalk): "Just like my Oscar. No sense of the time and place."

From this public spectacle, Marc blunders off to his office, Toffee smiling and glittering behind. Marc is the owner of the Pillsworth Advertising Agency. His staff is highly exercised at the the sight of the boss coming in at noon, escorting a red-headed dream in an evening dress.

They are not so interested as Julie Mason, Marc's chilly blond secretary. She has certain quiet plans for Marc, herself, and Toffee's appearance sends her temper flaring.

That evening, Marc and Toffee accidentally meet Julie and her date at a night club. Attempting to patch things up, Marc sends Toffee off to dance with the date. He remains behind to gaze deeply into Julie's eyes.

Now, as it happens, Toffee, being a dream girl, is slightly insubstantial. When Marc sleeps, she vanishes. When Marc day-dreams, she fades away. Thus, when Marc sits at the night-club table day dreaming about life with Julie, Toffee fades silently from the arms of her dancing companion. Through a series of complicated reactions, this causes a small riot. Everyone gets arrested, and Toffee and Marc make the first of their many appearances before a judge.

After a night in jail, they to return to Marc's apartment. There Julie waits for him. She wishes to resign her job. Instead, Marc proposes marriage to her and is accepted.

But what is he to do with Toffee?

He has discovered that she appeared, as a coherent dream image, after he had eaten Welsh Rarebit. So out they go to eat rarebit again. That, combined with a dose of sleeping pills, returns Toffee to the Valley of Marc's mind.

She is philosophical about her banishment. "I've served my purpose and it's time for me to return," she tells him. And so they part. And that, we may suppose, is the end of it.

But it isn't.

In "You Can't Scare Me" (March 1948), Toffee reappears when Marc needs her peculiar sort of help. He has married Julie, who seems short on common sense and long on jealousy. The plans for an advertising account have been stolen from him, threatening the agency. Toffee, eager to help, leaps into this mess and quickly plunges Marc from hot to scalding to boiling water. Soon a highly compromising photograph is made of him with Toffee. Clearly his world is becoming unglued. But after a novelette of dizzy complications, all trouble melts away.

Toffee hasn't changed. But Julie has. From cool, blond secretary, she has become that rather different thing, a cool, blond wife. Simmering with jealousy, inflexible, stuffy, snobbish, she rages across the scene, her mouth an icy line. She finds a semi-naked girl (Toffee) in Marc's office, and a naked girl (Toffee) in his bedroom, and surprises him being hugged by a vivacious young thing (Toffee), and her heart scalds with discontent.

In future stories, she will howl for divorce. She will storm out, slamming the door. She will teeter at the edge of indiscretion. She will grit her teeth and bring in the psychiatrist or the lawyer.

These emotional storms rage through each story. But at the end, Julie and Marc make up, shedding large drops of sugar water. Don't blame Julie for the way she behaves. She knows better. Only she has the thankless job of a supporting role in a farce. Meaning that she is given no inner coherence. Her function is to complicate the plot and provide tension.

But who cares? It's only cheap fiction.

"Toffee Takes A Trip," novelette, July 1947. Vacationing alone at the beach, Marc finds himself saddled with a murdered corpse. Toffee comes to his aid, generating chaos. The sheriff chases them; so does a deadly little man with a gun. Presently, they are taken prisoner by a scientific gang that threatens to blow up the world, unless they are paid off.

Toffee and Marc escape the gang, only to be arrested. Then they escape from jail, accompanied by a drunken plumber. After lunatic adventures, they blunder back to the gang's hideout. The police crash in; the hideout is blown up—rather than the world—because Toffee has accidentally reversed the deadly beam.

The author of these excitements, Charles F. Myers, was then in his mid-twenties. He was born in San Joaquin Valley, California, in 1922. He began writing while in the Army, when he prepared some special material for an USO show. He thought up Toffee during a "dateless Saturday night in a deserted barracks."

In his thinking, he was mightily helped by the novels of Thorne Smith, most of these available to servicemen in Armed Forces paperback editions.

Myers' debt to Thorne Smith is immediate and unashamed. Readers of *Fantastic Adventures* wrote asking if Myers were not Smith. It was hard to tell, for Myers wrote a clever pastiche of Smith's style—with certain differences.

Thorne Smith (1893-1934), author of about a dozen humorous novels, was born at the U.S. Naval Academy at Annapolis, Maryland. His father supervised the Port of New York during the First World War. After graduation from college, Smith worked at an advertising agency until the First World War, then enlisted in the Navy. While in service, he wrote his first book. During the 1920's he published a meager amount of fiction, having a hungry time of it until the success of his 1926 novel, *Topper*. Afterward, he worked in Hollywood. Many of his books appeared as films. He died, forty years old, at Sarasota, Florida, leaving an unfinished novel, *The Passionate Witch*, later completed by Norman Matson. The book was published in 1941 and immediately became a moving picture.

Almost all Smith's novels are joyous farces. All contain the same central situation: An inhibited man chafes against the narrow conventionalities of his life. Suddenly fantastic elements burst around him. He meets ghosts or gods or witches; he becomes intermittently transparent or tumbles into another dimension. Bohemian convivality reshapes his drab life. There is a great deal to drink, a beautiful aggressive woman, and assortment of demented companions, cheerfully amoral and full of bottled spirits.

All tumble through reeling adventures of riot and pursuit, nudity, falling-down confusion, underwear, conversations at cross purposes, dogs, bottles, and unrestrained bedlam. Social conventions are gleefully shattered. Also a good many laws and a few of the lesser commandments.

At the end, the hero is transformed. He has learned that repression and conventionality wither the heart, that there must be gaiety and play. There must also be love. His adventures may conclude with hangover, but he has become a whole human being.

Such material worked as a novel. However, as fiction in a pulp magazine, which had a second-class mailing permit to defend, many of Smith's more gaudy ideas could not be used. Although Myers adopted Smith's prose tone, scenes, character types, and favorite adjectives, much more was dropped.

Almost entirely omitted is the two-fisted drinking of the Smith characters. These spend their days and nights surrounded by bottles and having a high old time gettin tight. And very frequently, Smith's people end in bed together—men and women; oh, the scandal—and the worst sometimes happens.

Only pallid reflections of these revels entered *Fantastic Adventures*. Now and then a flash from Smith's lusty heroines ignites in Toffee. But it is only a flash, like a single diamond from some elaborate necklace, now broken and scattered.

Toffee crossed one lovely leg over the other and regarded it bleakly. Obviously, she thought it a waste in such scientific surrounding. Her determined belief in the idea that sex, if just given half a chance, could surmount any obstacle, seemed in grave peril of disproof.

That belief might be true of a Thorne Smith heroine but is not really true of Toffee. Granted that she is quite aware of the notorious differences in the sexes; she is also aware of that precious second-class mailing permit. With the result that her heaviest passes at Marc are curiously dimmed:

Toffee had already twined her arms around his neck and was kissing him. Finally she let him go.

"You never change, do you," Marc said shortly.

"Never," Toffee said. "Isn't it delightful? I know a game that's fun. We take turns...."

But what they are to take turns at is never explained.

In one matter, at least, Toffee remains close to her Thorne Smith originals. She is unable to keep her clothing on. Toffee's customary condition is close enough to nudity as to make no difference.

...Toffee stepped out, a wayward vision in a black lace negligee. The garment, inspired by the peek-a-boo idea, had been translated by Toffee's lovely figure into a wide open stare. In terms of visibility, the ceiling was practically unlimited.

"Good night," Marc said. "Did you have to pick that? It's darn near the nakedest thing I've ever seen. It's indecent."

"Thanks," said Toffee sweetly. "I knew you'd like it." She fell into a langurous pose beside the door. "By the way, what *is* the nakedest thing you've ever seen? It might be interesting to know."

"You and your evil mind," Marc sneered. "Anyway, we don't have time for that. We've got to get out of here."

What on earth ails the man. After all, she *is* his dream girl. Surely he could spare her a sidelong glance or a tender word. In this form of comic novel, however, normal sexual roles are reversed: the woman pursues, the man flees, timorous as a young deer, his melting brown eyes amazed.

In Thorne Smith's novels, the man is reluctant because social conventions have smothered his outgoing impulses. In Myers' stories, Marc is reluctant because that is a comic device. And because it is a comic device, not a personality trait, Marc does not develop as a feeling character until the final story of the series. Until that time, he remains a six-foot, two-inch caricature, cold at the heart, whose feelings toward the girl of his dreams are almost always annoyance. Myers has copied Thorne Smith's form, but the Thorne Smith substance eludes him.

By the July 1947 novelette, the series' story format is well developed. Marc faces a disagreeable problem. Toffee seeks to help him, creating even worse problems. They chase wildly about, spreading confusion and disorder. Wherever they appear, a riot explodes.

As at the old folks' home....

(The old folks) were magically transformed into a league of formidable warriors...no longer the slowly disintegrating remnants they had first appeared to be. Summoning hidden vigor, from heaven only knew what source, they rose as a body and swarmed toward the scene of outrage. One of their number had been attacked and they were plainly not to be found wanting. Crutches, ear trumpets and miscellaneous silverware were instantly pressed into service in lieu of weapons. One old gentleman, racing his wheelchair at break-neck speed, hurled himself into the fray with all the proud spirit of a knight astride a charger. Other ancient enlistees, in their near-sightedness, promptly engaged each other in ferocious battle. Crockery flew in all directions and crashed unheeded against the-walls. The orderly dining room was reduced to a raging ruin in only a matter of seconds.

Two or three of these explosions occur per story. As a result, Marc and Toffee frequently find themselves arrested. Hauled before a judge, they hear him cite an extended list of their transgressions:

Judge: "Now, taking it from the beginning, your crimes, since only this morning, include possession of lewd pictures, jail breaking, destruction of private property, resisting arrest, disturbing the peace, assaulting seven officers, collusion in an automobile theft, lewd and immoral conduct, two attempts at murder, harboring criminals and, now, grand larceny and perhaps an insurance swindle. That is just hitting the high spots."

Eventually, when the story is long enough, coincidence or author intervention blots out all problems. Toffee fades away to the Valley of Marc's Mind, and Marc is, once again, reconciled with Julie. Until the next time.

Two new characters join the series during the novelette "Toffee Haunts A Ghost" (November 1947). The first character is Memphis McGuire, a sensible fat girl, who occupies a minor role as Marc's new secretary; Memphis has considerable comic potential, but there is so much going on that her talents are not used.

The second character introduced is a major figure. His name is George and he is the ghost of Marc Pillsworth. A hard-drinking entity, capable of infinite disruption, George is patterned after George Kirby of Smith's Topper series.

After encountering several near-fatal accidents, Marc arrives at his office to find it haunted by the ghost of himself, swilling whiskey and chasing the girls. The ghost, who looks exactly like Marc, has been sent by the Spirit High Council to determine if Marc is still alive.

But although Marc lives, George enjoys the mortal world so much that he does not want to leave.

In the company of Toffee and George, Marc sets out on more wild adventure. They meet a moonshiner and a pair of ineffectual robbers. They drink too much moonshine and chase and get chased and cause a riot in an old folks' home. By then, George has plotted with the robbers to kill Marc, so that George can remain on Earth. But this dire plot fails. Eventually, George returns to Spiritland, and quiet settles. Quiet for an entire year—which is how long Toffee is absent from the magazine.

She returns in the November 1948 issue, the novelette being titled "The Spirit of Toffee," a glorious bubbling whirl.

Julie seeks a career as a musical comedy star, Marc footing the bill. The cost of supporting a Broadway production has almost bankrupted him. Thus the problem. After which Marc is knocked out in a car accident and, behold, Toffee returns.

So does George, the hard-drinking ghost.

The Spirit High Council, mightily annoyed by George's last visit to Earth, has sent him back to do Marc a good turn, thus making up for that last time. Since Marc needs money, George proceeds to get it for him—by robbing a bank. And away the money bags float, gripped by invisible hands. Followed by the usual wild chase, ending in a traffic jam that is immediately converted to a full-scale riot, as Marc and a partially dressed Toffee chase the floating money bags in and out of automobiles.

In the company of a fascinated cab-driver, Marc and Toffee proceed, through compounding confusion, to the riot at the movie, the riot at the diner. At last they reach the theatre where Julie is about to debut.

Toffee wanders out on stage during Julie's solo and proceeds to get undressed. That results in the theater riot, after which they are all arrested.

At this point, George does his good turn. Since he looks exactly like Marc, he has no trouble confusing all witnesses. The charges die. Or rather, they collapse, after George also demonstrates how easy it is to float up into the air and remove your head.

One byproduct of this interesting event is a conversation between two courtroom photographers. It is the pure essence of Thorne Smith:

...one of the photographers nearest this dreadful scene (George floating headless) turned to another of his kind.

"You know, Harry," he said in a controlled voice. "I've been thinking. You and me, we've been in this racket an awful long time now."

"Yeah," said Harry. "An awful long time."

"Yeah. And maybe too long. It's no kind of life for a man with any kind of sensitivity, you know. It's liable to take a bad effect on a guy after a while."

"I know what you mean," Harry said thoughtfully. "You get around too much, see too many screwy things. It might begin to give you a sort of distorted view, like."

"Sure. It could even get so bad you could get kind of unbalanced. Maybe it would start with you seein' things that aren't real."

"Uh-huh," Harry nodded. "Maybe like guys floatin' around in the air without they've got their heads on. Or something like that. Not that I've ever seen no such thing, mind you.... What say we get the hell out of here."

Even after George returns to the spirit world, events in Marc Pillsworth's life remain unstable. In "Toffee Turns The Trick" (February 1949, novelette), another magical gimmick shows up. It's pills—pills that can make you very young or very old. Both Marc and Toffee get a large dose. So do two criminals who are hot after the pill formula.

During this adventure, Marc, Toffee, and the pill inventor all get tight and remain tight. It seems that whiskey is the only fluid to counteract the pills' effect. This varies the device used in Smith's novel, *The Passionate Witch*, where large amounts of whiskey are required to rid the hero of voices in his head.

For a Thorne Smith imitator, Myers uses little drinking in his stories. Toffee is not adverse of a nice bottle of champagne or a good portion of moonshine, but she doesn't go panting after a drink. Nor does Marc.

George does. Ghost or not, he is a dedicated swiller, lured by any bottle. Since he is usually invisible, his quest for drink often has unpredictable results:

"There's nothing like whiskey to open the mind and the pores so the poison can get out," Jewel announced loudly. "It's wonderful stuff."

It was just at this moment that the invisible George drifted expectantly into the room. He stopped short and pricked up his ears. Whiskey! The very thing he was looking for, and here were mortals fairly wallowing in the stuff. Then he noticed Julie's glass languishing on the table.

...He waited till the turret-faced matron was looking in his direction, then lifted the glass with a broad flourish. Even to George the effect of the drink suddenly flying from the table and into the air seemed rather arresting....

"The glass!" Jewel blurted in tones of terror. "The glass!" Then suddenly she gulped and sat down again as the bottle, like the glass, leaped lightly from the table, upended itself over the glass, filled it, then replaced itself.

"The bottle!" Jewel boomed.

"She wants the bottle," May told Julie. "God, what a thirst that woman's got! Did you see her knock off that drink? And now she's yelling for the bottle. She's fairly lusting for the stuff...."

It's Myers' story but the situation and language are pure Thorne Smith, old and rare.

The final Toffee to appear in *Fantastic Adventures* was a full-length novel, "The Shades of Toffee" (June 1950). It is nearly the best thing of the series, blithely reproducing much of the lunatic merriment you find in the Smith novels. Marc accidentally invents an anti-gravity formula and two ineffectual spies are out to steal it. Toffee spends much of the novel wearing nothing but her agreeable skin and the frenzy never slows.

For some reason which escapes the casual reader, the novel alters several character relationships. For this story only, Marc seems never to have met Toffee before; and George, bottle-hungry as ever, is visiting the Earth for the first time. At all other points, it is the familiar farce, expanded, magnified, delightful.

After this novel, Charles Myers published no other fiction in *Fantastic Adventures*. Almost a year later, another Toffee short novel cropped up in *Imagination, Stories of Science and Fantasy*. *Imagination* was a thick, digest-sized magazine containing 162 pages (including the front cover) and costing 35¢. The editor, William Lawrence Hamling, had just completed three-and-a-half years as Managing Editor of *Fantastic Adventures*.

In the editorial column of the February 1951 *Imagination*, Hamling remarked that "My own personal discovery, Charles F. Myers, is in this issue...with his hilarious dream-girl Toffee. We're very proud of Charles Myers, and intend to give you more stories from his talented pen in the near future."

"The Vengence of Toffee" (*Imagination*, February 1951) is an uneven piece scattered with funny scenes and dialogue. Unfortunately it begins from the basic premise that it is humorous to see someone get kicked in the seat of the pants.

Well, it's that simple and it isn't.

By mental projection or some such thing, Toffee has thought up a ring which projects a ray which, when focused on the bottom of the spine, causes the tissue and bones of the human body to stretch apart, then snap together. That gives the effect of a kick in the pants. If that's clear.

Julie is an early victim and from there, the story is convulsed by people receiving invisible kicks and Marc being blamed for them and chased and etc. etc. etc.

The action occurs at the beginning of the Cold War Era. Everyone is sitting around, sour and depressed, feeling the atomic bomb and atomic war suspended over their heads, (This is a reasonably accurate rendering of the feelings people had at the time. No one had yet learned of the hydrogen bomb.)

After a lot of undirected play with her ring, Toffee gets herself introduced to a Congressman. Learning how serious the atomic war threat is, she soon takes herself to Russia (unnamed). There she gives Joe Stalin (also unnamed) a ray-induced kick in the pants and forces him to disarm the country.

Following this triumph, she returns to the United States and forces it to disarm by lavishly administering kicks to the Congress, and the War Department, and the President. (The President is a former radio personality elected by mistake to the nation's highest office.)

Subsequent issues of *Imagination* continued to promise a new Toffee novel, although nothing seems to have been published until the July 1952 "No Time for Toffee," another short novel. An additional two years would lapse before "The Laughter of Toffee" (October 1954), which may easily be the best story of the series.

Arrested as a dirty postcard peddler by error, Marc accidentally drinks a French elixir. This causes him to develop X-ray vision—X-ray to the extent of seeing through people's clothing. And off we go.

—To the riot at the lingerie shop, where Toffee strips the clothing from a live model and hordes of nude girls mingle in screaming confusion with a squad of police.

—To the department store, where Marc's X-ray vision so disconcerts him that he dons black glasses and has to be led around.

—To an excursion on a sightseeing bus, accompanied by a tipsy mob of gangsters and molls.

—To a frenzied chase at Marc's home in the country, where a group of nudists are having a picnic.

What with gangsters and molls and nudists and police flinging themselves back and forth, and Julie's entranced by a smooth-talking artist, and Toffee full of champagne and exciting ideas—with all this, Marc has an exhausting time.

As usual, it all ends in court. Whereupon Mr. Myers shakes his magic wand. All complications melt away. And the final Toffee adventure has been told, as far as this commentator can determine.

Although a sort of curtain call did appear in the 1954 *Imaginative Tales*. The September issue of this magazine reprinted "The Shades of Toffee," simplifying the title to "Toffee." In the next issue, November, two stories were reprinted: "Toffee Takes a Trip" and "Toffee Haunts A Ghost."

Thereafter, Toffee vanished permanently from all magazines. Gone back to Marc's mind, no doubt.

The Toffee stories made a charming series, full of irrational joy. Exactly what you want in a broad farce. Many more Toffee adventures would not be too many. There is not nearly enough Thorne Smith in this world, and Myers' continuations are gratefully accepted. Lord, knows, we need more stories full of falling-down confusion and hilarity. And a lot more warm-hearted red heads who have trouble staying dressed.

IV
Little Bits of Nothing

From time to time, Wooda N. Carr has asked me to share with him the labor of column writing. Nick is a prodigy, original and endlessly busy. Over twenty or so years, he has published more articles on the pulp magazines than most of us will live to read. Unconsumed by this blaze of words, he also corresponds with most of the English-speaking world.

But occasionally even a giant needs rest. And so I will receive a note, written in what seems druidic runes, suggesting a collaboration. Our shared columns rarely last long. Either the publication they are intended for vanishes like the road to Oz. Or I run out of ideas and sit there blankly, while Nick continues triumphant, moving from glory to glory.

In any case, my column work is unrelenting frivolous. Others can write of Nostalgia, Destiny, and Contemporary Sociological Interactive Patterning. My typewriter, less deeply disciplined, tackles more modest subjects. I may intend to analyze the archetypical structures of the heroic mythos in Clayton Publications. But what comes out is trivia about the way old magazine pages flake off.

It is profoundly depressing. I am prepared to write richly original contributions, showing every evidence of genius. But it never gets done. Nothing comes out but fluff. It's like heating up a blast furnace to toast marshmallows.

My typewriter is an old IBM electric, set in its way. Likely this is the problem. I may intend, through penetrating analysis and superb insight, to open new eras of literary criticism. But the typewriter would rather give the Old Pulp Collector another hearing. Literature calls, but Laurel and Hardy answer.

One of these days, that typewriter is going to expire. Then, in a glory of word processing, a new literary era will begin. I can hardly wait.

Until that time, it will be nothing but fluff, irresponsible fluff, little bits of nothing.

Let Me Call You Sweetheart

I love Ida Jones!

Now the secret is out and I don't care.

Let Nick Carr frown and whisper discretion. Let my wife sniff coldly. It is Ida I love, the slender, cool, lean-faced, self-possessed, sharp-minded Ida who sparkles so.

She's a detective, you know. Ida is part of Nick Carter's dime novel crew. She is invaluable, invaluable.

When Nick gets tied up and faces death, she slips in and unties him.

When Ida gets tied up and faces death, Nick slips in and unties her.

When not tied up, she investigates, often in disguise. And whatever she does, she remains cool, self-possessed, making no mistakes.

Oh, she's marvelous, Ida is.

Now it's true that when I was a lot younger, I had an immature pash on Nellie Gray. You may have met her—a tiny little blond lovely. She spent a lot of time in the company of a great hulking lump of a fellow, just one muscle stacked on another and never a brain to hold them together, I suspect. They were working for *The Avenger* Magazine at the time.

Nellie seemed to me to be a positive addition to any crime-fighting unit, such as the one I planned to set up. As it turned out, I didn't do this. My mother wanted me to finish high school, and then the years just slipped away.... After a while, I had second thoughts about Nellie; she was a bit quick with the ju-jitsu and I had no real confidence that I could handle a blond spitfire, what with all my homework and cleaning up the yard after school.

So I gave up on Nellie Gray. Then, for a time, I considered Pat Savage, the cousin of Doc Savage. Now there was a stunning woman: tall and glorious, with gleaming red hair, and an old Colt Peacemaker in her purse.

Pat was just exactly the right girl. She liked baseball and flying airplanes and banging people on top of the head. If violent adventure promised, she was ready to go. Right now. No waiting.

Thing was, about Pat, she was exuberant. She was very very exuberant. Having raised a daughter whose exuberance flares and blazes unrelentingly, I've sort of rethought my earlier passion for Pat Savage. Thing is, she always wanted to go. She wasn't really happy unless she was flying off across the Atlantic to see if she couldn't get her head knocked loose, and every place she stopped, a lot of people ended up dead.

It's probably lucky I didn't court Pat. Just too violent.

Now, Margo Lane, I never cared much for. If the truth is know, she was a feather-headed nitwit, a flighty pest who lacked any sense of personal danger. She liked the life of the high rich, too, and hung around with Lamont Cranston a lot, in *The Shadow Magazine*. The Shadow treated her rather humorously, as if she were a kitten full of catnip. She caused more trouble than she was worth. If you notice, The Shadow, in his true identity of Kent Allard, stayed as far from Margo as possible.

Allard, himself, seems to have had strong feelings about Myra Reldon, an efficient little thing brought up in the Orient; she was a professional investigator, herself. Whatever transpired between them, Allard kept very quiet. He would. I always thought that Myra was a little too close to The Shadow and would never have felt comfortable holding her hand. So I had no real ambitions in her direction. And Margo was just impossible.

Most of the big names in the pulp magazine world had a girl on the premises. The Phantom Detective was strongly drawn to Muriel Havens, daughter of the wealthy newspaper publisher who started The Phantom on his career. Muriel appeared rarely, more rarely had a significant part of the action, and left you with a sort of blank feeling. Toward the end of the series, she developed a wisp of personality. But not enough to make you care.

Diane Elliot was as much a tomboy as Pat Savage, or maybe more. She began as a newspaperwoman but, along the way, became regular army, so to speak. Her job was to help Operator 5 fight off monthly invasions. She was probably a sweet kid. But she knew too much about organizing counterattacks and gunning down sadistic troopers. If we had ever met, I'm afraid she would have burst out laughing. It upsets you to look into a girl's eyes and whisper "Darling" and have her burst out laughing.

Betty Dale, another cute newspaperwoman, was so tied up with Secret Agent X, that you knew immediately she was not for you. Besides, she had that special pulp heroine affliction—she kept getting captured and tied up. And if you went out with her, she was always finding excuses to pat your cheek to see if that was skin or make-up. She had Agent X very much on the mind.

Nita Van Sloan was another matter, entirely. She was one of these lovely brunettes with rich violet eyes. For years and years, she was engaged to this Wentworth fellow. They say he was the Spider, and if he was the Spider, Nita Van Sloan is the last person in the world I am going to go smiling up to. No, sir. That company's too hot for me.

Nita's family was old and respected, but they lost their money in the Depression. She supported herself by painting pictures of the Hudson River. After she became closely associated with Wentworth, she learned to drive fast, fly airplanes, and handle a gun like a match champion. There was steel under that glowing exterior and impatience with doing things in an indirect civilized way. A nice girl; a very nice girl. But a member of a closed unit that was protective of each other and most highly lethal.

You see the problem? all these are splendid girls—Nellie, Pat, Margo, Muriel, Diane, Nita. But to adore them, even from the other side of the page, is hard. Either they're too deadly, or their associates are fast, or they are too rich or sort of foolish.

Somehow I just can't love them the way I love Ida.

Ida is absolutely perfect, a living dream.

She'll be about 94 next month.

Negative Directionality and Other Difficulties

Exactly what are you supposed to do with those little brown chips that fall off your pulp magazines?

Most of them are too small to glue back on. Yet you can't really throw them away. They're actually part of the book. Only they get all detached, and there are so many of them.

I have a copy of *Unknown* whose pages are rimmed deep brown. Whenever I open the magazine to look at the Cartier illustrations, the page edges burst to confetti. You look down to see your shoes peppered with a sort of brown dandruff. Sometimes you can't even see the shoes.

This causes a certain analytical light to touch my wife's eyes. "I suppose," she says, looking at the chips littering the carpet, "that there's a reason for that mess."

ME: "Just a little aging of the collector's items."

HER: "They're past aging and into death."

Its annoying that every magazine you touch, sprays bits at the world. It's more annoying for it to shed large pieces. Irreplaceable chunks of the spine and cover, for instance.

On the second shelf of my center bookcase there is, right now, an inch-long chunk of purple and white spine. It reads "SUE 10¢." This is part of a 1936 *Clues Detective*, the bottom of whose spine reads "ALL STAR IS." When you put the loose piece in the proper place on the spine, you form an important message.

The spine fragment is too good to throw away. Yet if I rubber cement it into place, the first time I open the magazine, the repaired fragment will either crack lengthwise or vertically or in both directions.

Come to think of it, the whole spine is coming loose in long flakes. What is needed is a good swatch of transparent tape. But if you use tape on a pulp, you go to Hell when you die and you limbs are swaddled with tape and you are thrown onto a flaming mound of *Argosy* and there you fry.

But really, tape is the only thing to hold a torn cover together. You'll just have to take your chances with eternity. Once a friend told me that you could repair cover tears by placing the magazine face down and skimming a light gloss of Elmer's Glue along the back of the tear.

All this did was to glue the front of the magazine cover to my desk. This caused more problems than you want to hear about.

People say that the best way to keep your pulps from browning away, chip by chip, is to encase each in a transparent plastic bag. I'm also told that some bags give off noxious fumes which turn your pulps brown.

These problems come up all the time. I wish they didn't.

Because plastic bags are closed at one end and have an opening at the other, they present another pretty specialized problem. This is called "Directionality" by those who speak scientifically. To illustrate:

At one of the Pulp Conventions, I was inserting some magazines into plastic bags to improve their appearance. When I looked up, a fellow collector was regarding me with amused contempt.

"Why," he asked, "are you putting the pulps in upside down?"

This is one of those questions almost impossible to answer. I didn't know there was a right way to insert a pulp into a plastic bag. Usually I stick them in head-first because I like to look at the cover as the magazine slips into place.

Apparently that is wrong. Apparently you are supposed to slide them into the bag feet first. That causes you to look at the cover illustration upside down. Which hardly seems sensible. But I guess right is right.

Trouble is, I have hundreds and hundreds of pulps in plastic bags, and every single one of them is in upside down. I'm certainly not going to take each one out of its sack and turn it around. On the other hand, how can I show off the collection, knowing that everything is wrong way to inside the bag. When I display my treasured copy of *Spicy Zeppelin Stories*, the guest won't look at the magazine. All he'll see is the plastic bag's negative directionality.

I certainly don't know what to do about these problems. I don't even want to think about them. It makes me feel that little brown chips are bursting off the edges of my brain.

Once I gave a fellow a dollar for a 1938 *Phantom Detective*. That was the single most brittle magazine I ever met. As I read the novel, each page snapped off at the binding edge, while the force of gravity powdered the top, bottom, and right-hand margins. By the end of the novel, the magazine was reduced to loose squares of type on dunes of atomized paper.

The covers were OK and most of the novel was there. But the magazine had dissolved from around the type. Part of the paper was on the desk and part on the floor, and the rest floated around the room in the form of molecular gas.

I finally got all the fragments inside the covers, worked it into a plastic bag, and mailed it off to Frank Hamilton, the famous artist, with a note thanking him for past favors. Artists aren't daunted by disaster.

So the problem of brown paper chips remains. I can't stop them from forming and I can't throw them out, and I certainly can't mail all of them to Hamilton. Not even if he were deeply into brown chips.

Insoluble problems; insurmountable difficulties.

You Mean You Found That Jewel At A Flea Market?

This time of year, a few sunny weekends can lead to serious problems.

You get the idea that you can go out to the local flea market and find pulps. Last year's dismal failures are forgotten. This year, you'll find stacks of magazines. All over. In excellent condition or better.

That's what the sun does for you—inspires optimism.

If you get in the right place at exactly the right time, there's no reason why you shouldn't find a pile of 1923 *Weird Tales* or even that elusive second issue of *Spicy Mystery*. Such things have been known to happen. Dorothy found Oz, didn't she?

My luck has never been quite as grand as *Weird Tales* and *Spicy Mystery*. Once I found a very nice copy of *Indian Stories* (1950). That was the high point of 1979. Since then, luck has smiled less often.

Years ago, I was rooting around in a box filled with the *Modern Priscilla* and *Country Gentleman*, when up leaped a copy of *Green Book*. This was a general pulp from the 'Teens, one of a group that included *Red Book*, *Blue Book*, and (I think) *Yellow Book*.

Green Book is not exactly a treasure title and the magazine I found wasn't much of a treasure, either. At some point in its life, someone had soaked it in the river. When the magazine dried out, it mummified. It became a single stiff piece, like a floor tile. You would have had less difficulty opening and reading a floor tile than that magazine.

Most of the pulps you find at flea markets have had disastrous confrontations with water. I ran across a *Strange Detective Mysteries* last year in among a collection of *Popular Mechanics* and tracts. The cover and title page were gone, and so were pages 27 through 83. So you couldn't have called it entirely mint. Nor was it entirely dry, its owner having spilled a cup of coffee into the box just before I arrived. It was an issue I already had. Like as not, I'd never have bought it, even without the cream and sugar.

It reminded me of the *Argosy* issues a friend once gave me. He brought them over in a bushel basket. There were about two feet of them. He had been out to the farm and found them in a defunct chicken house. The roof had been draining into that basket for maybe ten years. The magazines had all melted together into a two-foot lump with curved sides and a strong sinister smell.

I fiddled with that lump for a couple of hours. But you couldn't expect much. Finally, I pried it apart enough to resurrect most of three covers. All the rest were memories. They were *Argosy* from 1930-1933 and it is a spiritual experience to toss two feet of those into the garbage can. No help for it, unless I decided to become a collector of black mold. There was plenty of that down in the center of the lump where the pages used to be.

You have to expect some damage to the magazines you find at flea markets. You're lucky to find a magazine in the first place. For years, I've gone at least twice a season to First Monday in Scottsboro, Alabama. (This is a huge flea market that fills up the center of town on the first Monday of each month; it's called First Monday because activities start the preceding Saturday.)

Twice I've found pulp magazines being offered at the little stands crowding around the Courthouse. That's twice in ten years, a feeble enough record. Both times, they were love and western pulps.

It's a hard blow. You leave home lifted up by sunlight. The least you anticipate is a stack of *Shadows*. Maybe a few *Avengers* in good condition or a run of *Daredevil Aces*. When you finally see the magazines stacked behind the depression glass or pushed off to the edge of the beer cans, you feel the familiar rise of hope. But what you've found are the usual love stories and westerns.

It just isn't understandable that people will put out for sale a stack of *Love Story, New Love, Thrilling Love, 10-Story Love, Fifteen Story Love,* and *Love.* Mixed in with these are a few copies of *.44 Western, Blue Ribbon Western,* and *Western Stories.* No dates are earlier than 1949. You can hear the frigid chuckle of fate.

Not that the love stories and westerns are even in good condition. Don't you believe it. They have been read to tatters. Where they aren't creased, they are folded. Large chunks are missing from the page edges, as if the former owner had absently chewed them while waiting for Prince Charming to roar up in his white BMW.

For these, the asking price is $2.00 a copy. (At the pulp magazine convention, you can get them by the ton for $1.00 each. But at the convention, you won't be bothering about *Love Stories* and *Blue Ribbon Western*.)

One of the great wonders of the world is the high value of pulps when they are displayed on the same table with depression glass. When tossed into a cardboard box and shoved under the counter, they are worth 25¢ each. But the minute they go out on the table, the price ascends. If they are encased in plastic bags, the price rises to $3.00 and the seller is very snooty about letting you open the sack to look at the magazine.

Once I found a 1946 *Detective Tales* at First Monday. Its life had been hard and, if it had been able to get around, it would have been on food stamps. Asking price was $5.00—almost double the usual dealer price. "It's a real old magazine," he explained. "Lookee there. 1946. That's a old one that is. They cost a lot more when they're old like that."

What can you say to that?

"Sir, you are misinformed. And you are also a grimy, tobacco-spit-dribbling cheat wearing last month's shirt..."

But if you haven't met that kind before, you haven't been scratching for pulps along the ragged edges of town.

When you come down to it, I can only remember two decent pulps coming out of my weekly excursions to flea markets. I've picked up lots of hardbacked mysteries, including some Edgar Wallace. But few pulps. Other than the *Indian Stories*, the only other issue worth mentioning was an October 1906 copy of *The Scrap Book* in lovely condition. It was priced around $4-5, in spite of being in a plastic bag. I started to read it but fell afoul of some of the poetry and dropped out early. The popular poetry of 1906 isn't something to take on when you're in your right mind.

That *Scrap Book* didn't come from Alabama but from a flea market near Dublin, Ohio. Every Sunday, one of the local drive-ins converts to a vast flea market. Maybe 20% of it is devoted to beer cans—empty beer cans. Someone's priorities are twisted. But in Ohio, you find a few more old magazines for sale than in Alabama.

No *Shadows*, however. The only good buy in *Shadows* I ever ran into, out in the wilds of America, was about 20 miles from Huntsville. I didn't find them. A collector in New Jersey found them advertised in the pages of the *Antique Trader* and wrote in and got them for about $2.00 each. Forty or fifty of them from the early 1940's. Then he wrote me and asked if I'd ever heard of the place that sold them.

I hadn't. But I went out there so I could wring my hands and cry. It was an Antiques and Treasured Trash store, just gone out of business. How they got the *Shadows*, the owner said, was easy. He'd bought them out in Oklahoma while driving through and advertised them and made a hell of a big profit, too.

But there were a couple of other things that hadn't been bought.

And he hauled them out—a copy of *Love Stories* and a *Double-Action Western.*

"Two bucks each," he said. "They're rare," he said. "See right there. They're from way back in the 1950's. Them jewels is old magazines. They's worth big money.

How To Deal With Dud Issues Of Magazines

Our friend, the Old Pulp Collector, stopped by the house last Wednesday night and, after taking a second slice of pecan pie, said, with increasing indistinctness:

"Now, every magazine collection ends up with a certain of dud issues. You don't want them. You never wanted them. But there they are, right on your shelves—*Ace Sports* or *Ten-Story Love* or *5-Novels Magazine.* Real authentic clunkers. I think the Easter Bunny must bring them.

"Well, all this stuff accumulates, you know. You start hunting for *World Man hunters* and all you can find are mid-1940s *Fantastic Adventures.* You can't even remember buying one *FA,* and there they are, all over the place, like kudzu. It isn't as if you can read them. They're like a government report— too dull to read and too thick to plough. I suppose you could rip off the covers and pitch the rest out. But that's a sin. I know a minister who says Hell has a white-hot room for people who tear off pulp covers. That's what he says. Of course, he collects The Shadow and you know what those people are like.

"So what do you do with all your junk magazines. They fill up the shelves and get in your way. But you can't throw them out. There's no way you're going to be able to sell them. You can't even trade them six to one for a copy of *Cowboy Romances.*

"Well, say, I read part of a *Cowboy Romances,* once. Made my eyelashes hurt. Didn't get over it for better than a week.'Course a real collector, he doesn't bother to read a magazine. Soon as he gets it, he slides it into a plastic sack. Then he seals it up air tight, so you couldn't get to it with a hand axe. Then he puts it up on the shelf and looks at the spine for the next fifty years. He might as well collect slabs of wood with spines pasted to them. Maybe spines and covers, if he wants to risk the white-hot room.

"Well, it's sure a problem. Myself, I weed the duds out of the collection about once a year. Stack them in cardboard boxes and store them in the garage. After a couple of years, you sort of forget how punk they are. Then you can pull the box open and take them out and look them over, like they're brand new. You'd be surprised. After a couple of years, some of those issues look pretty good. Or they do till you get foolish and try and read them.

"It's sort of dumb, hording a bunch of stuff you never look at. But it's better than getting rid of them. That's a fact. I know that doesn't make any sense. But, shoot, what's having sense got to do with collecting pulps?

"Got any more pie? It's tasty."

Why Those Early Black Mask Issues Are So Peculiar

The Old Pulp Collector wandered in Saturday afternoon and set a small cardboard box of magazines on the kitchen table. He said:

"I brought these over in a box. I was afraid they'd shed all over the floor and get your wife disjointed. Women get took funny about pulps flaking off all those little brown pieces. But that's how you know they're pulps. If they don't flake, they're probably forgeries. A real pulp'll shed like a collie in August.

"Thought you'd want to look at these covers before I ship them off. There's a couple of *Black Mask* in there. 1921 issues. Covers are about all they're good for. I'm going to stick that New Jersey collector, Walker Martin, with those. Every time he sees a real old *Black Mask*, he goes all tense and gets his want list out. I got no idea why. You can't read a 1921 *Black Mask*. The stuff they printed makes your eyes roll back.

"I had a goat once. He'd eat fish hooks and peach trees and tobacco and roofing tar. He ate the hood ornament off a 1938 Buick once and was starting in on the grill before I chased him off. One Sunday, it was, he got in the garage he ate a 1922 *Black Mask* from the cover through to about page 31. Then laid down and shook and blinked his eyes and I near lost him. He took bad right in the middle of a story about one of these rich young bored fellows who cleared up a murder the police couldn't figure out. They thought it was the butler, but it was the maid all the time.

"Why, nobody could stomach such guff and live. That goat never did get right again. I bet Walker doesn't read them, either. Just looks at the covers and stacks 'em up to keep his shelves from flying away. Man'd have to be lunatic to try and read them. See, the reason they're so punk, Mencken and Nathan were trying to keep their fancy magazine *Smart Set* alive. So they'd think up a couple of pulp titles and blow on them till they got going hot, and then sell them. That's how they come to invent *Black Mask*. It wasn't but a copy of *Detective Story Magazine*. They claimed they used the reject manuscripts in the *Smart Set* slush pile. Well, maybe so. You don't have to believe every thing you're told just because H. L. Mencken said so.

"What I think, he just collected the worst stories he could find and printed them. His idea was the worse the story, the better people liked it. That's the way he thought. I bet you, Mencken and Nathan and their buddies wrote some of those mysteries—wrote them just as bad as they could, laughing all the time and squirting cigar smoke around. They played lots of jokes like that. And now people collect these old *Black Mask* and look devout and handle them gentle and feel so proud and satisfied with themselves.

"Course a Red-blooded collector don't have time to read anything. He's too busy collecting. But I bet Old Mencken's up there looking down, watching them handle those dud issues like they were gold, and laughing all over himself.

"Lordy, now you've spilled paper chips all over the rug. Your wife's going to whang us both."

The Real Reason Argosy Is Better Than Fantastic Adventures

"I can't stay," said the Old Pulp Collector. "My wife's looking at thread and samplers and sewing kits. If I'm not there to help her carry out the sacks,I might as well be neck deep in ice.

"Well, you said you could use some *Argosy* and I got these here. 1930s Pretty fair condition. I don't know what you want *Argosy* for. Reading *Argosy* is like kissing a girl through a screen door. It's real interesting, but you just get one little bitty dab at a time. You get interested in a serial then it's 'Continued Next Week'. And just try to find Next Week.

"Now I got these down at the Antique Show. Fellow there from Nashville, he had a boxfull. I got everything that was any good, so don't bother tearing off down there. Not unless you want a bunch of *Fantastic Adventures* for about eight dollars each. I told him I'd give a dollar a foot for them. That didn't make him smile. So I got the *Argosy* and come away.

"Now these *Fantastic* covers are pretty good. But if you open them up and try to read them—why down you fall, deaf, dumb, and blind.

"If doctors knew their business, they wouldn't bother with sleeping pills. They'd just hand out copies of *Fantastic Adventures* at bedtime. In ten minutes, the place'd look like Sleeping Beauty's castle before the Prince got there.

"That's the difference between *Fantastic Adventures* and *Argosy*. *Argosy* wakes you up. You read four pages and then it's 'Continued Next Week.' You come right out of your chair with your hair on end, grinding your teeth, and wanting to kick somebody.

"*Fantastic Adventure*'s is OK for covers. But if you want to be up and around and real alert, give me *Argosy* every time.

"Drat it! I'm five minutes late to pick up the wife. Told you that *Argosy* makes people mad."

Disguise Is Pretty Impractical

"It's a dark and stormy night," said the Old Pulp Collector, extending his glass again. "Just like Snoopy keeps writing about.

"Those detective fellows—Sherlock Holmes and Nick Carter and The Shadow—now they can't resist a night like this. Let the sun shine, they squat at home all the day. But just you let the thunder and lightning start, and they got to go running out, hard as they can, and get soaking wet.

"Doesn't make any sense at all. You ever try hunting for clues with the rain pouring down and your shoes full of water? Shoot, no. Well, I guess it never bothered The Shadow cause all he did was slide around and listen at windows. But Nick Carter, now. What's he doin' out in the cloudburst with his false eyebrows and putty nose. Why, they'd melt right off his face.

"It makes you wonder about the others. Now you take The Phantom Detective and Secret Agent X. I mean, they were fixed up with waterproof faces. That's what they say. But I doubt it.

"Why, you ought to see my daughter. If she isn't working to improve her mouth, it's her eyes. Or she's readjusting her complexion. Dab, dab, dab, every five minutes.

"Now, the women are real professionals at this sort of thing. But you can't tell me any man's going to put lines on his face with eyebrow pencil so he looks old, and then go wandering out in the hurricane. Why, he'd get his face washed down to bedrock. Lordy, the women can't even keep themselves in repair when the suns' shining. And I don't think Nick Carter could, either.

"You take the Spider, now. He puts on a fright wig and false teeth and fixes himself up all hollow-eyed and scary. Then he gets all hunched up and goes out, and pretty soon the police have fifteen or twenty new murders to investigate.

"Say, did you ever try to jump around real fast in a fright wig and long cape. Why it's a wonder he didn't break his fool neck. I mean, you got to paste those wigs down. Or else you turn East and that wig's going to keep going North. And maybe the teeth, too.

"The Phantom, the same way. He wears all those spacers and pads and junk to change the shape of his mouth and make his nose fat. And he's all fixed up with eyebrow pencil and wig and colored greases and Lord knows what all. Why, if he'd go out in the sun, he'd scare a goat.

"See, I figure all this disguise stuff started back in the dime novels. You can blame dime novels for almost everything. Back then, all the fellows had facefulls of hair you could hide a rabbit in. You just change your whiskers and you were somebody else. If it rained, you might shrink a little. Didn't dissolve, though.

"Makes you feel right sorry for Secret Agent X. Having to stop every couple of minutes and look in his compact to see if he's who he's supposed to be. Makes you wonder how The Shadow stood it. One minute he's an old man and two minutes later, he's a full-faced business man. And then he squeezes his face a couple of times and goes to the Cobalt Club for lunch as Lamont Cranston. And all the time, he's Kent Allard underneath... Can you imagine the skin problems that man must have had, going around with a face full of putty twenty-four hours out of twenty-four? How he ever remembered who he was, beats me.

"Maybe that's why he kept sitting around in a black room, laughing to himself. He was just thinking how nice it'd be to get a suntan.

"Why, yes, I'd like another little taste. If you can stop yourself, try not to fill the glass clear up with ice. You got to leave a little space for the flavoring."

Why All Those Magazine Covers Of Girls In Space Are Dead Wrong
"For a fellow of your age and weight," the Old Pulp Collector said, "you ask the dizziest questions I ever did hear. Of course I look at those girly pictures on pulp covers. That's why they put them there for."

"You better have some more pizza," I said.

"Just one more. Before it gets cold." He took a large slice and fingered up all the loose mushrooms in the bottom of the box.

"Course, the girls never got to do much inside the magazine, you understand," he added. "But they made up for it on the outside. My land, yes. You don't think people bought *Thrilling Wonder Stories* to read, do you?

You can't read *Thrilling Wonder Stories*. It'd make your bones soft. You bought that magazine so's you could admire how they were wearing iron brassieres this month."

"Somebody must have read it."

"Well," he said, "you can't tell about these science-fiction types. They're liable to do anything—even read. Myself, I think the stories were just an excuse for the cover.

"Now I was over to see one of those science-fiction fellows last week. I carried along about three-four *Rapid-Fire Western* and a couple of *Startling Stories*. Thought he might want to trade for some of those *Pirate Stories* he's hoarding.

"Well, when I showed him those *Startling* covers, he kind of sighs and he says: 'I wonder why the men are always bundled up and the girls get to float around in a vacuum showing off their skin?'

"I said it was because science-fiction readers only looked at pictures. And that was the wrong thing to say. Because he starts telling me how everybody liked reading Harlan Ellison. It poured down Harlan Ellison for about two hours, a moderate heavy cloud-burst. So I went home and we never did get to talk about trading.

"But later I got to thinking about those covers. Now here're all those girls, and if a Bug-Eyed Monster ain't slobbering after them, then they're floating around out there by the Moon—and them bare from the toe-nails to ear lobes, except for about five cents worth of brass girdle.

"Now, a fellow who'd paint a picture like that don't know nothin' about women. First off, only time a woman goes around bare like that, she's near a swimming pool. Water just makes their clothes fly off. Show them a pool and a blue sky and then hide your eyes.

"Any other time, it's a blouse under a sweater under a coat. Then they cram on a scarf and pearls and beads and sun glasses. Why a woman isn't happy till she's wearing more clothes than she can walk around in.

"If a Bug-Eyed Monster ever caught a real woman, it'd die of old age before it got her shucked.

"Well, I think all those covers on *Thrilling Wonder* and *Startling* are hooey. The artists did all their painting by swimming pools. That's what's the matter. Only they couldn't put the swimming pool into the cover painting. I mean it's hard to think up a reason for having a swimming pool in orbit. So they just painted the girls."

I asked: "How come the men are in space suits?"

"Well, who cares what a man wears?" He examined the pizza box. "I suppose you'd rather I ate this last slice, so you don't have to throw it out. Course I could be wrong. I never read those magazines much. Maybe they're all about swimming pools in orbit. Maybe they're saving the lakes of Mars from Harlan Ellison. I don't know."

"You better have another beer," I said.

"Why, yes, I guess I will," he said. "No—a beer. Not a Coors. So that's the way I figure it. Bathing beauties in space."

"That doesn't make much sense," said.

"It doesn't have to make much sense. We're talkin' about girly covers. Just look at them and smile. You don't have to understand them. Even if you understood women, you still wouldn't understand women."

"I don't understand science-fiction magazines, either," I said.

"Then look at the pictures," he said. "For a fellow of your age and weight, you sure say the dizziest things."

Memoirs Of A Doc Savage Reader

Do you happen to remember the first Doc Savage novel you ever read? I do, and I have no idea why. It's one of the caprices of memory, clear, sharp recall when you don't need it. Although try and find the ignition keys or explain to your wife why the check for the fire insurance is still in your pocket.

My first Doc Savage had no cover and no spine and the back was gone. So were the first several pages. As I recall it, the magazine had a furtive, scrambled look, as if it had been detected crouching under a porch.

The place I found it explains the condition. The magazine was mixed in with a stack of *Police Gazettes* and outdoor sports magazines on a side table in Hick's Barber Shop.

This was in Charleston, West Virginia, around 1938.

Hicks was an extremely tall, soft-voiced mountaineer with a furrowed face and a great pile of blue-black hair combed glossy into a shining rise, so that his skull seemed about two inches longer than was decent. He had come to the city to earn his fortune. As it turned out, he was not apt to find it where he set up shop.

The price of a haircut was 5 or 10 cents, reasonable for the time. Possibly, even at those prices, Hicks might have earned a living. But he was also a perfectionist. When he cut your hair, it stayed cut for six weeks. With the precision of a scientist dissecting a microbe, he clipped infinitesimally along. Each hair was examined and nipped to within an atom's length of all the others. While Hicks trimmed your hair, whole geologic ages passed; the glaciers came and went; mountain ranges rose and were leveled.

To have Hicks cut your hair was, therefore, a major investment of time. So you can appreciate my horror when my turn in the chair crept around— and I discovered that I had nothing to read.

Appalling eternities gaped ahead. Nothing to read! The *Police Gazette* had no appeal and I had gnawed through all the outdoor magazines while waiting for my brother to get sheared. The only hope was that coverless wreck of an issue buried among equally disreputable *Gazettes*. This I grabbed up and climbed with it into the seat of honor. There the magazine proceeded to shower bits of page edge down my front and across the floor, for it was toast brown and brittle as last year's leaf.

So this is how I met Doc Savage—stting in a high chair, reading as the scissors circled my head with an eerie metallic chittering.

The story was "The Man of Bronze." What was left of the magazine began in the middle of Chapter II and from that point, we went on together.

It is now proper to say how much I was gripped by the driving story line and fascinating characters. How I was drawn on and on, shivering with excitement as the reeling adventure pounded along.

That would be proper. But not true. As a matter of fact, I found it mildly boring and slogged along with it only because anything was preferable to sitting in that chair until the glaciers melted.

Hicks was so slow that I managed to read all but the last few chapters before being released. As it happened, I didn't run across "The Man of Bronze" again for twenty-five years and never saw the original cover for almost thirty.

That's a long time to spend reading a story.

That was my first Doc. The second was "The Other World (January 1940) which I bought brand, shining new at the drug store. The cover shows Doc under the belly of what is obviously a dinosaur. No human being that ever lived could resist a story about dinosaurs, so I carried the magazine off, read it, was thoroughly, permanently hooked from then on.

Unlike The Shadow, which appeared gloriously every other week, and had done so since time began, Doc. Savage was published only monthly. Only monthly—the pity of it.

Since I could swallow the novel down in about an hour and a half, that left a long hollow space between issues. However, the pain could be eased a little by methodically rummaging the local magazine exchange. And, if you didn't mind wallowing in the sordid, you could search for magazines in those little stores that sold someone else's trash. The town was pimpled with them. Today, they are called Antique Stores or Flea Markets. Back then, they were Second-hand Stores and were packed with rusty offal and clothing too dilapidated to be worn, even in the Thirties.

No matter how noisome it was, every store had pulps. You hunted till you found them—coverless; two for 5 cents; otherwise 5 cents each. Had my mother any idea what I did on Saturday morning, she would have died thirty-five years earlier. In our home, pulps were barely tolerated because "they gave you funny ideas."

I never noticed that they gave me anything but satisfaction—and so early I learned that great principle of adult fallibility, which is the first step you take in becoming a fallible adult.

I still don't know where I put the car keys. But right now, I can tell you that my ragged copy of "Poison Island" (September 1939) and "Hex" (November 1939) came from a second-hand store. A fairly good copy of "World's Fair Goblin" (April 1939) and an almost new copy of "Mad Mesa" (January 1939) came from a magazine exchange.

(Notice that the dates were all 1939. For older issues, you either had to be lucky—even in 1940—or you had to find a long-established magazine exchange where the pulps coated the walls and loaded the basement. But those places were the exception. The more usual hunting grounds rarely offered anything more than two years old. To find a 1936 issue was to celebrate for a week.)

The magazine exchange handled magazines of all sorts, slicks as well as pulps, comics as well as digests. The larger exchanges even had shelves of hardbacks, most usually crowded into the back of the room, where they wouldn't fight with the rest of the stock.

You brought in your trade magazines and, if they were current (rarely) and in reasonable condition (more rarely), you traded two for one of the same cover price. Trades of comics for pulps were scowled upon, since comic books enjoyed the same status as a leper at the Symphony Ball.

If you had nothing to trade, you collected all the pennies that could be borrowed, begged and scrounged—pennies because nickels were few and dimes were unheard-of wealth. Then to the magazine exchange, where, in agony of mind, you selected a few Shadows, a few Doc Savage from great piles of those titles, always leaving behind more than the heart could endure.

For a few years at the end of the 1930's, there was a feeble sort of magazine exchange operated at the edge of the business district in Ada, Oklahoma. To this town, we came every summer or so, selecting the hottest time of the year to visit my father's family. At this time, Ada was about the size of a butterfly's sneeze. Out in the residential section, the roads were brown gravel and the sidewalks intermittent.

By 10 o'clock, the center of town reeled in a swoon of heat. Bare-footed boys meandering about town in search of amusement progressed from shadow to shadow, for if you stepped on the sunny part of the sidewalk, your toes burst into flame.

By careful hopping, you could work over two blocks to the south side of the business district. There the Ada Magazine Exchange slumbered. It was a vast, hollow room, with a ceiling of silver tin. The air glowed with entrapped heat, and the owner, in overalls, open shirt, and face bristles, sat limply before a small floor fan and glowered about his domain.

Scrap-wood tables circled the walls. The pulps were stacked across the rear—say, thirty feet of coverless, brown magazines, tattered, creased, folded to the point of death. Every magazine had been read to destruction by farmhands before being brought to town in cardboard boxes and traded for other issues in approximately the same condition.

By ploughing these shelves methodically, I found a copy of "The Men Who Smiled No More" (April 1936), a fascinating story, although the magazine was the usual coverless wreck. Mixed in with a sifting of loose pages was most of the cover of the May 1936 "Seven Agate Devils," showing Doc bending over an obviously murdered man, with a scarlet devil statue standing by.

The magazine, itself, was nowhere to be found. I never ran across it again until I was able to buy it in 1969. By then, it cost more that 5¢.

My real Doc Savage finds in Ada were not in the Magazine Exchange, but in a small storage shed, back of my grandmother's house.

The shed was a tiny out-building jammed with furniture cast off from the main house—chairs and tables and rolled carpets, all too good to throw away, but not good enough to use. Immediately inside the door was a small rolltop desk. This was crammed with miscellaneous and exciting things—pencils and old maps, marbles in glass jars, fragments of perished toys. And several ancient cigars, brittle as a mummy's smile. And two coverless *Doc Savage* magazines.

It was a moment of irrational joy to find all this together, just when boredom had made living intolerable. The Docs were 1938 issues—"The Living Fire Menace" (January) and The Mountain Monster" (February).

In "Living Fire," Doc and company get down in a cave and become so charged with electricity that their skins turn red and if they'd touch someone, he'd be blasted, as if with lightning. "The Mountain Monster" told of a towering huge gigantic spider that came stalking through the Canadian forest slavering for prey.

Magnificent I read those novels standing up before that crammed roll-top desk in a stifling semi-dusk, experimentally smoking the cigars. The stories seemed superb. There cigars were pretty good. I didn't get sick, didn't get caught, and had a grand time. Some moments are like jewels, glowing in your memory all your life. That's one of mine. To repeat the exploit now, would leave me in the Intensive Care Unit. But not then. How curiously joy comes and in what strange forms.

Well, it's harder to find the *Doc Savage* magazine now. People are more persnickety about condition than we were, way back when. Sometimes they read what they collect. Sometimes they merely collect.

But Doc Savage wasn't merely collected at the end of the 1930s. We read. We swooped eyes first into the adventure and let it swallow us up. It wasn't a matter having a collectible of value. The magazines were of no real value. But they spoke to us wonderfully, clutched us hard, filled us with heady fires.

We didn't grow up as smart as Doc, or as rich, or as strong. But he got into out secret minds and stayed with us. He was part of our past, part of our expectations. In just a few years, we, too, would move excelling among men. It was inevitable. The world would know us, just as it knew Doc.

And if we never, somehow, reached Doc's giddy heights, if the world beyond the pulp magazines was a flatter, less exuberant place—well, that was our poor luck. We knew it could be otherwise. We knew that out there, somewhere, just beyond out knowledge, Doc Savage was still adventuring. We knew that in our bones. And against all common sense, we know it still. Some articles of faith are too precious to be questioned.

Notes

Face Changer
[1]Albert Tonik, "D'Arcy Lyndon Champion," *Echoes*, Vol. 2, No. 1 (August 1983), pp. 7-9.

[2]Will Murray, "Who Wrote The Phantom Detective?" *Echoes*, Vol. 4, No. 1 (February 1985), pp. 23-25.

Jesse James' Ferocious Exploits
[1]Carl W. Breihan, *The Complete and Authentic Life of Jesse James*. Collier Books (1962), p. 58. See also p. 72, quoting a Jesse James letter concerning the Pinkerton attack. The biographical material used in this article is based on Breihan's book.

[2]Bob Younger died in prison. Cole and Jim were paroled in 1901.

[3]J. Edward Leithead, "The James Boys in the Saddle Again," *Dime Novel Round-Up*, Vol. 24, No. 4, Whole No. 283 (April 15, 1956), p. 30.

[4]Reasons for cancellation of the Jesse James dime novels are not clear. E. F. Bleiler, in his "Introduction" to *Eight Dime Novels*, NY: Dover, 1974, p. x, remarks that "Street and Smith cancelled its Jesse James series, when it seemed that public opinion was against the outlaws and their deeds." No publisher would risk too much public outcry for fear of cancellation of some portion of his second-class mailing privileges. Altruism is the public face of private fears for the bank account.

[5]In this series, names are consistently off, just a little. Thus, Dr. and Mrs. Samuel become Samuels, Jesse's half-brother Archie becomes Johnny, Quantrill becomes Quantrell, and Allan Pinkerton becomes his son, William.

[6]William Ward, "Jesse James' Revenge; or, The Hold-Up of the Train at Independence," *The Adventure Series* No. 13, p. 8.

[7]*Ibid*, p. 11.

[8]William Ward, "Jesse James' Narrow Escape; or, Ensnared By a Woman Detective," *The Adventure Series* No. 36, pp. 85-86.

[9]Daryl Jones, *The Dime Novel Western*, Bowling Green Popular Press, 1978, p. 96.

[10]Ward, "Jesse James' Revenge," pp. 74-75.

[11]*Ibid*, pp. 158-159.

[12]Ward, "Jesse James' Battle For Freedom," p. 12.

[13]Leithead, *op. cit.*, p. 26.

[14]In the opinion of this commentator, many of these Jesse James novels include material extracted from other sources and revised for *The Adventure Series*. To this date, however, no specific sources have been identified. It does no harm to point out that an opinion, unsubstantiated by fact, is also called a guess.

[15]Those fascinated by pretty coincidence may note that Frank James expostulates "By Jove" in "Frank James on the Trail," *Morrison's Sensational Series*, Vol.1, No. 46 (July 1, 1882), reprinted in E. F. Bleiler's *Eight Dime Novels*.

[16]Ward, "Jesse James' Mysterious Foe; or, The Pursuit of the Man in Black" (No. 42), pp. 171-172.

[17]Edward LeBlanc has pointed out that the Jeff Clayton novels in *The Adventure Series* were reprints of Sexton Blake stories from the English *Union Jack*. Clayton's brief appearances in the final two Jesse James novels were original. He appears infrequently and ineffectually, his presence serving mainly to prepare for the next *Adventure* series.

[18]Leithead, *op. cit.*, p. 30.

His Voice an Eerie Whisper

[1]*The Whisperer* and *The Skipper* replaced two older magazines, *Nick Carter* and *Pete Rice*, both of these being cancelled with the June 1936 issue.

[2]Information concerning the authorship and curious editorial sequencing of The Whisperer series was provided by Will Murray and is based on his examination of the Street & Smith editorial files. For further information concerning The Whisperer, refer to Murray's essay, "The Many Faces of The Whisperer," *Pulp* 7, Vol. 1, No. 7 (Spring 1975).

[3]Although "The Trail of Fear" was the first novel published, the first of the new Whisperer series to be written was "Killer from Nowhere." Somehow that got out of sequence and was published third, dated February 1941. That displacement makes no difference to the series, which was non-chronological.

[4]Hathway later rewrote "Heritage of Death" to eliminate The Whisperer. Pared down to novlette length, it was published in the August 1943 issue of *The Shadow* as "Murder at Floodtide."

[5]"Character magazines" is used here in the broadest sense, and includes such publications as *Double Detective* and *Red Star Adventures*, which featured major characters whose names did not appear in the titles.

Fourteen Issues

[1]In 1988, author and critic Will Murray published a comprehensive bibliography of Lester Dent in the *Pulp Vault #3*. Six Dent stories are cited as having been published in Scotland Yard: "Wildcat," "Doom Ship," "Teeth of Revenge," "One Billion—Gold," "Out China Way," and "Diamond Death." So now we know, at long last.

Index